Heirs to the Throne

THE LAST KING OF LEGEND

R. F. Steinhauer

Heirs to the Throne (The Last King of Legend, Book 1) by R.F. Steinhauer

Cover Design by John Palomares.
ISBN: 1537126105
ISBN 13: 9781537126104
Library of Congress Control Number: 2016913680
CreateSpace Independent Publishing Platform
North Charleston, South Carolina

For my son Alexander—

Anything in life is possible. Dream big.

The Witness

IT HAD BEEN a most peculiar Christmas Eve. Beginning with a lunar eclipse, which was followed by a ferocious storm that raged for precisely seven minutes, and then abruptly ceased. Afterwards bizarre and unexplainable phenomena had been reported all across the city. Some claiming to see stars falling from the sky as constellations fought with one another. Others witnessed seeing the moon weeping, or hearing unknown whispers in the wind. Among many such impossible things too numerous to name.

None of which compared to what had just occurred inside room number 66 on the sixth floor maternity ward of St. Peter's hospital. Where copious amounts of heavy dark red blood spotted the white floor. And though many eyes were present, only one pair had truly witnessed what had taken place here. Those belonging to an otherworldly visitor, who, despite all the nurses and doctors occupying the room, had gone unnoticed.

This specter, standing stoically in the corner, appeared an old man whose wrinkled skin contained a bluish tint, as if starved of oxygen. Dressed finely in a black suit and overcoat of a style more past century than present, carrying an ornate cane appearing far more ancient. He watched attentively through his mismatched eyes: the right a vibrant blue, the left a lifeless gray.

Wordsworth was his name, at least the one he went by now anyway. An experienced observer of extraordinary sights, his mismatched eyes had seen what most could not fathom. In ways it was his occupation. But even he was amazed by what they had glimpsed in this most unlikely of places.

In the laws of life and death, what had just transpired was entirely without precedent. The mother was dead as dead can be when the first child came forth from her body. Then the second emerged, and suddenly the deceased mother was alive once more. A medical marvel, some were calling it. Others, owing to the date, proclaimed it a Christmas miracle.

Wordsworth knew better.

For it was far more than that, for those like himself capable of perceiving it. It was magic of the most ancient and powerful kind, and it radiated from the two new born children as if they were the Source personified. And though they'd just been rushed off to another floor of the hospital, the room still glowed with their presence.

Of course, to those whose Eye was closed, like most magic, it would go unnoticed. But for those like Wordsworth, a seismic event had just occurred. The tremors of which would be felt across worlds. Though the fact that such power originated in this one, was most disturbing of all.

Wordsworth's gray left eye suddenly twitched. He was being summoned by his employer, who'd undoubtedly sensed the event. Before he departed, he filled two small vials with blood from the floor.

Outside of the hospital crimson flakes of snow were falling heavily in the city. While a large blood red moon loomed over it.

Wordsworth could still feel the charge of magic in the air. A strange sensation here. *Barriers are breaking*, he thought.

Late now, just past the witching hour, and the streets festooned with Christmas cheer were all but empty. Children were tucked away in bed awaiting anxiously the arrival of Old Saint Nick. Of course, if they knew the true story of Santa Claus they wouldn't be so keen to celebrate his coming. Then, so many things had taken on new meanings in this world.

Wordsworth had traveled to this world on numerous occasions on behalf of his employer, to whom it was of particular interest. Though time moved differently here, and every time he visited it was drastically different than the time before. So unlike his own in that regard, where change came not easily at all.

But then, life here was exceedingly short, and everyone trying desperately to make their mark before their little time ran out. Nevertheless, what they accomplished in such short lives was remarkable. A testament to what could be achieved with a true sense of urgency. And as he walked, he marveled at all the new sights, all the wondrous technology. The huge towering buildings, the whirling machinery, and bright lights. He understood why his employer so admired this world. It had exceeded all expectations.

He was also keenly aware of this world's dangers for those like himself. He had stayed longer than usual, tracking the disturbances which led him to the hospital. Nor was he as strong as he once was as age was taking its toll, and his powers were already beginning to fade. If he stayed much longer they would vanish. Until eventually he'd forget even his own name.

He turned abruptly and headed down a dark alleyway. When he reached the dead-end he pulled from his coat pocket a single golden key, and a wooden door appeared suddenly.

After taking a final look at the city, now covered in red snow, he braced himself for what would greet him on the other side of the door. Then turned the handle and disappeared through….

Gone was the city with its bright lights and Christmas cheer. Now a much different sort of place stood before him: the infamous Island of Flames.

A forlorn place in a forlorn realm residing in a dark forgotten corner of the universe. The wind blew cold and hard, abrasive to the skin. The sky was scorched and the air acrid. Everything about the place reeked of doom and destruction.

Black waters crashed violently upon the desolate shore below. Waters as legend told formed from the tears of the Titan Prometheus chained on a rock somewhere in the darkest fathoms of this forsaken ocean. Where he suffers eternally for his transgression, and for the secret he refuses, despite all manner of painful encouragement, to relinquish.

From afar the Island with its seven dark peaks resembled a crooked crown. And though thousands of years had passed steam still rose from the peaks as if the Eternal Fire once engulfing the isle were only recently doused. The realm had been one of the lights of the universe. But when the Eternal Fire was stolen in the Wars of the Fallen became a dead land. What remained were those belonging no place else.

Lately, his employer had spent a great deal of time in this abysmal place. And though one of the very last places he'd ever wish to be, Wordsworth found himself a frequent visitor. It never grew more comfortable, always eliciting the same feeling of impending dread and abandoned hope.

Wordsworth navigated the spiraling staircase carved into the side of the Island. Stopping momentarily, he gazed into the black obsidian rock, and a brush of fire swept across it. A reflection like everything else of what was lost. An eerie testament to a time forgot.

When he reached the top of the highest of the seven peaks a shiver ran up his spine, as much for the accursed place as for the face staring down at him.

Despite the ferocious wind, his employer's luminous long silver hair lay motionless. While his pale bluish face devoid of expression or emotion betrayed not the slightest thought or unspoken intention; as stoic and serene as a dying breath. His long black cape billowed as if it possessed a mind of its own; which if legend held true, it did. But most striking of all were his penetrating icy gray eyes that gazed down to one's very soul, and weighed it in the balance.

Standing before Wordsworth was the Great Lord of Death.

How he'd come to be in the employ of Death was a story for another time. But he served Death in many capacities. But then, everyone did in some respect.

Wordsworth appeared far older than his employer, who appeared a man in the prime of his life, with a face unblemished or unwrinkled by the hands of time. But his employer could not be said to be either young or old. Those terms did not apply to him. He was ageless, timeless, and eternal.

And though a demanding master, his employer was not cruel. For that term could not be applied to him either. For cruelty implied one had a choice to act otherwise. His employer had no choice. In the same way that a force of nature has no choice. One would not say that an earthquake was cruel.

His employer glanced at the golden time piece hanging from his blood red vest. "You're late," he said with reproach. His voice like a faint whisper, yet even from a distance there was no difficulty in hearing it.

"Apologies my Lord," said Wordsworth reverently bowing his head. To his employer time was always of the essence.

His employer did not walk so much as glide. He was pure terrifying grace. And as he spoke he paced. Clearly he was anxious. Or at least as anxious as an eternal being could be.

"Show me," his employer demanded.

Wordsworth removed his left gray eye and handed it over to his employer. Who took it into his hand and gazed through it. When finished he handed the eye back to Wordsworth, who returned it to its socket.

Wordsworth then handed his employer the two vials filled with blood. "I've never experienced such power."

His employer examined the vials closely. Then one at a time poured their contents down his throat.

"What is it my Lord?' asked Wordsworth, unable to contain his anxiousness.

After a long moment his employer replied, "The Heirs of Jove."

"A-are you certain?" Wordsworth's voice trembled despite itself.

His employer shot him a cold stare.

Of course he was certain.

"The Heirs of Jove...reborn in the Banishment?" said Wordsworth. For many even such a thought amounted to blasphemy.

"It seems we've all been searching in the wrong place," said his employer. "But that is not Fate's only surprise. The mother is also of my bloodline."

"Shall I bring them over?" asked Wordsworth.

"No. They were born in the Banishment for a reason, and there they shall stay, for now. Perhaps it is best," his employer mused, "The Veil will ensure that they do not realize their powers, or who they are, until old enough to choose for themselves. And even if sensed, few will believe the Heirs could be born in the Banishment. Or risk the journey to find out."

"But what will happen to the Banishment? It is already changing," said Wordsworth.

"The Veil will suppress their powers, for a time. But as the Heirs near their Coming of Age and their full powers awake, they will prove too strong. And without even realizing, they will rip the fabric of the world apart."

Wordsworth detected a distinct sadness in his employer. "Can it not be saved?" he asked.

His employer shook his head. "The Beast is already preparing to feast upon it."

"A shame," said Wordsworth.

"Yes...a shame."

"Could we...could we not end them now, and prevent it all from happening?" Wordsworth knew he asked a terrible thing, but the alternative was in many ways far worse.

His employer's fury was immediate, and Wordsworth's very soul trembled as the Beast roused. Wordsworth could feel it breathing down his neck, waiting to feast upon his life-force, to finish the meal started long ago.

"You shall not interfere." It was beyond a command. It was unbreakable law. "They must freely choose who they will become."

"And if they chose their appointed roles?" Wordsworth managed.

His employer paused for a long moment, before responding at last, "Then to the victor go the Eternal Throne."

The Darren's

Mrs. Darren stood in the kitchen dressed in a gunmetal gray jumpsuit. The uniform for the Mr. Scrub Company, where their motto, "We'll clean anything!" was taken quite literally, and while working there she'd encountered some of the vilest messes imaginable. The job didn't pay well, nor was it fulfilling or mentally stimulating. But it put food on the table, and a roof over her sons' heads.

Presently, however, the roof of her small rustic country cabin was badly leaking after being ravaged by another powerful storm throughout the evening, and appeared on the verge of collapsing. Though hardly the cabin's only problem. The foundation was perilously weak, the floor boards creaked, there were gaping holes in the walls, and when a strong gust of wind came along, the rickety wooden house, already slightly slanted, threatened to topple over completely.

But the surroundings were quiet. The only sounds those nature provided. Far better than sirens or honking horns or any other *noise* indigenous to the urban jungles the Darren's spent years struggling to survive in. And despite its many flaws, they had made it home. Or as close as they'd come in a very long time.

With Halloween just around the corner, and being Mrs. Darren's second favorite holiday, next to Christmas, the cabin appeared festively spooky. Over the years Mrs. Darren had amassed an impressive collection of Halloween decorations, most of which she'd handcrafted herself. There were ghostly clocks, gravely figurines, and everything in between.

One of the home's morbid features, however, remained up year round.

Adjacent to the fireplace stood a large dark wooden bookcase nearly completely filled with pictures of dead relatives. At the center of which was

Mr. Darren himself. The bookcase served as a memorial of sorts. One, unfortunately, that had grown at an alarming rate, as the Darren's had lost nearly every leaf on their family tree. Most meeting their demise far sooner, and crueler, than they should have.

To say the least, life had been hard these last few years, and like the cabin, Mrs. Darren was simply lucky to still be standing. And though clearly once a very attractive woman, life had taken its toll. She'd lost more weight than was entirely healthy on her athletic frame, and the twinkle in her emerald green eyes had long since faded, while her thick blond hair had withered and dulled. But for all she'd been through it was a marvel she still looked anywhere near as good as she did. And where most would've long given up hope, she persevered.

More than anything, it was because of her two sons—her little Christmas miracles—that she continued to battle on. And as long as she still had them she would be just fine. At least that's what she told herself time after time....

Thomas, the younger of Mrs. Darren's twins, was seated at the kitchen table finishing up some homework while he ate his breakfast. Today, and for the last four, a bowl of cold oatmeal with a glass of milk already a week past its expiration.

He was a baby-faced boy, appearing slightly younger than his thirteen and three quarter years would warrant, of slight build, and like his mother, a tad too thin. His skin was fair and he possessed a brilliant pair of baby blue eyes. While his cherubic face was framed by a mane of thick golden blond hair.

A sharp shaft of bright morning light pierced the glass of the small window above the sink, and there illuminated in the kitchen doorway was Jack.

Like his twin brother he was shabbily attired, wearing an over worn t-shirt that fit much too snuggly, and jeans that were in tatters. Though unlike Thomas, he somehow managed to make the second hand rags look stylish. Almost unnaturally handsome, with an angular face, strong jawline, and razor sharp cheekbones. He had penetrating dark eyes to compliment a shock of wild dark hair.

Phenomenally well built for his age, he already possessed the defined muscles of a full-grown man, along with the strength to go with them.

Jack looked down at Thomas doing his homework and smirked. "Still hard at work, I see," he said. His voice rich and deep.

"Almost finished," replied Thomas in a far weaker voice, one struggling these days to find its appropriate octave, going from high to low at a moment's notice. Something, along with a propensity for fainting, which caused him a great deal of embarrassment.

"I don't know why you even bother with homework. It's only the tests that matter," said Jack.

"How can I pass the tests if I don't do the homework?" Thomas countered.

"I guess *you* can't," said Jack, who of course never did homework, yet always aced the tests. He found it amusing that Thomas worked as hard as he did. For like everything else, when it came to school Jack was simply a natural. While Thomas struggled. Not because he wasn't smart. But because he was an avid daydreamer, and for him staying focused in class was no easy task.

As Jack devoured his oatmeal, complaining as always that it tasted like cardboard, he watched the family's small television set. As usual, it was tuned to SNN: the Standard News Network. Which lately with the brewing war Jack was practically glued to. Thomas, by contrast, was far less interested, having always preferred imaginary worlds to the real one.

Suddenly the cauldron shaped clock above the stove sent a witch's cackle ringing throughout the household, signaling the time had arrived for the day's journey to commence.

"Don't forget your coats," said Mrs. Darren standing at the front door holding matching brown jackets, purchased a couple months back from a second-hand thrift store. "It's cold out there."

"I don't need it," said Jack, being difficult as usual.

"You're gonna to take it anyway," said Mrs. Darren firmly, "And you'd better not lose this one like the last. You're not getting another."

Jack snatched the jacket from his mother's hand. Thomas already had on his, along with a scarf, skull-cap, and gloves, and was now thoroughly bundled up.

When Mrs. Darren opened the door the cold hit like a ton of bricks. Thomas felt his ears go instantly red and his cheeks start to chap. While Jack didn't seem to mind in the least and hadn't even bothered putting on his coat yet. Thomas swore his brother was cold-blooded.

Every morning, Mrs. Darren drove the boys to school in her old lime green station wagon. A hideous automobile, which to make matters worse, the doors when opened made a horrid, ear wrenching squeal.

Jack flashed a look of disdain for the embarrassing machine that he'd thought seriously about blowing up. Before climbing into the backseat where his brother was already waiting; whom he promptly pushed over, giving himself a disproportionate amount of space.

The car started up reluctantly with a hoarse cough of thick black smoke, and then off they went shaking and rattling down the road on their way to the Boonton Middle School.

Winter had arrived early this year. And as they headed down the road, they passed rows and rows of barren trees. Far from the only place dealing with unusual weather, over the last few years it had grown erratic all across the planet, with seasons coming on earlier and leaving later, while others failing to show altogether. Regions never knowing a single flake of snow before were buried in blizzards, while droughts turned lush rain forests into desolate deserts. Some claimed it was a drastic climate change, and that the world was heading towards a new Ice Age.

They arrived shortly at the blinking orange light strung up between two metal poles, followed by the crooked sign proclaiming—"Welcome to Boonton." To which some jokester had spray-painted below— "Leave while you still have the chance!"

The town of Boonton was once a beacon of modern industry, emblematic of the Empire's prosperity. But over the last decade it had fallen on hard times. When the town's lucrative manufacturing jobs were shipped to far flung provinces around the globe, where slaves in all but name performed the same work for pennies a day. Now the town was a mere shell of its former self, and every day the shell cracked a little more.

"I have to work the late shift tonight, so you'll be home alone again. There's some canned food in the cupboard—help yourself," said Mrs. Darren as they drove by the old steel mill, standing still as a reminder of glory days past.

"I'd rather starve," grumbled Jack.

"Suit yourself," said Mrs. Darren, "and no trouble tonight, Jack, I mean it. Yes—*you*. Thomas watch your brother."

"Yes mom." Of course Thomas knew watching his brother simply meant making a token effort to stop him when he inevitably decided it was time for a little excitement. One his brother would easily shrug off; or, if you were really foolish enough to stand in his way, a beating would befall you.

"How do you know Thomas won't get into trouble?" argued Jack, "He does have a troublesome look this morning."

"Do not!" responded Thomas.

"Look now he's getting mad—"

"I'm not mad!"

"Why are you yelling—if you're not mad?"

"I'm not ye-Elling!" Thomas' voice rose suddenly, causing his face to deeply redden.

Jack, catching it, smiled dangerously. "What do you think mom? Is Thomas ye-Elling?" he imitated his poor brother all too perfectly, causing Thomas to put his head down sheepishly, and wonder for the umpteenth time if his voice would ever stop cracking.

"I think both of you need to be quiet!" yelled Mrs. Darren, developing a headache.

"Now look what you've done Thomas, you've upset mom—"

"I'm not upset!" erupted Mrs. Darren before Thomas could respond.

To which, Jack predictably chimed in, "You *sound* upset...." amusing himself greatly at his family's expense.

It wasn't long that they arrived at their destination.

Like everything in Boonton, the schoolhouse was rapidly deteriorating, and looked more like an abandoned barn than an establishment of learning. Indeed it was a wonder the building hadn't been condemned.

"Have a good day now," said Mrs. Darren pulling up to the entrance. And no trouble—*Jack*, I don't want another call from Principal Bliss," she added with a look that said she meant it.

Jack gave his mother an obligatory kiss on the cheek and got out of the car, moving away from it as quickly as possible. Thomas then did the same.

Mrs. Darren blew them both another kiss, waved goodbye, and then sped off to go clean who knows what.

The Hunt

THOMAS BEGAN WALKING back home as he usually did after school. His mother unable to pick him up due to her work schedule, and there was simply no point in taking the bus when it was quicker just to walk, and far more peaceful at that. The bus had not always been kind to Thomas, bestowing upon him more than a few painful memories. It was so bad that at one point he was forced to beg his brother for help, which came with a price, as all deals made with Jack do. Jack took care of Thomas' bullies, in a rather ruthless and mean spirited way, but effective all the same as they never bothered Thomas again. For this service rendered, Thomas had to do Jack's chores for the rest of the year—a steep price to pay, but better than getting beat up every day.

Thomas started down towards Old Fisherman's Lake in his usual route home, which he'd whittled down to about an hour with a series of shortcuts through the forest, when suddenly he heard his brother calling out his name.

"Thomas—come here!" boomed his brother's unmistakably deep voice.

Thomas turned to see his brother standing on the other side of the road fashioned in his usual heroic pose: his black hair fluttering in the wind, his hands resting upon his hips, his broad shoulders spread, and his chest protruding outward. Thomas swore his brother always looked like he was having his picture taken.

He was surrounded by members of his sycophantic little gang, known simply as the Twelve. Appropriate given there were twelve of them, and Jack was their undisputed leader. He'd formed the Twelve his very first month at Boonton Middle after defeating the previous ruler of the school, a powerful eighth grader who bullied the younger kids. It gained him quite a following, and everyone clamored to be his friend. These were the lucky ones that made the cut.

Not seeing much of a choice, Thomas reluctantly headed over.

"You wanna play the Hunt with us?" said a coatless Jack in a tone making clear he wasn't really asking. "Joey's sick, so were one short."

Now normally the idea of playing anything with his uber-competitive brother for whom Thomas had never defeated in anything in his whole life, or his little gang, for whom he held a particular disdain, wouldn't appeal to him one bit. But today, for some reason, it did. And so with some legitimate enthusiasm said, "Okay, what park are we playing at?"

"Sherwood," said Jack.

"But that's a half hour's walk from here."

"It's the best place to play," said his brother decidedly, leaving no room for debate.

"Come on let's get going, I gotta be home by six," said Billy Wade impatiently.

Jack shot him a hard look of the kind Thomas knew all too well, having been its recipient on many occasions. It was the kind that chilled to the bone.

"I guess I really don't *have* to be home by six." Billy muttered feebly.

Billy or Colonel Billy as he was known, for Jack was fond of titles, was second in command. He was a fat, dirty, smelly kid, but being larger than most his age came in handy. Plus, like all the rest, worshipped the very ground Jack walked upon.

"So it's settled," declared Jack and everyone nodded.

They headed off for the park, setting a brisk pace as Jack order a forced march. They arrived in record time—a whole seven minutes faster than usual by Jack's watch.

The park itself was just a large field surrounded by a heavy brush of forest. The boys liked it because it was secluded and no one ever bothered them, unlike the other park in town where the cops hung out. There was a tall metal pole in the middle of the field. This served as home base.

In the Hunt there are two teams: the hunters and the hunted. There are three rounds, each lasting a half hour. Team with the most points at the end wins. The hunted score by reaching home base or remaining hidden for the entire period. While the hunters score by stopping the hunted from reaching home base and capturing them all.

It was a violent game, and reaching home base often involved taking a beating, especially if Jack was chasing you. And if so, then you might as well just give yourself up for the boy ran like a cheetah.

There isn't much to do in Boonton, and you do what you have to for fun. Nor were most kids inclined to want to be at home, as most learned from an early age that it was better to be gone when the yelling began.

The school did have a basketball team. But the team was a perennial loser, and received little respect. Jack had been their best player, and the team was actually undefeated in all five games in which he played. But all that ended the day they played one of the affluent schools from the eastern part of the state. The team hasn't won a single game since.

None truly know for certain what was said, but as closely as could be ascertained by those present had something to do with socioeconomic status, which Jack responded to by grabbing the ball and throwing it at the boy's unsuspecting face, shattering his nose. But it didn't end there, for the boy's snobby father seeing his son's nose gushing blood lost his marbles, and ran out onto the court to confront Jack. An impetuous mistake he'd live to regret. For Jack took the very same ball that had disfigured the son and threw it even harder at the father breaking his nose as well, and both lay together side by side screaming in horrid pain as they bled profusely in the middle of the court, while Jack laughed as security guards pulled him away yelling loudly—"Like father, like son!"

Later on he said his only regret was that the mother wasn't there. "I would've liked to disfigure the whole family of snobs. Then they wouldn't stick their noses in the air."

The boys promptly split up into even groups. Jack and Thomas, per usual, were on opposing sides. Thomas' team hid first.

Thomas was never great at sports, unlike his brother, but the Hunt he liked. It suited him: he was good at making himself invisible. Just ask his fellow schoolmates, for if it weren't for the enormous popularity of his brother wouldn't even know he existed. A fact Jack had on several occasions denied.

Thomas quickly found a tree in the middle of the forest and climbed up it. A perfect hiding spot, camouflaged by a surprisingly thick brush of crisp autumn leaves and standing a good height in which to watch the action.

By now it was getting dark as night crept steadily over the earth—a very good thing when playing the Hunt, especially when you're the hunted—and the hunting team was off to capture its victims. Thomas watched his brother lead the charge into the forest.

Why does he have to be first in everything? he wondered as he watched Jack directing his troops to precise locations.

Despite all his brother put him through, Thomas actually looked up to him. It was hard not to. His brother was bold, decisive, and absolutely fearless. A natural leader, people gravitated to him and sought his approval.

Of course, as much as Jack meant to others, who, particularly the Twelve, would do just about anything for him, they in turn were merely tools to serve him, means to ends. And Thomas had seen him throw them off with as much care as a change of clothes.

Being brothers, however, twins nonetheless, changed the dynamic. No matter what they were stuck with one another. And though he undoubtedly lived in his brother's shadow—a fact he was constantly reminded of—he would always be there for better or worse, in a place where others pined to be, if only to be so close.

It was then that Thomas' thoughts turned to their late father, as was often the case when he thought of his brother. Somehow it was a natural progression in his mind. Thomas was only ten when he died, but even when alive never really saw him much. Their mother called him a workaholic. Unfortunately, that wasn't the only kind of holic he turned out to be. Thomas remembered him as a hard man that spoke in short, blunt, commands.

Jack of course had been his favorite. He was even named after him. And after he died Jack began to act out and get into trouble, as if he blamed the whole world for the tragedy and the circumstances that followed, and every day plotted his revenge.

His father's death affected Thomas in other ways. He held his emotions inside, and whether it was for the better or worse he wasn't sure but it was his way of dealing with the pain. He missed his father, he was sure of that, and though their relationship wasn't half as close as Jack's, not a single day passed that he didn't think about him, wishing things could've turned out differently. But more than anything he missed those carefree days when they were a family, and life was simple and happy.

Suddenly Thomas' solitude was rudely interrupted when from beneath his perch came his brother's voice.

"I see you little brother. Now are you going be a good little boy and come on down, or do I have to come up there and get you."

He knew his brother could whip him in a fight and usually he'd do just about anything to appease him. But today for some reason he was feeling brave.

"I'm not coming down. If you want me you're going to have to come up here and get me. That's the rules," he responded with unusual defiance.

His brother simply smiled and shook his head. "Rules are meant to be broken. Besides it's a long way down—wouldn't want to fall if I were you."

Thomas looked down despite himself and felt a knot crop up in his throat. *It was a long way down… I could break a couple of bones…maybe it is best just to climb down on my own*, he thought, reconsidering his initial stance.

"Fine. You win. I'm coming down." Thomas conceded, earning a triumphant grin from Jack. Who of course knew all along what would happen in the end.

Thomas reached the bottom where Jack was grinning like a hyena. He held out his hand as Thomas braced himself for the inevitable blow, and then lightly tapped a cringing Thomas on the shoulder.

"You're dead!"

Thomas emerged from his protective ball to Jack laughing hysterically.

Dammit! he thought, looking like a fool, *Why did Jack always win?*

The boys played for a couple hours longer and then the game ended and they made their way back home. Jack's team as usual had won.

But Thomas had survived, something of a moral victory for him. He wasn't, however, completely unscathed, having been viciously tackled by Billy Wade when he made a mad dash for home base. He could already feel a bruise forming around his ribs.

By now it was getting late and the cold was biting down hard.

"We're going to get sick," said Thomas shivering as they walked back home through the forest.

"You worry too much," said Jack bluntly, himself not wearing a coat and exhibiting no symptoms whatsoever from the bitter cold.

"I'm telling you we're going to be sick and mom is going to be mad. You know she can't afford to bring us to the doctor."

"I don't believe you."

"Well, when you wake up coughing and sneezing you'll know why." Thomas' voice rising ever so slightly.

"I won't," replied Jack with complete confidence. "I never get sick," which was true he never did.

"…there's a first time for everything." Thomas muttered under his breath.

His brother smiled. "Not everything."

Thomas much preferred the forest during the day. At night it was an entirely different place. And tonight the forest was particularly spooky. There was a full moon out and a thick fog wafted about, giving the woods an eerie feel. The barren tree branches, gnarled and mangled, looked like hands reaching out trying to grab them. And to make matters worse, Thomas swore he heard a wolf's howling.

Jack, however, was as fearless as ever. He never got scared and equated fear with weakness. "A useless emotion," he called it.

Despite the ominous surroundings, they reached their house safe and sound around eight-thirty that evening. Late on all accounts if their mother ever knew, especially on a school night. But all the lights were out and their mother's car was missing.

Jack took the key from his pant pocket and promptly turned the lock, and they walked inside the dark house. Thomas quickly turned on the lights.

"Mom won't be home till later tonight…poor woman is always working," said Thomas as they entered.

"I'm starving. What is there to eat around this dump?" said Jack, peering in the cupboard with a noticeable scowl on his face.

"You know what we have, Mom told us this morning."

Jack pulled out a can of string beans and stared at it contemptuously.

"Beans, always beans—I *hate* beans!"

"There on sale this week at the grocery store," said Thomas happily pouring the contents into a pot to be heated.

"For once I wish we could eat something good...something that wasn't on sale," complained Jack as he often did about such things pertaining to their poverty. "Like steak...or lobster..." he said licking his lips, remembering the days when such foods were commonplace.

"You know we can't afford that kind of food any more Jack, not since—"

His brother shot him an angry glance.

"A, sorry," said Thomas weakly, and sat down at the table.

They ate their string beans in silence. Jack forced his down, trying mightily to hold back the vomit. While Thomas didn't think they were all that bad especially with a little salt and pepper. After they'd finished eating they got washed up, changed into pajamas, and headed off to bed.

They had bunk beds. Thomas slept on the bottom and Jack the top. They both hated that they still slept like little children. But once again economics had trumped their rapidly growing maturity.

The boys fell asleep quickly. Thomas didn't even get past the first few pages of the fantasy novel he was reading before dosing off.

Jack dreamed of nothing in particular, only random musings of the kind not wholly remembered upon waking, but that often return in the form of déjà vu, which for Jack was a frequent occurrence. Thomas on the other hand almost always dreamed and most of the times looked forward to them. Except for the nightmares, which were just terrible. The side effect of an overly active imagination. Lately, however, the nightmares had been far more frequent, and tonight the pattern continued.

It began innocently, and was actually quite delightful at first, as Thomas found himself standing in a great golden wheat field, the sun shining warmly upon his face, and a light soothing breeze gently brushing his cheek, a perfect summer's day.

He found that everything seemed better here. The sun was bigger and brighter than usual, and he bathed in its warmth feeling as snug and secure as an infant in its mother's arms. While the blue sky in which it hung held not a single imperfection to spoil it.

But abruptly his perfect scene changed its tone as a faint coldness took to his skin, and the light wind picked up its pace. Until it blew hard and cold like a northern gale. The sun faded back, cowering in the forthcoming storm's wake. Shadows of darkness crept ominously in obscuring the golden field into a colorless mass of gray.

He saw in the distance an enormous dark cloud moving towards him at an alarming pace. It sounded like teeth gnawing and gnashing, and as it passed over the field of wheat everything died as if consumed by a voracious swarm of locusts. And as it closed in upon him he saw that the dark cloud was actually a huge black beast, with vicious teeth and glowing red eyes.

Thomas ran frantically, fast as he could, and the insatiable beast gave chase. He ran and he ran, trying with all his might not to look back. He could feel it upon his tail nipping hungrily at his heels. But he stayed always one step ahead.

Then suddenly his legs betrayed him. He stumbled and fell to the ground. The beast pounced, rushing over him like a tidal wave, tearing the flesh right off of his bones….

Thomas awoke sweating profusely and covering his face protectively with his hands. His breaths were deep and heavy and his face ghostly pale. He clutched himself to ensure he remained whole.

Just a dream, he reassured himself, *It wasn't real…everything is okay…*

As Thomas was composing himself, however, there came a loud knock at the front door. Thomas quickly wiped the sweat from his forehead and arched to see the clock: 4:30 a.m.

"Go see who it is!" ordered Jack sleepily.

Thomas yawned, stretched his back, and then reluctantly got out of bed, a blanket wrapped tightly around him.

Probably Mom forgot her key again, he surmised as he headed towards the front door.

But when he opened it there standing before him were two uniformed police officers.

One of the officers was a tall, stern looking man with an exceedingly well groomed dark brown mustache. The name on his badge read Kent. The other an attractive petite female with short strawberry blond hair. Her badge read Valorous. Both wore serious no nonsense looks upon their face, the way only properly trained police officers can.

"Can—I—help—you—officers?" Thomas stammered, and not due to the brisk morning air.

"Are you related to one Janet Darren?" inquired Officer Kent.

"I'm her son," answered Thomas.

The officers looked at one another and then nodded very officially.

"You're going to have to come with us to the station." Officer Valorous informed him.

"What! Why? Have I done some—wait, what did my brother do?" asked Thomas. This wouldn't be the first time Jack had warranted the law's attention.

"Brother?" the officers replied in unison. Then they looked at one another and nodded.

"He's going to have to come to," said Officer Kent. "We'll wait while you get dressed."

"What is this is all about? If you need to speak with my mom I'm sure she'll be home any min—" and then he thought about it, why wasn't she home yet. She should be home by now, shouldn't she?

Officer Kent scratched his moustache nervously and Officer Valorous put her head down, and for a moment there was complete silence and an eerie calm of the kind preceding a thunderstorm. Then finally it came, like a swift, sudden, snap.

"I'm sorry to inform you," began Officer Valorous somberly, "but your mother was involved in an incident tonight at the Berkshire mall."

"W-what sort of an incident?" stuttered Thomas.

"There was a robbery attempt, and your mother was shot trying to stop them," said Officer Kent.

The words fell upon Thomas like a ton of bricks.

"Is she...ok?"

The officers looked at one another again. Then Officer Valorous turned and responded, "No, I'm sorry, she's dead."

Thomas' world spun upside down. His legs shook and his mind went blank. He fainted right then and there in front of the officers on his doorstep. As once again death had come for a visit.

Wordsworth

Jack and Thomas sat silently in Detective Cavanaugh's office at the Boonton police department. They'd shown little emotion since learning of their mother's tragic death only a few short hours ago. They hadn't even shed a single tear. Some may've said that they were in a state of shock, and perhaps they'd be right.

The office itself was standard police issued, aside from its general sloppiness. The work desk was engulfed in a sizeable pile of unorganized files haphazardly strewn together with papers shifting in and out of their respective folders. A half empty box of donuts sat atop the mountain heap, while Styrofoam cups smelling of old coffee were scattered about the room. A ragged leather chair slouched comfortably behind the desk, while the boys sat in two stiff wooden chairs situated opposite it.

The door behind them opened suddenly and then closed with a loud thud that would've grabbed most anyone's attention, and was designed to do just that. But the boys barely noticed, and didn't even bother lifting up their heads to acknowledge the Detective as he entered his office.

Detective Cavanaugh was a middle aged man on the heavier side with thinning red hair and tired hazel eyes. Much like his office, he was sloppily attired in an over worn cheap brown suit so wrinkled you would've thought it had never known an iron. Some excess food was crusted on the side of his mouth, blending into his prominent five o'clock shadow.

He carelessly cleared away files from his desk and sat down on the edge facing the boys with a serious, yet somewhat conciliatory look.

"This is a tough day boys," began the Detective in a voice doing its best to soften some of its natural gruffness, "but you'll get through it, mark my words.

I know it may not seem like it, but life goes on…things get better," he paused briefly allowing the words to sink in. "Lost my own mother when I was young, it hurt…hurt real bad. But you get over it, with time."

The boys continued staring blankly into space, betraying no hint they were listening to a single word the Detective said.

"Yeah, well, I know how you feel is all," he added, noting their complete lack of want for conversation. He sighed deeply, feeling the weight of the mood. "Anyway, we've a tried to locate some of your family members, but were having some trouble. Don't suppose you know of anyone we might be able to contact, do you?" he asked hopefully.

Once again the boys remained silent.

"Right, well, I suppose we'll just keep on looking then," and after a moment the Detective hopped off the desk and headed briskly towards the doorway, adding before he left, "I'll have someone bring you something to eat."

The boys sat in that dreadful room for what seemed like hours on end and slowly but surely the pain set in, as the numbness faded and the cruel reality came crashing down around them. It was then that they realized the unalterable truth: everyone they'd ever cared about was gone.

Thomas did what Thomas usually did: he tried to suppress what was happening, to push it down into that place where all things go that rot the soul. To hide it there, where it would never surface again, buried deep like all the rest in an overstuffed closet of bad memories and regrets….But this time the emotions proved too strong, and it all came tumbling out—tears streamed down the side of his face as the feelings burst forth from within.

Jack felt the anger, the rage, and he cursed the world for all it was worth. He wished upon it dark tidings and horrible plagues, misery and suffering to mirror his own. He banged his fist violently against the side of the chair causing the wood to split—trading one kind of pain for another.

It was then that Detective Cavanaugh opened the door once more and walked back inside his office.

It had been a strange day that's for sure, he thought scratching his scalp as he entered. He'd done all he could, but nothing turned up. It looked hopeless: orphanage, foster homes, and a life of constant upheaval. He'd seen it all before. It was a terrible way to grow up, and one he understood better than most, for it was the way his own sad childhood had played out.

All seemed lost and he was on his way to break the news when he received the phone call from out of the blue. At first, he thought it was some wacko playing a sick joke, but he had all the right information. He was legit, as absurd as that sounded.

Detective Cavanaugh sat back down on the corner of his desk and faced the boys. Thomas was still crying, while Jack was a block of ice.

"I got some good news. We located your Great Uncle, or I should say he located us. Royalty of some sort too, called himself the Lord of—hold on I got it here," he rummaged hastily through a manila folder, "Somulus. Never heard of it myself, but then geography wasn't my strong suit. But it's somewhere on the other side of the world. Anyhow, he's agreed to take full custody of you boys, being that he's your relative and all. Oh, and he's also going to pay for all the funer—" he stopped himself, "Well, a…" he smiled overtly, "you don't have anything to worry about is all. Your Uncle is sending someone over to pick you up. May take a few days though with the state of travel, so we're sending you home with one of our officers. Everything is going to be just fine." Detective Cavanaugh reassured them. Whether he believed it was another matter entirely.

Anything's better than the orphanage I suppose, he thought as he departed the room.

Three days past—three miserable, downtrodden, days. The boys barely got out of bed, and they weren't eating. Food had no flavor to them. Their tears had long dried up as all the fluid in their bodies was drained. Now there was only a deep feeling of emptiness, a void that felt as if it could never be filled again.

Officer Valorous attempted to cheer the boys up. But nothing worked and eventually she stopped trying altogether. *Best to let the mourning process run its course,* she thought, being herself no stranger to loss.

Finally, the day of the funeral arrived, and around 7:30 that morning a loud knock came at the door. Officer Valorous got up from her place on the couch, doubling these last few days as a bed, and answered it.

Standing on the doorstep was an older man with an impeccably trimmed white moustache completely encompassing the upper half of his lip. Dressed deftly in a finely tailored black suit that a dandy gentleman may have worn stylishly a century ago, complete with a black top hat and cane to match. He was tall, and it was evident had once been powerfully built, though the years had taken their toll. His eyes were mismatched: one gray the other a piercing blue. Speaking with a proper accent of the kind one would expect from a gentleman of old, he introduced himself as Wordsworth and said he'd come for the boys.

Satisfied that he was who he claimed to be, Officer Valorous allowed him inside.

The television blared with breaking news as Wordsworth entered the household. They both turned to watch an overly groomed anchorman announce that yet another country friendly to the Empire had been attacked. The third this week. They listened as he went into the grim details, using words like *catastrophe*, *tragedy*, and *disaster*.

Officer Valorous shook her head. "World is falling apart. Won't be nothing left to save soon enough."

Wordsworth smiled. "I suppose that depends upon one's perspective."

"Come here boys, your Uncle's—I'm sorry, what did you say were you again?"

"His assistant, you could say."

"Your Uncle's assistant is here to drive you to the church. So get dressed and ready to go!" she yelled back to them in a voice well accustomed to giving orders, or at least directing traffic.

The boys didn't answer. But they'd heard all the same and began putting on their black suits, which had been worn to more than their fair share of funerals and by now were several sizes too small.

"No rush," said Wordsworth.

"They have to be at the church by 8:15!" replied Officer Valorous, who prided herself on being punctual.

"I doubt they'd start the service without them, do you?"

"You have a point, still…"

"Time is always of the essence, isn't that right, Madam Valkyrie?" said Wordsworth.

"What did you…how do you …." her voice trailed off as if the words had been plucked from her mouth.

For a long moment they stood there in silence, with much being said yet unspoken.

Finally, Officer Valorous put her head down and her eyes welled with tears. Wordsworth placed his hand on her shoulder.

"You've been in hiding for too long," and she looked up at him like a lost child run away from home, "You cannot run from who you are. You belong with your family, especially in these darkest of hours. Though before you go, there is something you must do for me."

She bowed her head and listened attentively.

When Wordsworth finished she nodded and replied, "I'll do as you ask."

Just then the boys appeared dressed in their black suits, neither looking particularly happy or remotely comfortable. Especially bad for Jack, who looked as if he'd outgrown his suit years ago and was now clutching to his body for dear life.

"There you are," said Officer Valorous hastily wiping away the remaining tears from her eyes, "Now don't you look nice, such fine little gentleman. I bet the girls go crazy for you two. I know I would have when—" and then suddenly realizing she'd forgotten all about the man standing to her left gasped, "Oh! How rude of me! Boys, this is your Uncle's assistant, Mr. Wordsworth."

"Simply Wordsworth will suffice," he said humbly, and then bowed elegantly with hat in hand to each, revealing for the first time his white hair, surprisingly thick for a man his age.

The elaborate greeting took the boys back. They weren't at all accustomed to being bowed to—especially not in Boonton where a proper handshake was a rarity. Though Jack rather liked it and thought that everyone should address him in just such a manner.

"Please to meet you Mr.—err—Wordsworth." Thomas said politely.

Jack however said nothing and just stared coldly at the man, sizing him up like an animal, discerning what kind of a threat, if any, he posed to himself.

For a long moment they all just stood there staring at one another in silence.

"Such handsome little devils." Wordsworth said finally, breaking the increasingly awkward silence. "Now let me guess, you must be Jack, and you Thomas," he added, guessing correctly. "A tremendous honor to finally make your acquaintance. I've heard so much about you both."

"From who?" questioned Jack sharply.

"Why from your Uncle of course!"

"We've never even met him before," said Jack, "I didn't even know we had a Great Uncle until three days ago." Which was true neither boy could ever recall having heard mention of any Great Uncle before.

"All the same, he's very fond of you both. My word you should hear him go on and on. I haven't seen him so excited in years now that you're coming to live with him."

"I'm excited to meet him as well!" Thomas beamed, regaining for the first time in several days some of his natural cheerfulness. But then Jack shot him a nasty look that said quite simply—"shut up!" and the smile on his face wilted like the petals of a dying flower.

"We'll have plenty of time to talk at length later. But the good officer doesn't wish for us to be late, so we'd best be on our way. After you young masters," said Wordsworth beckoning them on with his hand.

Outside they discovered a beautiful shining black Rolls Royce parked in front of their house. Wordsworth walked up and opened the back door for the boys.

At first, they just stood there in complete shock. Neither had seen a car like this before, except for in a movie.

Could this really be for us? thought Thomas, opening and closing his eyes several times to ensure he wasn't dreaming. While Jack simply stood there wearing a smile worthy of a jackal.

"Coming young masters?" prodded Wordsworth, holding the door ajar.

They looked at one another and then both raced towards the car. Jack got their first.

When they were settled in on the plush white leather seats, Wordsworth shut the door, got into the driver's seat, started up the vehicle, and off they headed to the funeral.

The Dead of Winter

AS THEY DROVE the excitement of riding in such a luxurious automobile wore off and whatever magic the old man brought with him faded as bleak reality crashed their masquerade. Thomas wondered how he could've ever been so delusional as to have for even a moment forgotten his sorrow. But his mind it seemed was still playing tricks on him, for he swore at one point he actually saw the car steering itself. Though when he looked again saw the old man's wrinkled hands firmly clasped upon the wheel.

Saint George's was by far the oldest building in town. It was designed to look like a medieval cathedral, with a gothic architecture complete with ferocious stone gargoyles standing upon the crenulated rooftop. This was where Mrs. Darren would be laid to her eternal rest.

Mr. Darren by contrast resided in an ill-kept public cemetery in an unmarked grave—as they could not, on account of the heavy debts he'd saddled them with, afford to pay for an engraving.

Some random beggars were camped outside the church shaking their metal cans. When Wordsworth stopped the car in the front, several came up holding dirty washcloths offering to clean the windows for spare change. Wordsworth reached into his pocket and handed each a shining silver coin, though kindly informed them that the windows were in no need of a wash, and besides he suspected rain.

The church bells rang loudly from the church's highest tower. The boys looked up and listened as they chimed. Then made their way indoors.

The church was lined with rows of hard wooden seats, uncomfortable as any could possibly be and apparently meant to humble by assailing the back and knees. The rows were sparsely populated, as Mrs. Darren had little time or opportunity over the last few years for making friends, despite her amiable nature. Those few in attendance were co-workers. The boys and Wordsworth sat in the first row, while the rest sat sparingly in the two rows behind them.

Stained glass pictorials of various religious scenes and symbols occupied the triangular windows adorning nearly every wall of the church. The majority of which told the tale of Saint George himself. Outfitted heroically in shining silver battle armor, he fought a great fire breathing dragon to the death with his sword and shield, claiming ultimate victory in the very last window with the heel of his foot standing triumphantly atop the beast's head.

At the front of the church stood the parish priest Father Peter, a man widely known to be fond of the sacramental wine. Adorned in his finest ceremonial robes, he stood behind a large marble altar with several items used in accordance with the ceremony sitting atop it. Two altar boys dressed in red robes stood to either side awaiting his instructions.

As the ceremony began, Thomas couldn't help but think about what happened when you died, as he often did, having known so much death in his life. His mother had said that dying was just the ending of one journey and the beginning of another. That life goes on just in a different form and that even when a story ends it is only the reader that is cut off, while the lives of the characters carry on. Just as our loved ones do when their own stories are taken from our view and their part in the play of our life is over. They simply move on to their next role in another theater. But we remember them, as we remember any great tale or character. They stay with us in our hearts and minds. Until they become a part of us, a part of our own character in some way, and so we never truly lose them for we never lose ourselves.

Though, as cheery as that all sounded, Thomas always wondered if she'd just said that to give them hope, especially when times were at their worst. And what of the alternative: *What if there really is a place where people go to suffer forever?*

It was too terrifying to comprehend. *She can't be…she was a good person after all, wasn't she*? Thomas felt tears running down his cheeks. "I miss you Mom… wherever you are," he whispered as Father Peter spoke the final words of the sermon.

The pall bearers, many of whom were the beggars from earlier, carried the coffin shakily to the cemetery directly behind the church. It was quite the little miracle they arrived without dropping it once. The boys followed Wordsworth outside to say their final goodbyes.

None of the others who attended the church service actually came outside to the cemetery. Apparently having better things to do than watch Mrs. Darren go six feet under; that, or for the fact that the sky appeared ready to pour down rain at any moment. No matter. To Jack and Thomas it was only them and their mother anyhow.

A large black raven sat perched on the bough of an old twisted tree overlooking the grave site, as Father Peter managed to deliver the last rites in a remarkably sober fashion. After which, the casket was lowered slowly into the ground.

Thomas threw down a single red rose and two coins Wordsworth had given him before leaving to get the car, "For safe passage," apparently a burial tradition in his country.

The raven squawked three times and then flew off, and the funeral concluded. Mrs. Darren was laid to rest.

The rain which had held to this point began falling. The boys however stood there for a good while longer. They didn't mind, somehow it seemed appropriate. Their mother used to say that rain washed away the dirt of the world and the harder it rained the more there was. But when it finished the world was clean again and everything started over anew when the sun came out.

Jack hoped his mother was right and the rain would wash away the filth of the world. *But for that to happen it would have to flood...* and suddenly as if hearing his thoughts a roar of thunder shook the sky and the rain fell down harder—hitting the ground with brutal force, pounding itself into the earth as if echoing Jack's rage.

The boys walked back to the car where Wordsworth awaited them. Wordsworth got out of the car with an umbrella as they approached, though by now they were thoroughly soaked.

Thomas was weary at first about sitting on the white leather seats. But Wordsworth told him it didn't matter, it was only a car.

"Ready?" asked Wordsworth when they settled in.

"Yes," said Thomas.

"Master Jack," said Wordsworth, "Ready to go as well?"

Jack paused momentarily and stared back one final time at the graveyard as the rain fell torrentially. "Take us far away from this place," he said finally, and with that they were off.

Books and Covers

THE BOYS SAT in front of their small television set glued to SNN. The war had finally made its way onto the Empire's shores as several major cities along the eastern coast had been bombed by enemy planes in a surprise attack. The devastation was massive and reports claimed death tolls in the tens of thousands.

The President had given an address to the grieving nation. He promised they'd get through this dark time and be the stronger for it. He also made it clear—as he consoled the crying mothers and sobbing fathers who'd lost their only sons and daughters—that those responsible would soon gasp for their very last breaths.

In the wake of the attack, all planes had been grounded while other forms of transportation were severely limited. A fact particularly worrisome given that they were scheduled to depart for Somulus in the morning. But Wordsworth didn't seem the least bit concerned. The restrictions he said would have no bearing upon their travel arrangements, which apparently would take them far away from the war anyhow. According to Wordsworth, being so small Somulus was often overlooked by the rest of the world. Indeed few even knew of its existence. Of course, that still didn't explain exactly how they'd be getting there in the first place, Thomas thought. But decided to simply take the old man's word for it.

Before going to bed, Wordsworth mixed them up a cup of tea. "It'll help you sleep," he promised.

True to his word, the tea worked almost instantly and moments after drinking it both boys could scarcely keep their eyes open. It wasn't long before they were sound asleep....

To their complete and utter astonishment, when the boys awoke they found themselves traveling on a train.

"Welcome back." Wordsworth greeted them as they opened their eyes nearly in unison, putting down the book he'd been reading.

"H-h-how did we get here?" asked Jack with evident confusion.

"We traveled of course. Though I don't expect either of you to remember much of it. You two were dead to the world, as the expression goes. Why I practically had to carry you both!"

Thomas discovered that he'd no memory whatsoever of their travels. The last thing he remembered was drinking the tea and the next here he was. He didn't even recall packing. But there beside them were their suitcases.

"Surely you must remember something of the plane ride," said Wordsworth.

And just as he said it, something triggered in Thomas' mind, and though only a moment before he'd no recollection of traveling at all, let alone upon a plane, suddenly recalled, albeit vaguely, doing precisely that. And he wondered how he could've possibly forgot.

"Of—of course I remember the plane!" Jack snapped.

"Where are we now?" Thomas inquired.

"We're getting close to Somulus. Not much further now," said Wordsworth.

The train was old fashioned of the sort seen these days only in museums, and it appeared that they were its lone passengers. In fact, the only other person on the train was a tall, skeleton thin bald man with jaundiced skin, wearing a red vest and bow tie, who appeared to work there. Bizarrely, he was walking down the aisle calling out for tickets and stopping at each empty seat as if actually collecting them.

Must be really bored, thought Thomas shaking his head, *Or delusional.*

Abruptly, the train came to a screeching halt causing both boys to fly forward. Wordsworth must have anticipated this and taken precautions for he didn't budge an inch from his seat.

They waited for a few minutes. But no one got on or off.

"How long have you worked for our Uncle?" asked Thomas when they started up again.

"For many, many years," said Wordsworth.

"What's he like?" asked Thomas, curious about what sort of a person he was going to be living with.

"His Lordship," began Wordsworth in a reverent tone, "is a fair and just master. And once you get to know him I've no doubt you'll come to like him very much."

"How old is he?" asked Thomas.

"Older than he looks," replied Wordsworth simply.

"What does he *do* exactly?" asked Jack joining the conversation.

"As ruler of the realm, he does whatever duty demands of him," replied Wordsworth.

"Realm?" asked Thomas, unfamiliar with the term, at least as it applied here.

"You'll undoubtedly find some of our vocabulary different than what you're accustomed to. Though, you will also discover many similarities. Somulus is one of the seven lands, or realms, that encompass Mythil."

Thomas had never heard of either before. But then the world had gone through so many changes over the last decade, with countries breaking up and forming into others, that it was hard to keep track of them all.

"So our Uncle is like a king or something?" asked Jack.

"I suppose you could say that, yes. Though he'd never call himself one."

Jack shook his head. "He either is a king or he isn't."

"Not everything must be one way or another," said Wordsworth, "Besides one man's king may be another man's servant, while another man's servant, a king."

"A king bows to no one. Or they would not be a king." Jack declared unequivocally.

"Ah, but there are many kinds of kings, are there not? And one king may be more powerful than another. Everyone bows to someone Master Jack, even kings.

"So where will we be staying?" asked Thomas.

"In your Uncle's castle," responded Wordsworth, as if the most normal thing in the world.

Jack's eyes lit up, until practically glowing. "He has a castle?"

"Well, yes Master Jack, I thought I just said that."

And for once Jack didn't care about the sarcasm, being far too consumed with the idea of living in a castle, not to mention the implications.

Thomas too was excited beyond words. It was like he was in the middle of one of the stories he loved reading so much.

"Does he have any other family—I mean, besides us?" asked Thomas, hoping to encounter some distant relatives.

"I'm afraid not Master Thomas. Now that your mother has passed you two are his only remaining relatives, as he is yours. Precisely the reason he insisted upon you coming to stay with him. Family is very important to him."

"If it's so important then why didn't he come to visit us? Why haven't we ever met him before? Why did he leave us to rot—when he has a castle!" Jack erupted.

Wordsworth raised his eyebrows. "Master Jack, there is fire in those eyes of yours. You must learn to control your emotions, or they will control you."

But Jack's anger did not subside and only raged deeper for having been told to quiet. Though he'd heard much that piqued his interest, and beneath his outward anger was a kind of deceitful jubilation.

"As to your question, circumstances beyond his control have prevented him from seeing you. His position is a demanding one and his time not always his own. But I do know that he desires deeply to make up for time lost, and I'm sure he will, if only you give him the chance," said Wordsworth.

"It's going to take a lot for that to happen," said Jack, never one to hand out second chances easily, and when he did they came at a significant price. To which, he already had one in mind.

Just then the bald man with the red vest and bow tie arrived at their seat.

"Tickets!"

Wordsworth promptly reached into his breast pocket and handed over three tickets.

"How are things?" Wordsworth asked the man conversationally as he examined the tickets.

"Busy today, as I'm sure you can tell," he replied as he punched the tickets, "Been like this for some time now, running full capacity nearly every day. I haven't seen it this bad in—well—ages," said the man ruefully, and looking every bit exhausted with beads of sweat mounted like tiny soldiers on his forehead.

Thomas and Jack stared at one another incredulously, unable to believe what they were hearing.

This guy has lost his mind, thought Thomas, and Jack thought the same if only in harsher terms for the man's lack of mental capacity.

"These are difficult times my friend. And I'm afraid they're only going to get worse," said Wordsworth gravely.

"I know what you mean. But what ya going to do, eh? Can't stop em, can ya. Besides I got a job to do, don't have time to be worrying about the reasons."

Wordsworth nodded. "We all have our jobs to do. Speaking of which, how much longer is it going to be?"

"Let me see..." he pulled out a piece of paper and examined it, "Should be arriving shortly. Yours is the next stop."

"Splendid!" said Wordsworth.

"Right then, I'll leave you to yourselves. Author knows I got enough work to do around here."

"Give the conductor my regards," said Wordsworth.

"I'll do that. Enjoy the rest of the ride," and with a respectful nod he was off down the corridor of the train, shaking his head with every empty seat he passed.

"What in the world is he talking about? There's no one on this train but us," said Jack after he left.

"Yeah Wordsworth I haven't seen a single other person on this train. How could he possibly say it's full?" echoed Thomas.

Wordsworth shrugged. "I suppose he must be lying then. That, or you two are simply blind. It's one or the other. But are you perfectly certain you've given it a proper look around? Sure you're not missing anything? After all I wouldn't want the man branded a liar for nothing."

"We would've seen other passengers by now, especially if the train was full." Jack countered logically.

"That's true," agreed Thomas, "We would've seen at least *someone* by now."

"Hmm, you make a good point. Well, if you're sure then," and Wordsworth returned to reading his book.

The boys looked at one another and then simultaneously got up from their seats and walked out into the corridor.

As expected, it was empty. Not a single soul to be seen. To make absolutely certain, Jack walked to the end of the corridor checking every seat as he went.

"Empty," he yelled from the end, "There is no one else on this train—he must be crazy!"

Thomas couldn't see anyone either.

When they arrived back at their seat, Wordsworth glanced up from his book. "Were you successful?"

"If by successful you mean did we see anyone else. Then no, we were not." Jack answered brusquely.

"Oh, that is disappointing."

"What's disappointing?" shot Jack.

Wordsworth put the book down, and sighed. "That you weren't able to see the other passengers, I'd thought perhaps you might be able to. Apparently, I was overzealous. I wouldn't worry too much about it though, these things take time."

A flare of anger crossed Jack's face. "We weren't able to see anyone, because there is no one there—we aren't blind!"

"You are if you only see with your eyes," responded Wordsworth calmly.

"How else does someone see?" asked Thomas.

"There are many different ways to see, the eyes being merely one of them."

"What kind of nonsense is that? If I can't see something with my eyes then it's not there." Jack declared flatly.

But Wordsworth only smiled the way a patient parent would when dealing with a stubborn child.

"I tell you now that when we arrive in Somulus there will be many things that you'll not see if only you trust your eyes. While others you'll see and still not believe. You must open your mind and learn to see beyond mere appearances, beyond the façade."

The boys looked at him like he had two heads.

Seeing that he was making no head way, Wordsworth tried a different tact. "Perhaps an example would assist your understanding," and he held up the plain brown book he was reading, "Do you see this book?"

Both boys nodded that of course they did.

"Well that's a good start!" the old man laughed.

Neither boy was particularly amused.

"What would you say this book is about?" asked Wordsworth, after he'd finished amusing himself.

"How the heck should we know!" Jack snapped, "All we can see is its cover!"

"Precisely!" replied Wordsworth.

"Precisely what?" they both chimed in unison.

The old man sighed. "I see I'll have to explain further."

"A, yeah," said Jack, "We don't speak crazy."

Thomas stifled a laugh.

"Right," said Wordsworth, not taking their meaning. "A book is not just a cover, is it?" the boys didn't answer the clearly rhetorical question, "It's what lies *inside*, beyond the cover that matters most...what the pages hold. And though the cover may change, the book remains the same. This book happens to be one of the greatest ever written. But you'd never know it because your eyes could never see past the cover. Do you understand?"

"Not really," said Jack.

"Never judge a book by its cover," said Thomas reciting the old adage.

"Exactly right," said Wordsworth proudly.

"That doesn't explain anything." Jack countered derisively.

"Look *beyond* mere appearances, through the layers of consciousness, and you'll see the truth. Life is all just books and covers you see."

Jack shook his head. It was clear to him this was going nowhere. Nowhere sane anyway.

"What book is that?" asked Thomas, who of course loved books.

"It's a book of stories from our land. If you'd care to read it, be my guest," said Wordsworth handing Thomas the book.

"Thanks," said Thomas, always happy to have a new book to read. "Who's the author?"

"Being a collection of tales, it has many authors," said Wordsworth.

"Like fairy tales."

"Not all of them are about fairies," said Wordsworth.

Abruptly, the train came to another screeching halt that nearly sent Thomas flying off his seat, and surely would've if not for Wordsworth, who with surprising strength caught his jacket collar and pulled him back.

"T-thanks," said Thomas.

"This is where we get off." Wordsworth informed them, "Grab your suitcases—quickly there is no time to waste."

"What's the rush? It's not like there is anyone else on the train." Jack grumbled.

As they made their way briskly down the long corridor of the train, Thomas caught sight of something out of the corner of his eye. At first he thought he was hallucinating, or on the verge of one of his fainting spells when odd visions were commonplace right before he went down. But when he looked back, there they were staring at him: a family of four, a mother, father, and two young boys siting in the formerly unoccupied seat, as if they'd always been there. One of the young boys even waved at him, and Thomas found himself waving back. But when he blinked they'd vanished, and once more it was an empty seat with no hint it was ever anything else.

My imagination is playing tricks on me.

Nevertheless, as he walked he stared intently into every empty seat he passed to see if others would materialize.

As he reached the door where Wordsworth and Jack were getting off, he suddenly heard sounds coming from behind him of people speaking in a multitude of different languages. He turned around and saw the train completely filled with all different kinds of people.

Thomas stood there in utter disbelief. *How could I have missed all of them*? *How could anyone*?

"Coming Master Thomas?" Wordsworth called out.

"One moment," he called back. But when he turned back around the train was completely empty once more. *Hey, where did they—*

He shook his head as he hopped off the train.

The Fog

FRIGID AIR GNAWED upon Jack and Thomas' bones as they departed the train. Their feet crunched loudly when they hit the ground that was littered with a thick layer of dead leaves rustling about in a cold wind. Tentacles of fog drifted about, while a weak sun set low beneath snow covered mountains in the distance, portending the imminent onset of darkness.

The place facing them appeared utterly abandoned. The only remaining signs of life being a single lonely wooden bench that looked like it hadn't been used in ages, sitting beneath the flickering light of a rusted lamppost threatening to extinguish at any moment.

Thomas was just glad to be off the train. He wasn't sure what he'd seen, if indeed it was anything. Though this place he discovered wasn't much better. There was something off about it, something not quite right. There was an eerie silence, a soundless dreamlike quality that caused everything to seem a bit more dead than alive. Even the wind blowing cold across their faces only whispered, and the leaves dancing beneath their feet lay deafly silent. It all didn't seem real somehow.

The train's wheels churned as they prepared for departure. The train headed towards a dark tunnel cut crookedly into the side of one of the mountainous blocks of gray stone surrounding them.

Though as Thomas watched the train go, he saw something very strange—indeed impossible. The train's wheels weren't even touching the tracks, but hovering completely above them.

"Do you see—?"

But his brother wasn't looking.

And when Thomas turned back around, the train had disappeared down the tunnel.

Thomas couldn't believe his eyes, and not for the first time today. He was beginning to think that he was going crazy or….

"Now what?" asked Jack impatiently.

"We walk," said Wordsworth.

"Walk?"

"You know one foot in front of the other."

"I know what walking is," snapped Jack. "I mean no one is coming to pick us up?"

"Oh no, not here," said Wordsworth shaking his head, "Now come along… unless of course you'd rather stay here, though I wouldn't recommend it. You may find leaving far more difficult than you imagined."

Carrying their suitcases, the boys followed Wordsworth past the wooden bench and the flickering light of the rusted lamppost. After which they walked upon a narrow dirt path passing by a host of barren trees with gnarled branches. Before arriving at what could only be described as a wall of fog.

The boys stopped short, in awe of the natural wonder.

"Come now," prompted Wordsworth, noting their reluctance, "Keep moving."

As if anticipating their arrival, the fog opened up and allowed them to enter. Then like a mouth closed and consumed them whole.

The fog was so dense that it was nearly impossible to see anything. Wordsworth did his best to keep the boys close, and every few moments would call out their names to ensure they were still nearby.

"I'm right behind you!" snapped Jack after about the sixth time, "It's only fog!"

There was, however, Jack noticed a distinct nervousness in Wordsworth's voice, especially when they didn't immediately answer his calls. It was something up until now he hadn't heard before in the old man who always seemed so sure of himself.

He's afraid of something here, thought Jack, adept at sensing fear, and to test his theory would intentionally wait a few extra moments each time before responding.

"Jack?" Wordsworth called on one of his periodic checkups.

Jack didn't answer.

"Jack?" repeated Wordsworth, this time louder and with a strong hint of anxiousness.

"Still here," replied Jack finally, delighting in making the old man squirm.

"Thomas?"

But whereas Thomas would usually reply right away, this time there was silence.

"Thomas?"

Silence.

"Thomas!"

Finally, Jack heard Thomas' voice behind him say "Here," though it sounded weaker and wispier than usual. *Probably getting winded*, he thought. His brother was never much of an athlete.

"He's right behind me!" yelled Jack, making sure the old man heard it. He didn't need him having a heart attack. At least not before they got to the castle.

"Ah, good," said Wordsworth, sounding very much relieved, "Let's get a move on. We're nearly through."

Jack shook his head. *Foolish old man.*

Thomas was lost. He'd sworn his brother and Wordsworth were right in front of him. But then all of sudden were not. Now he'd no clue where they were.

"Jack! Wordsworth!" he called out frantically.

But for the umpteenth time there was no reply from either.

To make matters worse, there was definitely something moving in the fog. He kept hearing footsteps running and whispers brushing by his ears.

"Whose there?" Thomas asked finally, his head darting around.

Suddenly faces began forming inside the fog. Hundreds of them—cold, dead, faces. They surrounded him, and with foggy dead hands reached out towards him.

Thomas felt the all too familiar rush of paralyzing cold which preceded a fainting spell. He couldn't stop it. He fell...

As Wordsworth and Jack ventured on ahead, the heavy fog at last loosened its grip, as a bright yellow light began breaking through it. At first, the fog fought back against the light, but little by little the light forced its way through. Until the light was victorious and the fog was vanquished.

They stood in a grassy clearing directly between the bright light ahead, coming from just beyond a grassy hill, and the fog. Next to them was a giant white rock with hieroglyphic like symbols carved into it.

"Where is Thomas?" asked Wordsworth, looking around.

Jack shrugged. "He *was* right behind me."

Wordsworth appeared noticeably concerned. "When was the last time you saw him?"

"A few minutes ago…maybe. It's hard to see anything in that fog."

"Master Jack, are you telling me that you've no idea where your brother is?"

"I'm sure he's coming. He's a little on the slow side is all. Hey, where are we?"

"Thomas! Thomas!" Wordsworth yelled out into the fog, louder than ever before.

No response.

"Thomas—answer me!"

Now even Jack joined in. "Quit playing games and come on!"

But still there was nothing.

Wordsworth turned to Jack. "I'm going to look for Thomas. You stay right here. No matter what happens, don't move. Understood?"

"Whatever," responded Jack indifferently.

Thomas awoke lying face down on a tiled white floor that smelled recently mopped by some strong industrial cleaner, and was wet as a result. To which a yellow sign standing to his right cautioned any would be traveler that the floor was hazardous to walk upon.

He stood up slowly. His head was woozy, and everything appeared slightly out of focus and blurry. He rubbed his eyes to clear them of their malady. When he'd succeeded, he saw that he was standing in the middle of a hallway with stores lining either side.

Where am I? he puzzled, staring down the seemingly endless rows of stores.

Everything looked familiar to Thomas somehow, as if he'd been here before. But he couldn't place it.

He started down the hallway, staring at each of the stores he passed by, many of which he swore he'd been inside. But now they were all locked up.

As he walked, he heard music playing. One of those monotonous elevator jingles. He found himself humming the tune. Strangely, that too felt familiar.

He passed by a large floor buffer still plugged in by its orange extension cord, making him wonder about the whereabouts of the machine's operator.

Up ahead he saw a large toy store, a popular brand called Wonderblink Toys that you could find at any mall. He was certain he'd been there before. Not to another branch of the chain, but to this exact store. He even remembered the outdoorsmen's store next to it, "Nature's Call."

That's funny, he thought, scratching his head, *it looks exactly like the one I used to go to*, though he couldn't remember where or when he used to go there. It was like some far off memory, providing only glimmers of familiarity.

Thomas passed the toy store and turned around a sharp corner, and there standing just beyond the bend was a food court. The gray marble dining tables spanning the entire length of the checkered black and white floor, accompanied by a dozen popular brand name eateries all of which were currently—like the stores—barred.

I've definitely been here before, he thought as he stared at one restaurant called, "Mr. Fuji's Authentic Asian Cuisine" where a prominent sign alerted customers to a two for one egg roll special.

I know I've eaten there, and even remembered having one of Mr. Fuji's renowned egg rolls. *I wonder when they started the special*?

It was at that moment that it suddenly struck him, and he realized where indeed he was. *How could I not have seen it sooner*? he wondered, for it seemed now the most obvious thing in the world.

"I'm at the Berkshire Mall!" he cried out, his voice echoing through the food court.

He'd come here numerous times before with his mother who often worked there. But somehow he hadn't recognized the place, when it should have dawned on him immediately.

What's going on? he wondered, *How did I even get here? And how did I get inside when the mall is closed*?

Before he could attempt to answer, he heard a loud crash coming from behind him.

I bet it came from the other side of the bend, and he ran back towards the hallway.

Suddenly red alarms flashed throughout the mall followed by loud ear piercing sirens. Broken glass lay scattered across the tiled floor and the bars guarding the jewelry store were thrown off to the side, bent and smashed. Two figures wearing black ski masks bolted from the store carrying sacks stuffed with stolen loot.

"It's a robbery!" cried Thomas as he watched the masked thieves scurrying about. *I need to get to a phone and call the police.*

But before he could, he heard a woman's voice yell out, "Stop where you are—the police are on their way!"

Thomas' knew that voice. He'd heard it all his life.

When he turned, there standing only a few yards away was his mother holding a mop and blocking the exit.

"Mom!" he shouted, and forgetting all about the scene unfolding in front of him, ran towards her.

"Mom it's me—it's Thomas!" he cried, jumping up and down excitedly and waving his hands.

But somehow she didn't notice. Indeed she appeared completely oblivious to the fact that he was even there.

Maybe she can't hear me over the alarms, he thought, *or maybe she's too busy with the—robbers!* and suddenly realizing the severity of the situation. *I have to do something. I have to help her*, and he looked around for some sort of a weapon.

Utterly undeterred, the robbers stalked towards his mother. They laughed coldly under their masks as Thomas' mother commanded them repeatedly to halt.

"What are you going to do with that mop—clean us?" mocked one of the robbers, the heavier set of the two.

"Going to give us a good scrubbing, eh?" chimed the other.

"The police will be here any minute," threatened Thomas' mother.

But the robbers only laughed and kept walking towards her.

Thomas looked everywhere, but couldn't find anything to use as a suitable weapon. He was getting desperate and panic was taking hold as he watched the robbers close in on his mother.

There has to be something I can use, he thought scanning the mall. And then suddenly in a flash of red light he saw hanging on the wall next to the fire alarm an axe encased in breakable glass.

He ran over and kicked the glass which shattered on the floor. He grabbed the axe from out of its encasement, wielding it sturdily in his hands. "Hold on mom—I'm coming!"

Thomas' mother held her ground as the robbers approached. But despite the grim predicament facing her, showed no signs of fear. Not even when the heavier one pulled out a gun and pointed it directly at her head.

"You don't want to do this," she attempted to reason with them.

"Oh we certainly *do* want to do this," said the heavier one.

"If you surrender now you can get a reduced sentence," she told them as they came upon her.

"You hear that, Bob? Maybe we get forty years instead of life. What do you think about that?" asked the skinny one.

"What's the difference, I'll be dead in ten anyway." Bob replied, "But you know what Earl?"

"What's that Bob?"

"She'll be dead long before either of us if she doesn't get smart and move."

"Shame too, she's a pretty little thing."

"Stop right there!" cried Thomas' mother wielding her mop like a club. "I'm warning you!"

"And feisty," added Earl.

Bob nodded. "I like that."

"So are you going to move out our way like a good little girl? Or are we gonna have to send you to an early grave," said Bob tapping his gun to make perfectly certain she saw it, "Makes no difference to me," he shrugged.

"Me neither," said Earl.

But in spite of their threats, she didn't move, and simply continued standing there steadfast.

"Alright lady, it's your funeral," said Bob and he held up his gun and pointed it at her chest. "See you in the next life..."

Thomas arrived just in the nick of time, axe in hand, and swung it with all his might at the one holding the gun.

But the axe went straight through his body as if not even there and Thomas fell hard to the ground from the momentum of his swing.

Suddenly a door burst open at the other end of the mall and armed police officers flooded into the hallway.

"Time to go," said Bob, and he turned back around to face Thomas' mother, and fired a single shot.

Thomas watched the bullet fly out of the gun's barrel as if in slow motion and spiral through the air towards his mother. She didn't even see it as it pierced her chest.

Blood exploded from the wound and splattered onto the white tile as Mrs. Darren's body jolted backwards and the mop flew from her hand and rolled upon the ground. She hit the floor with a sickening thud.

The robbers ran past her body as the police gave chase. Thomas tried desperately to get to his mother through the commotion, crawling in her direction. With tears falling from his eyes, he finally reached her.

He knelt by her side. "Mom! Mom!" he yelled attempting to shake her. But his hands could not touch her.

"Why can't I touch her? Why can't I help her?" he pleaded to the lights above. But even his words found no ear to listen, and he watched on helplessly as the life seeped out.

"I love you mom," he whispered in her dying ear, hoping somehow, someway, it would reach her. But she gave no recognition that it did.

Thomas watched as his mother's eyes closed and her pupils drifted off into those far away depths lying in the back of the skull. Her body went limp and then the last gasp of air flowed weakly from her mouth. Then everything ceased. She died right then and there.

The entire mall began to quake and rumble. Then a sharp bright light dissolved the walls of the Berkshire Mall like fire through parchment, and his mother's lifeless face faded away before Thomas' tearful eyes.

"Don't leave me—not again!" he pleaded.

But it was too late, as the sight of his mother evaporated, along with everything else....

Thomas awoke with a thunderous jolt. His body slung forward like shot from a cannon and abruptly caught in midair and hurled backwards.

When he opened his eyes, he saw heavy snow falling upon a narrow roadway with mountainous cliffs and caverns on his right, and a flimsy steel barricade blocking a steep descent on his left.

I'm in a car! he realized, and when he saw the driver his heart nearly stopped beating.

A middle aged man with disheveled red hair and bloodshot brown eyes held the wheel absently with one hand, while the other hand poured whiskey down his hairy throat. The liquor missing his mouth was soaked up by his wrinkled white collared shirt. A poor wretch of a man. But one Thomas knew instantly as his father.

"Dad!" he called out as they sped on at a breakneck speed through the treacherous twists and turns of the mountain road.

"Dad—what are you doing!" yelled Thomas frantically.

But his father didn't hear him, or even acknowledge his presence, and only continued drinking down that foul inebriating substance.

Thomas' heart raced with every close call as the car threatened to fly right off the side of the road, and most alarming of all, his father didn't seem to notice or care in the least. Thomas held his breath as the car narrowly missed the side of the cliff. Inebriated as he was, his father was able to swerve at the last moment, laughing hysterically as he did.

It's like he wants to die, thought Thomas breathing heavily. *Like he doesn't care what he's doing to his family*, and it made him angry. So angry that he felt himself wishing his father would just go ahead and get it over with.

"Go ahead—kill yourself! We don't need you anyway!" he screamed at his father who continued swerving uncontrollably spilling whiskey everywhere and laughing like a drunken idiot. "Yeah that's right…laugh it up you fool…laugh your life away…cuz I'll be laughing for joy when you're gone. You hear me? I'll be laughing my head off when you're dead. We're better off without you!"

But try as he might, he couldn't suppress the sadness he felt, even if twisted by anger. It was still his father, still the man who'd once held him in his arms, and somewhere inside this wretched drunken fool he laid still, buried under an avalanche of broken dreams and booze.

"I'm sorry dad…I didn't mean it. Please forgive me. I don't want you to die. I don't want—"

But it was too late, as the car hit a patch of ice and fishtailed, spinning out of control, and then—

Boom!

The car broke through the guardrail and flew into the snowy night air and for a moment there was utter silence, a sweet serenity, as if time stopped right then and there.

Only a moment it was, as the car hurled towards the jagged rocks below with Thomas screaming loudly and his father laughing madly….

Wordsworth moved with utter determination through the thickness of the fog. He yelled out Thomas' name, but each time only the sound of his own muffled echo returned to him. Darting from left to right like a hawk, his eyes surveyed the field as he traveled further into the fog's icy grip. This was a dangerous place, and he'd hoped to get through it without incident. But that appeared now to be wishful thinking. For something had indeed happened, and there was no time to waste.

Suddenly he caught sight of Thomas' luggage lying only several yards away. He rushed over and picked it up.

He looked all around. But its owner was nowhere to be found.

"He's not yours to claim!" Wordsworth yelled forcefully into the fog.

The fog gave no recognition.

"I know you can hear me!"

The fog lay still.

"I'm warning you, return the boy…or there will be consequences."

The fog stirred.

"He is ours now," a cold dead voice responded.

"Return him to me." Wordsworth demanded.

The fog laughed: a cold, dead, laugh. "Never. His pain is…delicious."

"This is your final warning. Return him—now!"

"You have no power here…old man," the voice replied.

"Oh, we shall see about that."

Wordsworth lifted his cane, and suddenly a sharp bright light shot forth from out of it.

Shrieks and wallows emanated from the fog as the light attacked it, and they grew louder and louder….Until at last a billow of fog unraveled and there lying upon the ground was Thomas, shriveled up in a ball, unconscious.

Wordsworth rushed to his side. "Thomas, wake up," and he shook Thomas' body. "You must wake up," he implored. But Thomas would not respond. "Wake up!" he yelled with everything he had—"Wake up!"

Suddenly a sleepy voice responded, "W-Wordsworth?"

"Thomas!"

"Where—am—I?"

"In the very same place you were when you decided to take a nap," replied Wordsworth, smiling despite himself.

"I didn't…I must have… fainted," said Thomas. "H-how long was I out?" he asked, standing with the aid of Wordsworth's arm.

"Only a short while, nothing to get too concerned over," said Wordsworth, holding the still wobbly Thomas.

"Where's Jack?" asked Thomas, shaking out the cobwebs.

"Ah yes, Master Jack."

The clearing Jack discovered was like a small world unto itself, separate and apart from the two it stood between. There was something about this small area with the green grass and the white rock, a presence, a *feel*, that you could sense right away, and Jack struggled to decipher precisely what it was.

He felt strangely safe here, like nothing could harm him so as long as he stayed, as if an invisible shield surrounded the entire area. And somehow Jack knew—he wasn't sure how, but he'd always known things he shouldn't—that this place was a safe haven, and that many had come here for protection. Images suddenly flashed in his mind of a time long ago, during a great war, when this place had saved countless lives. He could literally feel their relief at reaching this place.

"Here they were saved," spoke Jack in realization, and for some reason he found himself despising this place. "They should have been punished. They *deserved* to be punished. And they were going to be, but this place saved them. Here they couldn't be touched," and a cold hard anger rushed over him.

"Cowards!" he erupted violently through clenched teeth in a voice deeper than usual. A great hatred and tremendous rage burned deep in the pit of his stomach, boiling up, begging for him to let it out, to release it, and suddenly his eyes alighted with fire and in a voice not quite his own cried out—"Vengeance will be mine!"

Then abruptly it vanished, and he completely forgot what he was mad about, or even that he was at all, and found himself standing there in the clearing with a blank expression on his face, wondering what was taking Wordsworth and Thomas so long.

"We don't have all day," he grumbled as he stared back into the fog. Jack's stomach growled loudly, "And I'm getting hungry."

Thomas couldn't believe that he'd actually fainted in the fog, and strangely he barely remembered anything at all about how it happened. Usually when he fainted he at the very least remembered having done so. But this time all he recalled was the fog, and then…nothing.

When they arrived, Jack was waiting for them in the clearing, between the light ahead and the fog, sitting impatiently atop a white rock.

"What happened to you?" asked Jack when they arrived.

"I...um...fainted." Thomas replied sheepishly.

Jack burst out laughing. He'd always found Thomas' fainting spells hilarious, and just another thing that made him superior.

Thomas didn't say anything. He hated the fact that he fainted. It was such an embarrassment.

"Shall we be on our way then?" suggested Wordsworth.

"As long as Thomas can keep himself upright," said Jack, still chuckling.

They soon discovered when they came over the hill that the source of the light emanated from a single lantern hanging on the bough of an elm tree standing a short distance away. The light was extremely bright, impossibly so, for such a small source. And as they drew close the boys were forced to shield their eyes, for it was like staring into the sun.

Wordsworth, however, simply walked up to the lantern and turned a knob on the side, and the light, though still quite bright, subsided.

"How is it so bright?" asked Jack, still half blind.

"Because it's a very special lantern. The Light of Apollo some have called it," said Wordsworth.

"As in the Greek god Apollo?" said Thomas, who'd always been interested in mythology.

"Yes," said Wordsworth, "The very same."

"Who does it belong to?" asked Thomas.

"It does not belong to anyone," said Wordsworth, taking the lantern from the tree.

"So someone just left the lantern for us?" asked Thomas.

"Not just for us, but for anyone who requires it," said Wordsworth. "Now come we have a schedule to keep, and as they say time waits for no one," and with that Wordsworth took the lantern and began walking briskly ahead.

Shortly thereafter they came to a crossroad. In the middle of which stood a post. Wordsworth placed the lantern on top of it.

"Now what?" asked Jack, growing impatient.

"We await the Horseman's arrival," said Wordsworth.

"We're traveling by horse?" said Jack.

Yes, I'm afraid we don't have any automobiles here. This is the old country, as they say," said Wordsworth.

But before the boys could begin to ponder what other staples of the modern world might be absent in their new homeland, they heard the sound of hooves approaching.

The Golden Forest

THE HORSEMAN WORE a heavy dark hooded cloak and had a long and exceptionally bushy gray beard that hung all the way down to his ankles. He kept his face covered and never once lifted up his head. He was oddly shaped, with a severely arched back, and his cloak protruded out in the strangest places, like several people were trapped inside fighting to get out.

The horses that pulled his black carriage were magnificent creatures, huge pale gray stallions that stood ever so proudly.

Wordsworth went up to the Horseman and said some words that neither boy could hear. The Horseman said nothing in return, only nodded his head. Wordsworth then pulled from his pocket three shining gold coins and placed them into the Horseman's outstretched hands, which Thomas noticed were long and hairy. Fascinated by the mysterious Horseman, Thomas continued closely observing him to the point of blatantly staring. Though the Horseman never once returned his glance and kept himself hidden beneath his heavy black cloak.

"Come Master Thomas, we're ready to depart." Wordsworth called out from inside the confines of the black carriage.

Reluctantly, Thomas tore his eyes away from the Horseman and entered the carriage where Wordsworth and his brother were waiting.

The oval shaped cabin was lit by a small lamp that gave off a shadowy light. Much larger than it appeared from the outside, the cabin sat the three of them comfortably, with room to spare. Everything was colored in shades of red, and the walls were padded and draped with dark velvet. The seats were soft and cushy like a feathered mattress, and neither boy could remember anything more comfortable.

Anticipating a bumpy ride, to Thomas' surprise it was smooth. Indeed, if he hadn't known better, he wouldn't have guessed they were moving at all, as they experienced not the slightest turbulence.

"Who is he?" asked Thomas.

"Who is who?" replied Wordsworth.

"The Horseman,"

"What do you mean?"

"He must have a name," said Thomas.

"If he does, then I do not know it," said Wordsworth, "And if asked, I doubt he'd give it."

"Why not?"

Wordsworth paused, and looked at Thomas pensively. "You're a very curious sort of a fellow, aren't you?" he observed.

Jack laughed. "Annoying isn't it?"

Thomas frowned.

"There are worse qualities," said Wordsworth with a genial smile, "But as to your question, he wouldn't give me his name, his real one anyhow, because names are powerful and dangerous things, for there is so much that comes along with a name. But to us he is known simply as the Horseman, for that is the role he plays."

Thomas found it rather odd to call someone by what they did, and not by their name. But perhaps he thought that was simply the way of this place.

"It'll not be long now, try and relax." Wordsworth encouraged them.

But the boys didn't need any further encouragement, having already settled in quite nicely. Jack for one was so comfortable he even forgot about his hunger, and anything else pressing upon his mind for that matter. Thomas too forgot all about his troubles, even his recent fainting spell seemed miles away.

The Horseman began to hum a lulling tune, and the sound carried into and throughout the cabin walls. It was a lovely sound, calm and soothing to the ear. The boys found themselves totally entranced by its sweet melody. Their bodies tingled and the hairs on their arms stood up, as their senses were enraptured by its rhythm. Soon their eyes began to close.

They slept like children before they come into the world….

The carriage stopped short with a hard jolt, rousing the boys abruptly from their slumber.

"Here we are young masters, the land of your ancestors. Welcome to the realm of Somulus!" declared Wordsworth loud enough to shake any lingering remnants of sleep. And to ensure they were fully awake, opened the carriage door widely, allowing the brisk air to invade their snug space.

"The castle is just this way," said Wordsworth pointing towards a dirt path lying up ahead which wound up into a heavily wooded forest and was lined by burning torches. "Now hop to it, were almost there, the journey is near its end."

The boys got out of the carriage slowly. Both were surprised that they'd fallen asleep, especially having slept so long previously. But there was something about being in that cabin, along with the Horseman's song, that proved irresistible. Indeed there was no doubt that if they stayed they would've fallen right back asleep.

Once outside, they were greeted by heavy flakes of snow. Though of a much different sort than they were accustomed to, for the flakes had a reddish tint, as if stained by blood.

Highly unusual, albeit not entirely unheard of Thomas knew. He remembered from Mr. Blue's science class that the natural phenomenon was generally caused when snow mixed with volcanic ash. So he figured, logically, there must be a volcano nearby—which of course caused him to worry that an active volcano had recently erupted and that they were now standing in its wake. But despite the terrifying implications, it was a beautiful sight all the same.

The Horseman turned his reigns, and within moments was driving off at a vigorous pace in the direction from whence he came. The boys watched their mysterious escort go. But the heavy flakes of red snow clouded their vision and soon he'd disappeared from view.

"Let's not just stand around. It's only a short ways. We'll be there before you know it!" said Wordsworth who began walking up the torch lit pathway into the surrounding woods. The boys followed suit.

It really is beautiful here. Thomas observed as he gazed out at the scenery before him. A deep, lush forest of tall oak trees filled with golden autumnal leaves, a wispy mist dancing between their trunks, while the red snow placed itself gently at their feet. The kind of scene one might expect to read about in a story or poem, some existential ode to nature, and Thomas thought it—*Lovely*.

The path was narrow and barely visible beneath the heavy coat of golden leaves and red snow, and if not for the torches providing the shape would've barely been distinguishable. The path twisted and turned bringing them further up and into the forest itself.

"Why aren't the trees bare?" asked Jack.

Something Thomas had noticed as well. For even though it appeared from the ground that a great many leaves had fallen, indeed the ground was mostly covered, the trees seemed not to have relinquished even a single one of their children.

"This is the Golden Forest," replied Wordsworth, "and as the name implies, the leaves are always full and golden—no matter the season."

"What kind of trees are they?" Thomas asked, never having heard of such a thing.

"The living kind," said Wordsworth.

"Aren't *all* trees living," countered Jack.

"Ah, but some are more alive than others," said Wordsworth, adding, "There are those that claim within these trees dwell the spirits of gods."

Jack burst out laughing. "That's ridiculous."

Even Thomas, an open minded fellow, found the notion difficult to swallow.

"Old gods, remnants from the first chapter of this world, now long forgotten by most… here they rest. This is their graveyard," said Wordsworth.

"A graveyard for gods." Jack scoffed. "That doesn't even make sense. Gods can't die, or else they wouldn't be gods."

"Everything dies Master Jack. But not everything dies in the same way. And though these gods have died in one form, they've been born in another."

"Why trees then?" asked Jack.

"Because trees are very important. Why it could even be said that trees have steered the course of the world. And sometimes the humble merely disguises the extraordinary," said Wordsworth. "But it is not the form alone that is telling, but the symbolism that is most important you see, for the old gods believed deeply in such things…" and he gestured out to the Golden Forest. "They remain eternally unchanged in the season of change, stuck forevermore between the heat of summer and the cold of winter; between happiness and melancholy; between life and death. Theirs is a state of permanence in a world of impermanence. They are rocks amidst dust…"

It was old country tradition Thomas thought. They didn't have technology and so people explained things they couldn't otherwise through stories. Gods were real in order to make sense of the world. It was charming he thought, and probably far more interesting than the actual reason why the leaves always stayed an autumnal golden—probably something do with the soil or the amount of rainfall, or some other mundane such thing easily explained away by science. *But then*, he knew *it's good to pretend sometimes.*

"Though," began Wordsworth again, "they say that sometimes in the stillness of the night, when the moon is just right, the gods emerge from their trees and retake their old forms and feast and drink just as they once did, like players reenacting their old plays."

Thomas couldn't say that he believed Wordsworth's tale about the trees really being the spirits of gods, but there was undoubtedly something peculiar about the forest, other than the golden leaves. Thomas even swore, amidst it all, that he heard singing. And he couldn't help but think that it was coming from the forest itself, perhaps from inside the very trees themselves. But every time he listened closely suddenly it ceased, only to begin again the moment he dismissed it. *This entire day has been one of the strangest in memory. I've got to get it together…before I lose my mind completely,* and he made a mental note to stop reading so many fantasy novels before bed.

Still, he glanced over at his brother to see if there was any indication that he'd heard it as well. But his brother gave none, and simply trudged on up the path behind him wearing an unreadable scowl.

Jack however had indeed heard the singing. The voice of a woman and one he found strangely alluring. But when he peered out into the deep trees there was no one there. Yet the singing persisted and seemed only to get clearer the more he listened—and listen he did. For her voice, whoever she was, was positively angelic and the more he heard the more he desired to listen. Soon he found himself desperately wanting to get closer to the voice, and the woman to whom it belonged.

The sweet song turned to even sweeter words when suddenly the woman's voice called out to him by name: "Jack...Jack..." she cooed, seeming to sing even as she spoke, "Come to me...join me in the woods...I'm waiting for you here...only for you Jack...come to me now...and I'll love you forever..."

She made him feel a way in which he'd never before known, a way he didn't even know possible. His feet turned and began walking of their own accord, taking him wherever they pleased. And there was only one place they wished to go.

"I'm coming," he whispered as his feet swept him over the threshold of torches and into the forest.

Thomas followed closely behind Wordsworth who took long healthy strides up the meandering dirt path with no end in sight. The red snow fell heavier the further up they traveled and by now Thomas' clothes had received a good dusting—giving him the appearance of being covered in blood. *Freshly fallen blood*, he thought brushing some off.

As they climbed, Thomas contemplated the enormity of the change he was going through. In some ways it was scary, as all unknown things are, but also exhilarating. He was being given a fresh start, a new chance at life. He'd lost everything he'd ever known or held dear, and his slate was once again blank. Whatever it was he could feel it, as if the change itself was palpable, and he felt somehow even now different. It was hard to explain, but the past seemed distant to him, and with every step up the path he took, the further away it became.

They arrived then upon a fork in the road, the path diverging off to the right and the left. Curiously, each way looked exactly like the other. In fact, the more Thomas examined them the more identical they appeared, right down to the very shape of the trees and the number of leaves.

Wordsworth stopped and stood there silently for a few moments muttering inaudibly beneath his breath.

"Which way now?" asked Thomas apparent they'd come to an impasse.

"Give me a moment," said Wordsworth, deep in concentration.

Doesn't he know the way back to his own home? thought Thomas worriedly. *Wait till Jack sees this, he'll never let it go…* and he waited expectantly for some snide remark, something undoubtedly to do with the old man's age and failing mental faculties. But none came.

Knowing Jack would never let a golden opportunity like this pass, Thomas turned around to see just what his brother was up to. But Jack was nowhere to be found.

Now where in the world could he have run off to?

"Wordsworth, I'll be right back, I'm going to look for Jack. He's run off somewhere. I wouldn't worry, he's probably close by," said Thomas, and knowing Jack he'd probably decided to do some exploring.

But Wordsworth just grumbled, which Thomas wasn't sure was meant as a yes or no, or whether he'd even heard in the first place.

"Right, you just stay here and sort it all out, and I'll be back soon with Jack," said Thomas, to which Wordsworth merely grumbled again. Thomas shook his head.

Thomas left Wordsworth standing there, still muttering to himself, and went off to look for his brother.

He couldn't have gone far, thought Thomas backtracking down the winding path.

The further Thomas went, however, the less he liked the idea of walking alone, and quickly began to wish that he'd waited for Wordsworth. The reason for his mounting trepidation was that he swore there was something lurking in the surrounding woods. For though he couldn't see anything, it was dark after all, he could hear the rustling of leaves, like something was running through them. And suddenly he heard what sounded like a growl, causing him to think instantly of wolves.

"Where are you Jack?" he whispered fearfully to himself, and beginning to get the distinct feeling that his brother might actually be in a great deal of trouble. The kind even he might not be able to worm his way out of. Still, despite his fear, he had to find his brother. So wolves or not he continued searching.

As he rounded an especially tight corner he heard the sound of a twig snapping and his eyes darted in its direction.

"Whose there?" he said much louder than he'd intended, his voice carrying deep into the forest. *Great tell the wolves exactly where you are so they can come and eat you,* he scolded himself, and he could just hear Jack's voice inside his head, "'Way to think things through genius.'"

Shut up Jack! Thomas found himself responding. *This is your fault. Couldn't just stay out of trouble could ya? No, no, not you, not the famous Jack, no. Always have to be the center of attention. Don't care who you bring down with you. Now we're both going to be dinner for a pack of blood-thirsty wolves*!

But as fortune would have it, the moon chose that very moment to show itself, and hung in the sky shining its bright luminescent light down upon the woods. In the moonlight, Thomas saw a figure standing alone amidst the trees only a short distance away from where he stood.

Jack? Yes, surely it must be! as he saw his brother's distinctive outline.

"Jack!" called Thomas, "What are you doing out there?"

Jack didn't respond and only continued standing in the middle of the woods.

He wants to play games. Just like him to pick the worst possible time. He probably has no idea there are wolves out there. Jack could be so pigheaded at times.

"Jack, quit playing and get out of there!" he called again louder than before.

But still his brother didn't move or respond at all.

He's not going to stop until I go in there and get him. Probably thinks I'm too scared. Jack had put him through tests like this before, and loved exploiting Thomas' fears.

But not this time. I'm not scared—I'm not Jack. If I have to go in there and get you, then that's what I'm going to do—even if there are wolves!"

Though as Thomas journeyed into the woods, he soon realized just how far in his brother truly was. In fact, his brother seemed to keep getting further away. It was like for every step he took, Jack took two more, widening the gap between them. Which to Thomas' dismay was exhausting the precious light of the moon, and if they kept on this way they'd soon be immersed in total darkness. To avoid this inevitability, Thomas started running towards his brother, leaving heavy tracks in the red snow.

When he finally caught up, Jack was standing with his back turned just beyond the last light of the moon. Thomas stopped running a few yards away from where Jack stood and suddenly froze. Surrounding his brother in the nearby thick of the forest were a dozen bright yellow eyes.

We're right in the middle of the wolf's den!

Instinctively, Thomas stood as still as possible.

Jack must've been thinking the very same thing, and was doing thought Thomas, a much better job than he was, as his brother stood rigid as a statue. A remarkable display of resolve and bravery. Trembling mightily, Thomas couldn't fathom how his brother was managing the feat.

The wolves, however, were far less impressed, as the yellow eyes closed in tightly.

We're going to have to make a run for it, concluded Thomas, switching into panic mode, *I have to get Jack's attention—before it's too late.*

"Jack—Jack—Jack!" cried Thomas loudly as he could within the constraints of a whisper. But again his brother didn't respond and only continued standing still as a rock.

"Stop playing games for once in your life would you? This isn't a joke. Get out of there—*now*!" Thomas pleaded desperately to his brother.

Once more Jack didn't respond, and a great panic swept over Thomas as the eyes closed in around his brother. He could hear their ravenous growling and the crunch of their paws stalking upon the snow.

"Jack!" Thomas yelled at the top of his lungs, his voice echoing loudly in the cold night air—"Move!"

"What!" Jack erupted with unrestrained fierceness.

The yellow eyes scattered like hares before the hound, and horrible shrieks filled the night air as the beasts fled back into the dark of the woods.

Thomas covered his ears for the shrieking was terrible, perhaps the single worst sound he'd ever heard. He'd no idea wolves could make such a wretched noise, or any other creature for that matter.

Jack turned around to face his brother, and when he did Thomas was suddenly no longer afraid of wolves. His brother's eyes burned with a raging fire that flamed in the darkness. It was an impossible, horrifying sight, and one that paralyzed him with fear.

Thankfully, Jack's eyes quickly cooled, and the fire inside them subsided. Until it disappeared entirely. And when he walked out of the darkness and into the moonlight appeared completely normal.

Though only a brief moment, Thomas couldn't believe what he'd seen. Nor would he ever forget it, or the paralyzing fear that accompanied it. *What—was—that?* he wondered as he stared at his now perfectly calm twin brother.

"What are you doing out here?" Jack demanded to know after a few moments of silence passed between them both.

"I…I was going to ask you the same thing." Thomas stammered, "Why did you come out here? Why did you come into the woods?"

"You know dam—" Jack began violently, but abruptly stopped short, and after a moment responded far more calmly, "I thought I saw something out here, so I came to get a better look. Guess I was wrong," he shrugged.

Stunned by his brother's response, Thomas began to open his mouth to say something about wolves and fire, but instead stayed silent and simply smiled back nervously.

"I'm sure Wordsworth is worried sick, and fun as it is to make him squirm, we should get back on the path," said Jack.

Wanting nothing more than to leave the woods as quickly as possible, Thomas fervently nodded his head.

"Why don't you lead the way?" suggested Jack, "After all you seem to know where you're going," he added with a smile that was, at least for him, entirely too nice.

"Um, sure," said Thomas.

Thomas followed his own tracks in the red snow. The entire way back neither spoke a single word, though Thomas did periodically check to ensure that his brother was still behind him. Every time he did, however, Jack simply smiled knowingly as if to say, "Stop worrying, I'm not going anywhere," which Thomas very much hoped was the truth. These woods had been eventful enough already.

As they continued walking back, Thomas couldn't help but reflect upon what he'd seen in his brother's eyes, the flames burning inside them. He'd seen his brother in fits of rage—which were terrifying enough—but this was much different. His brother hadn't even looked human, almost like he was possessed by something else, something...*evil*. Even the wolves were spooked by it, a fact lending credence to it not simply being a figment of his imagination. Speaking of wolves, strangely, he wasn't sure his brother had even noticed them, and if so, hadn't said a single word about it. *Whatever it was...whatever happened out there. I hope it never happens again.*

As he followed behind his brother, Jack stared obsessively back into the woods, and every time he did he hoped to hear that angelic voice once more. But to his great disappointment he never did, and it became obvious that the woman, whoever she was, would sing to him no longer. A fact which enraged him, for he missed desperately the feeling she'd given him, and yearned for its return with the entirety of his being.

Why did he have to come and ruin everything? he thought with utter contempt for his brother. *I was so close to her...so close to that beautiful voice...*and his anger grew...

As they crossed onto the path, Jack suddenly rounded on his brother. "Why did you come into the woods?"

Thomas paused momentarily, before responding, "I went in to get you. I thought you were in trouble," being of course the truth.

"You came to save…me?" said Jack incredulously, with a look plainly stating that the idea of Thomas saving him was utterly ridiculous.

"I did," insisted Thomas.

"Whatever you're *real* reasons, if you ever follow me like that again you'll wish you'd never been born." Jack threatened in a dangerous whisper, every word backed by painful promises.

"I-I won't Jack." Thomas swore. And though he'd no idea what he was swearing to, knew from experience that the better course was to simply acquiesce rather than dispute the claim, for knowing his brother, one caused far less pain.

"Good," said Jack suddenly smiling amicably again, "Glad that's settled," and he patted his brother on his back, and then without another word headed up the path, leaving Thomas behind with a puzzled look upon his face.

Can this day possibly get any stranger? he thought, shaking his head. Then followed his brother hurriedly up the path, wondering what could possibly be next.

Banshees

WHEN THEY ARRIVED back at the fork in the road, they were shocked, or at least Thomas was, to see Wordsworth still standing there in deep deliberation. He didn't even turn around to acknowledge their presence—assuming he even knew they'd left in the first place, which was doubtful.

Exactly where I left him, thought Thomas, who could scarcely believe that the old man was really still standing there thinking about it. *Must be going senile.* Thomas had seen the same thing occur with an elderly neighbor named Ms. Whitmier, who'd wander off and end up in the strangest places without the slightest clue of how she'd come to be there.

Jack possessed far less patience, and wasted no time in expressing his utter lack of regard for the old man's condition. "So which way is it already?" he snapped, "Don't you know the way back to your own home," adding in cruel mockery, "Even a dog knows that much."

But Wordsworth refused to dignify the ridicule with a response, choosing instead to continue unperturbed on the task at hand.

"We could just flip for it," suggested Jack taking a coin out of his pocket, "Let fate decide. Better than standing around here waiting for you to figure it out—a person could grow old." Jack laughed, "Oh wait, one already has!"

"Quiet now," said Wordsworth, "I've almost got the lyrics....Right or left the path does go...one is hope, while the other is doom..." and then suddenly cried out, "Best to go right if you want to get home! Yes, that's it, we go right!"

Jack and Thomas glanced over at one another, and then at the same time replied in unison. "Are you sure?"

"Why of course I'm sure!" said Wordsworth with supreme confidence, and promptly followed the path to the right.

"This had better be the right way," said Jack, growing tired of all the delay.

"What happens if it's not?" asked Thomas with evident concern.

Jack shrugged. "Only one way to find out," and followed Wordsworth down the path.

Thomas caught up with Wordsworth and walked beside him. The old man had pulled out a pipe from his jacket pocket and was happily smoking it. Jack hung back a bit. Something Thomas was thankful for after their encounter in the woods, which he was doing his best to try and forget.

The path to the right as it turned out was literally a path that veered to the right, consisting of nothing but a series of right turns, making Thomas wonder what the point was of going in one giant circle. But the day had already been filled with so much absurdity, that he figured perhaps, paradoxically, more absurdity simply made for good sense. *We're already down the rabbit's hole*, he thought.

The torches still burned brightly around him, keeping the forest at bay, and hopefully whatever lurked inside it. Thomas still worried about the prospect of the wolves returning to finish the meal they'd been deprived of.

"Do the wolves ever come out of the woods?" Thomas asked Wordsworth, hoping very much the rule "don't bother them and they won't bother you" applied here.

"Wolves know far better than to enter these woods," said Wordsworth.

"There aren't any wolves in these woods?" replied Thomas, "Are you certain?"

"As certain as I can be about anything. Wolves around these parts keep strictly to the White Woods, and even those that stray wouldn't dare enter this forest, and if they did they'd never come out. For these woods are filled with beasts that make wolves look like cuddly little puppies; namely, banshees."

"What the heck is a banshee?" asked Thomas, never having heard the term before and wondering fearfully what sort of creatures they must be to scare off wolves.

"A banshee is one of the most horrible creatures you could ever have the misfortune of encountering. They are extremely dangerous and never miss an opportunity to feed. After all, it's really the only thing they have to live for anymore."

"What do you mean…anymore?"

"Like most things in this world, banshees have their story," said Wordsworth, adding, "Stories around here are taken very seriously."

"What's the banshees' story then?" asked Thomas, who loved a good tale.

"Well, if you were to believe the legends—and there are many around these parts that do—then you would believe that long ago in the days of old banshees were a tribe of extraordinarily beautiful nymphs. So beautiful that if a man but looked upon them he'd fall completely in love, such that from that moment forth he lived only to serve them, caring nothing for his own needs or wants, preferring their approval to food, their lightest touch to life itself. And they'd stay that way until the banshee released him from their spell, if ever they did.

"But instead of using their power for good, the banshees used it for their own personal gain. Their ambitions knew no bounds. They sought to rule over the world. To be worshipped by all the inhabitants of the earth. In order to achieve their ends, they made armies of men, and waged a great and terrible war…."

Wordsworth took a prolonged puff of his pipe before continuing on, as if to store up oxygen for a long talk.

"Now men were not then as you think of them now, but far stronger beings. They were man as he was always intended to be—man before the Fall. They were capable of feats now thought impossible, able to cross boundaries which now confine them. Why even the sky was their domain, and they traversed it as naturally as they walked the earth. Though despite their incredible abilities, they were mostly peaceful beings, desiring nothing more than to work the land, love their wives, and raise their children. Theirs was a simple and happy existence.

"Banshees changed all that, forcing them to abandon all they loved, and thrust their entire being into the art of war. Something which they discovered they had a profound talent for. Indeed, they became so skillful at war that the destruction they wrought upon the earth has few rivals in the annuals of history.

"It was during this time that the women of the land, whose husbands, brothers, and fathers, had been enslaved and used as tools of destruction by the banshees, banded together. These abandoned wives and discarded daughters, desperate mothers and forlorn lovers, sought their revenge. But the banshee, with an army of men at their command, along with many other opportunistic creatures that had joined their side, could not be defeated by mere force, for none could oppose them, so strong they were.

"The women heard tell of a very old and very powerful creature that could help them. It was a creature though not of the light, but of the shadows. A remnant of a war long ago, when the Kingdom of Darkness and the Kingdom of Light clashed, and the night became their truce. But they were desperate, and in their desperation sought the creature out.

"The creature, whose true name can no longer be spoken by the tongues of man or beast, dwelled in a cave deep in the heart of a fiery mountain range. A perilous journey to undertake, many did not see it through to completion. But for those that did, found that when they arrived the creature was already waiting for them. It took the form of an old man, though one side of him stayed ever in the shadows. The creature said it knew why they'd come, and that it could help them. But there was a price for his service: a single soul.

"A steep price indeed, for nothing is worth so much as one's soul, and none of the women were at first willing to pay it.

"But seeing no other choice, a strong woman named Lilith stepped forward and offered up her own soul to the creature in payment.

"The creature gladly accepted. He produced then from out of thin air a small black box. Inside of which was an unfathomable darkness. Lilith disappeared into the darkness, and the lid shut.

"True to the creature's word, he placed a very powerful and sinister curse on the banshees, turning them for all time into horrible monsters as hideous and repulsive as they once were beautiful. Their spell was broken. The war ended. And the world was saved.

"Transformed into hideous monsters, the banshees fled to the woods and hid themselves in caves and other dark secluded places, never to come out during the day again, or in any light for that matter for they cannot stand to see what they've become. Nor were their looks all that was transformed, so too were their voices, said to be nearly as beautiful as they once were in appearance. Now from their mouths comes one of the world's worst noises, a shriek as grating to the ear as it once was enchanting.

"It is said, however, that despite losing their looks and voices that they retained something of their ability to influence men. It is said they are still able to enter a man's mind and become again inside it everything they once were. And it is believed that to this very day they lure unsuspecting men into the woods, singing for them to come…"

There was a long pause after Wordsworth finally stopped speaking. Despite what logic, or his brother surely would've said, there was still a part of Thomas that couldn't help but believe that the story could be true. A part of him that had always believed that such fantastical things were real, or perhaps still held out hope that they were. A part dulled by the cold reality of the world. And yet, what about the singing he'd heard.

"Do you believe the legend?" asked Thomas.

"You mean do I think it's true, in the literal sense?" replied Wordsworth.

Thomas nodded.

Wordsworth smiled. "All stories contain kernels of truth. This one is no exception. But most stories, the good ones anyway, also have a lesson to impart. Some call it the moral of the story. And the moral of this story is an important one to be sure," he turned to Thomas, "Can you guess it?"

Thomas thought for a moment and then responded, "Hell hath no fury like a woman scorned."

Wordsworth burst out laughing, louder than ever before, and it seemed to break through the dense silence of the forest and echoed throughout. "Ah Shakespeare, one of my all-time favorite storytellers," said Wordsworth, "I've always enjoyed his work immensely. What a wit!"

Thomas too was a fan of Shakespeare's. His English teacher Mr. Joyce had made the class read several of his plays, including Hamlet and Julius Caesar. Most kids hated it, complaining about being forced to read something so old and antiquated. But Thomas absolutely loved it. *The man was a genius*, he thought, and wished one day to become even a hundredth as good of a writer.

"I'm afraid however," said Wordsworth, "true as it undoubtedly is, that's not quite the lesson I had in mind. No, the main lesson of the story regards the corrupting nature of power. The banshees were corrupted by their power over men and what that power could bring them, namely, more power. They had the ability to seduce men into doing whatever they wanted, and yet, in the end, it was power itself that ultimately seduced them—enslaving them as completely as they had men. The cycle of power some have called it."

"But do you believe the story is true," said Thomas, "That banshees really were nymphs and all that stuff."

Wordsworth paused, and took a deep draw of his pipe. "I'll say this much," he said finally, "Banshees are quite real, no matter their true origin, and they are extremely vicious creatures who dwell in this forest. But as for the rest," he shrugged, "to each their own."

Thomas stopped and stared out into the surrounding forest, unsure of what to believe.

"But then," Wordsworth called back suddenly, "do you honestly believe that all these torches are simply here just to light the way?"

"What—"

But it was too late for the old man had gone on ahead, leaving Thomas to wonder.

Ravenstead

WORDSWORTH AND THE boys came around another bend for what was the umpteenth right turn they'd taken, when suddenly they emerged from the forest and stood face to face with a breathtaking sight. The night sky held in it more stars than they'd ever dreamed possible. It was like looking out upon an ocean of sparkling blue diamonds, appearing so close you could almost just reach up and grab them.

Is this what the sky looks like without pollution? wondered Thomas staring wide-eyed at the astronomer's paradise before him.

Soon however their attention turned away from the sky to what lay beneath it. They were standing upon a cliff overlooking a deep valley that glowed with fiery bright lights, presaging the existence of civilization. Off to their right, looming over the valley, was a small mountain standing amidst the back drop of a series of larger mountains in the distance. Upon the small mountain's peak was a magnificent dark castle with numerous turrets, battlements, and sharp pointed towers. Next to it hung a yellow sickle moon cutting through the night sky like a scythe.

"Behold Castle Ravenstead!" Wordsworth announced as the boys stared up at the grand structure standing majestically upon the peak. A sight so spectacular it caused the stars to be almost uninteresting in comparison.

"We're going to live there?" said Thomas.

"Yes, Master Thomas, that is your new home. I hope it is to your liking."

"It's incredible!" exclaimed Thomas, who had never—not in his wildest flights of imagination—seen anything to compare to it.

As for Jack, well, he'd never worn a bigger grin in his entire life. *That will be mine one day*, he thought with his usual sense of certainty, as if simply stating a fact of life. *All mine, and no one else's*… and he flashed his brother a suspicious glance; though Thomas didn't catch it.

"Well don't just stand there drooling, it does have an inside after all," said Wordsworth, and without further delay they headed off towards the base of the mountain; only a short distance away from where they currently stood by way of a winding dirt road.

As they walked, Thomas' attention turned back to the wondrous sky above. "Are there always this many stars?" he asked.

"Not this many, no," said Wordsworth, "It appears they have all come out tonight. Perhaps the entire Host even. Why I haven't seen so many gathered together at once in well, a very long time."

"Must be a really clear night," surmised Thomas, observing not a single cloud in the whole sky. It appeared to have stopped snowing as well. If ever it had fallen here in the first place, for there was no evidence that it had. Yet another peculiar thing to add to the rapidly growing list.

"They're curious," said Wordsworth.

"Who's curious?" asked Thomas.

"Why the Stars of course," said Wordsworth, as if the most obvious thing in the world.

"How can a star possibly be curious?" asked Thomas, "They're just balls of gas." Something he'd learned in science class.

"B-b-balls of what did you say! My word, please don't let them hear you say that. I can only imagine," said Wordsworth shaking his head.

Thomas thought momentarily about protesting that such a notion was preposterous, but instead asked, "Curious about what?"

"Well how should I know, I'm not a bloody Star now am I!"

"Oh, right," said Thomas. *How ridiculous of me.*

They came then to an enormous stone statue of a bird, which held in its beak a set of dangling scales of the sort painted upon the wall at the Boonton courthouse.

"Is our Uncle a judge or something?" asked Jack as they drew close.

"Being the ruler of the realm, your Uncle has many responsibilities, and that includes on occasion handing down judgments. But don't worry Master Jack he's not going to put you behind bars or anything like that," said Wordsworth, adding with a grin, "Unless you really deserve it."

"Let him try," said Jack under his breath.

"The statute is meant to symbolize balance," said Wordsworth. "That the scales should not tip too far in either direction, for with extremes there is chaos."

"Why are the scales being held by a bird?" asked Thomas.

"A raven, to be precise," said Wordsworth. "This castle is known as Ravenstead for a reason. Your Uncle is quite fond of ravens, along with being the family's symbol."

"Symbol?" said Jack.

"Every great House has a symbol," said Wordsworth.

"House?" said Thomas.

"Noble families are known as Houses," said Wordsworth, "The head of the House takes the name. Being the head of House Hades, your Uncle is known as Lord Hades."

"Wait, Hades as in the Greek god of the underworld?" asked Thomas, and recalling the lantern named for the Greek god Apollo.

Wordsworth nodded. "You may find many names that you recognize from tales you've read. The tales and the names had to originate somewhere after all, and this is the old world," said Wordsworth. "And as I told you before, these lands are known collectively as Mythil. The reason many stories originating here came to be referred to as myths. Of course, like any story, they have changed and evolved with each subsequent telling, adding embellishment along the way. For example, the reason Hades became synonymous with the underworld is that Somulus resides below the Line of Light, in the region commonly called the Underlands. Being that we are under the Line, it is darker here more often than it is light. For those above the Line, the opposite is true. Ah, but where they have the sun we have the moon!

"Unfortunately, however, those above the Line are not so fond of those below it, and the Line has served to separate us in many respects, with numerous prejudices arising as a result."

This newest revelation made Thomas wonder about other myths he'd read, and how they'd come into being.

"How long has House Hades ruled Somulus?" asked Thomas, knowing Greek mythology went quite a ways back.

"Oh, a very, very long time," said Wordsworth, "It is an ancient House, one of the oldest. But the name itself derives from this valley, which was known as Hades by the Ancients. And when your family came to settle here they adopted the name as their own. Though you must understand that time is measured differently here; for this land was old long before yours was even young."

When they came at last to the mountain, they saw a road cut deeply into the side of it, encircling it in layers and spiraling upwards like a drill.

"How are we going to get all the way up there?" asked Thomas.

"With our feet of course," said Wordsworth.

"That's going to take forever," said Thomas, whose feet were already starting to hurt.

"On the contrary, I think you'll find that with the wind at our backs it should take no time at all to reach the top," said Wordsworth.

Thomas was understandably more than a little skeptical. Even Jack, the supreme athlete, looked dubious about the prospect.

But true to his word, the wind did indeed seem to whisk them effortlessly around the mountain. Thomas felt like he was simply being swept along, almost like there were a sail tied to his back. And before they even knew it, they'd reached the top, in what must've been record time, and with hardly any physical exertion at all.

In full view, the castle was even larger and more magnificent than it had appeared from below. It had numerous archways and a gothic style of architecture reminding Thomas of St. George's. And ravens were perched everywhere, staring down watchfully through their beady black eyes.

Being so high, they had a fantastic view of what lay out around them, and one sight in particular held their focus. In the distance, just beyond a series of jagged mountains they saw—in stark contrast to the one above them—a tempestuous sky full of raging thunder and lightning and swirling black storm clouds.

And amidst it all a fiery light emanated from a single lone peak which looked, Thomas thought, a great deal like a fang.

"What's out there?" inquired Jack.

Wordsworth paused. "Another realm," he said finally, not caring to elaborate. "Come along now. Your Uncle awaits."

Wordsworth led them through two giant archways and past two huge statues that Thomas thought looked a great deal like the jackal headed Egyptian god Anubis. From there they came to the front of the castle, where a great triangular iron door stood. Carved into the center of which was a full moon, with each side of the door containing a half.

What an interesting door, thought Thomas, marveling at the craftsmanship.

Wordsworth fumbled in his pocket and pulled out a single golden key, which he put into the lock located in the center of the moon, and turned. The doors creaked loudly, and began to slowly open....

Reunion

THE BOYS COULD scarcely believe their eyes when they glimpsed the confines of the castle for the first time. The hall they entered was absolutely enormous in scale with an arched ceiling rising to such great heights Thomas swore a giant must live here. Etched upon the white flagged stone floor were strange symbols, and everything glowed in a fiery light from wall mounted torches. In the very middle of the hall, stood the most incredible spiraling stairwell descending through the ceiling as if from the heavens above. It divided the hall into two distinct corridors, each lined with gray columns appearing to go on forever.

"Not quite what you're accustomed to," said Wordsworth, delivering perhaps the understatement of the century.

Suddenly a clock standing on the wall to their right began to chime loudly. Standing about fifteen feet tall and intricately carved, the massive clock contained three large dials within which were numerous smaller ones.

The chiming was soon replaced by the sound of footsteps coming down the stairwell, moving closer towards them—one deliberate step after another.

"Ah here your Uncle comes now!" Wordsworth announced, and the boys readied themselves to meet their only remaining relative.

Emerging from the darkness of the great winding stairwell was a figure wearing an extraordinarily long black cape appearing to carry the very shadows along with it. A tall man, with exquisite posture, he moved with effortless grace, as if gliding on air. He had long flowing hair, more silver than gray, which lay gently upon his slender shoulders. And though years had undoubtedly passed before his pale gray eyes, his face, despite the distinction of age, was youthful, and strikingly handsome. While his skin, appearing not to have seen the sun in years, contained an almost bluish tint. A red vest stood out colorfully amidst the rest of the black he adorned, and a shining golden pocket watch hung from his breast.

As he drew close, Thomas felt an undeniable presence that he swore he'd felt somewhere else before, but could not place it.

"May I introduce the sovereign ruler of the realm of Somulus, the Great Lord Osiris Pluto Hades." Wordsworth pronounced in a voice befitting such a regal introduction.

"Thank you Wordsworth. Welcome my nephews, it is good to finally make your acquaintance. It has been long over do," said Lord Hades, who spoke almost in a whisper, like a faint breeze, but one in which they'd no trouble whatsoever in hearing. "Now you must be Thomas, and you must be Jack."

"Yes," they answered in unison, for he'd guessed correct.

"I was deeply saddened by your mother's...passing. Please accept my belated condolences," said Lord Hades somberly.

Until that moment, the boys had nearly forgotten all about their mother and the terrible circumstances that had brought them here. She'd somehow been misplaced in all the excitement. But their Uncle's words abruptly jarred their memories, and it all came flooding back like a deep wound painfully reopened. Jack felt the rage, while Thomas forced back the tears.

But when their Uncle spoke again, the thoughts fled once more from their minds, and they dwelled upon them no longer, forgetting even for that brief moment they ever had.

"I know the journey here can be a trying one, being that we are a long way from your home. But I am pleased to see you've arrived safely," and Lord Hades' gray eyes glanced over at Wordsworth who nodded ever so slightly. "These lands can be unusual at first, especially in relation to those you're accustomed, and will take time to adjust to. But soon I hope you will call them home."

"It really is beautiful—your, um, realm," said Thomas, "But I've never heard of it before Unc—I mean, um, Lord Hades," he added, not certain what to call him and not wishing to offend by presuming.

"Uncle Hades will suffice. No need for added formalities amongst family," replied the newly christened Uncle Hades. "As to your question, not many have.

We are very small and easily overlooked by the rest of the world…something which admittedly has its advantages."

"How'd you get this castle?" asked Jack, greatly interested in how one acquired such things.

"This castle is very ancient Jack, as are most things in this realm. Our family came into possession of it several centuries ago. It once belonged to another ruler. But he was dispossessed of it, and our family stepped in to fill the vacancy."

Jack was pleased to hear his family had taken the castle.

"Now then," Uncle Hades continued, "I do have a few rules. I apologize for bringing them up so soon, as you have only just arrived. But I feel it prudent to get them out of the way before we proceed any further. I'd appreciate if you would strictly abide by them while you stay, as they are as much for your benefit as for my own," and after a barely audible grumble from Jack began then to set them forth.

"This castle is very large as you can plainly see, and larger still where you cannot, and one can get lost quite easily. I myself still do from time to time. There are many locked doors and they are locked for a reason—do not try to enter them, for some are not for entering. The forest is also not a place for you to go, unless accompanied by myself or Wordsworth, for some have gone in that never came out," to which Thomas shot Jack a quick glance as Uncle Hades continued on. "I will be gone most of the day and return sharply at the seventh chime of the clock for dinner. I expect you both to join me. Please do not be late, my time is precious. Those are the rules, for now. The rest we will make up as the need arises. Do you have any questions?" asked Uncle Hades finishing at length.

The boys both mulled it all over. Thomas found the rules sensible enough, though he did wonder where his Uncle would be going during the day. *What does a king or lord really do anyway? Probably whatever he wants*, he presumed.

Jack on the other hand didn't like them in the least. But then, they were rules and he didn't intend upon following them anyway. *At least not for long*, he thought mischievously.

"No, Uncle Hades," Thomas responded after a moment, "It all sounds perfectly reasonable."

Jack simply smiled and nodded his head.

"Very good," said Uncle Hades, "Now then, we can move on to more pleasant things. Are you hungry by chance?"

Upon the mere mention of food, Jack remembered just how hungry he was and responded brusquely, "Starving."

After a slight frown for his brother's lack of manners, Thomas replied more politely, "Yes. Thank you."

"Unfortunately, it is well past dinner time. But I think we can scrounge up something. Wordsworth, would you be so kind as to bring my nephews something to eat, while we retire to the sitting room to get better acquainted."

"Of course my Lord," responded Wordsworth, and he hastened over towards a door next to the enormous clock.

"Now, if you would follow me," said Uncle Hades, "I will take you to more comfortable accommodations, so that we may sit and converse with one another at length. Leave your suitcases. They will be brought up to your rooms."

A Dragon's Tale

UNCLE HADES LED the boys through an archway to a formidable wooden door. Through the door they entered into a large oval room with the most incredible fireplace at its center. Carved from gray marble, the enormous fireplace had two exquisitely detailed sculptures of horned satyrs holding up the mantle. A bright fire of dancing green flames roared inside, casting shadows up and down the walls.

"This is the sitting room," said Lord Hades. To which, true to its name, an elegant Victorian style couch and several large chairs of the same period were arranged around the spacious room. Uncle Hades held out his hand encouraging them to make themselves comfortable, adding to ensure they took his meaning, "Please sit down."

Thomas sat on the couch in the middle of the room, Jack lounged in one of the throne like chairs to the right, while their Uncle sat in the adjacent chair. His absurdly long black cape covered him like a blanket, making Thomas think of a bat with its wings folded.

On the walls hung portraits bearing the likenesses of what appeared important personages; namely, Lords and Ladies. All extremely well painted—immortalizing their respective subjects in flattering circumstances.

Thomas was especially taken with one portrait in particular hanging prominently above the fireplace. That of a stunning auburn haired young woman with gentle emerald green eyes and fair porcelain skin dressed all in white with a wreath of bright yellow and purple flowers wrapped around her head. He found he could scarcely take his eyes off her without them instantly wanting to return. *Who is she?* he wondered, so much that he decided to ask. "Who is that?" he said pointing up at her portrait.

Uncle Hades stared at the portrait for a long moment and then gave a slight smile. "That," he began in a reminiscent tone, "is a very special woman I knew long ago. Perhaps one day I'll share the story that goes behind her. But tonight we've much else to discuss."

"It really is a wonderful portrait," said Thomas, for it truly was an exceptional painting, as they all were for that matter. "Who's the artist?"

"I am," said Uncle Hades, "I've painted all the portraits in the castle. Painting is one of my passions, portraits in particular."

Thomas noticed then his Uncle's hands. They appeared nimble and dexterous, an artist's hands.

"Are they family members?" asked Thomas, hoping to learn something of his family's history.

"No," replied Uncle Hades, "Merely lives I have taken an interest in throughout time."

"Why are the flames green?" interjected Jack abruptly.

"On account of the wood," said Uncle Hades, seamlessly switching topics.

"What's so special about it?" asked Jack.

"It comes from a special tree indigenous to these lands. When the bark is burned the green fire it creates is far stronger, and burns for much longer, than other wood. A single log can burn for weeks on end," said Uncle Hades, adding, "Some even claim it has magical properties."

Jack scoffed loudly, while Thomas' eyes lit up.

"What sort of magical qualities?" inquired Thomas eagerly.

"There is no such thing as magic!" snapped Jack.

Thomas threw his brother a defiant look—one thankfully his brother didn't catch. He knew Jack couldn't accept such a fantastical thing as magic.

"There is a legend about the tree, if you'd like to hear it," offered Uncle Hades.

"I'd love to hear it!" said Thomas.

Jack emitted a pronounced groan. "Always needs a little bed time story," he grumbled. "Might as well tell it, or he'll never be able to sleep."

"Very well," said Uncle Hades, "There are many different versions. But I will tell it the way in which it was first told to me so many years ago…"

All fell suddenly silent as Uncle Hades stared deeply into the blazing green fire, and soon the boys found themselves doing so as well. And as he spoke the green flames flickered with his words…

"A long time ago, there came upon the land a great and powerful dragon that the people of the age called Khan, meaning scourge of the earth in the Ancient Tongue. And indeed he was just that. For Khan burned all of creation wherever he went, leaving nothing but ash and scorched earth in his wake.

"The people believed that Khan was a terrible curse set upon them. And no matter what they tried, no matter how many they sent to face him, the dragon Khan survived.

"Eventfully, the people abandoned all hope and fled to the refuge of the highest mountain ranges. There they hid in caves while the world was ravaged.

"They stayed in hiding for a very long while, fearing ever to go back out into the world. Until one day the young son of the king, a boy named Aloysius, was out playing amidst the rocks far from the others, when he came upon a strange man. Older, and with a long white beard, he wore a gray cloak and carried a tall staff. The strange old man called to Aloysius by name.

"Surprised, Aloysius asked how it was that the man knew him.

"The old man told Aloysius that he knew a great deal about him, more even than Aloysius knew about himself.

"'Who are you?' Aloysius asked.

"And the old man replied, 'My names are many, but you may call me Mosiah, for that is who I am now. I am here to help you fulfill your destiny.'

"'What is my destiny?' Aloysius asked.

"To which Mosiah replied, 'Your soul will be re-born in many forms, live many lives, and from your line the greatest kings shall come to rule, and countless will be saved. I am to prepare you for all that you will face. For our destinies are linked: I am your teacher and you are my student.'

"Not understanding, Aloysius asked. 'What is it that I am meant to do?'

"'Many things,' Mosiah told him. 'The first of which is to slay the dragon Khan,'

"The young boy jumped back in fear, and cried, 'No one can slay Khan!'

"Mosiah shook his head, and said, 'Only *you*. For it is your destiny, and yours alone.'

"But Aloysius could not comprehend such a thing. 'How am I to slay Khan? He cannot be defeated," he despaired.

"Mosiah answered, 'I am the bearer of three gifts given to me by the Author Himself, and with these three gifts I bear you shall slay not one Khan, but three. But since now there is only one, only one shall you receive. The others will be bestowed at a different time, in a different place, when we are, all of us, different. Now open your hands and receive the first.'

"Aloysius did as Mosiah asked and opened his hands.

"Mosiah produced then from the air itself three golden orbs bright as the sun. The orbs spun with unfathomable speed twisting and turning in the air, crashing into each other. It was chaos….

"But when it was over, only one orb remained and it floated gently into Aloysius's arms. Upon touching his skin the orb turned into a shimmering golden bow with a quiver of golden arrows.

"'Behold, the weapon you shall slay the dragon with,' said Mosiah.

"And young Aloysius responded with tears in his eyes, for he wanted to do all that Mosiah asked, 'I don't know how to shoot an arrow.'

"To which Mosiah replied, 'I will teach you,' and true to his word he did. So well the boy was said never to miss.

"After months of training under Mosiah's tutelage, the day finally arrived for Aloysius to fulfill his destiny.

"His parents the King and Queen pleaded for him not to go, for they did not wish to lose their only son and heir. But Aloysius told them it was his destiny, and they should not fear. Knowing that they could not stop him, his parents accepted their son's decision. And after a long night of difficult goodbyes, and many tears, for in truth the people did not expect him to return, Aloysius set out to face Khan.

"The journey was a hard and perilous one. Aloysius was the first to return to the world for many years and what he found there made him weep. The beautiful world he'd once known was gone, barren scorched earth taking its place, where no life could be found.

"Aloysius tracked Khan for several years, until finally one day his search led him to a desolate land of smoke and fire, where the dragon had made his lair. There the battle ensued.

"By now a young man, Aloysius fought with extraordinary courage, and the battle raged for many days. At last, he stood atop a high peak facing the mighty dragon, and as Khan swooped down upon him, Aloysius fired a golden arrow which pierced the dragon's eye. Khan fell, and was vanquished, just as Mosiah had promised.

"From Khan's body sprung forth new life, and it covered the land that had been burned and destroyed. New plants, animals, and creatures of all kinds emerged. Even mankind was changed, enlightened by new knowledge and powers. And led by King Aloysius the Lightbringer as he came to be known, the world entered a golden age.

"A tree is said to have grown from Khan's very mouth, and it grew larger and higher than any other. It came to be known as Dragonwood for its origins, and because of its enormous size and the scaly feel of its bark. The bright green flames it creates when burned are said to be the breath of Khan trapped inside for all eternity and released only when ignited by fire once more. A great good from a great evil…"

Ask and Ye Shall Recieve

At first, the boys didn't realize that their Uncle had stopped speaking and continued staring silently into the fire, entranced by the flickering green flames. Both had been quite overtaken by the story and the almost hypnotic voice in which it was told. And in the flames it all seemed to come alive before their very eyes. Why even Jack—despite his best efforts to resist—had become totally engrossed by it.

Soon however they snapped out of their trance as their Uncle began speaking again. "So what did you think of the story?" he asked.

Thomas, who had very much enjoyed the tale, had only one question. "Are there any dragons left?"

"It's just a story," snapped Jack, "Dragons aren't real—don't be an idiot!"

Thomas began to open his mouth to protest, but Uncle Hades beat him to it.

"You must understand Jack that the people who dwell in these lands have a great many legends and beliefs. Stories are very serious things here, and taken as such. And yes, there are those who believe dragons still exist."

"Just because people believe something doesn't make it true," countered Jack, adding "The fire is probably green because of some chemical in the soil, that's all."

"Perhaps you're right," allowed Uncle Hades, "But belief is an extremely powerful thing. Sometimes by simply believing in something it can become true. Sometimes belief exists before even the thing itself. You must also understand that this is not the world you once knew, and perspectives can change quickly here, I assure you. Nor can everything be explained away so easily by your science. But, as they say, seeing is believing."

A loud cough came from the doorway disrupting their conversation. They all turned to see Wordsworth standing there with a silver cart chalked full with pastries and other assorted treats. "Pardon the interruption, but I have the food you requested."

"Yes, Wordsworth come in." Uncle Hades beckoned, "I'm sure my nephews are far more interested in what's on your tray than in my old stories. I know I would've been at their age."

Wordsworth wheeled the cart over to where the boys were seated and placed it directly between them. Then stepped away from the cart like he'd just fed a pack of wild animals.

The boys quickly made the metaphor apropos as they grabbed handfuls of pastries and furiously stuffed them into their mouths without the slightest regard for the mess they were making. Being famished from the journey, they voraciously made up for all the meals passed. Not to mention how absolutely delicious the food was, especially in relation to their usual fair. When they finished the cart was picked completely clean, with nary a crumb remaining. Wordsworth promptly took it away wheeling it back through the doorway and out into the hall.

Thomas and Jack sat back in their seats thoroughly satisfied. At least with their stomachs that is, for before long they began again with their questions.

"Where are we going to school?" asked Thomas.

"You will continue your education of course, but not in what you might call the traditional sense. We have no formal schools of the kind in which you're accustomed. Instead, we have the guilds. Depending upon one's talents, one is chosen for entry into an appropriate guild through a rigorous process. Once chosen, their skills are nurtured and developed in their respective trade," explained Uncle Hades.

"So what will our trade be?" asked Thomas anxiously, having not the slightest idea about just what sort of trade he'd be good at, or want to devote his life to. It was something he'd never really given much thought to in truth. Though, he had in all honesty dreamed of becoming a writer. But from what he'd heard that was impossible. *Better to try and become a dragon slayer.*

Unlike Thomas, Jack had always known what he wanted to be, and before Uncle Hades could answer he broke in, "You're a king, aren't you?"

"I am the ruler of the realm, so yes you could say that I am the king. I don't particularly care for the title, however. But if I chose, I could wear it."

"And we are your only family," said Jack.

"This is true," allowed Uncle Hades.

"So that would make us your heirs wouldn't it?" said Jack.

Where is he going with this? Thomas wondered.

"Under the Common Laws, yes, I suppose that's true as well." Uncle Hades confirmed.

"So...that would make us princes, wouldn't it?" said Jack.

Uncle Hades didn't say anything for a long moment. While Thomas was mortified that his brother could be so blatantly audacious—not that he hadn't come to expect it by now, his brother was the very epitome of boldness. But even for him this was going too far.

"Would you like to be princes?" Uncle Hades asked finally, a response catching even Jack by surprise.

Jack simply nodded his head, rendered speechless for perhaps the first time in his entire life.

"And you Thomas? Would that be suitable?"

"I...um...a..."

"Of course he would!" Jack answered for his brother, triumph in his eyes.

"Then so be it. From this day forth you and your brother shall be princes of Somulus." Uncle Hades declared.

Thomas' jaw nearly hit the ground, while Jack simply smiled smugly.

"Let's make it official then shall we? Wordsworth, come here if you would," called Uncle Hades, and within a moment the old man stood before them.

"Yes, my Lord."

"Draw up papers declaring my nephews princes of Soumlus, with all according rights and privileges. Ensure word spreads throughout the realm."

"Yes, my Lord," replied Wordsworth obediently, and if surprised certainly didn't show it.

By now, Thomas had nearly lost it and his mouth—if not for the hinge of his jaw—would've hit the floor. Thomas couldn't believe what had just transpired. *Did he just say what I think he said? Are we really—princes?*

"Now we have a trade," said Jack, grinning triumphantly. "We'll learn to rule."

Lord Hades rose abruptly from his seat. "I apologize but I must retire for the evening. Wordsworth will show you to your bedrooms. You'll find your closets stocked with clothes I have provided. They are a bit more appropriate for this land. If they are a tad large, do not worry you'll grow into them soon. I bid you both good night," and with that Uncle Hades walked purposefully towards the doorway, his long black cape following behind him like a loyal dog.

"Ready to see your rooms?" inquired Wordsworth after Uncle Hades had left.

"Yes, show us to our rooms," said Jack, and Thomas detected greater smugness than usual in his brother's voice. *He's going to push this prince thing as far as he can*, he realized, and he wondered what that would mean for everyone else. *His ego is going to go through the roof*!

Wordsworth led the boys up the long winding staircase in the middle of the main hall, the one from which Uncle Hades had descended earlier. Which ascended into the very heights of the castle, traveling so high up that after a certain point it just disappeared altogether, like a mountain into clouds.

"How many floors are there?" asked Thomas, staring upward.

"This staircase has thirteen floors," said Wordsworth.

"Oh. What floor will we be staying on?" asked Thomas.

"You will both be staying on the third floor. The Gemini hall. Most appropriate since you are twins."

"Are all the halls named after astrological signs then?" asked Thomas.

"All accept for the last one," said Wordsworth.

"That's pretty cool," said Thomas, who like his mother had always been fascinated by astrology.

Jack on the other hand could've cared less, if he was even listening at all, which he wasn't. He was far too busy planning what he was going to do now that he was a prince.

Just then they arrived at the first floor.

"Here, you see, is the hall of Aries," said Wordsworth.

There was a symbol on the floor in front of them of a shield crossed by two swords. Both boys stopped and looked down its length curiously. But they found it impossible to see anything, as the hallway was covered in shadowy darkness.

"Why can't we just stay on this hall?" asked Jack, admiring the symbol.

"I am sorry Prince Jack, but your rooms have already been made up for you," said Wordsworth.

Jack began to open his mouth to voice his displeasure. But before he could, as if anticipating the complaint, Wordsworth headed it off, "I assure you Prince Jack that the Gemini hall is far more appropriate for royalty."

Jack paused, and then responded, "Fine, we'll stay there then," as if the decision were his to make.

Only a few moments later they reached the second floor, which Wordsworth informed them was the hall of Taurus. Though they probably would've guessed as much—or at least Thomas would've—since the symbol was a horned bull.

Once again their vision of the floor was obscured by darkness, and Thomas wondered why there wasn't any light on these hallways.

Finally, they made it to the hall on which they would be staying. The symbol was that of the Roman numeral II.

Thankfully, this hallway was sufficiently lit up by several torches hanging on the walls lining the breadth of the hall, which consisted of only two doors.

Wordsworth stopped at the first door on the left side of the hallway and pulled a single key from his jacket pocket. He quickly unlocked it and then walked a short distance across the hall to the adjacent door and did the same.

"You'll be staying in this room, Prince Jack," he said indicating the door to the left, "And that room is yours Prince Thomas," pointing to its counterpart on the right, "I hope everything is too your liking. If it is not, don't hesitate to call. I'm always around."

"We won't," replied Jack brusquely.

"Good night Wordsworth and thank you for everything," said Thomas graciously.

Wordsworth smiled genially. You're very welcome my Prince."

Jack however said nothing and barely deigned a glance at the old man.

When he'd left, Thomas and Jack stood across the hall from one another, standing just outside the door to their respective rooms in silence, as if each were waiting for the other to say something.

"Weird day, huh?" said Thomas finally.

"Weird?" replied Jack, "You mean greatest of our entire lives! We've just become princes! Do you have any idea what that means?" It was not a question Jack wanted Thomas to answer for before he had a chance, Jack responded, "It means we're royalty now—meaning we're better than everybody else. This is the best day of our lives and we've only just arrived here. Stick with me and we'll accomplish great things—I can feel it!" and suddenly Thomas saw a flash of fire dash across his brother's dark eyes, and it caused him to take a couple steps back. Until stopped short by the door to his room, bumping into it awkwardly.

"What's wrong with you!" barked Jack.

"Um, nothing, I just can't believe we're princes is all." Thomas managed hastily. *Does he know that I saw it? Does he even know that it happened? Did I really just see it again*? the questions mounted.

Jack smiled. "Get used to it. There are going to be a lot of changes ahead."

"I will," replied Thomas weakly.

"And remember, we deserve this—we've earned it," said Jack, and Thomas wondered if his brother really meant them, or just him.

"Now I can't wait to see what it feels like to sleep like a prince. I bet they even do that better than everyone else," and with that Jack opened the door to his room and walked inside shutting the heavy wooden door behind him.

Thomas stood there by himself for a moment longer before heading into his room as well.

The Story and the Dream

THOMAS HAD NEVER had his own bedroom before, always forced to share one with his brother. Needless to say he rather liked the idea of being alone for a change. *At least I'll finally have some space of my own*, he thought as he entered his new room.

As for space, he certainly received his wish and then some, for the room possessed more sheer floor space than his entire house back in Boonton. Why the bed alone was as big as his old living room, appearing as if it could sleep ten comfortably. Upon seeing it, he wasted no time in doing what any boy would've done in his place: a full speed run followed by a leap onto his massive new bed, which caught him with the greatest of ease as he sunk delightfully down into the soft royal blue sheets.

I could get used to this, he thought spreading himself out to his fullest length, and with no fear—unlike his bunk bed—of tumbling off. He wondered what size it was. *Probably a king*, he thought, barely able to contain his joy. *Though this room is fit for a prince.*

Not ostentatious, nor overly simple in its décor, but a pleasant compromise between the two, and Thomas found the room quite tasteful, as far as such things go. There were no portraits or paintings adorning the walls, which were painted a shade of blue perfectly replicating the sky on a clear mid-summer's day. No lavish indulgences, except for perhaps the white rug sprawled across the center of the room appearing made from the fur of some sort of animal.

Beside the bed was a small table with a single lit candle atop it, providing the perfect light for reading. The rest of the room was visibly lit by larger candles that hung on the walls, providing a warm welcoming light. A large glass window stood off to the left of the bed, while an enormous dark brown wooden closet stood to the right, which Thomas was certain could've fit all his worldly possessions with room to spare.

On the other side of the room, separated by the white fur rug, stood a sizeable dresser with a very long mirror above it, appearing quite old and what his mother surely would've termed "antique" with elaborate designs carved into its dark wooden frame.

There was a bathroom at the end of the room, another feature Thomas found very much to his liking, being yet another thing he'd always been forced to share with his brother. Thankfully, he discovered it to be relatively modern, with everything one would expect to find in a typical bathroom.

There was a fireplace at the center of the room near where the rug laid. He made a mental note to ask Wordsworth for some wood. Maybe he could even acquire some Dragonwood. *How cool would that be,* he thought, imagining his very own fireplace roaring with hot green flames.

The room had everything he needed, everything he could ever ask for in a room, apart for perhaps a television set. Though to be honest, Thomas much preferred books anyway.

Not everything turned out perfect, however, for when he opened his suitcase he discovered that all his clothes were ruined. How it had happened was a mystery, but somehow they'd all been torn to shreds, and lay in his suitcase in tatters. It looked like an animal had burrowed inside and had itself a field day. He held up his favorite shirt and stared at it in dismay. *No amount of sowing is ever going to salvage this*, he thought, shaking his head, and he found not a single piece of clothing had been spared—they hadn't even left him a sock!

Despite this apparent tragedy, he was determined not to let it ruin his good mood. Besides it wasn't as if they were expensive designer clothes, most coming from secondhand-shops and thrift stores.

It was then that he remembered what his Uncle had told him earlier about having put clothes in the closet for him. So he quickly made his way over to the massive dark wooden structure and opened the doors.

Thomas could scarcely believe his eyes at all the clothes he saw. The huge closet was completely full! There had to be more than quadruple his entire wardrobe in there. These clothes, however, were of a much different sort than those he was accustomed to.

"What in the world is this?" he said taking out a frilly black shirt that looked like it belonged to a pirate. "They'd make fun of me forever at school if I wore this. Is this really what they wear around here?" he wondered aloud, putting the shirt back into the closet where he found it.

It quickly became apparent that the rest of the clothes weren't much better. He did have to admit, however, after giving them a good perusal, that though they certainly weren't of the kind he'd normally think to wear, and certainly not what one would call the popular style that they nonetheless appeared finely made. Some being cut from the most superb cloth he'd ever felt in his life, and it was obvious that a great deal of time and care had gone into crafting them.

It was like a thespian's closet filled with theatrical costumes. There were long multi-colored coats with extensive embroidering, pants as sturdy and rugged as they were soft and comfortable, cloaks and capes Thomas couldn't figure out the purpose to, but found magnificent all the same. There were hats and gloves of the kind worn by gentlemen in the days when the word was still apropos, boots made from fine leather and suede, and many other articles you'd be hard-pressed to find in any department store.

He pulled out a set of full length silk pajamas, sky blue to match the color of his bed. *These will do*, he thought and headed off to the bathroom to wash up and change for bed.

Upon returning from the bathroom, wearing his new pajamas which were slightly large, but not a bad fit, and undoubtedly the most comfortable thing he'd ever put on his body, Thomas took out the book Wordsworth had given him earlier on the train, and decided to do a bit of reading before going to bed, as was his custom. He blew out the candles, all except for the one at his bedside, and settled into bed. Then he opened the book, entitled ***Tales of Principle and Folly*** and turned to the very first tale: ***The Story and the Dream.***

Interesting title, he thought, and quickly turned the well-worn page and began to read…

Long ago, in a great kingdom of old, two friends were out walking the land. Both were brave and honorable men who had accomplished great deeds in their lives. But had grown old and frail, and their heroic feats of yesteryears were largely forgotten by the people.

This did not sit well with either man, for they were understandably very prideful of their accomplishments, wishing for them to be remembered long after they had gone to the dust. But how to ensure such a precarious thing neither did rightly know. And it was the cause of great angst for them both as their lives were coming to an end.

Upon their walk they came upon a small stream and decided to take a drink from its waters, for it was a hot day and their mouths were parched.

They knelt each upon the water's bank and proceeded to drink. When suddenly they heard a voice from behind them speak, and this is what it said: "Memories fade and memories go…time makes the sturdiest rocks into pillars of dust, and idle men of even the greatest heroes…woe, woe, woe, for those who are forgotten!"

The men darted around to see who was speaking to them in such a fashion. But to their surprise saw no one. Except for a stately raven sitting high upon the perch of an elm tree.

"Whose there?" asked the first man.

"Who dares speak to us so?" echoed the second.

Then they both replied at the very same time, "Don't you know who we are!"

"It is I!" answered the stately raven at last, and both men their eyes not deceiving, were immediately humbled, and bowed low before the stately Raven.

"Oh great Raven, you honor us with your voice. Tell us what you desire with such men as ourselves?" they asked.

"I've come to you both with a simple proposition, a choice between two paths, as you are twice a man in number and stature," responded the Raven. "Though be forewarned, one must choose one path and the second then must choose the other. It is up to you to decide which. But there must in the end be a decision. Do you agree to my terms?" he inquired of each.

"We do," the two men responded in unison, not wishing to upset their visitor.

"Very well, listen close," and the Raven began thus: "There are only two ways known to man to be remembered for generations hither. The first is to become a story written by a great pen and read by all who come after. The other is to become a dream,

a memory replayed out in the minds of men when their eyes close to sleep....Each is quite different from the other, each possesses its own unique properties, its pluses and minuses. Listen closely for I shall not repeat them. Remember, you may only choose one..." and began listing the merits of each.

"A story depends upon the hand of another, an author to write the letters; yet a dream is untouched, not by the hand of a scribe or the song of a bard, and is interpreted solely by the dreamer.... A story can be viewed in its entirety for as many times as one may wish; while a dream is not always remembered whole, and the dreamer may only occasion it once.... A story can be read far and wide, and people in all different lands may come to be inspired by its tale at the same time. But a dream inspires only one at a time, though its inspiration is far greater.... A story influences the waking mind, while a dream dwells deep in the unconscious. One is freely chosen by the reader, the other forced unbeknownst upon the sleeper. And though both may spur men on to accomplish great things in their lives, only a story will truly get the credit. Yet in the end it is the dream that shall bring the greatest glory....

"Now the time has come for you to choose which you will become after your lives are done and over," said the Raven having finished.

Both men thought long and hard on their decision, weighing each option according to their own scales. Until at last they had each decided, and conferred with one another to ensure they'd chosen different.

The first man faced the Raven and said: "Oh great Raven, of the choices you have presented, I have chosen to become a story, written by the hand of a great author, to be read over and over after I meet with my end. So that children may grow up with my tale and be inspired to become great men, like myself, and greater than I still."

"Very well then," the Raven replied, "A great story you shall be, heard by countless throughout this land and in a thousand others...and your name shall forever be Legend."

The Raven turned then to the second man. "So then you shall be a dream...a divine inspiration to change the course of men's lives in the breadth of a single night... an Omen, a Prophecy, you shall guide them through—"

"No!" interrupted the second man, "I shall be both!" and he pulled a knife from his belt and stabbed his friend to death.

When he'd finished his dastardly deed he turned back to the Raven, sitting still upon his perch, unmoved in the least. "Now I shall be part of his story forever, for it will never be told without me. Therefore I shall be both, a story and a dream," and he laughed at the cleverness of his plot.

"Yes," replied the Raven ever so calmly, "both shall you be. But in both, and forevermore, shall you be a murderer..." and suddenly the Raven flew straight over the man's head, and he dropped dead right there. The bloody dagger still clutched in his hand.

The story ended on that ominous note and the Sandman arrived shortly thereafter. Thomas fell asleep with the book on his chest and questions dancing in his head.

That very same night in the room directly across the hall a strange and most vivid dream came to Jack as his eyes finally closed. It was one that when he awoke he would not wholly remember, though it would stay with him always. It began simply...

Upon the lofty heights of a palace balcony there stood overlooking a vast and beautiful kingdom of gleaming white towers and sprawling city houses, a handsome young man of flawless olive skin and heroic stature, with an angular face and long shining dark black hair to complement his equally dark features. His flowing silken robes of brilliant bright red and shining black were rich and regal, befitting the highest nobility. Yet clasped hard in his left hand was a great spear as tall as a man—though none taller than himself—marking him clearly as a warrior.

The city he oversaw was a wonder to behold, with bountiful hanging gardens of unmatched beauty gracing the sides and tops of the sun-drenched white marble buildings and houses, creating a primitive jungle paradise amidst the throngs of civilization. And colorful exotic birds lay perched upon the rooftops singing sweet melodies to the crystal blue heavens above.

The white marble streets beneath were bursting with life and activity, lined as far as the eye could see with people of all different sizes, shapes, and colors. The sights and sounds of celebration captivated the crisp morning air as an enormous parade marched through them. Adults cheered and children laughed as the spectacle passed, complete with jugglers, fire-breathers, acrobats, cages filled with a menagerie of exotic creatures, and many other marvels and curiosities.

The man, however, joined not in their revelry, and stood stoically upon the palace balcony carefully surveying the action below. His blood red cape flapping ever so gently in the wind behind him, and his spear clasped firmly in the iron grip of his left hand. He stood deep in thought, his keen black eyes coldly analyzing all in their path, as if discerning the outcome of some unforeseen event.

"Today my Prince you shall become the king and all shall be yours at last," purred the melodious voice of a woman from directly behind him, interrupting the solitude of his thoughts.

Her hand, appearing as if sculpt from porcelain and adorned with an exquisite ring of gilded gold fashioned into the shape of a snake, placed itself lovingly upon the man's thick shoulders.

"Ours, my Queen," responded the man, his voice deep and full, "For you and I shall rule Jove together."

A smile crossed her sensuous dark featured face as she appeared then beside him.

"You make me happier than any woman could ever hope to be. I am yours always and forever my King...I am your servant... I am your slave..." she moved in closer to him, and he no longer had eyes for anything else.

"And I yours..." he whispered in return as their lips finally met, and they kissed passionately upon the balcony until their lips could kiss no more.

"Today history itself shall come this day to pay homage," he continued tenderly stroking her cheek as he spoke, "And when you sit upon the Eternal Throne no one will ever again question the legitimacy of our love."

Suddenly her beautiful face twisted into a hateful scowl, as it roused with rage. "We will wipe the smug smiles from their haughty faces, and scourge the laughter from their lips. And for the rest of their days they will know only sorrow and pain!" she erupted.

"Be still my Queen," his voice calm and soothing, "All shall receive their just deserts. But on this day let us pay no mind to our enemies. For this day is ours, and when the crown is placed upon our heads, their happy days shall be at their end. But wait for vengeance my love, all good things in time," he said, holding her hand firmly as it shook with unbridled rage.

She broke free of his grip, walking back inside the confines of the palace room. He paused momentarily, taking a final glance at the festivities, then turned to follow.

The room was exotically decorated with colorful silks and elaborate tapestries hanging from the walls, intricately woven carpets spanned the breadth of the floor. Large golden bowls of burning incense were placed around the room, making for a smoky veneer.

She began then to pace, moving in and out of the smoke like a Medusa stalking through the columns of her lair. As she spoke her words were full of bile and hate. "I shall hang them from their entrails and bleed them dry as the desert sands. Until all the noble blood they are unfit to carry—every last drop of it—drains out. Their very souls shall our family possess, and from their weakness we shall build great pillars of strength. From their envy we shall forge the foundation of an everlasting empire. I swear upon our love all shall come to pass!"

The Prince merely regarded her with a loving glance. Until her own face softened once more: her lips parted, she smiled, her beauty returned.

"You truly are my Queen," said the Prince, looking at her the way only a man completely in love can.

"Yes, my King," she gazed back, equally entranced, "truly, I am."

They moved towards one another to embrace once more, when suddenly there came a knock at the door.

"Come in," commanded the Prince and the door opened instantly.

There standing before them was a tall, slender man with a stern face, dressed in white robes with gold embroidering. The symbol of a blazing sun prominent upon his breast.

"Sorry to disturb my Prince—" and then upon seeing her standing next him, added begrudgingly, "—and Princess."

"What is it?" demanded the Prince.

"Your father wishes to speak with you before the ceremony begins. He is waiting for you in his chambers. And he requests," he shot a glance over at the Princess "you come alone."

The Prince looked at him hard for moment, as if deciding whether to decline the request. But then nodded his head and replied, "I'll be there shortly."

"I will inform his Lordship, my Prince," and after a quick bow the man departed shutting the door behind him.

After he was gone, the Prince turned back to the Princess before she could say a word, "Do not worry my love, I am sure it is nothing."

"But he does not—"

"There is nothing he can do," said the Prince flatly, "It is his choice no longer."

"But he is still—"

He grabbed her arms firmly and stared deeply into her opal eyes. "Not for long my love," and then he kissed her softly on the forehead and whispered, "I shall return soon…" Then with his spear leading the way headed purposefully towards the doorway, his long streaming jet black hair and bright red cape trailing him faithfully.

The Princess watched him go with deep concern etched upon her face.

It was at that moment that the dream began to fade and blur. It began changing into something else, melting from one scene into another like paint being washed away, only to be reformed into an entirely new picture…

The Prince stood atop a large hill. No longer adorned in fine silken robes, but fearsome black battle armor. A thicker, coarser red cape draped down from his back, to go along with the red dragon insignia displayed upon his breastplate. Upon his head rested a heavy crown with sharp iron spikes protruding out of it, making it appear more burden than blessing. He appeared different than before, hardened by the grindstone of life, his face a living testament to all his many trials. For there was a wild, savage, animalistic look about him, as if he'd been through much, survived, and was stronger for it. He wore a beard now upon his face. It suited him, as if his face was destined to wear it.

One of his gauntleted hands clasped his faithful spear, while the other gently held the Princesses'. Wearing a long silk dress as dark as his own, she appeared more seductive and alluring than ever. In her other hand, she held a black wand, with a green snake painted upon it. While upon her head was a lavish silver diadem of sparkling, multi-colored jewels.

Together they overlooked the breadth of an enormous expanse nearly every inch covered with the mechanisms of war: siege works and cruel killing machines of all kinds stood amidst legions of soldiers dressed in black armor to mirror the Prince's. Above dozens of fire-breathing dragons flew. In the distance, stood the city encircled by high white walls.

"I never thought I would see this day," the Prince spoke in a solemn tone, staring out at the city of his birth, "Never did I think that it would come to this: an intruder marching upon my own home…that I protected for so long, from countless enemies. Now I return at the head of an army, and *I* am the enemy. Who will protect them now? Who will come to their defense? My brother—the coward," he laughed at the absurdity, "There is no one. It is a graveyard, though it does not yet know it." He put his head down. "They have brought this judgment upon themselves by their arrogance, their deceit…and their betrayal," and he lifted his head up once more, "And for the dagger they stabbed into my back, I shall break theirs!"

"Destroy them all my love," urged the Princess, "lay waste to the city of Jove. Burn every building, level every house. Do not cease until it is ashes. Until it is wiped clean from the earth. Do this for me my King, I beg of you, for I do not wish to look one moment longer upon that vile place that has wounded you so…nor the pathetic creatures dwelling within its walls."

"What will that make of me?" he asked with evident uncertainty in his voice, "How will history judge me for such an atrocity? A monster without comparison—a second Khan?" he pondered aloud the terrible ramifications of such an act.

"No one would blame you my love, many already support your claim," her voice like the sweet purr of a cat, "They have betrayed you my King. It is the only acceptable punishment for such an offense. They have denied you what was yours by right. What was yours since the day of your birth. But today you take it all back, and embrace your destiny. And as for history, it is written by the victors…and today you shall be its author."

She broke away from his hand, and lifted her black wand to the heavens, and as she did the skies darkened, and the wind picked up.

"Today you take control of your own fate," the skies grew more and more violent, "For you are Draconis, the Dragon King, and all shall bow before you!" and the thunder ripped through the sky.

He closed his eyes and breathed in deeply. "Yes..." he paused for a long moment, relishing in the sound and feel. Finally, he opened his dark eyes once more, and as he did they burned with fire, and the spear in his left hand shook as if alive. "I am."

Everything suddenly calmed and the turbulent sky grew silent and still once more, as footsteps came from behind them. They turned to see a man approaching them on the hill.

A short, ugly man, too thin by far with drawn out features and pale, squalid skin stretched much too tightly over his bony face. His nose was long and pointed like a beak. His head was bald and frail as a new born babe's. His eyes were dull, lifeless, and gray, showing no apparent sign of a soul beneath. He wore elegant blue satin robes appearing completely out of place upon the body they adorned, and upon his scrawny fingers were several loosely-fitting golden rings. He held in his hands a large black book with a single symbol on the cover etched in gold: a snake wrapped tightly around a tree.

"A thousssand pardonss for the interruption my King," hissed the man, his voice like the slither of a snake, "And to you mossst radiant Queen," he bowed so low that the beak of his nose nearly scraped the dirt.

"What is it Moloch?" commanded the Prince shortly, his voice stiff and unwelcoming, fraught with obvious displeasure for the interruption.

"The Generalsss are getting anxiousss my King. They wissh to know your orderss for the attack." Moloch licked his lips, as if the mere thought was delicious.

The Prince paused for a long moment as he overlooked the vast landscape covered by the mechanisms of war, and his sight went further still, past the troops gathered in their endless masses, out to the horizon and to the great city shining brilliantly amidst the rolling knolls, lush green hills, golden wheat fields, and majestic snow-covered mountains that nestled it. And it was at that moment that the sun rose up over the horizon, large and bright, and it hovered above the city as if preparing to defend it, as if visibly choosing sides in the battle to come. The Prince's face hardened to stone. "Burn it all to the ground, and bury it deep beneath the ashes. Purge it from the pages of history."

"What of the citizensss my Lord?" asked Moloch anxiously.

"Kill them all," said the Prince without hesitation, and his eyes lit once more with fire and his voice grew colder and more sinister than before. "Let Death feast until it bursts!"

Suddenly the scene began to change again, but this time it changed far more rapidly, with scenes going as quickly they came, providing only glimpses of the past for the eyes of the future….

….Fires rage uncontrollably and people run for their lives screaming for help that will not come. Destruction and carnage fill the city streets, staining the spotless white marble red…

….Thick ashes and dust lay heaped atop the remains of a thousand bodies' times a thousand. They lay contorted and twisted beneath the ruins and rumble. Just beyond the city stands an endless field of ditches each filled to the brim with decomposing bodies. A dense fog lingers over all…

….A man with thick golden hair leads his people up a treacherous mountain path. They carry upon their backs everything they own and their faces are smeared with dirt and anguish….

….Hundreds of weary sweat drenched men and women trudge up a steep slope carrying upon their whipped-lashed backs enormous black stone blocks. They place one upon another in endless procession, laying the foundation for the massive structure to come in the future. The sky above them is black and ominous as dark storm clouds hover and dragons circle, overseeing the toil of production…

….The golden haired man clutches a sword of blinding bright light and holds it up to the sky as his people kneel before him…

….A moon hangs high and full in the night sky as the golden haired man, adorned in glimmering white battle armor, places a banner bearing the symbol of a white lion upon the steeple of a tall tower. Thousands cheer below…

….A young boy yells to a crowd, "We've got her! We've captured the Queen of lies! She's to be judged this day…"

…The Prince sits upon a black scorched earth, steam rising up from it. Behind him wooden spikes as far as the eye can see hold countless dead bodies, impaled gruesomely. Yet he is concerned with only one. He clutches in his arms the lifeless, hideously charred body of his Princess. No longer held in by their sockets, his dark eyes burn with uncontrollable fire. He cries out suddenly to the heavens above "Vengeance will be mine!" and his voice echoes throughout the land...

....Atop a jagged mountain peak, the Prince stands in full black armor holding his spear which burns with fire like his eyes. Across from him is the golden haired man in white armor holding his sword glowing with light. Behind the Prince is darkness, dense and deep. Behind the golden-haired man a light brighter than the sun. They face one another, preparing for battle.

"It ends now!" declared the golden haired man.

"But not the way you think little brother," responded the Prince, and he turned his flaming spear and held it at arm's length, the blade facing his chest. "Every ending is another's beginning....We shall meet again soon and settle this once and for all..." and he plunged the flaming spear deep into his heart....

The dream ended thus, fading from memory as sleep from the very first light of day. Though somewhere in the deepest recesses of Jack's heart he remembered it all, and would never, ever, forget.

Slepnir

Thomas awoke feeling quite good about the day ahead, surprising given the turbulent night he'd endured. The main culprit being a mischievous tree branch that began tapping noisily on his windowsill during the middle of the night, and continued on incessantly from that point forward until he finally went back to sleep from sheer exhaustion in the wee hours of the morning.

Nevertheless, he felt right as rain, even despite what appeared a dreary fog-filled day. Though he couldn't help but eye the wayward tree branch suspiciously one final time, standing innocently right outside his windowsill, and imparting a few last remarks. "Oh, don't want to tap now do you? No, it's only at night when I'm trying to sleep. There's no fun in it now, is there?" and he vowed to deal with it later. Once he'd found himself an axe. "This isn't over," he swore.

He went to his closet and promptly changed into some of his Uncle's clothes: a pair of brown suede pants, a double-breasted dark green overcoat of the sort a dandy may have worn stylishly in the days when the word was still in vogue, overlaying a long white button down shirt with golden cufflinks, along with a pair of black leather boots. It all fit perfectly, as if specially tailored just for him.

Not bad, he thought taking a longer look than usual at himself in the mirror. And as he did he actually thought—though not a vain boy—that he appeared rather handsome, dashing even. And whether it was simply the clothes, he swore he appeared noticeably older. Indeed, it was like he'd aged a couple of years overnight. And perhaps it was just the boots, but he felt like he'd sprung up a couple of inches too. "How long was I asleep for?" he joked.

Fortuitously, Thomas walked out of his room at the very same moment that his brother was walking out of his, and when Thomas saw him he stopped cold in his tracks. For his brother looked strikingly different than he had only the night before, and it wasn't just the clothes, though they certainly stood out. He wore a long dark blue velvet cape draped over his wide shoulders, his shirt was a pristine white with elaborate gold embroidering and sapphire cufflinks, and his pants were an elegant dark blue velvet. His solid black leather boots had a silver buckle polished to a gleam.

But his clothes were far from the only change in his brother, or the most drastic. His black hair looked like it had grown an inch in length, and he was larger in size and stature, with his shoulders, chest, and arms appearing more imposing than ever. There was even a noticeable hint of stubble on his angular face.

Jack stared at Thomas, and then after giving him a discerning once over replied, "Those clothes suit you."

Even his voice is deeper, Thomas thought, noting the precipitous drop in octave.

"Thanks, um, yours too," said Thomas.

"How did you sleep?" asked Jack.

"Well, actually—"

"I slept wonderfully!" said Jack completely cutting him off, "In fact I don't believe I've ever had a better one in my entire life. It's so much better to sleep in a proper bed, don't you think? We really have been deprived all these years, living in our other life. But that's all in the past now."

Has he forgotten where he came from after only one night of becoming a Prin—?" and that's when it struck him, he'd nearly forgotten, or perhaps he'd thought it all a dream, or something his imagination cooked up. *We're princes*! he nearly cried out, *princes!* the shock nearly as great as when they'd first been named.

"Let's go to breakfast," said Jack, adding, "Hopefully the butler has something for us worth eating."

"The who?" replied Thomas not taking his meaning.

"The butler," reiterated Jack squarely, "You know, Wordsworth. He is the help—nothing more," and made a dismissive gesture with hand, as if brushing crumbs off a table.

"I didn't—"

"You must learn to tell the difference, now that you're a prince. Can't have you associating with the wrong kind of people," and he grimaced as if the mere idea of it was distasteful.

Thomas was stunned. *Has he lost his mind? Calling Wordsworth a butler? And why does he keep talking like that?*

"Um, right, sorry. I'll remember that. So breakfast?" said Thomas, not letting on to his true feelings.

"Yes, let's go," pronounced Jack decidedly, and without another word whipped his cape around—which nearly hit Thomas square in the face—and headed down the spiraling staircase.

As Thomas followed his brother down the staircase, he began to wonder if Wordsworth was indeed a butler. *He does dress a little like one*, he supposed, though not exactly certain what a butler dressed like except for what he'd seen in movies and television shows. *And he does work for our Uncle, doesn't he? Serves us food and all. Maybe Jack's right, maybe he is a butler. Speak of the devil*!

Wordsworth awaited them at the bottom of the staircase holding a tray of freshly baked pastries. Thomas' mouth watered the instant the tantalizing aroma hit his nose.

"Hurry young Princes, eat some breakfast. We have things to do today, and you have slept late," said Wordsworth, holding the tray out to them.

"What sort of things?" asked Thomas quickly grabbing a pastry, while Jack was already chomping down on one with another in tow.

"We're going into the town of Everfall to pick up some supplies. Your Uncle also thought it beneficial for you to experience a bit of the realm."

"Splendid," said Jack, "I want to meet my subjects."

Wordsworth gave Jack a curious look, before responding, "Um, yes, I'm sure that'll be quite a thrill for them."

Thomas thought he caught just a hint of sarcasm, though far too subtle for Jack to hear, as he paid the 'butler' scant attention. *Easy Wordsworth, tread lightly.*

All the same Thomas too was excited about the prospect of going into town. *I wonder what the people are like*, he thought.

"All finished? Fantastic. Let's get going then? No time to waste!" said Wordsworth hurriedly snatching the tray away before either had eaten their fill.

"Hey I wasn't—" But before Jack could get it out, Wordsworth had already left with the tray, leaving Jack with a half-eaten pastry in his hand and a fierce scowl upon his face.

"Oops," said Jack nonchalantly tossing the half-eaten pastry onto the floor.

"What'd you do that for!" cried Thomas.

"The butler has to learn his place," said Jack coldly.

Thomas didn't like the sound of that at all. *There is going to be trouble between those two. I just know it.*

"Don't you want to see the—um—your subjects," said Thomas attempting to divert his brother's attention.

"Your right, we shouldn't deprive them of my—" he stopped, smiled, "*our* presence. I am anxious to see the state of things. From what I've seen changes will need to be made."

Who does he think he is? thought Thomas, shaking his head, *He's been a prince for less than a day and already thinks he's King Arthur*!

Just then Wordsworth returned.

"Ready young Princes, follow me if you—"

It was then that he saw the half-eaten pastry lying on the floor. He frowned, then took a handkerchief from his coat and cleaned it up.

Jack smirked smugly. "You missed a spot."

Thomas shook his head.

Wordsworth led the boys outside the great triangular doors to where three horses stood saddled and waiting. Thomas and Jack both stopped cold when they saw them standing there, for these were no ordinary horses. They were far larger than normal horses, and most unusually of all had eight legs instead of four.

Thomas blinked several times in disbelief.

"What sort of horses are these?" asked Jack giving them a queer look.

"They are known as Sleipnir. They were given to your Uncle as a gift by the King of Asgard in exchange for hospitality your Uncle showed a relative of his some time ago. Magnificent creatures, they can run twice as fast as a normal horse, leap twice as high, and the ride is infinitely smoother," said Wordsworth.

"The King of Asgard?" said Thomas, "As in the Asgard of Norse mythology?"

"Yes," replied Wordsworth, "As I told you these lands are responsible for much of the world's so called mythology."

Thomas remembered Wordsworth telling him that these lands were collectively known as Mythil, and that stories originating here had become known as myths as a result. But he had claimed that they were really just old stories which had been embellished over time. Before Thomas, however, stood three giant eight-legged horses. *Where's the embellishment?* he wondered. He was beginning to think that perhaps there was a reason—other than the name—that myths emanated from here.

Even Jack appeared to be thinking along the same lines, begrudgingly acknowledging that something odd was afoot, something perhaps even…fantastical. But then suddenly his logical mind reclaimed hold. "A genetic defect is all," he said dismissively, as much to himself as anyone else.

It was then that Thomas remembered what their Uncle had said about not being able to explain everything through science. Though so far at least his brother was doing a pretty good job at it.

"Climb on," prompted Wordsworth.

"Wait, we're actually going to ride them?" asked Thomas fearfully, having never ridden a horse before, never mind a massive eight-legged mutant one.

Jack walked fearlessly up to the largest of the three, an enormous white stallion, and placed his hand on it. "This one is mine!" he declared.

"Ah, Helmud, a fine choice Prince Jack," said Wordsworth applauding his decision. "And I shall ride Olaf," and he grabbed the reigns of a dark brown stallion smaller than Helmud yet larger than the third: a tan horse that appeared to be the runt of the group, yet still extremely large. "That leaves Prince Thomas with Snorri."

"H-how do you ride?" asked Thomas uncertainly, keeping his distance.

Wordsworth laughed. "Nothing to it, just hop on and Snorri will do the rest. Trust him and he'll not fail you." Wordsworth promised, and then with but a single leap sat atop his own horse, an astonishing feat given his age, and one which took the boys thoroughly by surprise. "You see even a decrepit old man can do it!"

Not one to be outdone, especially not by a 'decrepit old man,' Jack immediately followed suit, and was soon perched triumphantly atop his great white stallion as naturally as if he'd done it a hundred times before.

Thomas' cheeks went red as all eyes turned suddenly to him. *Why do I always have to be last?*

He crept slowly up to Snorri mouthing words of encouragement beneath his breath, "You can do this…just jump up…nothing to it…" and he reached out his hand timidly and touched the animal for the first time. It didn't budge. *So far so good*, and gaining a bit of confidence began positioning himself for the leap.

He took a deep breath, and then with all the effort he could muster, and using Snorri's back for support he leapt—

Whew, he wiped his brow after barely making it up. *That could've been disastrous.* Thankfully, Snorri had adjusted at the very last moment allowing Thomas to reach the saddle safely. "Good horsey," he said patting the animal's head and growing a sudden fondness for him.

"Let's ride!" cried Wordsworth and he turned his reigns and the horse headed steadily down the side of the mountain. Which was on the other side of the castle in relation to the way they'd come up yesterday. The two paths meeting at the castle and then forking with one leading down to the forest, the other to the valley below.

"Not scared are you?" asked Jack, in a way suggesting otherwise.

"I'm fine." Thomas lied, and trying desperately to keep his balance.

"You don't *look* fine," replied Jack with a smirk, "Are you sure you're not scared?"

"Yes I'm sure!" snapped Thomas angrily.

"Good," said Jack, and then he quickly turned his reigns mimicking Wordsworth's form perfectly and galloped down the mountain.

Thomas took a deep breath and then followed suit.

Barbarians at the Gates

To Thomas' great surprise he turned out to be a more than adequate rider, perhaps even something of a natural. Though he did wonder whether it was really him or Snorri. But nevertheless he made it down the mountain without incident, and even thoroughly enjoyed the experience. *Way better than riding in a car,* he thought.

The valley was cool and damp, with tendrils of fog wafting from off of the surrounding mountains. A pastoral setting, where one might expect to see a shepherd tending a flock of sheep. There were rolling hills, gentle knolls, and meadows spotted with a beautiful array of colorful flowers—blooming in abundance despite the lush green grass being coated by a thick layer of glistening frost. There was a large variety of trees as well, with many tall pines, firs, spruces, and cedars scattered about. Off to the right stood a wood of long white poplars lined up in perfectly straight rows, seeming to go on forever. Wordsworth referred to them as the White Woods, which, as Thomas remembered, was where the wolves were.

Thomas was hoping very much to see some Dragonwood trees. But Wordsworth informed him that they grew further to the south, past the mountains. They were so large he said that giants often dwelled amidst the Dragonwood groves. Jack of course laughed uproariously when he heard this. While Thomas found it harder to dismiss, especially when riding upon an eight legged horse, giants hardly seem all that far-fetched.

"Such a nice day," commented Wordsworth as they continued down the meandering dirt road, "the sun shining brightly and all."

Both boys looked up into the gray sky and saw just the faintest glimmer of a sun. Indeed it appeared more an imprint of the sun than the actual sun itself, as if merely the reflection of a sun shining brightly somewhere else, and it gave off little warmth, if it gave off any at all. Even gloomy Boonton received more sun than this on an average day, let alone a good one.

Apparently, however, there was enough light to cast a shadow, as Thomas watched his silhouette riding beside him. And looking at it, sitting tall and straight atop a horse, he felt strong and brave in a way that was for him unusual. He felt like one of the characters from the books he so admired, like he was a great hero on a daring quest of adventure. And the more he looked at his shadow, the more it seemed to morph into that very image. He even swore at one point that he saw a sword in his hand and a crown atop his head. But then all of a sudden the shadow disappeared.

As they rode, they saw gleaming silver flowers growing in abundance along the roadside.

"What kind of flowers are those?" inquired Thomas, never encountering their like before.

"They are known as Luna Lilies," said Wordsworth, "They grow exclusively in this valley. And if you think they're something now, you should see them at night. When the moonlight hits them they shine brilliantly. They're considered sacred by the locals."

"Don't tell me they have magical properties too," said Jack.

"Indeed, some believe they do," said Wordsworth.

Jack shook his head. "I'm going to have to weed out all of these—" his face curled into a snarl, "—superstitions."

"You may change your mind about so called 'superstitions' once we arrive in Everfall," said Wordsworth cryptically, "Which we'll be doing shortly," and he pointed out to a wooden sign standing in the middle of the road reading "Everfall" in red with an arrow pointing up ahead.

Not long thereafter they glimpsed the town of Everfall looming like a small gray mountain in the distance. Standing in the epicenter of the valley, its formidable stone walls encircled it like an impenetrable fortress, making one wonder whether it was intended to keep intruders from entering or its inhabitants from leaving. A single solid gray bell tower rose high into the gray sky like a beacon marking the town's existence for miles around.

As Thomas stared at the veritable fortress before him, and then back at Castle Ravenstead looming high above them casting its shadow onto the valley, he couldn't help but think that they'd been transported not simply to another country, or even another continent, but to another time entirely. It was hard to believe that such a place could exist in this modern day and age. Yet it appeared completely untouched by modernity, like the world had simply skipped over it and gone on, forgetting it was even there in the first place.

While Jack, on the other hand, contemplated just how many people lived inside those steep gray walls, how many subjects he could command, and the nearer he came, the more excited he grew. *I bet there are enough people in there to raise a small army,* he thought hopefully, and suddenly found himself calculating the town's defenses, measuring from afar the high gray stone walls with an eye towards their vulnerability. He surveyed the surrounding landscape, paying special attention to the makeup of the terrain. Making mental notes as to what hills would be advantageous for attack, and which for defense, drawing demarcation lines across the terrain with his eyes, plotting out potential traps. Until plans formulated in his mind of strategy and tactics, grand maneuvers, sieges and flanks.

As they neared the massive gray walls of Everfall, they saw a sizeable line gathered just outside the entrance, stretching out a few hundred yards at least. It didn't seem to be moving fast, if it was moving at all. The line's occupants appeared to have relegated themselves to the long wait, many sitting on the ground in circles around small fires. Some were playing music and games while others were cooking or reading to pass the time. An eclectic looking bunch, any one of which would've stood out like a sore thumb where Jack and Thomas came from.

"Why is there such a long line?" asked Thomas.

"There is nearly always a line to enter the gates of Everfall, especially during the daytime hours. Merchants from all over the realm come to sell their wares, and given its proximity to several waterways the town always has its fair share of outsiders as well. Though with the Moon Festival fast approaching it will be even more crowded than usual," said Wordsworth.

To which Thomas and Jack responded in near unison, "What's the Moon Festival!"

Wordsworth was taken aback by the outburst. "Oh, I nearly forgot that you're, um, not from around here," and after a moment responded, "The Moon Festival is Everfall's most sacred holiday. Its origins go back to the town's founding. As the story goes, the thirteen founders followed a comet for three days until they arrived here in this valley. Upon which they were greeted by the largest, most spectacular moon they'd ever seen. So they settled here, and started new lives in what they named the Valley of the Moon. And every year since the comet returns, and three days hence the moon shines once more in its fullest glory, just as it did when the founders first arrived."

It was certainly a little strange, thought Thomas regarding the origins of the Moon Festival. But then he thought, was it really any stranger than some of the holidays back home. *Compared to Santa Claus and the Easter Bunny following a comet to a valley seems downright normal.*

"The comet comes around the same time every year," continued Wordsworth, "This year it's actually later than usual, historically speaking. But it should be arriving anytime now. And upon the third night after the comet comes, the Festival begins. A grand celebration, with dancing and drinking and all kinds of festivities."

"Can we go?" asked Thomas hopefully.

"That is up to your Uncle," said Wordsworth.

"Do you think he'll let us?" asked Thomas.

"I'd say there is a good chance," said Wordsworth with a smile.

"Do we get gifts?" asked Jack.

"Some do."

Jack smiled.

Being highly interested, Thomas wanted to learn more about the Festival, but just as he began to inquire further, Jack declared abruptly, "I'm not waiting in line with these peasants!" and then violently snapped Helmud's reigns and sped off towards the front gate—kicking up clouds of dust as he went.

"No—wait!" cried Wordsworth. But it was too late for Jack was already racing up the line at a breakneck pace.

"This is not good at all," muttered Wordsworth grimly.

"Why do you say that?" asked Thomas, noting the high level of concern in Wordsworth's voice.

"No one storms the gates of Everfall, prince or not," said Wordsworth, looking all together worried as he watched Jack go. "Come, we must get to your brother before he gets himself in real trouble," and he snapped Olaf's reigns and bolted after him.

Why does Jack always have to do these things? thought Thomas, taking off as well.

Thomas and Wordsworth flew up the line after Jack, receiving many crude remarks as they did. It was obvious that the people did not take kindly to being skipped over. Thomas even had a rock thrown at him by an elderly woman wearing a bright yellow bonnet.

At last, they reached Jack at the gate.

He was surrounded by a dozen extremely large men wearing gray plated armor and bright red capes. The symbol of a white tree emblazoned on their chest plates. Some carried long swords, while others equally long black stakes sharpened to a deadly point, both of which were currently aimed directly at Jack's chest as he sat defiantly upon his horse.

"I am your Prince! Lower your weapons now or I'll have your heads stuck on those stakes in your hands." Jack threatened them, his face seething with rage.

But the guards did not lower their weapons and only appeared more resolute for having been told to do so.

"Stop this! Stop this now!" cried Wordsworth riding upon the scene like a white knight to the rescue.

The guards glanced uncertainly at one another and then back at a tall thin dark-skinned man standing at the entrance of the gate wearing a pristine white cloth wrapped around his head with a dazzling blue gem in the center. Rather than a long sword or a stake like the others, he carried a curved scimitar in the sash of his red belt. Thomas thought he looked like a character straight out of Arabian Nights.

"Stand down," the man commanded, his accented voice full of authority, and the others immediately lowered their weapons and stood at attention, awaiting the next order.

"Wordsworth," the man bowed his head slightly, "It has been too long," and the dark-skinned man walked over to where they were all standing, his men parting to let him pass. He had the appearance of a hardened man though his years appeared not greater than thirty. His eyes were the color of sand.

"Indeed, Captain Allac, I dare say it has. You're looking well as ever," said Wordsworth affably.

"You as well," returned Captain Allac politely.

"No need to lie. Even a fool can see I look worse now than I ever have and tomorrow I'll look poorer still. Such is the way of age. But I shall take your compliment as I have found them in short supply as of late," said Wordsworth, smiling.

Captain Allac's face suddenly softened allowing a slight smile to escape. "At least you have a sense of humor about it."

"That's about all I have. That and a very bad back," said Wordsworth, and they both laughed.

"So, this one here is with you?" asked Captain Allac, returning to a much more serious tone. "And is he really a prince as he claims?"

Wordsworth sighed deeply. "He is with me," and then after a pause added, "and he is a prince."

"And now you're all going to—"

"Please allow me my Prince." Wordsworth interrupted.

Jack paused and grudgingly nodded, allowing the old man to speak on his behalf.

"Captain Allac, it is my great privilege and honor to present Prince Jack and Prince Thomas of House Hades, and the realm of Somulus," said Wordsworth.

Along with the other guards, Captain Allac wore a face which made plain that he wasn't quite buying it.

"I wasn't aware that Somulus had princes," said Captain Allac, "I admit I am at a loss as to why I was not informed, being that I am Captain of the First Guard," and some of the guards grumbled, echoing their commander's malcontent.

"The reason you have not been informed is that they were only formally named as princes of Somulus this past night. You may therefore consider *this* your notice, Captain," said Wordsworth, handing over a piece of parchment.

"His Lordship's nephews?" said Captain Allac as he read over the paper, "I did not know his Lordship had any family."

"They are his only family. So I expect them to be treated accordingly, or you'll have to answer to his Lordship."

There was a collective grumble from the guards. But Captain Allac smothered it with a withering glance.

"I will ensure that word spreads. And you can assure his Lordship that his nephews, the Princes, will be treated with the utmost respect and honor befitting their station from this moment forth. Please give his Lordship our deepest apologizes for this…misunderstanding," said the Captain, but then added forthrightly, "I would, however, remind our new Princes that even they are not above the law."

Jack began to open his mouth, but Wordsworth again quickly cut him off. "Of course Captain, you are correct. No one is above the law."

Just then a heavy set man yelled out from the line behind them, "We ain't got all day ya know! Night is coming!"

The guards instantly turned their attention to him. He froze from the glare of their cold stares and fell silent.

"Wordsworth, as delightful as this has been, I have a duty to perform, as I'm sure you have yours," said Captain Allac, and he made a welcoming gesture towards the open gates, "Welcome back to Everfall,"

"Thank you Captain for your patience and understanding," said Wordsworth, adding as one friend to another. "Perhaps we can share a drink soon."

"Perhaps. Until then Wordsworth…my Princes…" and Captain Allac gave a slight bow to each as they rode past.

Jack, however, hung back a bit as Wordsworth and Thomas went on ahead through the gate. The Captain stared up at him as he slowed his horse.

"My Prince," said Captain Allac, "Is there something that you want?"

Jack smiled. "There are many things that I want, Captain. And I intend to get them all."

"I have no doubt you will prove successful in your endeavors," replied Captain Allac.

"I could use someone like you, with your authority," said Jack, "You would be richly rewarded for your service. I am Prince after all. Besides, I think you owe me after this… misunderstanding, don't you?"

"My Prince, I am not quite certain I understand what you're proposing. But I will answer in the way in which I assume. As Captain of the First Guard, I am sworn to uphold the law and protect the citizens of Everfall. That is my duty, and my oath. I serve only the law and the citizens—"

"—And you serve your Prince." Jack interjected, and suddenly his voice grew deeper and darker, a voice that was at once Jack's, and yet in the same another's. "Let me be clear, if you will not serve me then you are my enemy. . .and I will burn your life to the ground. Now, choose your allegiance."

Upon seeing that Jack was not following, Wordsworth called back, "Prince Jack—are you coming?"

Jack paid him no attention, nor did he take his eyes off of the Captain.

"I think you should catch up with your companions, my Prince," said Captain Allac.

"Not until I have your decision." Jack insisted, his voice deep and dark.

"I think you have it," replied Captain Allac resolutely, "And I pray you never ask again."

"I never will," and with that Jack snapped the reigns of his horse and sped through the gates after his brother and Wordsworth.

Captain Allac stood there for a moment watching Jack as he rode away. His hands shook despite themselves. "Those eyes," he whispered.

Everfall

UPON ENTERING EVERFALL, Wordsworth paid a man to shelter their horses in a nearby stable; a necessity given the sign up ahead forbidding them beyond it.

As they made their way, the boys discovered that the town had a labyrinthine shape, with winding roads and slender alleyways that wisps of white fog slithered through like a snake. The streets were cobblestone and the buildings stone and wood. There were many sculptures, statues, and elaborate fountains, making it clear that art was fully celebrated here. And everything was decorated for the Festival, which appeared a bit like what would happen if Halloween and Christmas had a child. Merry and macabre all in the same breadth, with wreaths of skulls, trees festooned with spooky ornaments, and mistletoe appearing to actually have toes in it, along with many other such things. *Mom would've loved it.* Thomas thought.

"Why is everyone dressed up?" Jack asked suddenly, "And I thought horses weren't allow—" but then stopped abruptly, and just stared ahead. Thomas turned to see as well.

Suddenly their eight legged horses weren't so extraordinary, as two horses with bare-chested torsos and the heads of men galloped by them. The boys stood utterly aghast as they watched them pass.

"I'm guessing you haven't seen many centaurs before," said Wordsworth, "Usually they keep to the woods, but the Festival brings out all kinds."

"Centaurs?" said Thomas, "Those—are—centaurs?"

"Yes." Wordsworth confirmed.

"Like...*real* centaurs?" asked Thomas uncertainly.

"What other kind are there?" said Wordsworth.

"W-we don't have centaurs where were from." Thomas mumbled.

"Well, you've plenty of other things that we don't have here. Why should it be any different in reverse?" said Wordsworth.

Thomas opened his mouth, but stopped. He didn't know how to respond. Even Jack looked thoroughly perplexed, as if for once he didn't know what to believe.

"Costumes." Jack muttered finally. But didn't sound sure in the least.

"Not costumes, I assure you," said Wordsworth dispelling the notion, "Of course, if you'd like I could arrange a thorough inspection. Though centaurs aren't the friendliest of creatures and would undoubtedly take great offense at the request. I suggest, however, you simply take a good look around you first."

Jack and Thomas surveyed their surroundings, and what they saw amazed them. Strange creatures were everywhere, simply going about their business like everyone else. They had pointed ears, elongated noses, glowing eyes, scaly skin, even horns sticking out of their heads! And many other oddities too numerous to recount. Some were very tall, while others very small. Some looked almost human, while others appeared the farthest thing from. It was like every mythical creature was standing right there in front of them.

"How—is—this—possible?" Thomas mouthed in wonderment.

Wordsworth smiled. "I told you this is the old world, and just because the new world has forgotten some things, doesn't mean those things cease to exist. After all, there had to be something to forget in the first place."

"But—how?" asked Thomas.

"There will be plenty of time for explanations later. For now, we've things to do," said Wordsworth, walking ahead.

Thomas turned to Jack and their eyes met. It was a silent acknowledgment that everything they'd known had just been turned on its head. Thomas remembered then his Uncle's prescient words about perspectives changing quickly. *He wasn't kidding*, he thought, *we're in a whole new world*. World perhaps the opportune word.

Wordsworth was at least kind enough to identify the various creatures as they passed. So far they'd encountered trolls, dwarves, elves, and satyrs, along with creatures Thomas had never heard of before including trogs (a cross between an elf and a dwarf), ballehorns (a cross between a troll and a griffin), and wropples (which appeared to be a mixture of several different kinds of creatures all brewed into one). Thomas couldn't stop blinking his eyes in disbelief, and pinching himself to see if he'd wake up. But never did.

As Thomas searched for more mythical creatures, he noticed the almost ubiquitous presence of the armored soldiers of the First Guard, themselves a hodgepodge of creatures. They stood on every corner surveying the crowd like hawks. He wondered what sort of a threat they were guarding against, which in a land filled with fantastical creatures could literally be anything.

Jack must've been thinking the same. "Why are there so many guards?" he asked.

"With so many coming in and out of town it is imperative that order be maintained," said Wordsworth. "And with the Festival approaching everything is exacerbated."

A dozen guards clustered around the entrance to a particularly formidable black building upon which was painted a golden shamrock.

"What's that?" Thomas asked.

"The bank of Everfall," said Wordsworth. "It was founded by Artimus Callahan with a pot of gold he stole from a leprechaun. Hence the shamrock."

Thomas mentally checked leprechauns off his list of once imaginary creatures that now existed.

Thomas glanced over at his brother to see his reaction. His face almost seemed to be fighting against itself—a reflection no doubt of what was occurring inside. One half looked like it wanted to laugh out loud, while the other was adjusting to the new reality that leprechauns and the like were real, and it was foolish to believe otherwise.

Thomas had to admit it was rather satisfying knowing that for once his brother didn't have everything figured out. Or that so many things he'd been ridiculed for believing in throughout the years were turning out to be true.

They came to a large square courtyard. In the middle of which stood a barren white tree with sprawling branches, like the one pictured on the armored breastplates of the two burly guards beside it. Around the square were shops and restaurants, most, if not all, with their fair share of customers.

Many had tree themed names, such as: The Sapling, The Acorn, The Twig and Limb, and The Falling Leaf, which appeared built from the trunk of a massive tree.

"What's with the white tree?" asked Thomas, which was surrounded by candles, like some kind of shrine.

"The Tree of Everfall. It has been here since the founding. The town was literally built around it," said Wordsworth.

Suddenly a loud voice called out from behind them, "Wordsworth—is that you!" and they all turned to see standing there in the middle of the street wearing a gigantic toothy grin, a short, exceedingly plump man with a thick walrus mustache dressed in an absurdly tall black top hat and long tailed suit.

Wordsworth looked like he wanted to hide. But seeing as that was not an option, put on a blatantly fake smile and responded cheerfully, "Mayor Tweed—what a delightful surprise!"

"The delight *and* the surprise are all mine Wordsworth. It's been far too long since we had the honor of your presence. Where have you been hiding?" asked Mayor Tweed, flagged on both sides by two hulking guards, along with a creature only but the size of a child with a sharp beaked nose and glowing green eyes. *Maybe he's a leprechaun,* thought Thomas, only half joking.

"I've been away, traveling on his Lordship's business," said Wordsworth.

"Well you're back now—that's all that matters!" said Mayor Tweed flashing a toothy grin. Then upon seeing Jack and Thomas added, "And you haven't returned alone I see. Just who might these two strapping young lads be?"

"Mayor Tweed may I present Prince Jack and Prince Thomas of House Hades," said Wordsworth.

"P-p-princes—did you say?" replied Mayor Tweed, as if he hadn't heard correctly.

"They are his Lordship's nephews," said Wordsworth.

Mayor Tweed paused for a long moment, as if mulling it over. "You know," he said finally, "I wasn't aware his Lordship had any family."

Recalling Captain Allac earlier, Thomas saw a pattern developing. *I wonder how many people will ask that.*

"They're his only family," said Wordsworth.

"Well—well! This is quite an occasion isn't it!" boomed the Mayor, "If only I would've known, I would've held a grand celebration in their honor!"

"I'm sure the town's time—and funds—would be better used in preparation for the Festival," said Wordsworth. To which Jack, no doubt relishing the idea of a parade in his honor, shot him a menacing glare.

"Um, yes, that's true." Mayor Tweed admitted, "Nevertheless it's a tremendous honor to meet you both. And anything you need, anything at all, I'm the one to see!"

The Mayor must've seen Thomas staring, for he said then, "How rude of me! This little fellow here is my most trusted assistant Garrick. Even amongst goblins there is no finer mind for figures."

Thomas mentally checked goblins off his list.

"So you govern the town for my Uncle?" asked Jack.

"You could say that. For the most part his Lordship allows Everfall to govern its own affairs. We have a long standing arrangement," said the Mayor.

"I see," said Jack, "How long have you been Mayor?"

"I'm in my tenth term now, and hopefully the voters will see fit to grant me an eleventh!"

"How often are the elections held?" asked Thomas.

"Once a decade," said the Mayor, "The next being only but a few short phases of the moon away."

"That would mean you've been Mayor for over a hundred years!" gasped Thomas.

"And every one an honor and a privilege. Which reminds me Wordsworth, his Lordship will be attending the Festival?" asked the Mayor, in a way suggesting he may not.

"He wouldn't miss it for the world." Wordsworth assured him.

"And the Princes?" the Mayor added anxiously, "Will they be attending as well?"

"We wouldn't miss it for the world," said Jack.

Wordsworth paused, and then nodded hesitantly.

"Splendid! Marvelous!" exclaimed the Mayor, "It'll be a night to remember! Best one we've ever had. Why Madam Currie has been working overtime on the arrangements and—"

"My apologies," Wordsworth cut him off abruptly, "But we've some pressing errands, and want to be back before nightfall. So, if you'll excuse us we really must be on our way."

"Yes, yes, perfectly understandable. I'll leave you to it," said the Mayor.

"Farewell," said Wordsworth.

"Farewell Wordsworth...my Princes," and he bowed before them both, earning an approving smile from Jack.

A mayor bowing to us, thought Thomas, something unfathomable only a few days ago. *But then that seemed to be the ways things were going lately.*

The boys caught up to Wordsworth, quickly putting distance between the Mayor and himself.

"He seemed nice," said Thomas when they were out of earshot.

"Don't be fooled. He is crooked as the night is long," said Wordsworth bluntly, "And for a pocket of gold he'd sell you his soul."

Mom always said never trust a politician, thought Thomas. *Maybe not everything is so different here after all.*

"Why does Uncle allow the town to govern itself?" asked Jack, in a way strongly suggesting his disapproval.

"That's the way it's always been," said Wordsworth, "Your Uncle stays out of the town's affairs, provided they adhere to the laws of the realm. He only interferes when absolutely necessary. He's extremely busy, and doesn't have time to play babysitter."

"Nothing lasts forever…" muttered Jack.

"Why was the Mayor concerned about Uncle not coming to the Festival?" asked Thomas.

"Because his absence would not reflect well upon the Mayor, and with an election coming up, and his popularity waning, he can ill afford something of that magnitude," replied Wordsworth.

"Do you think he'll win again?" asked Thomas.

"Hard to tell. He's a very good politician. While his opponent is only but a very good man," said Wordsworth. "But he's never been on shakier ground, due to recent scandals involving the misappropriation of funds. Even some of his staunchest allies have turned against him."

"How can he possibly be that old?" asked Jack.

"I wouldn't call him old," said Wordsworth, and then seeing the boys faces added, "You'll find that time moves somewhat differently here."

They arrived then at a sign that read, "Nevermore Road," and followed Wordsworth down it.

Not long thereafter, they came upon a tavern called The Crooked Raven. Two pale faced gentlemen sat on the tavern's front porch, evidently in the midst of a heated discussion for their voices were loud and their gestures animated.

Upon seeing Wordsworth and the boys, they abruptly stopped talking.

"As I live and breathe—Wordsworth is that you!" called the younger of the two, who had a slightly effeminate appearance and was dressed in a black cape coat with a red scarf around his neck. Extremely well groomed with a perfectly straight razor thin mustache and nary a strand of his wavy black hair out of place. "We've missed your wit in our everlasting conversation. Why we were just having a discussion regarding ethics."

"Yes, he doesn't have any," quipped the other, who, it was apparent, in contrast to his friend, cared little about his appearance. He wore an old dusty gray suit and had shaggy unkempt brown hair with an equally untidy mustache.

"Quite right you are—why limit myself! I say the ends are justified no matter the means."

"I think you have that backward," said Thomas.

"No, I don't think so."

"Mr. Poe," said Wordsworth nodding his head to the older, disheveled one, and then turning to the other, "Mr.—excuse me—*Lord* Byron," he added with more than a hint of sarcasm.

"You're a Lord?" asked Jack taking a sudden interest.

"I am!" he replied, "Not by blood perhaps, but certainly by merit."

"How'd you become a Lord then?" asked Jack.

"I am a Lord simply because I choose to be one."

"You can't just choose to be a Lord." Jack countered sharply.

"Why ever not?"

"Because what's the point of being a Lord if anyone can be one?" Jack retorted.

"A fair point," said Mr. Poe.

"True. But let us admit too that not all royalty deserves their title, for what accomplishment is it to be born—why anyone can do it!"

"A good point my friend. What say you Wordsworth on this most important of subjects?" inquired Mr. Poe.

Both boys turned expectantly towards Wordsworth.

"My opinion is that we've wasted precious time talking to you two blabbering idiots. And whether you wish to call yourself a Lord, and have others do so is of little consequence. For like your title, it is utterly worthless."

"You sting my heart with your cutting words," intoned Lord Byron, holding his breast, "Must be jealousy, for though your age is far greater, your wit will never be my equal."

"Nor mine," echoed Mr. Poe.

"And just wait till Mr. Milton arrives, and you'll be thrice overshadowed. Must hurt being embarrassed in front of your grandchildren," said Lord Byron.

"We're not his grandchildren," snarled Jack.

"They're his Lordship's nephews. The new Princes of Somulus," said Wordsworth, "May I present Prince Jack, and Prince Thomas of House Hades."

Both men were momentarily stunned into silence.

"I didn't know his Lordship—" began Mr. Poe.

"They're his only family," said Wordsworth.

"Well, I propose a toast," said Lord Byron, and picked up the tall black cup sitting in front of him filled with a smoking liquid that smelled, Thomas thought, like formaldehyde. "To our new princes—may they be better than our last!"

"Hear! Hear!" seconded Mr. Poe.

"The last prince?" interjected Jack, to which Wordsworth was attempting to covertly shake his head.

"Oh—um—never mind," said Lord Byron hastily.

"Tell me." Jack demanded.

"Cats out of the bag," said Mr. Poe.

"I think Wordsworth should tell the tale, don't you?" said Lord Byron, and all eyes turned to Wordsworth, who looked none too pleased.

"Very well," Wordsworth grudgingly conceded. "Somulus' last prince, which was a long time ago, far before any of us were around, was a bit of a terror."

"That's putting it mildly," interjected Mr. Poe.

Wordsworth frowned. "Yes, the Prince was cruel and perpetrated many atrocities upon the citizens of the realm."

"Like feasting upon the blood of children," added Mr. Poe.

"What!" cried Thomas aghast "Is that true?"

"I'm afraid so," admitted Wordsworth. "He was a monster, quite literally."

"What happened to him?" asked Jack.

"He was cast out of the realm, never permitted to return again," said Wordsworth.

"If only he would've stayed away," bemoaned Lord Byron.

"Yes, well, now we really must be on our way," announced Wordsworth hastily.

"Nice to meet you both," said Thomas.

The two men rose abruptly from their seats and each gave a truly ostentatious bow, as if trying to outdo the other. "Our Princes," they chorused.

Thomas had to stifle a laugh, so utterly ridiculous they both looked.

"Wordsworth, do come around more often," said Mr. Poe, "I dare say our little club has not been the same without you." Lord Byron nodded in agreement.

Wordsworth smiled. "I shall do my best," and with that on they went.

Doctor Von Wolfenhauer

STANDING BEFORE WORDSWORTH and the boys was a slightly slanted nondescript gray stone building on the corner of the street with a large wooden sign reading:

> ***Doctor Von Wolfenhauer***
> ***Master of Concoctions***

"Here we are," pronounced Wordsworth.

"Why are we going to see a doctor?" questioned Jack. "We're not sick."

Wordsworth shook his head. "Doctor Von Wolfenhauer is a doctor of magic, specializing in alchemy. He is a true genius, albeit an eccentric one. But then," Wordsworth mused, "most geniuses are I've found."

"Magic?" said Jack, his voice filled not with the derision such a word usually elicited, but something closer to intrigue. While though Thomas said nothing, inside could barely contain his excitement. It was like all his dreams were coming true at once.

"Yes, magic," said Wordsworth, "Now come along, the day is fading fast."

Jack and Thomas looked at one another and then took off after Wordsworth, already at the door marking the store's entrance.

"The Doctor is the best at what he does...and along with his famous concoctions his store contains many rare magical items..." explained Wordsworth as they entered.

The store had a fair amount of customers and was bustling with activity. There were shelves upon shelves cluttering the dark dusty floor lined up in not so straight rows packed to the brim with jars of powders, vials filled with colorful liquids, and many other odd and fantastical items. Each row had a symbol etched on it. *Like hieroglyphics,* Thomas observed. There was a row with the symbol of a snake trying to eat itself; one that had a single opened eye; while another a half moon combined with a half sun, and many others too numerous to recount. Customers clamored about the shelves scrutinizing their contents the way one would produce at the grocery store.

Wordsworth grabbed a small basket from the front and began going about his business with the familiarity of a loyal patron, moving from shelf to shelf inspecting items with an eye as to whether or not to buy them.

The store had a strange odor Thomas noticed as they ventured through the shelves. *A mixture of mildew and burnt rubber with a hint of pesticide mixed in*, as he placed it. The store was not well lit either, most of the light being provided by the glowing liquids themselves. Thomas thought the place had something of the look and feel of a mad scientist's laboratory.

Jack decided to do some exploring of his own, and took off in the other direction without saying a word. Thomas by contrast stayed close to Wordsworth, for there were many questions he desperately needed answering.

"How does it work?" Thomas asked eagerly when they came to an area without many other customers.

"How does *what* work?" replied Wordsworth, examining a vial containing a bright blue liquid.

"Magic," whispered Thomas as if some big secret.

Wordsworth smiled. "I was wondering how long it would take you to ask. Another thing you don't have where you're from I suppose."

Thomas shook his head.

"No doubt this entire day has been something of an eye opener for you."

"I feel like my whole world has been turned upside down. I don't know what I know anymore," said Thomas.

"I've known the very same feeling on more than a few occasions throughout my long life," said Wordsworth, "In fact, when I first came to this realm I too was quite overwhelmed. New places mean new changes…some more so than others."

"I suppose this is what Uncle meant by us experiencing new things," said Thomas.

Wordsworth laughed. "I believe the intended message has been relayed."

"I have so many questions Wordsworth—I mean how's this even possible! How could there be mythical creatures and magic and—"

"Your questions will be answered in time." Wordsworth assured him. "But I will not be the one to answer them all for you. I'll say this much, the world you once knew is a thing of the past."

Thomas didn't need to be told that. "That much I figured out on my own."

"I can, however, explain something of the nature of magic to you." Wordsworth offered, and seeing Thomas' eagerness proceeded then to do so.

"To begin with, you must understand that there are many kinds of magic—magic being a general term for tapping into the power that connects everything in this world. This power, referred to as the Infinite, among many other names, flows throughout the world like a river. But a river with many tributaries, each being both apart of and separate from the river itself. So it is that magic comes in many different forms as well. For example, this section—symbolized by the hammer and anvil—is magic dealing with the transmutation of metals. The potions here transform one metallic substance into another. This particular kind of magic commonly falls under the discipline known as alchemy. Doctor Von Wolfenhauer is himself an alchemist. But there are many other schools or disciplines of magic, including mysticism, sorcery, shamanism, and witchcraft, to name a few. Each has its own rules and properties, methods and expertise," explained Wordsworth.

Magic was like science in that respect Thomas thought. For science too was a broad generalized term encompassing many different branches or fields, including chemistry, biology, geology, and physics.

"Can anyone do magic?" asked Thomas, hoping that very much to be the case.

"Like anything it can be taught, to a degree. Though like anything some have more natural potential than others. Most possess an affinity, or what is commonly called a Gift, for only certain kinds of magic. For example, some are natural conjurers, while others, like Doctor Von Wolfenhauer are natural concocters. There are also summoners, channelers, charmers, diviners, and animists, to name a few. All tap into and manipulate the Infinite in a different way.

But whatever Gift or Gifts one possesses they must be developed, and the guilds are highly selective and guard their knowledge fiercely. Only those deemed worthy may enter their ranks and be taught. So most, unfortunately, never fully develop their Gifts, and like anything without cultivation withers and dulls."

"When do you know if you have any Gifts?" asked Thomas, as Wordsworth began eyeing a jar of yellow powder.

"It varies. Some discover their Gifts earlier than others, particularly depending upon the race. Faeries, for instance, are born with their full powers, the reason few things are more dangerous than a baby fairy. But most don't receive their true powers until they are old enough to understand and control them. Nature's way of regulating, one might say," said Wordsworth, "Thirteen however is commonly known as the Coming of Age, when our Gifts are fully awoken, and the true extent of our abilities begins to manifest."

"I'm thirteen, and I've never done any magic before," said Thomas, disappointingly.

"Have you ever tried?"

"No," admitted Thomas, "But wouldn't I have done something by now, even by accident."

"Perhaps. But some are late bloomers, and your situation is…unique. It may be that you're simply in a period of adjustment, or that your magical abilities are merely waiting for a spark to ignite them. Or, that you aren't even thirteen yet."

"But I've had thirteen birthdays," replied Thomas.

"Ah, but that would depend entirely upon how long a year is, would it not?"

"I-I suppose," said Thomas, "How long is a year here?"

"It depends,"

"Depends on what?"

"Upon what kind of time you're talking about."

"There are other kinds of time?" asked Thomas confusedly.

"Oh yes, many. Of course, we use the moon to tell what is known as Common Time, for there must be some uniformity. But there are other kinds of time as well, and each person's relation to time differs, one's own internal clock you might say," explained Wordsworth. "So we simply rely upon nature to tell us when we've Come of Age."

"How do you know?" asked Thomas.

"There are signs, changes begin. It can come on very quickly, overnight even. We awake one day and all of sudden are different. Certain events may trigger the changes as well. The Moon Festival, for example, is an especially common time for Coming of Age's to occur, as the moon's transformative magic is extremely strong."

Thomas was literally bursting with questions. But before he could ask them, Wordsworth smiled and said, "I think that is enough for now. We could be here forever talking about all the intricacies of time and magic. Let's finish up here and get going."

Jack moved briskly through the store's many aisles. The store was far larger than it appeared, and for some reason he felt compelled to journey further into its depths. The further he went the less populated it became. Until there was no one around but him.

Jack stopped and looked around. He was in a section of the store where the shelves were sparsely populated and everything appeared old and dusty. The items were of a different sort than the ones earlier—the liquids and powders not colorful and bright, but dark and shadowy. And only a few candles hanging on a nearby wall provided any light.

Just then a tall slender man came darting through the aisle and ran straight into Jack, nearly knocking him over.

"Watch where you're going!" snapped Jack, furious at nearly being run over.

The man stopped. His face was exceedingly pale, and he had long flaxen hair that was nearly white. He wore expensive looking clothes with a velvet cape and carried a straight black cane. His eyes were obscured by the dark glasses he wore.

"My sincere apologies," he said at last, "I should've been more careful."

"You should've," said Jack angrily.

"Allow me to introduce myself. I am Count Lucian of House Feratu, and to whom do I have the pleasure of addressing?"

"*Prince* Jack of House Hades."

Count Lucian barely hesitated. "Your majesty," he bowed his head reverently, "I implore your forgiveness for my…carelessness."

Jack paused, and considered for a moment. "You're forgiven," he said at last, "But only this once."

"A magnanimous gesture my Prince," said Count Lucian, "As you could strike me down for interfering with your royal person."

Jack smiled, relishing all his new found power.

"You are Lord Hades' son then," said Count Lucian.

"His nephew." Jack corrected him.

"His only heir?"

"I have a brother."

"But you are the older?"

"Yes."

Count Lucian smiled.

"Are you a *real* count, or do you just go around calling yourself one?" asked Jack sharply.

"I am a real count. Not of this realm of course," said Count Lucian, "You know, I wasn't aware that this realm had princes. I thought your Uncle eschewed such trappings of nobility in favor of more…*equality*," he uttered the word disdainfully.

"Does your realm have a king?" asked Jack.

"Unfortunately, the throne of my realm lays unoccupied at the moment. Though I suspect the vacancy shall be filled very soon," said Count Lucian. "Tell me are you looking for anything specific? Perhaps I can help. The least I can do after my transgression. I'm quite knowledgeable when it comes to this particular section."

"Everything in this section is old," replied Jack derisively.

"Ah, but the most powerful items are those that have been around the longest," said Count Lucian, "And some things are so old they become new again."

"So what's in this section then?" asked Jack, noting the symbol on the shelf of a snake coiled tightly around a barren tree.

"Are you familiar with the magical arts?" Count Lucian inquired, "I only ask because you appear new to these lands."

"It's that obvious?"

"Not all realms deal in magic, and those coming from them lack a certain... scent, shall we say, acquired by those who practice regularly. The same way those born in realms distant from the sun are devoid of color," said Count Lucian, referencing his own paleness, "It is clear that magic is new to you, for the scent is only faint. Though, I sense in you vast magical potential waiting to awake. Indeed, I have never sensed so much dormant potential."

"Until recently, I didn't believe magic existed." Jack admitted.

"You still sound skeptical my Prince. Would you care for a demonstration perhaps?" offered Count Lucian.

Jack nodded. "Show me."

"A simple bit of elemental magic will suffice," and Count Lucian took his black cane and began to wave it around in concentric circles towards the ground. He moved it rhythmically and as he did whispered the words, "Inferium... maelstrom.... serpento..." over and over again....

Suddenly a snake of fire emerged from the ground itself. The fire snake hissed and bared its fiery fangs. All the while Count Lucian controlled it with his cane—making it dance like a puppet on strings.

"Incredible," whispered Jack, wide eyed.

"A mere parlor trick," said Count Lucian dismissively, and with another casual flick of his cane the snake disappeared in a cloud of black smoke.

"Teach me." Jack ordered.

"As flattering of an offer as that undoubtedly is my Prince, I am no teacher, and you are no ordinary student. Not anyone can be *your* teacher. But I've no doubt one worthy of the task will soon present themselves. Great teachers and great students have a way of finding one another."

"Well, at least tell me about this section, as you offered," said Jack, slightly disappointed.

Count Lucian nodded. "This section contains items of a darker kind of magic, one unfortunately out of fashion at the moment, though beginning to make a comeback. Some simply fear what they don't understand," said Count Lucian, lovingly stroking his pale white finger over one of the shelves, "The Doctor's selection is better than most in these parts, though to find the best you must venture outside these walls to my realm, just over the mountains. There is, however, one item here that cannot be found anywhere else—a rare prize indeed."

"What would that be?" asked Jack, his curiosity peaked.

Count Lucian walked over to a shelf in the far corner, the last in the entire store, where no light could reach, where there was only shadows. He emerged holding an old black wooden box.

"What's in the box?"

"Open it," said Count Lucian handing it over, "And you shall see."

Jack took the box, which was about the size of a jewelry box and not heavy, in fact it felt empty. There were odd markings on it.

Jack unlatched the box and opened it.

"It's just a stone," said Jack thoroughly unimpressed as he stared down at a shiny black gem half the size of his fist.

"Look inside, and tell me what you see." said Lord Lucian.

As Jack peered into the stone, he saw a red and black iris staring back at him.

"It's an eye!" blurted Jack, taken back by the sight.

"Not just *any* eye my Prince. The eye of the Dragon King."

"Who?"

"He had many names, and played many roles. To some he was a villain, to others a savior. But none deny that his power was without equal. He was a king of kings," said Count Lucian with utmost reverence, as if speaking not of a man, but of a god.

"And *this* is his eye?" the question was pregnant with skepticism.

"Oh yes,"

"How did it get in the stone?" probed Jack.

"That is a story all its own my Prince, a long and winding one. But the eye is the window to the soul, and no soul was more powerful than his. What things it has seen, what knowledge it contains!"

"Why don't you want it for yourself?" questioned Jack sharply, "If it's so great?"

"It's not that I do not wish to possess it, but that I am unworthy of it. It is an item befitting only—" he smiled allowing his sharp white teeth to show "— a prince. And it is my gift to you. Consider it paid for."

Jack took the gem from the box and held it in his hand. Suddenly he felt its presence, its power literally pulsing through his veins. It was like he held all the mysteries of the world within the palm of his hand. The eye in the stone alighted with fire, and as it did, so too did his own…

When Jack finally looked up Count Lucian was gone. Jack stood there for a moment longer and then put the gemstone into his pocket. Whether it really was paid for or not did not concern him. No one was ever going to take it from him.

By now Wordsworth and Thomas had filled their small basket with a plethora of potions and other magical ingredients. Some came in jars or vials, others in palm sized velvet sacks. Some smelled particularly odorous, such as one labeled, "Ground up wings of a bat with eye of newt added," a literal translation Thomas was certain. Though none smelled worse than the dreadful, "Knarble's tail, sliced extra thin," which positively burned the nostrils like fire had been poured into them. *Whatever a Knarble is I don't ever want to meet one,* he thought.

They finished their shopping and were ready to check out, when Thomas saw Jack striding towards them looking triumphant.

"Ready to go?" said Jack upon approach, as if just because he was, they should be also.

"Almost, we just have to pay and we'll be on our way," replied Wordsworth stepping in line behind a short pointy eared gentleman wearing a green frock coat.

"If we must," said Jack, as if such a thing were unnecessary.

Thomas turned to his brother, and behind Wordsworth's back so as not to be heard, whispered, "Did you take something?" he knew his brother had stolen before. He'd never actually caught him in the act of course, Jack was too clever for that, but Thomas had discovered things he was sure his brother couldn't possibly afford.

"Do I look like a thief to you!" snapped Jack.

Thomas was about to inquire further when suddenly a heavily accented voice yelled out. "Next!"

Standing behind the counter was a thin bespectacled man with a scraggly brown beard as unkempt as the hair on his head, which flew out in every direction. Dressed in a long red woolen coat, he smiled sharply as they approached.

"Verdsverth, is dat you?"

"It is I, good Doctor, in the wrinkled flesh!" pronounced Wordsworth placing his basket upon the counter.

"It as been quite avhile since last you visited my shop. I vas beginning to tink you ad chosen another for your concoctions," said Doctor Von Wolfenhauer.

"Never worry about that Doctor. There is no other shop to buy what you sell. You have, as they say, the market cornered," responded Wordsworth.

"Dat is because my competitors are hacks, vith no talent in da art of concoction," said the Doctor with a hint of arrogance, "Though nice of you to say so nonedaless. For dere are many who cannot see my genius as you do. But, let us not harp on such un-pleasantries. Vhat ave you got dere?" and promptly began taking items out of the basket, "A very good selection as alvays."

Doctor Von Wolfenhauer gestured sharply to a small brown haired girl dressed in shabby attire, who promptly began putting the items into a large sack.

"Vill dat be all for today?" the Doctor inquired.

"Not quite, I also need the usual for his Lordship," said Wordsworth.

"He as already finished vith da last batch den?"

Wordsworth nodded.

It was then that the Doctor's eyes shifted perceptibly from Wordsworth to Thomas and Jack.

"I've forgotten my manners, allow me to make a proper introduction," said Wordsworth, "These are the new Princes of Somulus. May I present Prince Jack, and his brother Prince Thomas. His Lordship's nephews."

The Doctor barely hesitated. "My Princes vhat a great honor it tis to ave you in my shop," he bowed.

"It's wonderful," replied Thomas, "Your shop."

The Doctor smiled. "I am glad you like it my Prince," though strangely even as he spoke to Thomas one of his eyes remained focused on Jack. "I hope dat you vill come more often, for I ave many tings dat may be to your liking, tings dat you cannot find in any other place."

"Yes Doctor, you are very good at what you do." Wordsworth affirmed the man's boasting, then added hurriedly, "And I'm sure we'll return to try all that your incomparable skill has to offer, but now, if you please, we really must be going."

"My apologies, I ave kept you too long. I vill get da other items," and taking his glance from Jack, quickly turned, walking back towards an unmarked door, and disappeared inside.

Shortly thereafter, he returned carrying a wooden box that looked very much Thomas thought—remembering his father who'd often smoked them—like a cigar box, though something told him there weren't cigars inside.

"Please inform his Lordship dat dis is a slightly different batch dan da last, and may take some getting used to. Nothing to be concerned about," said the Doctor.

"I'll inform him," said Wordsworth and then handed over a small felt purse, "Will this cover it?"

The Doctor weighed the purse in his hand. "Dis should be more dan adequate," he replied with a rather greedy smile Thomas thought.

"We'll be on our way then," said Wordsworth grabbing the box and sack from the counter.

"Come back and visit me soon," said the Doctor giving a slight wave as they left his store.

Nightfall

WHEN WORDSWORTH AND the boys emerged from Doctor Von Wolfenhauer's store they were greeted by a commotion. A dozen women of various ages dressed in long shimmering green dresses with golden stitch around their necks and flowers coloring their hair, were gathered right outside. Highly agitated, some held up signs that read "Defiler of Nature" and "Poisoner of Everfall," among many other unflattering epitaphs. Several guards stood between them and the store.

"What's going on?" asked Thomas.

"They're protesting," replied Wordsworth.

"Protesting what?"

"Doctor Von Wolfenhauer."

"Why would they do that?"

"Because they do not approve of his methods."

"What's wrong with his methods?" interjected Jack.

"Well, according to the witches—"

"Witches!" blurted Thomas before Wordsworth could finish.

"Yes, they're witches," said Wordsworth calmly.

Certainly nothing at all like the picture of witches Thomas had in his mind, the one popular culture had supplied. They didn't wear black garments or pointy hats, or fly on broomsticks, or any other such things. Indeed, they appeared quite normal. Some were even stunningly beautiful.

"The guilds do not always get along with one another," continued Wordsworth, "The witches' guild, which is called a Coven, and the alchemist's guild have long been rivals. But ever since Doctor Von Wolfenhauer's arrival in town their rivalry has burned hotter."

"Why are they rivals?" asked Thomas.

"It boils down to a difference in philosophy really," said Wordsworth. "Witches worship Mother Nature and seek harmony with her. While alchemists seek to improve upon nature. Each has their valid points, and there is certainly room for both, provided there is balance."

"Why don't the guards put a stop to it?" asked Jack.

"Because unlike in some other realms, here opinions may be expressed freely, provided they are done so peacefully."

Jack grunted his disapproval.

As Thomas watched the protest continue to flare, he caught sight of one of the witches. She was young as he, or very nearly, and he found that he couldn't take his eyes off her. *Who is she*? he wondered as he stared starry-eyed at her rosy red cheeks, her flowing auburn hair, and emerald green eyes. A yellow light seemed to radiate from her skin, giving her an almost angelic aura.

"Come, we've seen more than enough of this," said Wordsworth brusquely, and before either could respond the old man was off in the other direction, moving quickly away from the protest.

With extreme reluctance, Thomas tore his eyes away from his fair maiden, and followed his brother and Wordsworth.

After stopping briefly at a couple of other shops to pick up some additional supplies they retrieved their horses from the stable and made their way out of Everfall. As they departed, they saw that the line to enter had completely dissipated, and torches had been lit all around the tops of the walls.

"What happened to the line?" asked Jack, "They couldn't have all made it inside by now, not at the pace they were going."

"The walls of Everfall are sealed for the night, and will not reopen until day returns." Wordsworth informed him.

"Doesn't look like night to me," said Jack, noting that it appeared no closer to being dark than it had on their way into town. Thomas nodded in agreement.

"The darkness comes swiftly here. You may not see it yet, but it is coming, I assure you. It'll be upon us soon, and I suggest we get a move on before it does," said Wordsworth.

"Why?" asked Jack, "What's the big deal?"

Thomas had noticed that since the moment they left Wordsworth had been intent upon returning to the castle before nightfall. He had never much cared for night himself, but Wordsworth's fear of it seemed extreme.

"The night holds many dangers, best avoided if it can be helped," said Wordsworth.

"What sorts of dangers?" inquired Jack, with evident interest.

"The night brings out the worst kind of elements…and lately those elements have grown bolder."

"It was night when we arrived." Thomas noted.

"Yes, and we were lucky. We also enjoyed certain advantages that we do not now."

"What advantages?" asked Jack.

"For one, the fact that you two weren't named princes yet, and no one knew we were traveling. Now everyone knows who you are, and you can be sure that eyes are watching us."

Both boys looked around suspiciously.

"Why aren't guards patrolling the roads, if it's so dangerous?" asked Jack.

"Not all protections are seen Prince Jack, some are only felt. Same with enemies," said Wordsworth cryptically.

"Hey what's that?" asked Thomas pointing to a nearby house standing between two foothills with heavy black smoke pouring copiously from its chimney. Next to the small cottage stood a most unusual tree, one side completely barren, the other filled with luscious red apples.

For a long moment Wordsworth did not answer. "A place of ill-repute," he said finally. "And if you're wise you'll stay far away from it."

This only served to further their curiosity.

"Why is it so bad?" asked Jack, adding, "It doesn't look bad."

Wordsworth at first appeared as if he wasn't going to answer, but then acquiesced. "It has a sordid history. It was once home to a dark witch, who dealt in forbidden magic. And the taint of the evil she performed there lingers still."

"What kind of magic is forbidden?" asked Thomas, wanting to learn as much about magic as possible. To which Jack too appeared quite interested.

Wordsworth hesitated, it was clear this was not a topic he wished to explore. But again finally acquiesced. "There are kinds of magic, the darkest of the dark, that take a part of a person, a part of their very soul. It corrupts them…turns them into something monstrous…something evil. And once cast, there is no turning back. That is why it is forbidden."

"Why not just burn it to the ground then?" asked Jack.

"Some things cannot be rid of so easily…some things leave deep scars," and Wordsworth turned to the boys with a serious look. "It's best to pay no mind on that place, and forget it even exists."

Something far easier said than done. For though Thomas tried his best to do as Wordsworth said and put it out of his mind, the more he tried not to think about it, the more he did. And he kept looking back at the house despite himself, until it finally disappeared from sight, and its hold released from his mind.

They made their way to the path spiraling up the mountain to the castle at the top. Going up, however, turned out to take quite a bit longer than it did going down. Thomas wondered what happened to the helpful wind they'd enjoyed the night prior, which seemed to have disappeared altogether.

Though, when they finally reached the top, a strong bone chilling gust of wind struck them like a knife.

"What was that?" asked Thomas, shivering.

"The Changeover," said Wordsworth. "Nightfall is here."

The boys looked out upon the land and saw that the sun, though still shining faintly, showed no apparent signs of receding.

"I don't see anything," said Thomas.

"Watch closely. It won't be long," said Wordsworth, pointing out towards the horizon.

"What are we looking for?" asked Thomas.

"You'll see soon enough." Wordsworth promised.

At first nothing happened. Then something moved in the far off distance. It began as a dark glimmer, like a storm cloud approaching. But as it neared it grew exponentially larger until it was rushing towards them like a tsunami, consuming everything in its path, leaving only darkness in its wake.

As the wave closed in on the mountain, Thomas felt a cold fear grip his body, a dread that clung to his very bones, and he began to feel faint. His body went completely numb, and as the wave rushed over them cried out desperately, "NooOOO…."

A fair golden haired boy of adolescent years wearing a wooden chest plate and holding a wooden sword, walked down a vast white marble hallway with columns aligning each side. Between the columns stood enormous statues of men masterfully sculpted, each appearing so life-like it seemed at any moment they'd cease to be inanimate. The boy stared up at them as he passed with a somber expression upon his face.

"Great kings," he spoke, slowing his pace, "and every one my ancestor—my blood," he continued aloud, "Though I do not deserve to share it with them." Shame looming heavy in his crystal blue eyes.

He stopped walking and stood before one of the statues. A stern faced man with rigid, sharp features, wearing a crown atop his head and dressed in battle armor after the ancient fashion showing off his muscular arms and legs. His stone eyes were penetrating and focused, appearing to judge all who stood before them. He held a book in one hand, while the other grasped a sword pointed towards the heavens. The inscription below him read: King Sigrid the First.

"The rock that built the Empire…you unified the tribes and brought order to the world. Defeated the dark wizard Ishmon and his armies in the Chimera Wars, and then bound him to the Mountain of Chains, bringing peace after so many years of war." He sighed deeply, "I wish I could be like you Sigrid. But if you were here, you'd probably disown me, or worse send me into exile. Not that I'd blame you."

He began walking again, his head held low.

"What does it matter anyway!" he erupted suddenly, "Jaden will be king, and he will be a great king—like Sigrid. While I remain a weak prince, whose only glory was to be born to an important family—as if that is any accomplishment!

Better to be a blacksmith, at least then I could forge a sword to be carried by a great hero into battle. I'm pathetic!"

In the midst of his self-flagellation, a hurried voice called out from behind him. "Prince Abram! Prince Abram!"

He turned to see a plump man with a pudgy face covered by a light brown beard and crowned with a shiny bald head, running towards him at a breakneck pace. His iron breastplate, adorned with the symbol of a golden sun, clanged nosily as he ran.

By the time he reached Prince Abram he was sweating profusely and breathing heavily. He paused for a long moment, attempting to compose himself before beginning to speak.

"There you are," said the man thoroughly relieved, "I've been looking all over the palace for you."

"I'm sorry Sir Hammond but you'll not get what you came for," said Prince Abram decidedly.

"But my Prince you must—"

"I'm not going, and you can't make me, or have you forgotten that I am a prince, albeit a completely useless one. You can't make me do anything that I do not wish to," said Prince Abram.

"My Prince, your brother is in the arena awaiting your presence—as is half the kingdom. If you do not face him, as tradition requires, you will bring great dishonor upon yourself. And your father will be ashamed." Sir Hammond pleaded.

"It will be much worse if I face him," said Prince Abram, turning away, "For then father will know just how weak I truly am. At least now he still has some hope that his second son is not a total waste."

"My Prince, I cannot believe what I am hearing. Surely you do not speak the truth of your heart!"

"What's the point of going out there when you know with absolute certainty that you will be defeated? Why not save yourself the humiliation?" Prince Abram argued, "And that is exactly what I intend to do Sir Hammond, save myself and everyone else a great deal of embarrassment."

"The point—the point!" Sir Hammond's voice rose along with his tone. "Now you listen here fool boy, prince or not, I'm going to teach you a thing or two about what it is to be a man, and when I'm finished you're going to go out there and face your brother in the Games. For I'll not have you bring dishonor on yourself or your House. Now listen, and listen well to what I have to say."

Thoroughly taken aback, Prince Abram recoiled like a child about to be spanked, and nodded his head sheepishly.

"Now, you say that you'll lose if you compete, and that may be so, but never, *never*, shall you ever fear to do so. Never shall you ever be afraid to try, because if you do not try you'll never accomplish anything of worth. Failure is a natural part of life—as certain as the sun rises; we lose, just as we win. You say it is madness to compete when the chances are that you'll lose, while I say that it is the highest form of courage. To fight when duty calls, to do what you must though faced with insurmountable odds, to stand up bravely in defiance and say I will never give up, and I will never give in! That is honorable—that is heroic! And that my Prince, is the truest measure of a king," finished Sir Hammond his chest puffed up and his head held high, looking every bit the great soldier he was.

"So my Prince," continued Sir Hammond far more calmly, "you have a choice. You can either run away like a coward, or you can stand up and fight like a man, like a *king*. The decision is yours."

Prince Abram paused for a long moment then answered weakly, "I-I will fight."

"What was that? I could not hear you!" boomed Sir Hammond.

"I will fight," said Prince Abram a bit stronger.

"Well then dammit, say it like you mean it!"

"I will fight—I will fight—I will fight!" the words burst forth from Prince Abram's mouth and echoed throughout the corridors of the hallway bouncing off the walls and returning back to him.

"That's more like it! Now I believe you may even have your ancestors' attention. It's time to show them all what you're made of. Come, the arena awaits!"

Brimming with new confidence, Prince Abram followed Sir Hammond down the hall towards the sounds of the thunderous crowd.

Storytime

THOMAS AWOKE TO the sight of the woman in the portrait from the prior night regarding him with sympathetic eyes. He was lying on the couch in the sitting room next to the green fire. His brother and Wordsworth sat in adjacent chairs. Wordsworth was smoking his pipe, while Jack looked incredibly bored.

"Oh look who finally decided to wake up," remarked Jack snidely as Thomas sat up.

"Welcome back," said Wordsworth.

"How long have I been out?" asked Thomas, still woozy.

"Nearly two strokes of the clock by my count." Wordsworth informed him.

"W-what happened?" asked Thomas, afraid of the answer.

"You fainted," replied Jack bluntly.

"I did?" said Thomas, feeling instantly ashamed as his face turned a scarlet red.

"No apparent injuries though." Wordsworth reported cheerfully, "Could have been much worse, falling off your horse like that. Though, it did appear as if you were having a rather lucid dream."

"Yea you kept mumbling some nonsense about not giving up," laughed Jack.

"Nothing to be ashamed of Prince Thomas, nightfall can have strange effects," said Wordsworth, adding, "Just ask the werewolves!"

Suddenly Thomas' fainting spell wasn't so interesting.

"There—are—werewolves?" said Thomas. Not completely shocking given all the other things they'd recently discovered were real, but still....

"One of the more unfortunate Changelings," said Wordsworth, and seeing their faces added, "Changeling is a general term encompassing those with one nature during the day, and at night another one entirely."

"Aren't werewolves controlled by the full moon?" asked Thomas, recalling popular lore.

"Werewolves are highly susceptible to the transformative magic of a full moon, during which the beast is nearly impossible to control without years of training or strong potions. But they are not exclusively ruled by the moon's cycle. Changelings have two distinct natures, two completely separate identities, and each constantly strive for domination. The battle renews each and every night as the beast fights to break free."

"What about vampires?" asked Jack, perfectly serious.

The sheer fact that Jack would even ask such a question was testament to just how far things had come over the past few days.

Wordsworth paused before answering, "Vampires are one of the creatures known broadly as the Undead. Those skirting the line between the living and the dead, belonging at the same time to both and neither."

"Vampires can't walk in sunlight though, right?" said Thomas.

"It's true that long exposure to sunlight will kill a vampire, while at night they are at the height of their powers. But they are not, strictly speaking, confined to walking the night. Some of the older vampires have built up a tolerance to sunlight. And there are places where the sun never really shines, while others where it shines only faintly."

Thomas got the distinct feeling that Wordsworth was referring to Somulus; not a comforting thought in the least. The existence of vampires and werewolves would certainly make going out at night perilous. *Are those the worst elements Wordsworth referred to earlier*? he wondered. *And what about the stakes the guards were holding?*

But before they could delve any deeper, the great clock in the hall rang out.

"Ah, dinner." Wordsworth announced cheerfully.

"About time," grumbled Jack.

They followed Wordsworth to the hall where the door next to the clock was opened. Inside, they discovered a lengthy dining room lit by a series of torches lining the breadth of its brown stone walls. Large portraits, like those in the sitting room, hung on the walls. While in the center of the room stood an obscenely long wooden table stocked full with an equally obscene amount of delicious looking foods. When the boys saw it they sprinted to the table, sat down, and began grabbing at everything they saw.

"It would be best to wait for your Uncle," said Wordsworth, abruptly interrupting their feast.

Reluctantly, Thomas put down the roll in his hand. While Jack, on the cusp of biting into a biscuit, didn't look like he was going to listen, until Wordsworth added, "He would not be pleased if you started without him."

Thankfully, they didn't suffer for long, as shortly thereafter their Uncle emerged through the door at the end of the hall—his exceptionally long black cape trailing behind him. Without a word he sat at the head of the table. His face, Thomas noticed, appeared strained and more aged than it had the night before. *Must've had a rough day*, he concluded. His mother having come home looking similarly drained on particularly strenuous days.

"Please, eat." Uncle Hades implored them, his voice nearly as weak as his appearance. "We'll converse after you've finished."

Needing no further encouragement, they dove headfirst into the feast, stuffing handfuls of food eagerly into their mouths. Their Uncle by contrast ate nothing, and merely watched as the boys gorged themselves on sweet meats, biscuits and pies, fruits of all kinds, and deserts stacked so high you could barely see over them. Though at one point during the course of the meal Wordsworth brought over the wooden box purchased at Doctor Von Wolfenhauer's, opened it, took out a small glass vial containing a gaseous white liquid, and poured it into a chaliced cup sitting in front of Uncle Hades; who drank it down with a ravenous thirst.

Thomas swore his Uncle's face rejuvenated before his very eyes, the youthful vigor of the night prior returning as if never gone. *What the heck was in that vial?* he wondered, astonished by the drastic transformation.

The boys tasted everything, eating their fill and then some. Until they couldn't possibly stomach a single morsel more, and sat back in their chairs nursing bellies on the cusp of bursting.

"Did you enjoy the meal?" Uncle Hades inquired.

"It was amazing," said Thomas rubbing his swollen belly and relishing without a doubt the greatest meal of his life.

"I'm pleased. You'll dine this way every night in which you stay," said Uncle Hades.

"Who cooks it all?" asked Thomas, thinking of the tremendous labor that must've gone into creating such a feast.

"The chef, of course," said Uncle Hades.

"I'd like to thank him," said Thomas.

"I'll pass your compliments along," said Uncle Hades.

"I'd like to do it myself, if that's alright," said Thomas.

"That's not possible," said Uncle Hades brusquely, adding, "He's already left for the day."

"Tomorrow then?" asked Thomas hopefully.

"Perhaps."

"What did you do today?" asked Jack, joining the conversation.

"Nothing particularly noteworthy. The usual business," said Uncle Hades vaguely. "Though your day, I gather, was quite extraordinary, life changing even. I'm sure you have many questions."

The boy glanced over at one another and then nodded fervently.

"Perhaps it's time for some answers then. Let's retire to the sitting room and you'll have them," and with that Uncle Hades rose from his seat.

After they'd settled in, Uncle Hades continued. "It's time you knew the truth, and as family I thought it appropriate that I should tell you. Therefore, I instructed Wordsworth to be less than forthcoming in certain respects. I also thought it beneficial for you to witness some things with your own eyes, in order to save time."

He paused for a long moment before beginning again.

"You're not simply in another country, or even another continent, but another world entirely." The boys glanced uncertainly at one another. "You're in the magical world of Mythil. The True World," said Uncle Hades, "Those in your world once belonged to this one, but the Great War changed everything."

At the mention of war, Jack's eyes lit up.

"It is largely the story of a man commonly known now as the Dark Prince or the Pretender King, among many other names. But first he was simply Prince Jaden of Jove, eldest son of the great King Insun.

"Jove was the greatest kingdom of the age, or of any age for that matter. It was the light that guided the world. The ruling House of Mourning traced its lineage back to Jove's founder Aloysius the Lightbringer, of whom we spoke earlier. Like his famed ancestor, Prince Jaden was the greatest warrior of the day. Extraordinarily gifted, the feats he performed were legendary.

"One day a powerful dark witch named Darmania appeared in Jove. None know from where she came. But shortly after arriving she caught Prince Jaden's eye, and he fell deeply in love with her. Playing upon his ambition, she twisted his mind, and corrupted his spirit.

"So much, that despite Jaden being the rightful heir to the Eternal Throne, as King Insun lay dying he chose Jaden's younger twin brother, Prince Abram, as king. Robbed of his birthright, Jaden left Jove, vowing to return and exact his revenge.

"True to his word, Jaden returned at the head of an army, and burned the great city to the ground. But he did not stop there, for the throne he was denied he decreed that all thrones should be his. He proclaimed himself King Draconis, and waged a war against the entire world.

"Countless joined his fanatical quest to rule over all—a quest carried out with single minded ruthlessness. With his army he scourged the world as only Khan before him had. None were spared. All were forced to choose sides. Kingdoms standing for thousands of years fell to ashes…entire races were wiped out…the world ripped itself to pieces….

"But led by King Abram, a legendary warrior in his own right who came to be known as the White Lion, the Alliance fought back. And finally, after years passed and lives beyond counting were lost, the war ended in the Pretender King's defeat.

"In the aftermath, the victors came together to decide what was to be done with those that had joined him. There were far too many to simply imprison. Nor could they all be executed; though some advocated for it. In the end, it was decided that they should all be exiled. But to where?

"The Grand Council of the Alliance arrived at a solution. A fake world was constructed, a mirror image of this one, known as the Banishment. To separate the Banishment from Mythil a great wall of magic known as the Veil was constructed. More than simply a wall, it was a curse that caused the Banished to lose all their powers and knowledge of Mythil, becoming dumb beasts condemned to brutally short existences."

"So our world—" began Thomas.

"Is the Banishment," Uncle Hades confirmed.

So our world is composed of the villains from this one. Thomas thought. Having experienced enough cruelty in his lifetime, the prospect wasn't entirely unbelievable. *It would explain a lot actually.*

"But the Banished proved resourceful beyond all expectations, creating ingenious tools and building a world filled with wonders. While in ways magic held this world back, its absence liberated the Banished to develop new sources of power," explained Uncle Hades with more than a hint of admiration.

"And though stripped of their powers and knowledge, the Banished retained vague remembrances of the world they'd been cast out of—glimpsed in dreams and other moments of altered consciousness. And though forbidden, many in Mythil ventured over into the Banishment to visit their banished brethren, even to start new lives. But those staying too long paid a heavy price, eventually succumbing to the curse and forgetting even who they were…."

Uncle Hades turned then towards Thomas and Jack. "Before I go further, do you have any questions? I know this is a great deal to digest."

"What happened to Prince Jaden?" Jack asked.

"In the midst of the War's final battle on a peak known as Ragnarock, he claimed his own life, plunging his infamous spear into his heart."

"Why would he do that?" asked Jack.

"Because he swore that when he returned, he would wage an even greater war and take vengeance on his enemies," said Uncle Hades.

"Return from the dead?" said Jack, "Like a vampire?"

"Not return as an Undead," said Uncle Hades, "But be reborn to an entirely new life."

"Like reincarnation?" said Thomas.

Uncle Hades nodded. "Just as we have blood ancestors, so do we have spirit ancestors as well, those for whom we share a soul. Soulcestors, you may call them. And each new life in a soul line adds to the soul. For life, like time, is a continuum, and we are not simply who we are now, but who we have been."

Thomas could scarcely believe it. Not only was magic real, but so was reincarnation. "How would you know your soulcestors?" he asked, curious about who might inhabit his own.

"Those adept in soul magic have ways of telling," said Uncle Hades, "But have you ever had déjà vu or perhaps a particularly lucid dream in which you were someone else. These are memories of past lives. And in this way our past lives communicate with our present."

"But some souls are extremely powerful," continued Uncle Hades, "One in particular beyond all others. Known as the Soul of Legend, its bearers have been history's greatest heroes, including Aloysius, and its original bearer, Samson. Many believe, however, that in Jaden and Abram the Soul of Legend split, becoming two separate souls. And that Jaden's soul was corrupted by the Lord of Nightmares, creating a dark soul to rival Abram's light."

"Who is the Lord of Nightmares?" asked Thomas.

"Time for yet another story, it would appear…"

Like the night prior, their Uncle's words became images in the green flames of the fire.

"In the beginning, a powerful being we call the Author wrote the world into existence. The Author required rulers to order and guide his new world, along with finish the task of creation, filling in his blanks. So directly from his mind he conceived thirteen sons and thirteen daughters, known as the Dream Kings and Queens. The Author bestowed upon them the ability to wield the Infinite nearly as great as his own, the ink the Author used to write the world. And for centuries they ruled Mythil as the Author's surrogates, carrying forth his designs and purposes.

"But there was one Dream King, the oldest and most powerful, known as Setus, who wanted more. He wanted to create his own beings…even his own worlds.

"Setus discovered a new power, a dark perversion of the Infinite. But the dark magic used to wield it came with a cost. It thoroughly corrupted Setus, preserving only his will to dominate and rule. He became a Dark Creator, and brought forth an army of monsters conceived in darkness. For this he was known as the Lord of Nightmares.

"Setus persuaded many of his brothers and sisters to join him, and together with his army of monsters rebelled against the Author in the First War. A war fought on many different planes, the scars of which remain to this day.

"But the Author could not simply un-write what had been written. It is the first rule of this world, and one he is bound to. In order to win the war, the Author required a warrior to lead his army. So he created a soul like none other, imbued with a piece of his own, and dipped into the Source of the Infinite itself. Then of all the races the Author chose Man as the soul's vessel. And with a woman named Danya conceived a son called Samson.

"Samson was a force the likes of which the world had never known, a superman in every respect. And he led the Author's army to victory over Setus and his monsters.

"Setus was sentenced to a specially constructed prison at the center of the world, to remain there unto the End of Days. But alas, that was not the end of the tale. The Lord of Nightmare's abominations still lingered, and even locked in his prison his influence seeped out and corrupted the world, along with the dark power he'd unleashed upon it. Throughout history he has turned many minds, offering a dark path to rival the Author's light. Thus was evil born into the world…"

After the story ended there remained to Jack one burning question left unanswered.

"So why are we here now?" he asked.

"Like so many others," Uncle Hades began, as if anticipating the question "our family line was split after the Great War, as many of our bloodline joined Jaden's side and were exiled to the Banishment in the Purge. I tracked our line in the Banishment, keeping a close eye. When your mother passed you were all that was left, and I knew the time had come for the bloodline to be reunited. So I arranged for you both to be brought over."

"Why did you wait so long?" asked Jack in an accusatory tone, "Why didn't you just bring us over earlier, including our mother."

Uncle Hades paused before answering, "I regret not doing so sooner, given your circumstances. But you must understand to bring one over from the Banishment, let alone two or more, is neither an easy task, nor one easily hidden. You also had to be able to survive the journey…something the strongest struggle to accomplish. It simply couldn't be done any sooner. I'm sorry."

Forgiving by nature, Thomas accepted his Uncle's apology, while Jack, never known for his sympathy, wasn't ready to forgive or forget.

"Are there many others like us?" inquired Thomas, "Those who have, um, been brought over."

"I would not say many, but there are some," said Uncle Hades, "As I explained, it is forbidden for those here to journey over into the Banishment, and the penalties are severe. But to bring one of the Banished over is a far greater crime still. In the eyes of the Grand Council few are worse."

"So you risked punishment to bring us here," said Thomas with growing appreciation.

Uncle Hades nodded. "Not all laws should be followed…and some should be broken all together."

Jack smiled appreciatively, being himself of a similar mind when it came to rules, at least those written by others.

"That being said," Uncle Hades continued, "the law is hardly the only danger. There are places where the Veil is thin and can be crossed. But every route is perilous. The crossing is also best done when death is near, and life is weak, because in a way one is already between worlds. Few survive long in this transitory state."

"What was that tea Wordsworth gave us?" asked Jack suddenly.

"A powerful potion to facilitate the journey."

"So it almost killed us," said Jack bluntly.

"It masked your life-force, suppressing it for a time, allowing you to travel by means otherwise unavailable."

"The train?" said Thomas.

Uncle Hades nodded.

"So the fog we passed through that was the Veil," said Thomas.

"A manifestation of it, yes," said Uncle Hades. "You must not think of the Veil as something physical. The Veil is pure magic, and its own entity. The fog was how the Veil manifested itself to you."

"What about the Horseman?" asked Thomas, fascinated by the peculiar hooded figure from the moment he'd laid eyes upon him.

"The Horseman is an extremely old character, one who has taken on many different forms throughout history. He provides passage for a price."

"What was his price?" asked Jack.

"The price was steep." Uncle Hades admitted. But instead of going into further detail stood abruptly from his seat, and like the night before announced that he had urgent affairs requiring his attention. On his way out, however, he stopped at the doorway and turned to face the boys a final time before departing.

"Now that you're free of the Veil, you may find yourselves going through some… changes. Do not worry, it is perfectly natural."

Thomas opened his mouth to inquire about what sort of changes his Uncle meant, but he was already out the door.

Shortly thereafter, Wordsworth escorted the boys up to their rooms, and then retired himself for the evening.

Like the prior evening, the boys stood just outside the doorway to their respective rooms.

"What'd you think about, you know, everything Uncle told us?" asked Thomas, dying to discuss it all.

Jack pondered the question for a long moment. "We're meant to be here," he said at last.

Something of an odd statement Thomas thought. His brother had always had a certain sense of fate or destiny—in fact he often spoke in those terms, as if things were predetermined; a fact seemingly at odds with his otherwise logical mind. But above all else his brother believed in himself, in his own "star" as it were. Thomas too found a great deal of truth in the statement, and ever since he'd arrived had felt a sense of belonging he'd never known before, as if this really were home.

"Yeah," nodded Thomas, "I know what you mean."

But much to Thomas' disappointment, instead of engaging in further discussion, Jack simply opened the door to his room, walked inside, and shut the door behind him without another word. To which, after a moment, Thomas did the same.

When Jack arrived in his room he discovered the gemstone he'd acquired at Doctor Von Wolfenhauer's store lying on his bed.

How did you get there? he wondered. He certainly hadn't put it there. Indeed he'd stored it away safely in a dresser drawer.

He walked over and picked it up.

It was smooth like glass, and its color was dark and black. Inside the gem the red iris stared up at him. And he stared back at it, until lost in its gaze.

Suddenly the gem began convulsing in his hand. Startled, he dropped it on the floor, and suddenly it ceased.

But as he went to pick it up, inside appeared the vision of a girl where the iris had been, as if trapped in the gem itself.

Dressed in a red and black dress, she had midnight dark hair and opal eyes, while her skin was fair and radiant, and her lips so sensuous they could've cured any ill with a kiss. She was simply the most beautiful girl he'd ever seen in his life, and he felt instinctively compelled to her. His heart raced, his breath grew short, and his hands trembled. He felt like he'd felt only once before—in the Golden Forest.

Who is she? he wondered, desperately wanting to know. Indeed he'd never wanted to know something so badly before.

But then, as abruptly as she'd come, she vanished, and the red iris returned.

"Come back!" Jack commanded.

But she would not.

He shook the gem forcefully and yelled at it. But no matter how hard he shook or how loudly he yelled she would not return to him. His heart ached with a deep sense of loss—like the world's greatest prize had just been stolen from his grasp.

Anniversary

"THE COMET HAS come! Two nights to the Festival!" they proclaimed joyously at Mrs. Clauses' abode. Thereafter the candles were lit and the celebration begun. As the witches of the Primrose Coven rejoiced for the coming of one of their holiest of nights.

But there was one present not in such a cheerful mood, and who refused to partake in the festivities, despite her Sister's pleas that she do so. A beautiful young girl with emerald green eyes and auburn hair whose name was Catherine.

"No, go on, have fun. I'm going to stay up here and read some," said Catherine to Mrs. Clause, in whose house she'd lived for the past few years.

"My dear, I wish you'd reconsider, everyone keeps asking for you. We're going to boil some sweet pumpkin soup. I know how you like that." Mrs. Clause cajoled; a plump woman whose rosy red cheeks and snowy white hair made her appear the quintessential grandmother.

"Perhaps I'll come down later," said Catherine at last.

"I'll save you some soup," promised Mrs. Clause shutting the door to Catherine's room.

Catherine sighed deeply at the arriving solitude.

It wasn't that she didn't *want* to join her Sisters in merrymaking, or that she was some sort of recluse. But tonight was the anniversary of the day five years ago when she lost her parents. The reason she lived here now. And as she sat on her small bed in her small room—made even smaller by the many stacks of books—she thought of how much she missed them both.

When she was a child they'd lived together happily in the realm of Avalon, where her father was a knight of the elite Order of the White Lion, the Guardians of Creationdom. A hero of the Vampire Wars, and a member of the Round Table, some even claimed he'd one day be king. While her mother was a distinguished Lady, and renowned to be the most beautiful woman in the realm. Catherine loved both dearly, and couldn't have asked for a better family in which to grow up in.

But everything changed when her happy life was consumed by tragedy.

The circumstances were mired in mystery—the way of the White Tower and the wizards who rule it. But the story goes that upon returning home from a quest her father went on a murderous rampage, killing her mother and then attacking the Patriarch himself, nearly taking his life, and striking down several knights coming to his rescue. For his crimes, he was stripped of his knighthood and sentenced to being burned alive in the Holy Fires.

Catherine never believed a word of it, and had always suspected a conspiracy that ran deep into the highest chambers of the Arch. Of course, she hadn't the slightest shred of evidence to support her suspicion—only what she knew to be true in her heart. But that was more than enough.

Because of her father she became a pariah and was cast out onto the streets like refuse. Eventually, she was caught stealing food and sentenced to a House of Reformation. Where the women who ran it—known as the Maidens of Creationdom—believed pain the only true path to salvation. She tried to run away several times, but was caught, and punished severely, "Seven lashes with the rod!" she remembered each one vividly, and the scars on her back would never allow her to forget. But everything changed that fateful day near three years ago when her Grandfather showed up out of the blue.

She'd never met the man before that day—never even knew he existed. Her father had never spoken of him. But then, her father spoke so little about his own childhood that she'd come to believe he hadn't even had one. Though she knew from the moment she laid eyes on him that he was her Grandfather, for the resemblance to her father was uncanny.

Her Grandfather told her the reason he hadn't visited was that he served a powerful Lord in a faraway realm in the Underlands known as Somulus. But they would have plenty of opportunity to make up for time lost as she was coming back there with him.

Leaving that dreadful place was one of the happiest moments of her life. Though, even as she departed Avalon, she swore one day to return and exact her revenge. A promise she fully intended upon keeping.

Upon arriving in Somulus, she found herself in a much different sort of a place. Whereas in Avalon the sun shone so bright that everything was bathed in a perpetual golden glow, in Somulus the sun barely showed its face, and when it did was blanketed by fog. And whereas in Avalon the darkness of night was a mere interlude to the play of the day, in Somulus the night decidedly held the starring role.

She was given over to the care of Mrs. Clause, as her Grandfather resumed his duties in the castle and she was unable to stay there with him. But Mrs. Clause provided her with a fantastic home, treating Catherine like her own flesh and blood. Mrs. Clause had never had the privilege of having children of her own, though wanted them more than anything in the world. But fate had not deemed it so, and her husband had died many years ago. And though she'd never fully replace Catherine's real mother, was undoubtedly the next best thing.

The other wonderful thing about Catherine's new home was the witchcraft. Mrs. Clause was Head Witch of the Primrose Coven and took Catherine on as her apprentice when she showed signs of her magical potential. Catherine took to the Craft like a fish to water. Now she was widely considered—young as she was—to be the most talented witch in all the realm. Some even claimed that she would take over as Head Witch when Mrs. Clause retired. But that was a day far off in coming.

Just then there was a knock at the door.

"Come in," said Catherine, annoyed at the interruption.

"Sorry to disturb," said Mrs. Clause opening the door, "But you have a visitor."

"Who?" asked Catherine, not expecting anyone.

"Come and see."

Catherine followed Mrs. Clause to the front door, and her eyes lit up when she saw her Grandfather standing there.

"Grandfather!" she ran over and gave him a big hug. "I've missed you!"

"Not as much as I've missed you," he replied.

"I'll leave you two alone. Nice to see you again Wordsworth," said Mrs. Clause with a warm smile.

"And you, Mrs. Clause," said Wordsworth with a gentlemanly tip of his hat.

"Would you care to accompany me on a stroll?" her Grandfather inquired.

"I'll get my coat," said Catherine eagerly.

It was a nice night. The air cool and crisp. The moon hung large and full in the sky and with the Festival so close already appeared fit to burst. The streets were busy as many were out celebrating the comet's arrival. Its red streak could still be seen cutting across the sky. Red candles were alight in many of the windowsills and would remain burning throughout the night to honor those who had come before, just as the comet preceded the Festival.

As usual, her Grandfather smoked his pipe as they walked.

"So are you ever going to tell me how you always manage to find a way into town after dark?" asked Catherine.

Her Grandfather smiled. "I have my ways."

"I have no doubt," said Catherine.

"I'm sorry I've not been around much lately," said her Grandfather.

"It's okay," said Catherine, "I know you have your responsibilities."

"Yes, and you are one of them, and I have been neglecting you."

Catherine didn't say anything. She knew what he said was true.

"But that's going to change," said her Grandfather firmly. "I promise."

Catherine smiled, and hoped very much that would be the case. But she'd heard the same promise many times before.

"I brought you something from my travels," said her Grandfather pulling from his coat a dark leathered bound book appearing very old. "It is known as the Malahrati, which means, words of enlightenment. The mystics claim it as their most sacred text. I hope you enjoy it."

"It's wonderful," said Catherine eagerly taking the book into her hands. Catherine loved books and her Grandfather fed her passion.

"I am also," he began again, "sorry that when I saw you earlier today that I did not come over. That was in poor taste. It's only—"

"You couldn't be seen sympathizing with the protests." Catherine finished for him. She knew he was often forced to do things he wouldn't otherwise for the sake of duty. Her father had been forced to do the same.

Wordsworth sighed. “Doctor Von Wolfenhauer is very influential, and his Lordship has granted him special status.”

“His magic is an abomination. He perverts nature, and peddles poison!” raged Catherine, anger and disgust thick in her voice.

“You know some claim witches to be the Lord of Nightmares’ handmaidens,” said her Grandfather.

“That’s ridiculous! We serve Mother Nature. No one hates the Lord of Nightmares more than us.” Catherine protested.

“Perhaps. But all magic has its light and its dark aspects,” said her Grandfather, “And witches have certainly had more than their fair share of bad apples, need I remind you.”

It was a point difficult to argue with. There had been many evil witches. The Dark Coven was filled with them. Not to mention the Queen of Lies herself.

“So those boys with you today are our new princes?” said Catherine, changing the subject. The whole town had been abuzz by their arrival. And there was something familiar about the smaller one with the golden hair, as if she’d met him before, but couldn’t place where.

“Yes.”

“So what are they like?” she asked, curious like everyone else.

“They are boys on the cusp of becoming men, and like all in that category still have a great deal of learning to do. Speaking of which, if I’m not mistaken, you’ll be a woman soon,” said her Grandfather, growing suddenly serious.

Catherine had sensed the change as well, and over the last few months her powers had been gaining in strength. A witches’ Coming of Age usually coincided with one of the five holy nights of the year, and she knew that hers’ would occur at the Festival, which the witches also called Samhain, when the transformative magic was at its peak.

“It is a time of passage,” her Grandfather continued, “A transition from one phase of life to the next in which we begin to become the person we are destined to be.”

“What if I don’t like the path chosen for me?” asked Catherine, “What if I want another?” A question looming heavy upon her mind for some time.

Her Grandfather smiled. "A question many have pondered at their Coming of Age. It is the great paradox: are we merely slaves to destiny, or do we choose our own fate?"

"Which do you think?" asked Catherine.

"Like so much in life, the answer lies somewhere in between," said her Grandfather.

"I'm not sure I understand what you mean." Catherine admitted.

"Allow me to show you then…" and suddenly her Grandfather turned down a side street, veering off the main road they were traveling upon.

"From the moment we're born we are placed upon a path formed by the choices of others," said her Grandfather, and he turned abruptly down another side street.

"This path long predates our birth, going all the way back to the beginning of the world, when the first letter was wrote. The consequences of the choices of our ancestors become our fate…"

Yet again he turned down another street, until they were in a part of town that Catherine had never been before.

"But fate only determines where we begin, not where we end up. We are not condemned to the consequences of those before us. Each of us is given the opportunity to forge our own path."

They came then to an alley that had three different adjoining streets. Her Grandfather abruptly stopped walking.

"Which way?" asked Catherine.

"You tell me," replied her Grandfather.

Catherine smiled. "I see what you're doing," and after a moment to think about it answered. "To the right."

As they rounded the corner they came upon several First Guardsmen restraining three individuals, clearly goblin juice addicts, easily recognizable by their glowing green eyes.

"Of course we must be careful where we end up," cautioned her Grandfather with a smile.

Her Grandfather led her back out onto a main street.

"What was my father's Coming of Age like?" Catherine inquired.

Her Grandfather opened his mouth to speak, then stopped abruptly, and stayed silent for a long moment.

"I don't remember it," he said at last, profound sadness in his eyes, "I wasn't there."

"It's okay Grandfather," said Catherine, placing her hand on his shoulder. "What about your own Coming of Age then?"

"Mine!" replied her Grandfather with a chuckle, "I can barely remember yesterday, or even what I had for breakfast this morning, let alone several centuries ago."

"Surely you must remember something of it," said Catherine hopefully.

"Well…maybe a little," responded her Grandfather, a tiny twinkle appearing in his blue right eye.

"Tell me," said Catherine anxiously tugging on his arm the way she used to when she was younger, "Pleaseeeeeeee…."

"Alright, I'll try," he conceded finally, earning a loving hug from Catherine, and he wondered how he could've ever refused her anything.

"I remember there was a great deal of uncertainty, and that I was so worried, so anxious about the future. I could barely sleep at night, and I laid in my bed for hours on end pondering all the possibilities. It was enough to drive a person mad," he laughed. "But my parents assured me that everything would work out for the best, and the transition would be as natural as leaves changing colors. In the end, they were right. It happened with barely a notice, something just clicks all of a sudden, and you see the world differently, with a purposeful eye. You feel the burden of responsibility upon your shoulders. But it's not an unwanted feeling, for it makes you stronger and you carry it almost like a badge of honor as you begin to journey into a new stage of life. At least, that's the way I remember it anyway," said her Grandfather.

Catherine put her head down upon his shoulder. "I wish my parents were here to see mine."

Her Grandfather placed his hand upon her head. "They see everything you do, I assure you. And they are extremely proud."

"I miss them so much," said Catherine, tears streaming down her soft cheeks, "I wish I could see them again, just one more time."

"I know my child. But you must be strong for them…and for yourself. You cannot live in regret for what could have been. It will eat at your soul. Everything happens for a reason, remember that too. The past is not who you are, or who you will become. Cherish their memory, and honor it by moving on..." and suddenly he grabbed her firmly by the shoulders, "Promise me that you'll not allow what happened to them to haunt you."

I—"

"Promise me," said her Grandfather adamantly.

"I promise," she replied weakly.

"Catherine."

"I promise," she responded more strongly.

"Good."

They walked awhile longer and then returned to Mrs. Clause's where the celebration was still ongoing.

"You could stay," said Catherine.

"Much as I'd love to, I must return to the castle. But I'll be in town tomorrow on some business. Would you care to meet me for a meal perhaps? I've heard The Sapling has a fantastic new chef."

"I'd like that very much," said Catherine.

"Then I shall see you tomorrow," and after a warm hug her Grandfather departed.

A Time for Exploring

THOMAS HAD SLEPT terribly, worse even than the night before. The tree branch had tapped incessantly against his window sill, only seeming to grow louder and more persistent. *Either that tree goes or I'll never be able to sleep again*, he thought as he gazed at the window where the branch stood now ever so innocently. But it wasn't only the tree that had kept him awake, there was also a strange blinding bright red light that flooded into his room as he was about to fall asleep. He still wondered what it was, and whether he was the only one to see it.

Thomas put on some clothes from the closet: a long white and gold trimmed coat and dark blue pants with black riding boots. Like the prior morning, after taking a long look at himself in the mirror he swore he appeared older, taller as well. *These clothes are doing wonders for me*, he thought.

Again like the previous morning, when he headed downstairs he found Wordsworth waiting at the bottom holding a silver tray full of pastries, which he offered to Thomas as breakfast.

"Fresh from the kitchen," said Wordsworth.

"Don't mind if I do," said Thomas, taking a couple and shoving them into his mouth.

"Did you catch the comet last night?" Wordsworth inquired.

"The comet?" responded Thomas with a mouth full of pastry.

"Came right at the stroke of midnight, a most spectacular sight."

So that's what that bright light was—a comet, thought Thomas.

"That means the Festival will begin soon right?"

"Only two more nights," said Wordsworth.

"I can't wait!" replied Thomas excitedly.

"A splendid time to be sure."

Thomas looked around. "Where's Jack? Is he still sleeping?"

"Certainly not, Prince Jack has been up for a while actually. He's in the sitting room, and has been there ever since I awoke," said Wordsworth.

"Doing what?" asked Thomas.

"I haven't the foggiest. I recommend finding out."

"I'll do that," said Thomas, "What are we doing today by the way?"

"Well, I don't know what *you're* doing, but I have to attend to some business for your Uncle and will be gone the better part of the day."

"We can't come with you?"

"I'm afraid not. Besides it's a very dull piece of business. So you will stay here in the castle while I am gone. I'm sure you'll find something to pass the time. I'll be back before you know it," said Wordsworth with a smile.

Thomas nodded his head, and then headed off to see what his brother was up to.

Jack hadn't slept a wink. His mind was preoccupied with more important things, and the weight of his thoughts drove him downstairs at some point during the night, and ever since he'd sat there next to the green fire, the black gem caressed in his hand. He'd tried just about everything he could think of to bring the girl back, even throwing it into the fire to see if that might trigger some reaction. But nothing worked.

Suddenly, Thomas walked into the room disturbing Jack's thoughts. He hastily put the gem back into his pocket.

"Morning!" Thomas greeted him cheerfully.

Jack cringed at his brother's cheerfulness.

"How'd you sleep?" asked Thomas sitting down in the adjacent chair.

"I didn't," replied Jack shortly.

"I know what you mean. I barely slept myself with the comet and all. Did you see it?" asked Thomas anxiously.

"No."

"Oh, well, that's okay," said Thomas. "But now that it's come the Festival will start soon."

Jack stayed silent.

"Anyway, Wordsworth said he has some errands to run today, but we don't have to go. So we're on our own for a while. What do you want to do?"

This immediately peaked Jack's attention. "Really?" he responded his head swimming with possibility.

"Yeah…why?" replied Thomas suspiciously, "I know that look, and whatever you're thinking the answer is no."

"This is the perfect opportunity to see what this castle is all about. To do a little exploring. Can't tell me you're not curious," said Jack goading his brother.

"What do you mean—exploring?"

"You know, do a little snooping, like detectives. We can make a game out of it," said Jack knowing how his brother loved to pretend.

"Yeah, okay!" responded Thomas far too quickly. But then added as a caveat, "I don't want to get into trouble."

"Don't be such a baby. Always worrying about getting into trouble. Where's your sense of adventure?" challenged Jack, "Not afraid are you?" he added, knowing how to push his brother's buttons.

"I'm not afraid!" Thomas declared defiantly.

Jack smiled, knowing he had him. "Prove it."

"I-I will."

"So when Wordsworth leaves we go exploring," said Jack, sealing the deal.

Wordsworth came into the room shortly thereafter.

"I'm leaving my Princes, I'll be back later. Try to enjoy yourselves while I'm gone."

Once he left Jack turned to Thomas, "You see he *wants* us to have fun."

Thomas wasn't sure they shared the same interpretation. "I don't think he meant for us to go sneaking around."

Jack shrugged. "Has to expect it, leaving us all alone."

Thomas had to admit his brother's logic was sound. *After all who leaves two teenage boys in a castle unsupervised? Especially when one of them is Jack.*

Once it was clear that Wordsworth was gone and the castle free to roam, they set out on their mission.

They started down the corridor on the left side of the main hall. The candles on the walls were spaced such that the light from one would end before the light from another began, with patches of darkness in between. On both sides of the corridor portraits hung upon the walls. Many of which Thomas found appeared to reflect those who'd lived in the Banishment.

When they passed the portrait of what looked like an old general in full military regalia, Thomas swore that the soldier winked at him. But when he looked again the portrait was as lifeless as ever. Normally, the possibility of such a thing would've been disregarded as a figment of his overly active imagination, but in a world of magic nothing could be dismissed out of hand. Thomas made a mental note to keep a sharp eye out for similar occurrences.

Further down the corridor they came to a wooden door with the symbol of a sun carved above it.

Jack went straight up to it and pulled the handle.

"Locked," he grumbled after the door refused to budge.

"Remember what Uncle said about locked doors." Thomas cautioned.

"They can't all be locked. Let's find another."

It wasn't more than the length of a candle's light before they got another chance. Once again Jack pulled the handle, and once again found it locked.

From that point forward a door followed every torch. Many of which had elaborate designs carved into the wood. For example, one door had a long ship shaped like a sea monster with a handle fashioned into the form of a boar, while another a very fat bald man with an enormous round belly wearing nothing more than a towel around his gargantuan waist. But no matter the door's design they all had one thing in common: they were all locked.

Jack's frustration was showing and with every successive door that would not open his anger grew.

At last they came to the very end of the hallway, where but a single door stood.

"Last one," said Thomas.

"It better open," threatened Jack, as if there would be consequences.

"That's strange," said Thomas, scratching his head.

"What's strange?" shot Jack.

"This door doesn't have any markings."

"So?"

"So, I don't know. It's just different is all."

"Well, different could be good, if it means it isn't locked. Why don't you give it a shot," said Jack hitting his brother on the back for encouragement, as if he needed it.

"Here goes…" and Thomas pulled back on the handle with all his strength. But like all the rest, the door wouldn't budge.

"Locked again." Thomas shrugged, "I guess that's it then—end of the road."

"Dammit!" yelled Jack angrily, and he kicked the wall violently.

"Easy Jack, you're going to break your foot!" cried Thomas, and worried his brother may have done so already, though Jack hardly seemed to notice.

"They can't all be locked!" Jack raged, "They just can't!"

"Maybe Uncle *knew* we'd be snooping around so he locked all the doors. Maybe that's why Wordsworth wasn't worried about leaving us all alone," said Thomas.

By now it looked like an entire day wasted. But just as Jack was about to turn and head back, the black gem stirred in his pocket, and he felt its power surge through him.

Jack walked back to the door.

"What are you doing?" said Thomas who'd already begun to head back.

"This time you open." Jack commanded the door, and pulled back hard on the handle.

The door creaked and moaned… and slowly, but surely, it opened.

Thomas stared in disbelief at the now opened door.

"How did—it was— locked!"

"Apparently, you're just not strong enough," said Jack triumphantly, "Time for exploring!"

The Wayward Forest

THOMAS AND JACK stood outside the now opened door peering out into utter darkness and freezing cold.

"Now what?" asked Thomas, hugging his shivering arms.

"What do you mean now what? We're going in of course," said Jack.

"You can't be serious. Its pitch dark and free-zing," said Thomas, his teeth chattering, "Besides who knows what's in there," his imagination stirring with grim thoughts of what lay lurking in the dark.

"That's the fun of it! See you on the other side." Jack declared, adding with a smile, "Unless you're too scared…" and with that walked into the cold darkness and disappeared from sight.

"Jack—wait—"

But it was too late.

Thomas stood at the foot of the doorway, gazing warily into the foreboding darkness dreading what would happen next. He knew he didn't really have a choice. Jack would ridicule him mercilessly if he didn't go. So he mustered his confidence and proceeded to put one foot begrudgingly in front of the other through the doorway and into the abyss….

Thomas hit the ground with a hard thud.

When he opened his eyes he was lying on a hard barren earth.

Where the heck am I? he wondered when he got to his feet. *And how did I even get here?*

Wherever he was the castle was completely gone, and equally strange despite the fact that it was day when he walked through the doorway now it was decidedly night. And what a dark night it was, with no stars in the sky or moon to be seen, just ominous dark clouds.

Despite the complete absence of light, however, Thomas discovered that he could see far better than by all rights he should be able. And what he saw was that he was smack dab in the middle of a forest. Not just any forest either, but an utterly frightening forest, everything a dark scary forest could be. Dead barren trees twisted and weaved into one another like thorn bushes. The ground steamed like it had been freshly burnt and the fire only recently doused. Eerie sounds emanated from unseen sources. As far as forests go, it didn't get much worse.

Where's Jack? He has to be here. I saw him go through the same door.

"Jack!" he whispered loudly, "Jack!"

But there was no response.

He tried several more times, but received nothing in return.

Even Jack would've said something by now, he thought dreadfully.

The whole situation feeling a bit like déjà vu all over again. *I hope there aren't any wolves here…or banshees.*

But just as he thought it, Thomas heard a twig crack loudly, and then several others. They were followed by the sound of a dozen footsteps headed in his direction.

He had no time to react as hooded figures cloaked in black robes emerged from the slanted trees and surrounded him. He thought about running, and then seeing the futility thought better of it. So he just stood there waiting to see what would happen next.

One of the dark figures stepped forward. He held a long black cane with the golden head of a jackal at its peak. Fiery red hair protruded from his black hood, and his chin stuck out to obscene lengths.

"Thomas, isn't it?" he said with a grin reminiscent of the Chesire Cat. His voice, like his face, had a certain unhinged quality, as if on the verge of breaking out into a hysterical fit of laughter at any moment.

"Who are you? What do you want?" asked Thomas, a bit more bravely than he'd intended or felt.

A massive paw grabbed his neck forcefully and pulled him up into the air holding him there with his feet dangling. Steamy breath coated Thomas' face along with the sound of guttural, animalistic groans and grunts.

"Now, Cadmus where are your manners? He simply doesn't know who we are yet. Put him down," the red haired figure insisted.

Cadmus growled angrily, and then the strong hairy hand gripping Thomas' neck released and he fell roughly to the ground.

"Good boy!" the red haired figure exclaimed as if talking to a pet. "Perhaps a treat is in order," and Cadmus, more bear than man in nearly every respect, licked his lips in anticipation and clapped his massive hairy hands.

"On second thought, wouldn't want to spoil your appetite," said the red haired figure and Cadmus emitted a disgruntled growl. "Now to business!"

Thomas' head turned by some unknown force toward where the red haired figure was standing, and held there firm. He couldn't move, no matter how much he struggled. Nor had he a voice in which to speak, for when he opened his mouth to protest nothing came out.

"Apologies, but I do need your full attention. We have things of grave importance to discuss you and I, and Time is a fickle friend—one moment you have Him, the next—" he blew into his hand "—gone."

It was then that he threw back his hood and his long fiery red hair burst forth from its confines, like a bird freed of its cage. His face was absolutely cartoonish in its dimensions. Everywhere it was sharp and pointed, and Thomas swore his cheekbones could cut through glass and his chin poke out an eye.

"I suppose a name is in order…something for you to know me by. Though names are such precarious things you know, and must be carefully guarded. Hmm, let me see now, just what shall it be?" he pondered, stroking his obscenely long chin, "Ah, I know! Call me…Mr. L." and he laughed as if he'd just told a particularly funny joke—a laugh sick and maniacal.

"I suppose you're wondering why you're here?" he continued after the laughter subsided, "Well aren't we all!" and the newly minted Mr. L laughed wildly once more, expanding the outer lengths of his face with the obscenity of his grin.

"Get on with it!" shouted one of the hooded figures.

Mr. L stopped abruptly in mid-pace and turned towards the interrupting voice. His grin disappeared, replaced by an equally pronounced frown.

"Cadmus, if you please," replied Mr. L calmly.

The great bear suddenly grabbed the figure by his neck and with one massive hand hoisted him off the ground. An impressive show of strength for he wasn't small by any means, though compared to Cadmus—who was simply enormous—appeared but a child.

"No, no, please, I didn't mean it!" the figure pleaded as he squirmed for his life. But no one seemed to care in the least, and if they did kept it to themselves.

"I cannot abide by rudeness," said Mr. L, and he nodded his head.

Cadmus flashed a childlike grin, and then with his other hand made a fist and drove it deep into the figure's chest, ripping out his still beating heart. The rest of the body fell to the ground limp, and then burst into flames. Until nothing more than tattered cloth and ash remained.

No one moved so much as a muscle while this took place. Though Thomas surely would've screamed out in bloody horror had he the use of his mouth, or run for his life if he controlled his legs.

"You would think vampires would have a bit more patience," mused Mr. L shaking his head. Then he turned towards one of the other black hooded figures standing to his right, "Not one of yours I hope Lady Miranda."

"He wasn't even a noble." Lady Miranda scoffed, indicating how little she cared for her fellow vampire, of which she most certainly was, a vampire, for while most of her pale skinned face remained hidden beneath her cloak, two razor sharp fangs were easily glimpsed when she spoke.

"Then he won't be missed!" said Mr. L and there was a collective chuckle from the other members of the circle.

"Now, if there are no *further* interruptions, I shall continue," and everyone fell deathly silent. Except for Cadmus, chewing on the heart like a dog with a bone. Mr. L shook his head, "Cadmus, look at you—you're a mess!"

Blood and guts dripping down his mouth, Cadmus abruptly stopped chewing on the heart and gave Mr. L a dumbfounded look, as if unsure what to do, and obviously not wanting to part with his prize.

"Put it away Cadmus, you can finish it later."

Cadmus hung his head like a scolded child, and then reluctantly put the half-eaten heart into his pocket for safe keeping.

"As I was saying, we've been waiting such a very long to meet you Thomas. And here you are—right on schedule. So what makes you so special?" mused Mr. L in rhetorical flourish.

"Well, that's a complicated question, but I'll do my best to answer it. Though, I wouldn't want to give it all away and ruin the surprise—for what a surprise it'll be!"

Mr. L began to pace and twirl his cane as he spoke.

"Something very big is on the verge of occurring you see—a story long in the making. And at last all the characters are gathering...the pieces taking their places. You have a special role in this unfolding story. In fact, you're one of the main characters."

What the heck is he talking about? Thomas thought, listening intently as Mr. L continued on.

"But one must be sure of such things. Too much is at stake to get it wrong. So we'll be requiring some of your blood—just a bit, it won't be missed, I promise. It will tell us all we need to know. For where words may lie, blood never does....So without further delay, Lady Miranda if you'd be so kind?"

"My pleasure," replied Lady Miranda, and from her cloak with one hand pulled out a small-yet brutally sharp-dagger, and with the other a purple vial with the golden symbol of a snake shaped like an S written upon it.

Though Thomas couldn't move, his eyes showed just how terrified he was. But there was nothing he could do to stop what was about to occur. His body being paralyzed from head to toe.

"Relax, it'll be over before you can blink." Mr. L joked and Thomas' eyes blinked rapidly on their own.

The sleeve of Thomas' shirt pulled back and his bare arm lifted up and held there firm.

"Proceed," said Mr. L.

Lady Miranda grabbed hold of Thomas' arm tightly and bared her fangs. She licked her lips slowly. "Next time we'll do this a better way...for us both," she whispered, as Thomas stared straight into her bloodthirsty red eyes.

Thomas felt the knife pierce his skin as the blade slit into his wrist. He watched silently as the blood spouted from his veins.

Lady Miranda cupped the vial under his wrist and collected a heavy dose of blood until Mr. L said at last, "Come now, we don't want him to bleed him completely dry."

After a moment she closed the vial and brought it over to Mr. L, licking the end of the knife like frosting from a cake.

"Exquisite," she said continuing to sample the goods, while the other vampires stared hungrily at the blood flowing freely from his arm.

Noticing the growing hunger, Mr. L made a slight gesture with his hand and suddenly the blood stopped flowing, and the cut instantly healed, leaving only a small scar.

"Test it," ordered Mr. L handing the vial over to another black hooded figure who took the vial into his distinctly male hands with the utmost delicacy. His face remained hidden as he headed over to where a makeshift table had been set up on a tree stump.

"Shouldn't be long now," said Mr. L with a cartoonish grin, "Soon we'll know all about you my little friend. Curious as a cat I'm sure you are…but you do know what happened to the cat now don't you?" Mr. L laughed.

True to his word, it wasn't long before the testing was finished and the cloaked figure returned to Mr. L and whispered something into his ear. Mr. L nodded and responded simply, "I see," and for a long moment just stood there silently.

"Bring him," said Mr. L finally.

Cadmus' massive hands grabbed hold of Thomas and lifted him up into the air.

It was then that something wholly unexpected happened, something his captors had not planned upon. A bright blue light streaked through the top of the trees and landed directly in front of them. They hissed and snarled as the light blinded them.

The blinding blue light formed into the shape of a man. Beautiful and brilliant, he illuminated everything around him. He had massive wings of pure light which fanned out several feet on either side.

Everyone froze, except for Thomas, Mr. L, and the mysterious visitor. Thomas, still under Mr. L's spell, watched on silently while the two conversed.

"Twinkle, twinkle, little star..." sang Mr. L.

"What are you doing with him!" roared the visitor's voice, hard, uncompromising, and otherworldly.

"Why nothing Gabriel, merely talking is all," said Mr. L.

"You know the rules," replied Gabriel sternly.

"I wouldn't *think* to break the rules," said Mr. L.

"Then why have you brought him to the Wayward Forest? Why do you hold him against his will?" asked Gabriel sharply.

"I do no such thing. He's free to go any time he likes."

"Liar!" Gabriel raged and his blue light flared out wildly all around him, causing Mr. L to take several steps back—"Trickster!"

"No need for name calling is there?"

"You have been called much worse—Loki."

The name stuck hard in Thomas' mind.

"Brother, you wound me," intoned Loki, holding his hands to his chest.

"You are no brother of mine—you are an abomination!" roared Gabriel, and the world shook.

Loki grinned widely, obviously deriving pleasure from Gabriel's growing anger.

"You know all Stars fall, only a matter of time..." replied Loki grinning dangerously.

"Enough!" roared Gabriel with an air of finality, "Send him back!"

Loki sighed. "Very well, I suppose I can wait a tad longer. But be advised that when it begins the boundaries will no longer be observed...and next time we meet," he smiled widely, "for the very first time in your long existence you will truly know pain."

Gabriel stood firm in his place, unmoved by Loki's threats, and replied with absolute resolve, "Send him back—now!"

Loki frowned. "I've grown bored of this little game anyway," and he turned and looked at Thomas still being held tightly in Cadmus' frozen arms.

"Tragically, it appears we must now part company. I'll miss you Thomas and I'm sure you'll miss me. But alas this is not the end. We'll be seeing one another again sooner than you think. And when we do— " a grin came upon his face, larger and more evil than before "—I'm going to eat your soul!" his maniacal laughter filled everything and suddenly the entire scene, the forest, the black cloaked figures, Gabriel, even Loki himself began to blur, and then the entire scene faded out of view.

It was as if someone hit the rewind button and time reversed. Thomas was hurled back at lightning speed. His body sailed upwards through a dark airy abyss and up and up he went at an unfathomable speed…

With a gasp of air, as if coming up from an extended period underwater, he emerged.

Thomas rolled to a hurtling stop, and a door behind him shut. He heard footsteps coming towards him. A hand touched his shoulder. He braced for the worst.

"What took you so long?" said a familiar voice.

Thomas looked up.

"Oh. You don't look so good," said Jack.

The Library

"WHAT HAPPENED TO you?" Jack asked Thomas in a tone that was a bit more curious than concerned.

"I..." Thomas began and then abruptly stopped. He'd no clue how to explain what had just happened to him, and still quite shocked himself. "Wait, where were you?" he asked instead.

"I was in the room with all sculptures," said Jack, "Where were you?"

He has no idea what I've just been through? Thomas realized. *He wasn't in the forest. He wasn't even there.* And he began to wonder if perhaps he really had fallen and banged his head. But then he looked down and saw a small scar on his wrist. *Maybe it really did happen.*

"Are you going to tell me or not?" said Jack, growing impatient.

"I took a wrong turn and...fell and banged my head." Thomas conceded at last, not knowing what else to say.

Jack looked at him for a moment in utter disbelief. "You—fell—again?" and he burst out laughing.

"Are you finished?" said Thomas angrily, made even more so by the fact that this time at least it wasn't actually true.

"I'll be finished when you're done falling—which at this rate will be never!" said Jack laughing uproariously.

Thomas was about to say something in retort, but was diverted when he saw just where they were standing. An enormous room filled with rows upon endless rows of giant bookcases stacked full with books.

"We're in a library," said Thomas, in awe of the sheer scale of the place, not to mention the seemingly endless amount of books.

"Bit of a bookworm," said Jack.

"Or a collector," suggested Thomas, noting the time it would take to read even a single shelf's worth of books, let alone all of them.

"Let's get out of here. I'm bored just looking at them all," said Jack.

Thomas laughed. His brother was never much of a reader. In fact, he found the entire act tiresome. "Let them write a book about me, then maybe I'll read it," he was fond of saying.

They made their way through the rows of books, zigzagging around the massive shelves. They soon discovered, however, that no matter how far they traveled there was always another shelf, always another row to go down. And to make matters worse the rows would split into two or three different rows forcing them into choosing which way to go. It became apparent that they were lost in a giant maze.

"There has to be a way out of here!" yelled Jack frustratingly after they'd weaved in and out of rows for what seemed like an hour. "Let's just go back the way we came."

"No!" cried Thomas.

Jack shot him an odd glance.

"I mean, we've come this far already it would be silly to go back. Besides, I don't remember the way out do you?" said Thomas covering his tracks.

Jack paused, and then shook his head. "No," he admitted, "Let's keep going," and so onwards they journeyed through the never ending rows, searching for the elusive way out.

The search continued to prove fruitless, and after a long while of walking Thomas' began to tire. But knowing Jack they wouldn't stop unless he said something.

"Can we take a short break?" Thomas asked finally.

At first, Jack looked as if he were going to refuse the request. But then shrugged and said, "Might as well, not like we're going anywhere fast."

Thomas decided to peruse a book while he rested. It would keep him from dwelling on what happened earlier, something he wasn't prepared to confront just yet. So he grabbed one from a nearby shelf and sat down.

The book was thick and weighty. The black leather bound cover appeared old but in good condition. Thomas opened to the first page.

"The Red Plague," read the heading in bold lettering and directly beneath in smaller print, "Volume 10999."

The book turned out to be nothing more than a long list of names with corresponding dates.

It's a record book, thought Thomas. A record of what though he wasn't sure. But from the looks, it appeared to be either births or deaths; likely the latter given the subject matter.

After putting the book back in its place, he went over to the adjacent shelf and grabbed another. Just as thick and old as the last, but with a red cover.

"The Purge: Volume 336" read the heading and like the other was nothing more than a long list of names with corresponding dates.

"I think we're in the reference section," said Thomas.

"What?" replied Jack, who was pacing restlessly back and forth like a caged animal.

"You know, where you do research and look things up," said Thomas, remembering several school projects in which the section had come in handy.

"Unless it can tell us the way out of here, I don't care," said Jack.

"No, I don't think so." Thomas admitted.

"Then these books are worthless like all the rest," and Jack walked over and snatched the book from Thomas' hand.

"Hey!"

Jack opened the book and proceeded to tear out a handful of pages, which he ripped in half and threw, along with the mangled book, onto the ground.

Thomas' was horrified. "What'd you do that for!"

Jack shrugged. "No one will know the difference."

"You've ripped out at least twenty pages—you don't think someone will notice!"

"There are thousands of books here! What does one matter?"

"It—it—just does!"

"Not to me."

"Just wait till Uncle finds out."

"He won't find out…unless you tell him. But you're not going to tell him, are you?" said Jack giving Thomas a menacing glare that promised excruciating pain.

Thomas put his head down. "No," he mumbled. "But you still shouldn't have done it."

"Why? What's going to—" Jack stopped abruptly.

The torn out pages were moving about, joining with one another like a puzzle being put back together. Until the papers were once again whole, and one by one flew back inside the book.

Thomas and Jack stared at one another, both thinking the very same thing—*Magic*.

Jack promptly grabbed another book from the shelf and ripped out even more pages and threw them to the ground.

After a few moments, the pages once again put themselves back together and returned to the book.

Jack then grabbed several books and ripped pages from all of them, which he tore into far smaller pieces and threw into one heaping pile.

Soon the pieces began whirling around their heads floating and falling like flakes of papered snow. The paper danced in and out trying desperately to find its partner, and amidst it all they stood like figures in a snow globe.

But in the midst of their fun, suddenly something went terribly wrong. A strong force pulled the boys towards one another. Then one of each of their arms locked tight against one of the other's, joining as if just another piece of paper striving to become whole.

"I can't move!" cried Thomas in horror, his left arm fastened to Jack's right.

"Push away from me!" Jack ordered, taking control.

"What?"

"Do it!"

Jack pushed out in one direction and Thomas the other. Their arms were like elastic and the more they pushed the further they stretched. Thomas shrieked at the sight of his own arm distorting into his brother's, while Jack continued forcing his way outward stretching their symbiotic arms to obscene lengths.

"Keep going!" commanded Jack.

"I can't feel my arm anymore!" cried Thomas.

"Just keep going!" shouted Jack continuing to relentlessly force his own side as their conjoined arms became the rope in a twisted game of tug of war.

"It's not working!" yelled Thomas, his eyes bulging from the strain.

"Don't stop!" responded Jack, tugging hard as he could.

The pages completed their reformation and returned to their respective books. Except for one, which remained opened.

The remaining book began pulling them into it. Jack's body lifted off the ground, and then Thomas' did as well. But as it did, Thomas was able to grab hold of the edge of a shelf with his right hand.

"Don't you dare let go!" shouted Jack, his face flapping nauseatingly in the intense current as he dangled in the air.

The strain of holding onto the shelf was immense. But Thomas steadied his focus and held fast, digging his nails into the wood. He had to hold. There was no other choice. *I won't let go*!

But despite all his willpower, the physical exertion proved too great and Thomas was down to only two remaining fingers, threatening to give out at any moment. Soon they'd be sucked into the book.

It was then, however, that Thomas saw a figure come straight out of one of the nearby shelves: a middle aged bespectacled brown haired woman wearing flowing white robes. She had a spectral quality and appeared to float in the air. Thomas watched in astonishment as she floated over and shut the book.

Thomas and Jack fell separately onto the floor, no longer attached and exhibiting no signs that they ever were.

"Let's get out of here!" yelled Jack, and began running full speed down the hall. Thomas paused to look for the woman who had saved their lives, but she was gone. He took off after his brother.

They ran through the meandering rows, quickly putting distance between themselves and the voracious book.

They kept running until finally Thomas stopped abruptly, his lungs burning a hole through his chest. "I...I can't run anymore," he gasped.

Jack stopped as well, though unlike Thomas wasn't even breathing hard. "I guess we're far enough."

They'd entered a noticeably darker and less maintained section of the library. Cobwebs spread copiously throughout and a sense of forgetfulness clung to the books which lay jumbled upon their shelves.

Thomas, still catching his breath, collapsed to the floor thoroughly exhausted.

"What happened back there?" asked Jack taking a seat as well, "I thought we were going to get sucked into the book, and then it just closed."

"The woman saved us," said Thomas breathlessly.

"What woman?"

"You didn't see her?"

"No."

But for once Jack didn't simply dismiss Thomas as delusional. "What'd she look like?" he asked.

"She was wearing all white…and it was almost like she was…" Thomas paused.

"Like what?" Jack prodded.

"A ghost."

Jack hesitated only momentarily, and then shrugged. "Wouldn't surprise me."

"It—it wouldn't?" replied Thomas incredulously.

"There are witches and vampires and werewolves here, why not ghosts," said Jack.

Do I tell him about what happened in the forest? Thomas wondered, *if there was any time Jack would believe me it would be now….Ok, I'll tell him*, he decided.

But just as he opened his mouth to do so he heard a noise.

"What's that?"

"What's what?" asked Jack.

"I heard a noise," whispered Thomas, his head on a swivel.

"I didn't hear anything. Now you're just being paranoid," said Jack.

"Maybe your right," said Thomas, beginning to relax. *Maybe I am paranoid.* Of course ghosts and man-eating books will do that to a person.

Then suddenly there came what sounded like a loud growl.

They looked at each other and at the same time cried—"Run!"

As thoroughly exhausted as Thomas was his adrenaline kicked into gear and he gained a second wind inspired by fear. They ran through rows of books at a speed they'd be hard pressed to duplicate again. And for good reason, for something very large was most definitely hot on their tails and making up ground by leaps and bounds. A low deep growl followed the thunderous footsteps like a shadow, and both grew louder by the second.

They turned the corner to yet another row and suddenly Thomas' heart sank. It was a dead-end: a vertical wall of books sealing the row off.

"This is so not happening!" Thomas yelled out, feeling desperately around the solid wall of books for an opening.

The footsteps stopped. The creature stood in the darkness only several feet away. They backed up until their backs hit the wall. The creature stalked slowly from out of the darkness and for the first time they saw it.

An enormous dog, bigger than any they'd ever seen before, with thick dark blue hair and a massive head. It gave a vicious growl that sent shudders down their spines. Its huge sharp teeth were bared and saliva dripped menacingly from its jowls.

"Gaaaooood doggy," said Thomas, trying to pacify the beast. Which didn't work in the least, as the dog let loose an earth-shaking bark, causing books to fall from their shelves.

Jack stared back unflinchingly into the dog's dark eyes. "If you want this meal, you're going to have to earn it," he said defiantly, challenging the beast to a fight.

As the dog stalked towards them like a predator about to consume its long awaited prey, the boys each prepared in their own way: Jack with a perverse sense of anticipation for the fight to come, while Thomas prayed for another miracle, another saving grace. But three in one day, he wondered if he was just being greedy. And then, to his surprise, one came.

A voice called out "Down Achilles!" and everything ceased. The dog so terrifying only moments before, sat obediently with its tongue hanging out and its tail wagging, looking no more threatening than a puppy. In fact, Thomas felt the sudden urge to go over and pet its massive head.

Then from out of the darkness emerged their Uncle. His gray eyes fixated upon his nephews.

"What are you doing in my library?"

The First Blood

LOKI STRODE DOWN the long bridge towards the entrance to the mountainous Red Dome in the heart of the great vampire city of Shadaman. Sacred to the vampires, inside the Dome the seven oldest of their kind were entombed. Those known as the Eternals.

The Dome was utterly massive, indeed in all the six lands of Tartarus only the Dark Pyramid loomed larger. It was a wonder. Taking almost an entire century to complete, it was forged from stone mined from the deepest depths of the Fire Mountains of Muspelheim. While blood from a thousand souls provided the mortar holding the stone in place.

Lining the long stone bridge leading to the Dome's arched entrance were torches burning with a blood red fire. The wood which produced the red flames came from the infamous Bleeding Trees indigenous to the Black Plains. A tree growing up out of the blood soaked soil of a great battle long ago. Loki remembered it well. *Ah, the memories*, he thought recalling fondly the many lives he'd ended that day. *Some of my finest work.*

Looming over the high crenulated towers of the city stood the sharp mountain peak resembling a fang known as Ragnarock. Upon which stood the burning spear, as it had ever since the day the Dragon King plunged it into his heart. And there the legendary weapon shall remain aflame until its master returns to reclaim it. A day Loki knew was not long in forthcoming.

It was night, as always in the realm of Nott, the Land of the Endless Night. Though a night where no Stars dared shine their face. For here their gaze could not penetrate, as powerful spells clouded the vision of even the most far-sighted amongst them. Nevertheless, whether they could see or not was irrelevant. They could not quell the impending tempest. Already their fallen brethren—whose light had gone dark—were awaking in the perpetual darkness of Erebus. Soon their chains would break and they'd roam the world once more.

The moon by contrast shone full above the Dome, nearly duplicating the shape. The moon was beloved by vampires, for in ways it was family.

Loki of course was no vampire. He was something...different. Vampires were merely his allies of the moment. They shared common interests and common enemies. They also served the same master. And vampires had their uses, even if they were relatively new beings, at least to Loki anyhow. But then to him most things were.

As Loki neared the entrance to the Dome, he encountered two giant albino vampires guarding it, each standing three times his height. Known as draugs, their intelligence was limited, but their physical prowess was virtually unmatched. They'd been instructed to allow Loki to pass. If not, they undoubtedly would've attacked; a fight which would've ended badly—for them.

Upon entering the Dome, Loki was greeted by the fountain of blood. An extraordinary piece of artwork sculpted from pure bone into two giant fangs. Blood poured down from the massive fountain into the pool below. Into which he submerged his hands—as required of all entering this holy place—and splashed the blood upon his face.

He then headed into the main chamber, a cavernous oval room with moonlight shining down through a hole at the center. Elaborate murals adorned the tiled walls depicting great vampire victories of the past.

The sarcophagi of the Eternals lay around the room. The six Chosen, progenitors of the noble houses, lined the edge of the room. While the sarcophagus of the First was displayed in the center directly beneath the moonlight. Next to which stood a figure dressed in dark robes holding a long black and gold staff and wearing a golden mask carved into the shape of a skull.

"Lord Demus," said Loki as he approached.

"Do you have it?" Lord Demus inquired. His voice cold and hollow as it echoed through the metal of the mask.

"Of course."

"Bring it here," ordered Lord Demus, extending his gauntleted hand. Into which Loki placed the vial of blood.

Lord Demus held up the vial and examined it in the moonlight. "Has it been tested?"

"A perfect match," said Loki.

"Did you encounter any resistance?" asked Lord Demus, continuing to examine the vial.

Loki grinned. "Nothing I couldn't handle."

Lord Demus traced his finger along the ornate markings of the stone sarcophagus of the First. "Soon the Dark King will rise...and all the Generals will awake...and the End shall begin..." and he removed the top from the vial.

"I'm bursting with anticipation," said Loki, giddy with excitement as he imagined all the lives he'd soon be ending.

Lord Demus poured several drops of blood from the vial through a hole on the side of the sarcophagus. "Awake again," and he lifted up his staff and began to chant in the Ancient Tongue.

"I'll leave you to it then," said Loki as he turned and left.

In the outskirts of the city amidst the charred black hills Loki found Cadmus waiting. His loyal companion was playing with a boulder, tossing it up into the air and catching it. Next to him stood another figure beside two huge monstrous horse like beasts with horns sticking out the side of their heads, and a nub of a horn in the middle. Their eyes glowed red and smoke shot forth from their nostrils. Known as birons, they had once been unicorns. But when their horn was cut off became entirely different beasts.

Cadmus grumbled as Loki approached.

"Yes Cadmus we're going to kill someone soon," replied Loki sounding nearly as impatient as his notoriously impatient friend. Even amongst ogres, Cadmus was especially eager.

Cadmus grumbled again.

"Complaining isn't going to help."

Cadmus shook his enormous hairy head like a small child.

"You know the rule, work before pleasure," said Loki. "Speaking of which, Commander Arnault is everything prepared for our little trip?" he inquired of the other figure.

"All is prepared Lord Loki," replied Commander Arnault, who cut a foppish figure with a haughty air to go along with a perfectly quaffed head of white hair. He wore a long red coat with gold trim and polished black boots.

"Splendid!" said Loki, and suddenly a wide grin crossed his face like a thoroughly delightful idea had just popped into his head.

"Could you come here for a moment Commander, I have something to tell you, something important...something secret." Loki whispered.

"What is it my Lord?" inquired Commander Arnault eagerly.

"Come close now, we can't risk being overheard. You never know who may be listening." Loki whispered cautiously, and the Commander leaned in close. Until his face was nearly touching the tip of Loki's protruding chin.

"That's better," replied Loki grinning wildly.

Suddenly a blade protruded from Loki's cane and he drove it into the core of his unsuspecting victim, relishing every moment as the blade drove deeper into the flesh, which he twisted to increase the pain, and his own pleasure.

Commander Arnault's face went lifeless. His limp body hit the ground and Loki stood over it wearing a look of utmost satisfaction.

Cadmus grunted angrily, interrupting Loki's euphoria.

"I know what I said!" Loki snapped, "But I see no reason why work and pleasure shouldn't be the same thing on occasion. Besides he was a traitor. It was only a matter of time before he betrayed us as well. Oh, don't give me that look," said Loki lowering the blade from his mouth.

Cadmus grunted even louder than before.

Loki sighed heavily. "Come, you'll have plenty to kill soon enough," and he hopped atop the biron. "To Everfall!"

The Great Books

Jack and Thomas looked at one another and then blurted out at once, "We got lost!"

Their Uncle raised an eyebrow. "Is that so?"

"This place is a maze!" said Jack, continuing to eye the large dog now sitting harmlessly with his giant tongue hanging out.

"I suppose it can be rather tricky. The question, however, is not what happened when you arrived, but how you came to *be* here?" said Uncle Hades, gazing deeply into his nephews' eyes as if searching them for answers.

"There was a door and—"

"It was open," said Jack interrupting his brother. "So we thought we were allowed to go inside."

Thomas nodded in confirmation. *Technically, he's right,* he thought, *though we were snooping around in the first place.*

Their Uncle looked at them for a long moment, and then replied, "It should not have been unlocked. This can be a dangerous place. A fact which you may have discovered. Nevertheless, I do not blame you."

"So…we're not in trouble?" ventured Thomas uncertainly.

"One cannot be faulted for mere curiosity. Though curiosity does have its consequences," said Uncle Hades. "Shall we depart? I imagine you've grown tired of my library."

That's for sure, thought Thomas, having been nearly killed on several occasions.

The boys followed their Uncle through the rows of books, who unlike them appeared to have no difficulty in deciphering the way. The great dog Achilles followed along obediently.

"This is your dog?" asked Thomas, petting the head of the now tamed beast.

Uncle Hades nodded. "Achilles has been with me for many years. You must excuse his earlier behavior. He did not know you. Though it appears now that all is forgiven."

"What are you doing down here?" asked Jack.

"Searching for a book," replied Uncle Hades.

"You certainly have enough of them," said Thomas, "Where did you get them all?"

"The collection was begun by a dwarf named Orisius, who was known as the Bookeeper for his obsession with books. He devoted his entire existence to accumulating them. I procured the collection and carried on his legacy."

"So you bought all these books?" said Jack, scarcely able to think of a bigger waste of money.

Uncle Hades nodded. "The collection was sold to me by one of the Bookeeper's heirs who did not share his ancestor's passion."

"It must have cost a fortune," said Thomas.

"For him, it was undoubtedly a fortune. Though for me a mere pittance compared to what I received in return. This library contains every kind of book imaginable. There are books from every realm, including the Banishment, which I have discovered to be some of the finest. There are enchanted books that cannot be destroyed—not by ripping, not by shredding, not even by fire." Thomas gave his brother a look. "There are even books here that are…alive."

"How can a book possibly be alive?" asked Thomas.

"Everything in magic is possible if one is willing to pay the price," said Uncle Hades. "In order to create a living book, the author must insert into it a part of their own spirit."

Upon hearing this, Thomas' mind turned instantly to the ghostly woman who saved them from being sucked into the book.

"Why would someone want to create a living book?" asked Jack, never caring much for books, living or otherwise.

"There are those who desire to persist after death, to leave their imprint upon this world and influence it long after they have perished. Many sorcerers have sought to continue on by creating a living book, and witches often create them as Grimoires so that their magical knowledge remains within their coven."

"So can you talk to the book?" asked Thomas trying to puzzle it out.

"Yes, the book contains its creator's consciousness. But rather than try and explain, allow me to show you…" and Uncle Hades grabbed a book from off a nearby shelf; as he did Thomas jumped back, eliciting a queer look from his Uncle.

"This book was created by an elven sorcerer called Elohim who belonged to a tribe of forest elves possessing an unusual kind of magic, a power over death. For that reason, they were known as the Deathless. Not wishing for others outside the tribe to know their secrets, they wrote nothing down and all their knowledge was passed by word of mouth. But something terrible happened to the tribe: they were beset by a mysterious plague causing them to all go mad, to literally lose their minds, and their knowledge along with it. Elohim was the strongest amongst them, and before the plague claimed his mind, in order to save the tribe's knowledge, he created a living book. This book. Known as the Book of the Deathless. Though it will only divulge its secrets to one of the tribe's own bloodline."

From within the binding of the book itself, Uncle Hades pulled forth a small dagger. He then took the dagger and pricked his finger. He allowed the blood to drip onto the book, which absorbed it all up.

Suddenly the book began to shake, and then…

"Greetings ancestor," the book spoke in an old resonant voice, "I am the consciousness of Elohim Arandock of the Deathless. What do you seek?"

"Tell me of the last days of the Deathless," requested Uncle Hades.

The pages flipped at a furious pace and then abruptly stopped and Elohim's voice began to speak:

> *"The last days of the Deathless came swiftly, without warning…the plague was a dark curse…where it came from we knew not…perhaps we brought it upon ourselves by our hubris, by our defiance of the laws of nature….It was incurable, and it drove us mad one after another, addling our minds, making us forget even our own names....Our powers were lost…our knowledge gone…and at long last Death had its revenge…"*

"Thank you Elohim. That's enough," said Uncle Hades and the voice ceased, the book closed, and Uncle Hades returned it to its place on the shelf.

"So...you're part elf?" asked Thomas.

"As are you both, for Elohim was your ancestor as well."

Discovering they had elven blood flowing through their veins may have been the single most incredible thing Thomas had heard to date, which was certainly saying something given the many incredible things he'd heard as of late. And it made him wonder just what other kind of ancestors he had.

"By now, the Great Races have all mixed and mingled to some degree. Being not nearly as forbidden as it once was, even amongst the royal families," explained Uncle Hades.

"Great Races?" said Jack.

"Man, Elves, Dwarves, Faeries, Naturerals, the Mer, and Centaurs compose the so-called seven Great Races. They are those that stayed loyal to the Author during the rebellion of Setus. In return for their loyalty, they were given dominion over the world," said Uncle Hades.

"What about the Stars?" asked Thomas suddenly.

Uncle Hades gave him a curious look. "When did you learn about the Stars?"

"Wordsworth was talking about them." Thomas managed hastily. He didn't know why but for some reason he didn't want to tell his Uncle about what happened in the forest. In fact, strangely enough, even when he thought about doing so his mind seemed to stop him, as if there were a mental block.

"Stars are very unique beings. Said to have been forged by the Author in the reflected light of the Source. They are at once a part of this world and beyond it. They dwell in the Celestial Gardens, in the World Beyond."

"What's the World Beyond?" asked Thomas.

"Composed of the spirit realms that reside in the Astral Planes, the World Beyond is a mysterious place. As the tale goes, when the Author finished writing the story of the world he fell into a deep slumber, and in his dreams another world was formed—the World Beyond. A world that even the Author does not fully understand for it was not a conscious creation. It is a world with its own rules. What little we do know of it comes from the Great Books."

"What are the Great Books?" asked Thomas anxiously, scarcely able to keep up with all the new information.

"The Author gave a Great Book to each of the Great Races after the First War. They were meant to guide the Great Races in their rule of the world. Each Great Book was written specifically for the Race to which it was intended, in a language they could understand. Unfortunately, the Great Books have led to as much ill as good in this world. They contain invaluable knowledge, but are contradictory in many respects and not always clear upon their meaning, leaving much to interpretation. That being said, they are all perfectly clear on one thing: the Ending. An apocalyptic war between the forces of good and evil to decide once and for all which shall rule."

"Good is supposed to win though right?" said Thomas, for in nearly every story he'd ever read that had been the case.

"None know for certain," said Uncle Hades, "The outcome is unclear."

"But good always wins!" Thomas protested.

"If only that were true. But I'm afraid evil has won more than its fair share in this world. And evil has its Great Book as well."

"Well then how can they be so certain it will even occur?" asked Thomas.

"Because it must," said Uncle Hades, leaving it at that.

Shortly thereafter they came to a door. Through the door they entered into another part of the castle. One which appeared older than the rest of the castle, almost primeval in comparison. Lit by torches, it was crude and cave-like with no portraits or other adornments on the crumbling walls—just rock and shadows and several severely rusted iron doors.

"This is the eastern wing. The oldest part of the castle," said their Uncle, "It was part of the original castle which I expanded upon. Come, I have something to show you."

He walked up to one of the oldest looking doors with the symbol of a tree carved at the top. He pulled out a thick brass ring holding keys of all different shapes and sizes. He took one appearing as old as the door itself and put it into the lock. The door opened with a pronounced groan as if awaking from a long slumber. Like the door Jack opened earlier, darkness and cold greeted them.

"Stay, Achilles," commanded Uncle Hades, and the giant dog obeyed; though appeared none too happy about being left behind.

"Sorry." Thomas whispered to Achilles giving him a pet upon his massive head.

"After you," said Uncle Hades.

Without hesitation, Jack walked into the darkness and disappeared.

"Now you Thomas."

After his last experience, Thomas was understandably reluctant about going through the door. *This feels eerily familiar*, he thought peering out into the cold darkness.

"Nothing to fear," his Uncle assured him.

Thomas took a deep breath, braced himself for what he was about to face, and followed his brother through the doorway....

The Cave

THOMAS AND JACK found themselves someplace else completely. And what a strange place it was. It was like they'd entered a dream, as all around them huge trees floated about in white space with glowing yellow orbs growing off of them. They stood upon a pathway of pure bright light that wound through the floating forest.

"Where'd the castle go?" asked Jack, looking around as if it were merely hiding.

"We are far from the castle," replied Uncle Hades.

"Where are we? What is this place?" Jack demanded to know.

"We are in what the Dream Kings once called the Dreamtime, or simply the Dreaming. It is an extremely old place. So old some claim it existed before the world was even created. Some claim it is where the Author wrote the story of the world. This particular section is known as the Orchard."

"How did we get here?" asked Thomas.

"Some of the doors at Ravenstead provide passage from one room to another...while others lead to entirely different places. The reason opening doors can be so dangerous—you never know where you might end up," said Uncle Hades.

Now you tell me, thought Thomas.

"How do we get back?" asked Jack, noting the fact that the door had vanished.

"The same way we arrived," said Uncle Hades, "The door will return when it is summoned. It is a doorway of Janus."

"How do they work?" asked Jack, his curiosity fully peaked.

"Very powerful magic," said Uncle Hades, "They were created by the Dream King Janus so that he and his siblings could move around the world. He created these passageways all throughout the world. But the doors do not go everywhere. Few come to this place for example. Ravenstead was originally built by Janus himself, and there is no other place from which one can travel to so many others."

"Can a single door go to several different places at once?" asked Jack, "Or does each door only go to one place."

"Most of Janus' doors go to only one place, and by way of that same door you may return from where you came, for the door swings open on both sides."

"You said *most*," noted Jack, ever the keen observer.

"There are skeleton doors, you may call them, which can go nearly anywhere. The opener need only specify the place. Janus constructed very few of these doorways, and for good reason, as they have proven extremely dangerous in the wrong hands. They were utilized by the Dark Prince to frightening effect during the Great War."

"Can anyone go through them?" asked Jack.

Their Uncle shook his head. "Every door requires a key."

"Are there skeleton keys?" asked Jack.

"There are," said Uncle Hades, "But like skeleton doors they are exceedingly rare, perhaps even rarer."

"What are the orbs growing on the trees?" asked Thomas as they walked along the winding path of light.

"Choices," said Uncle Hades.

"Choices?" echoed Jack.

"Not ordinary choices, of the mundane sort we engage in daily which come and go without any real consequence. These are life changing choices...world changing even. Each has the power to set into motion a sequence of events, for within each of these choices lie the seeds of countless others."

"Whose choices are they?" asked Jack.

"They belong to whomever they are meant. They grow on the tree until they are ripe, fed by the maturation of individual lives. Then at last when they are ready they fall to those to whom they are intended. They will come in many forms, even in dreams, and their impact will be profound."

"So it's like fate?" said Thomas, trying to grasp what seemed an exceedingly difficult concept.

"You could say that. Though fate only provides the door. We decide whether or not to walk through it. In the end, we make our own choices," said Uncle Hades.

As they walked through the Orchard along the winding path of light they saw many of the orbs falling from their trees, falling down into the white space. No doubt they'd soon be popping up in someone's head, changing the course of their life forever. When they came upon a tree unlike all the rest. It was completely rotted and held dark orbs upon its withered branches.

"What's with that tree?" inquired Thomas.

Uncle Hades paused. "That tree," he began at last, "is one of the Lord of Nightmares' most devious plots. Setus planted in the Orchard a tree of his own, a tree of dark thoughts, plucked from his twisted mind. The choices from this tree have turned many souls dark."

In a way it reminded Thomas of the cottage they'd seen in the valley, the one with the tree half filled with apples and half barren, and it gave Thomas the same eerie feeling.

When they passed by the tree, the gem twitched in Jack's pocket. He hastily put his hand upon it, and it ceased.

They continued walking until they came to the end of the path. At the end, the boys discovered a giant oak tree the height of a skyscraper standing in the middle of a placid lake of crystal blue water, which, like everything else, was suspended in the middle of space. The tree had all kinds of creatures carved into its bark.

"This is the World Tree," said Uncle Hades, "The axis connecting all the realms of Mythil. Come, I want you to meet someone."

"Who?" asked Jack.

"An old friend," responded Uncle Hades, leaving it at that.

There was a small wooden boat docked at the water's edge.

"After you," Uncle Hades gestured towards the vessel. Once they were all inside, he began rowing towards the enormous tree. They headed for an opening at the tree's foot, which the boys soon discovered to be a cave.

The water continued on through the cave, which was lit by the flickering light of fire. Yet the source of the fire was never seen. As they journeyed deeper into the cave, they saw shadows upon the walls, of plants and animals and all other sorts of things. It was like a puppeteer were making the shapes on the wall. But like the fire, no source to be seen.

At last, Uncle Hades docked the boat upon a shore. When they disembarked they saw a light emanating from up ahead, just around a corner.

"Just there." Uncle Hades pointed towards the light.

Upon turning the corner they came to a nook. Inside was a rickety old wooden chair standing next to a wooden table where sat an extremely old man—by far the oldest person they'd ever seen. He made Wordsworth appear the very picture of youth and vigor in comparison. His obscenely long white beard hung upon the ground in front of him. Dressed in raggedy brown robes, he was writing on a wrinkled piece of parchment. On the table beside him stood a single candle, an inkwell, a dusty cup, and an old fashioned hourglass. The sand of which was nearing its end.

"He wasn't lying about the old part," whispered Jack.

"No kidding," Thomas whispered back. *If anyone could be said to be on death's door it was him.*

The old man abruptly stopped writing and looked up as they approached.

"Right on time," said the old man, his voice frail as his appearance.

"I brought—"

"I know," said the old man turning towards the boys, "I've been waiting a long time to meet you both."

Thomas heard something similar from Loki in the forest. *Why is everyone waiting to meet us*? he wondered and beginning to get the impression that there was a great deal they weren't being told.

"I'll leave you three to get acquainted," said Uncle Hades.

"I wish to speak with you briefly afterwards," said the old man.

Uncle Hades nodded, and then departed the room.

"Come now, I don't bite…I don't even have teeth left," said the old man gesturing for the boys to come close.

As they moved in closer the boys got a better look at him. He had a genial demeanor, and his brown eyes were kind and welcoming. But he appeared worn out, and the shabby rags he wore hung loosely from his withered body.

"Forgive me for not standing, but my bones are weary and growing ever wearier these days."

"Who are you?" asked Jack bluntly, beginning to interrogate the old man.

"Friends have called me Sam…while my enemies, well, they call me other things," he laughed, and for a brief moment regained some of the life he'd so clearly lost, "But for you Sam will do. Can't forget it—only three little letters!"

Of all the peculiar names they'd encountered as of late, Sam seemed all together mundane. Indeed it was hard to imagine one any less ostentatious Thomas thought.

"Why do you live in a cave?" questioned Jack sharply.

"It's peaceful, and I enjoy the solitude. But then, this is no ordinary cave."

"What's so special about it?" replied Jack, clearly unimpressed.

"This is the cave of Hypnos, one of the Dream Kings of old. This was once his dwelling place," said Sam. "He was a dreamer, and as peaceful as the sleep he loved."

He speaks of Hypnos the way a father would a child. Thomas observed.

"But alas Setus proved too strong for him…too strong for them all," said Sam shaking his head, "He knew their weaknesses well. For Hypnos it was the Moon Goddess Luna. He loved her, but she loved another….Setus promised Hypnos the Moon…and Hypnos believed him."

"What happened to him?" asked Thomas.

Sam paused for a long while. At last he responded, "If drank the waters of the stream flowing through this cave will make one forget….It's good sometimes to forget…"

On the table beside Sam Thomas noticed a cup.

"What are you writing?" inquired Thomas, noting the long piece of parchment in front of Sam.

Sam suddenly perked up again. "Ah, just scribbles. The useless musings of an old, tired, mind. In my youth I was quite prolific. I could write for days on end, and create such…such wonderful things," he laughed. "Makes one wonder where the inspiration comes from," he mused. "Now though my mind has gone stale, and like Hypnos I am simply a dreamer. But then, in the end, all writers are just dreamers I suppose."

"I want to be a writer one day," volunteered Thomas.

"A noble calling. To create something from nothing, to bring forth into existence what has never existed, nothing is more joyous...or more painful… " and Sam took a long drink from the cup.

"Why did you want to talk with us?" snapped Jack, growing impatient. "And how do you know who we are?"

"I know a great many things. That is my curse: to know too much. Though, it is also a curse to know too little. I wonder, do you even know who you are?" asked Sam.

"I'm Prince Jack Darren!" declared Jack proudly.

Sam laughed. "That is a name, nothing more. Names come and go, and one may put them on and slip them off as easily as clothes. A name does not make one who they are—especially not one bestowed by another."

"So who are we then?" asked Thomas, finding as of late that perhaps he didn't know himself as well as he thought.

"That is something for *you* to figure out," said Sam, "Our birth does not define us, nor our parents, only we decide who we ultimately become. In the end, we are all either the writers of our own tale or characters in another's… and if you don't decide who you are, someone will decide for you."

Thomas and Jack looked at one another.

"But enough philosophizing, I have something for you both," and from out of a nearby box Sam produced two dusty rolled up parchments with a red wax seal, "Here," he said handing one to each.

"What's this?" asked Jack.

"It's a rolled up piece of parchment," said Sam, stating the obvious.

Jack tried unfurling his, but discovered that he couldn't. "I can't…it won't open."

"The seal will not break until the appropriate time." Sam informed him.

"When will that be?" asked Thomas, unable to unroll his either.

"I suppose you'll just have to wait and see," said Sam, "For everything there is a time…or is it a season. I can't recall."

"What does it say?" demanded Jack, never one for waiting.

"You must learn patience Jack. In my youth, I was like you, always rushing headfirst into things. But I discovered that when we rush we miss so much. For the destination is not nearly as valuable as the journey…and the lessons learned from the road… " and once again Sam's voice drifted off and his mind along with it.

"Sam?" said Thomas finally.

Sam returned his attention to them. "I apologize, but I am tired now and require rest. Please send your Uncle back in would you," said Sam, "Goodbye... until we meet again…"

"Nice meeting you," said Thomas.

Sam nodded, and then returned to his 'scribbles.'

The boys found their Uncle waiting just outside.

"Your turn," said Jack.

Uncle Hades nodded, and then went in to see Sam.

A few minutes later he returned wearing an inscrutable look upon his face.

"What did he say to you?" asked Jack, adding, "Old man has clearly lost his marbles."

"Perhaps…or perhaps he's the only sane one left," said Uncle Hades.

Thomas noticed then that Uncle Hades' right hand was trembling slightly. But he quickly took control of it with his left hand, and it ceased.

"Time to leave this place," declared Uncle Hades, and suddenly the door appeared from out of thin air. He put the key inside and opened it.

Upon returning to the eastern wing of the castle, they were greeted by Achilles wagging his massive tail. Thomas began petting him.

Uncle Hades led them to a winding staircase at the end of the hall. They made their way down it, until they came at last to another door. They went through the door and emerged back near the sitting room with the green fire. As they did, Wordsworth was just returning from his errands.

"M-my Lord," cried a startled Wordsworth nearly dropping the items in his hands, "W-what are you doing back so soon?"

"It's alright," said Uncle Hades, "I ran into the Princes in the library. It was quite fortuitous."

"But how—they couldn't…"

"The door was unlocked."

"But all the doors were—"

"Apparently, we'll have to check again. But I think they have learned their lesson about going through doors when they do not know what awaits them on the other side," said Uncle Hades.

Just then the clock rang out.

"Time for dinner. Shall we?" said Uncle Hades.

An Offer

After dinner Jack and Thomas returned to their respective rooms. The dinner had been a quiet and uneventful one. Their Uncle hadn't said much, and seemed consumed by the weight of his own thoughts. Wordsworth appeared preoccupied as well.

Upon returning to his room, Jack removed the black gem from his pocket and began examining it. He was certain the door opening today had something to do with it.

"What secret are you hiding?" he asked the gem, as if it would answer back.

But then suddenly it did.

Like the night prior the gem began to shake, and then again abruptly stopped and the girl appeared once more where the iris had been.

Jack stared at her, and she stared back at him.

"Who are you?" he demanded to know.

But she only continued staring silently back at him from inside the gem.

"Answer me!" he raged.

"You can have her Jack, along with everything you've ever desired. If only you wish it," a distinctly male voice whispered in reply.

Jack jumped up, and though at first startled, quickly recovered and scanned the room for the intruder. He saw no one.

Must be hiding, he thought, and being a master from his days of playing the Hunt of finding those not wishing to be found, decided to coax his new friend from whatever dark place he lurked. "Who are you?" he asked calmly.

"The one who can give you your heart's every desire," replied the shadowy voice, "The one holding the keys to unlock all that you seek."

"You haven't answered my question," said Jack impatiently, "Who—are—you?"

"I have given kings and queens riches beyond their wildest dreams, made men into gods and gods into men...I have destroyed mountains with a touch... quieted the raging oceans with a whisper...I am knowledge. I am glory. I am *power*. And now I come to you Jack, and offer the world," said the voice.

"The world?" replied Jack with a sardonic laugh, "Which one?"

"Which would you like?" the voice replied.

"All of them," said Jack.

"Then all shall you have."

Jack laughed. "You're going to give me everything I want and we've never even met before?"

"To the contrary, we have met many times," replied the voice, "In many different forms, in many different ages."

"I would remember someone offering me the world," said Jack.

"You do not wish to rule?" questioned the voice, "To be a king of kings?"

Jack shrugged. "Who doesn't? But what makes you think I need your help, or even want it. You're too scared to even show your face and hide in the shadows like a coward."

"I do not hide from you," said the voice, "I am right in front of your eyes."

"Where?" replied Jack, his eyes darting around the room.

"Allow me to show you..."

The shadows lying in the corners of the room began moving about. They crept down the walls and slid to the middle of the floor, where they gathered into a pile, which shifted about like clay being shaped and molded. Until it formed into a living breathing creature.

Dressed in a long sinewy black robe, the creature's face, at least half of it anyway, was that of an older man's with an exceedingly long black beard which appeared made of ash. His eye resembled a dying ember still smoldering in the socket. His skin was the color of gray suet and his hand was long and thin with nails severely overgrown. The other side of him could not be seen and stayed covered entirely in shadows.

"I am Jinn," the shadowy creature pronounced with a slight bow.

"What—are—you?" asked Jack as he stared at the strange figure who only moments before was shadows on the wall.

"What I am and what I am called are one in the same." Jinn answered, and along with his words black smoke emanated from his mouth.

"So what's a Jinn then?" asked Jack, still staring warily at the peculiar being before him.

"A facilitator of desires and a purveyor of dreams," said Jinn.

Jack raised his eyebrow. "And you're going to give me everything I want?"

"I am."

"Why?"

"Because your desire is the greatest," said Jinn.

"If you really have the power to do what you say, then why not just take it for yourself?" asked Jack.

"I only desire to fulfill the dreams of others," said Jinn, flashing a smoky grin.

"I don't believe you," replied Jack bluntly.

"Perhaps you need to see for yourself..."

Suddenly the room vanished and Jack was standing high atop a mountain cliff overlooking a vast expanse of earth and wealth. He could see far as the strongest telescope could gaze, and farther still. He could see everything—all the worlds and the worlds within worlds.

"All can be yours," said Jinn, "All the kingdoms of all the worlds."

Jack stared out at what lay before him, the great castles, the magnificent cities and massive structures, and all the innumerable creatures inhabiting them. "You're just going to give it all to me?" he asked uncertainly.

"And much more....Behold."

Standing beside Jack in the flesh and blood was the girl in the stone. She grasped his hand tightly and he felt her skin against his as real as anything could be. A crown sat atop her head and below for untold miles creatures of every kind bowed low before them pledging their undying fealty.

Jack saw then his mother and father standing there on the other side of him. Seeing them alive brought tears to his dark eyes. "Mom...Dad..."

"Son," they replied.

"Even the Kingdom of Death shall be yours to rule," said Jinn, "If you wish it to be."

"Yes," whispered Jack, unable to deny his heart's desire, "I do."

Jinn smiled. "I knew that you would. It's what you have always wanted…it's why you were born—to rule."

"What do I have to do?" asked Jack.

"Only choose."

"That's all," responded Jack skeptically.

"Yes."

But Jack knew that nothing was free. *Everything has a price.*

"Must not be worth much, if you're simply giving it away," said Jack, and his hand released from the girl's as he began walking away from the edge of the cliff.

"Of course, every choice comes with its costs," replied Jinn hastily.

"Then tell me the cost of this choice!" Jack demanded.

Jinn bowed his head. "Very well," and began then to tell Jack everything he needed to know…

Like the previous night, once Thomas was comfortably settled into bed, he opened the book Wordsworth had given him entitled ***Tales of Principle and Folly*** for his customary nightly reading. Curiously, he discovered that one of the pages was bookmarked, and turned to it.

On the page was a tale entitled ***The Tragedy of Dorian the Great***.

He began to read.

There once lived a very powerful wizard named Dorian Ignatius Aquarius, or Dorian the Great as he was known by the creatures of the day. The greatest sorcerer of his age, with such mastery over the magical arts that even the Stars sought his guidance.

But for all his vast power and knowledge Dorian remained unsatisfied, for he possessed an unquenchable thirst. What he desired more than anything in life was to slay the Beast of Death.

Dorian devoted his entire being to the study of Death. Stretching even the outermost limits of time and space to delve more deeply. One by one, he unraveled the mysteries and revealed the unknown. Until at long last, he discovered a solution, a way to control the Beast.

And he set a trap for Death.

In a mystical valley on a night of powerful magic, Dorian laid in a circle of ancient runes under a white oak tree beneath the light of a full moon. Then by potion induced his own dying to entice the Beast into coming…and come the Beast did.

As Death bore down upon him, preparing to feast upon his life-force, Dorian sprung his trap. With Death imprisoned inside the circle, Dorian cast a binding spell like none before it. The Beast fought for three days and nights. But at long last, Dorian triumphed, and they were bound together. Two entities sharing a single soul.

But Dorian had miscalculated and underestimated the Beast. For the Beast could not be controlled as Dorian thought. Nor could he free himself from the bond that he had sired. Thus was Dorian's tale a tragic one, for in the end he became that which he hated most….

A Spirited Breakfast

Once again Thomas found himself gazing into the mirror, bewildered by the reflection staring back at him. Again he swore he'd sprouted up another inch overnight. He also seemed to have developed some new muscles. *Maybe it's all the food I've been eating,* he thought admiring his growing physique.

He remembered then what his Uncle had said about changes occurring, and wondered if perhaps this was what he meant. Not that he was complaining, quite the opposite, he'd never looked so good in his life. Though, the way things were going, he was afraid he'd wake up one morning and find himself staring at someone else entirely. Someone he did not recognize.

Unlike the previous two mornings, when he came downstairs Wordsworth wasn't there to greet him with a cart full of pastries. He wondered how early he'd risen. Something difficult to gauge given the lack of sunlight. The great clock in the hall wasn't much help either, for there were so many different hands moving in so many different directions, along with numbers and strange symbols all whirling about, it was impossible to decipher anything. *Just what sort of clock is this*? he wondered.

He ventured into the sitting room to see if perhaps Jack was there like the previous morning. But found that he was not.

He'd resigned himself to sitting and waiting when he heard a noise coming from the hall. He discovered that it was coming from the dining room—the door of which was opened. He figured it was probably Wordsworth getting breakfast together, and decided to see if he could use a hand.

When he arrived in the dining hall—in stark contrast to dinnertime—the long table was devoid of food, and no one was inside. But the door at the end of the hall was slightly cracked open.

On account of the prior day's events, Thomas was understandably weary about going through unknown doors, discovering they could transport you to places far away from the castle. But the door was already opened, and unlike the ones yesterday, a warm welcoming light emanated from inside. So Thomas decided to venture in.

Thomas found himself standing in the most extraordinary kitchen. It was large and grand with marble walls and numerous gleaming pots and pans. But what made it so unusual was that while activities associated with cooking were indeed occurring, not a single cook was present. Pots were being stirred by floating spoons, spices sprinkled themselves, and knives sliced and diced unguided by hands!

Thomas stood there in utter amazement.

Then suddenly Thomas remembered the train. *I wonder if…maybe if I just…* He closed his eyes and concentrated on seeing the unseen.

When he opened his eyes there standing before him were a half dozen people, all possessing the same ethereal quality as the woman who had saved them in the library. A tall chef wearing a white chef's hat with a long thin mustache curled up at the ends barked out orders in a heavy French accent, which were instantly carried out by the others.

Having seen them must have in turn enabled them to see him, for suddenly they turned at once and everything ceased: the spoons stopped stirring, the knives ceased slicing, and the dishes went un-seasoned.

"Who—are—you!" the French chef barked, "And what are you doing in my kitchen!"

Thomas was utterly speechless, having no idea how to respond.

"Well!"

"I-I just wanted to…um…to tell you your food is delicious—best I've ever had." Thomas managed hastily.

The Chef paused, and then bellowed loudly—"Well of course it tis! Do you have any idea who I am!"

"S-sorry, no. I'm afraid I don't. I've only been here a few days."

This served not to pacify the ghostly chef one bit, and appeared on the brink of yet another explosion when mercifully Wordsworth entered the kitchen.

He paused momentarily and surveyed the scene before him. Then turning to Thomas said, "I see you've met the renowned Chef Jacque."

"Please to meet you," replied Thomas politely, "I'm Thomas."

"Wordsworth!" Chef Jacque yelled—as he seemed so fond of doing—"I cannot work with these distractions—strangers interrupting my masterpieces!"

"Of course, it's completely unacceptable. Come Prince Thomas let's leave the Chef to his work."

"Those were ghosts!" Thomas blurted out when they arrived back in the dining hall.

"And prickly ones at that," replied Wordsworth, and seeing Thomas' face added, "This castle is tended by ghosts. Except of course for me, that is."

A castle run by ghosts? Thomas was beginning to think that perhaps the House of Hades was closer to the myth in truth.

Wordsworth gestured for Thomas to sit down at the table. When he was seated Wordsworth brought over the cart of pastries. At the moment, however, Thomas possessed a far greater appetite for answers than food.

"Tell me about ghosts," said Thomas eagerly.

"Very well," said Wordsworth, and sat down in the adjacent chair and pulled out his pipe. After a few long puffs, he began speaking at length on the topic.

"Sometimes upon dying a person's soul does not go on to the spirit realms, sometimes it lingers upon the earthly planes. These are ghosts. They are like words that have not been fully erased on a page. They are in-between. Not quite here…and yet they remain. Of course without their physical presence their ability to interact is limited. Though magic can compensate for some of the deficiencies, as you have seen, and admittedly being transparent has advantages, walls for example. But theirs is largely an unenviable state, for they possess a lingering sadness, a perpetual feeling of being lost."

"Why do they stay behind?" asked Thomas.

"Each has their own reasons," said Wordsworth, "And like souls, ghosts come in many different forms. Most are quite harmless. But some are so thoroughly corrupted, so evil, that they become wraiths and fiends and other foul creatures that seek to possess the bodies of others," and then upon seeing Thomas' face added, "Don't worry the ghosts in the castle are all of a benign sort known as shades. They do exactly what they loved to do in life. Your Uncle brought them here and gave them purpose again."

Thomas decided then to tell Wordsworth about the woman in the library.

"...she saved us..."

"Ah yes, Ms. Dickinson," said Wordsworth "The castle's librarian."

Thomas committed the name to memory and promised to thank her for what she had done. "What happened to her? Why did she stay behind?"

"That I do not know," said Wordsworth, "For each ghost there is a story... some will tell their tale, most will not."

"Why?"

"Because to a ghost nothing is more personal, or closely guarded. The reason it's so difficult to get them to move on, for without knowing what caused them to stay behind in the first place you cannot help them to depart."

"On the train, there were ghosts there too," said Thomas.

Wordsworth smiled. "I thought you couldn't see them."

"I saw them as we were getting off. But only for a moment. How come I couldn't see them at first?"

"Because you couldn't see past your eyes, which saw only the emptiness of the train, and in turn your mind could not conceive otherwise. But once you believed it was possible your magical eye was opened."

"Magical eye?"

"Some have called it the Third Eye, or the Infinite Eye. Not all possess it, and it requires years of training to use it properly. It allows one to see the world as it truly is. The fact that you were able to see the ghosts is testament to your magical potential. And contrary to what you told me earlier, you have done magic before: you have made the unseen appear."

Thomas was positively elated to discover that he had magical potential and that he'd even performed a magical act. *I actually did magic—I can do magic!*

"Where were they headed, the ghosts on the train?" Thomas asked.

"To the spirit realms of the World Beyond," said Wordsworth. "Beings called Valkyries transport them there."

"So the guy collecting tickets on the train—"

"Was a Valkyrie. One of the choosers of the dead," said Wordsworth, "The ticket each passenger carries is earned in life. For as they say, that which we sow in this world shall we reap in the next. Of course, we were just hitching a ride."

"You really know a lot about this stuff." Thomas observed.

"I've known a lot of death in my life," replied Wordsworth somberly.

"So have I," said Thomas, and for a long moment they sat together in silence.

Until Wordsworth smiled and said, "Come let's see what that meddlesome brother of yours is up to. No doubt getting into some form of trouble."

Thomas nodded. *Wordsworth was beginning to understand Jack.*

They discovered that Jack still hadn't come down from his room. *What's he doing up there*? Thomas wondered. His brother was never one to sleep long.

They made their way up to Jack's room and Thomas knocked on his door.

"Go away." Jack barked.

"Are you coming down?" asked Thomas.

There was a pause. "I'm sick," said Jack finally.

"Sick?" said Thomas. Jack never got sick, not once in his entire life.

"I have potions that can cure whatever ails you." Wordsworth offered.

"Leave me alone!"

Thomas walked away shaking his head. *He's getting stranger every day.*

Preperations

CATHERINE STROLLED DOWN the streets of Everfall admiring the multitude of decorations that had sprung up all over the town, and would continue growing up until the Festival began. Citizens displayed their festive cheer with elaborate arrangements as each attempted to outdo the other in an effort to claim the coveted prize. Mrs. Clause, a past winner, wanted desperately to claim victory again and had been working feverishly throughout the night. She'd sent Catherine out to pick up some last minute supplies to complete her masterpiece.

The streets were filled with an eclectic mix, as creatures from all over had come to join in Everfall's famous celebration. Some coming from as far away as the Lands of Light. A rarity here, as most dwelling in that part of the world dare not cross into the Underlands, unless they absolutely had to, or were merchants engaged in trade. This year, however, they appeared in greater numbers than usual. Easily spotted by their rosy complexions and distinctive golden glows, causing them to stand out like sore thumbs amidst the translucent locals. Having lived half her life in the Lands of Light, Catherine still possessed a tinge of her golden glow, faded as it was from years without the beaming sun, and rapidly replaced by the blue sparkle that came from being so close to the moon.

To her surprise, and dismay, she'd even seen Emissaries of Creationdom, or Wordspreaders as they were infamously known, walking about the town. Wearing their ubiquitous long red cloaks and white sash, and carrying, as always, the Book of Light. The book they claimed the first wizard Mosiah had given Aloysius to enlighten the world. They had declared it the new Great Book, meant to supersede all the others. To which, the wizards who ruled the Arch had dispatched Wordspreaders all over the world to convert nonbelievers.

But for all of the Arch's professed piety, Catherine had witnessed firsthand their extreme cruelty. Their methods were harsh and conversion often exacted through torture. Nor was tolerance one of their virtues. In Avalon, witches were burnt at the stake just as the Queen of Lies had once been. What the Arch didn't care to admit was that without witches the Queen of Lies never would've been caught in the first place. In those days witches and wizards worked together. Now witches were demonized, along with any others the Arch deemed to be practicing dark magic.

Despite their vow to bring enlightenment to the world, however, the Arch had long forsaken this realm. Claiming it so far from the Light—figuratively and literally—that those dwelling here were beyond saving. Though according to her Grandfather, the real reason they kept away from this place was fear, plain and simple. His Lordship couldn't stand them, and had warned them in no uncertain terms that their brand of proselytizing wasn't welcome in his realm. So to see them here now was a strange portent. Especially when all they supposedly eschewed was being fully celebrated.

The First Guard was out in force patrolling the streets. In this hectic time, with so many new and foreign faces abound, maintaining order was a daunting task. But through the years they had, for the most part, kept things relatively peaceful. Barring a few isolated incidents, mostly on the notorious Bacchus Street where the drinks flowed especially freely. But the Festival always brought dangers, owing to the strong transformative magic present.

Many Changelings began showing for the first time during the night of the Festival, in what was commonly known as the Awakening. For this reason, Changeling parents generally kept children Coming of Age far away from the town. But there was always a few unaware they carried Changeling blood, and would to their tremendous shock transform for the first time during the Festival. Even so, most Changelings were relatively harmless, transforming into only benign creatures. There were only a few really dangerous ones—werewolves the most notorious.

But Changelings weren't the only ones who had to worry about awakening hidden traits during the Festival. The Festival was also a time when young witches came into their full abilities, as the moon's transformative magic awoke latent talents. Some witches for example suddenly discovered they could speak with birds or beasts. Others that they had the eye of prophecy or could levitate. Catherine wondered what hidden talents she may soon discover.

Just then Catherine spotted Captain Allac standing on the corner, and went over to say hello to her friend.

"Morning Captain Allac," she greeted him cheerfully.

"Lady Catherine," he replied with a graceful bow.

Catherine always found the Captain's comportment to be impeccable. She noticed, however, that there was something not quite right with him today. She'd always possessed a sixth sense about these sorts of things.

"What's wrong?" she asked.

Captain Allac at first appeared unwilling to say, but then answered, "Commander Arnault has gone missing. Until he's found I'm in charge of the First Guard."

Catherine knew Commander Arnault to be an extremely pompous man, who along with leading the First Guard was also a member of Everfall's governing Council. He was thoroughly disliked by the witches for his blatant favoritism of the alchemist's guild.

"No one knows where he is?"

"He's not been seen or heard from in two whole nights," said Captain Allac displaying an uncharacteristically worrisome expression upon his usually sphinx-like face. "I've dispatched several Guardsmen to search for him. Though they are resources we can ill afford to lose at the moment."

"Do you think something happened to him?" asked Catherine.

"I cannot say. But there have been many strange occurrences as of late, even for Everfall."

Everfall was known for odd things, owing to its eclectic nature. It was a cauldron brewing with all sorts of strange ingredients, especially during the Festival. But this year had perhaps been stranger than usual she thought, recalling the Wordspreaders she saw. But her grandfather hadn't mentioned anything to her. *Though he was acting rather odd yesterday.*

"What sort of things?" she prodded.

"It's not your concern," replied Captain Allac brusquely.

Catherine shot him a disapproving glance.

Captain Allac sighed. "The Festival is always a dangerous time and we take extra precautions to keep out undesirable elements." Catherine knew the First Guard kept watch on everyone entering the town through the seeing stones known as the Eyes of Everfall. There were other defenses as well, many of which the witches had helped design. "But lately our defenses have not been working as they should, and the Eyes have been losing their sight. I informed Commander Arnault of my concerns. But he would not hear of it. Now he has gone missing. There have also been many disturbing—"

Captain Allac was abruptly cut off by a loud commotion coming from behind them. They both turned to see what it was.

Miss Thisbe, appearing thoroughly crazed as usual, was accosting a well-dressed man, grabbing his expensive looking coat and screaming loudly, "Pyramus! Don't you remember me? It is I, Thisbe—your love!" while the man appeared completely horrified.

Captain Allac shook his head. "Not again," he muttered, "Excuse me Lady Catherine, I must attend to this."

Catherine felt bad for Miss Thisbe, who was endlessly searching for her long lost love. Not wanting to watch as Captain Allac and several other First Guardsmen restrained her, Catherine turned to walk away. But as she did, she ran straight into what felt like a brick wall and was nearly knocked over.

Before her stood two figures: one an ogre as big and hairy as a bear—the one she ran into—while the other had the sharpest features, and widest grin she'd ever laid eyes upon, along with the wildest fiery red hair. He carried a black cane with the golden head of a jackal.

"You should be more careful where you're walking my dear," said the one with the wild red hair, who seemed to laugh even as he spoke, "You could've been hurt. What a pity that would've been for one pretty as yourself...and so tenderly young," and his bearish companion emitted an animalistic groan.

"M-my apologies, I-I did not see you," she stammered.

"Don't fear little flower. I'll forgive you this. *If*, that is, you point me in the direction of Doctor Von Wolfenhauer," he replied with a toothy grin.

Catherine quickly pointed out in the direction of Wolfenhauer's store, only a short distance away from where they presently stood. "His store is just around the corner to the left."

"Splendid! Now run along little flower before you start to wilt. I feel the chill of winter approaching...and it's going to be a nasty one this year," and with that they headed off in the direction of the shop.

Who in the world were they? she wondered as she watched them go.

Dark Risings

Lord Demus strode purposely across the hard marble expanse, his boots reverberating sonorously as they assaulted the ground. Beneath the mask of solid gold carved elaborately into the shape of a skull was an expression of hardened resolve. And as he walked, he felt a rush of anticipation. The time was drawing near, a new chapter on the verge of beginning. One written by a dark hand.

This was the epicenter of the Kingdom of Darkness, the temple of Setus, the pyramid standing in the darkest heart of Tartarus. It was a place he'd entered many times before, yet the effect of it never lessened upon him. The proximity to such unfathomable power was both exhilarating and terrifying, and highly seductive. For directly beneath this pyramid his Master laid imprisoned—his influence seeping up through the cracks, filling the very air itself.

He made his way into the antechamber at the apex of the pyramid. In the center of which stood a great golden triangular table marked in ancient symbols of the Dark. Twelve unoccupied thrones sat around it. While at the triangle's pinnacle laid the thirteenth, a throne larger than the others.

Lord Demus traced his finger across the table admiring the elaborate markings with reverence. *Soon you'll be filled.*

He made his way across the room to where two gargantuan iron doors marked the entrance to the main chamber. Two black cloaked figures stood guard. Their faces were dark shadows. They had many names, and took many forms. They were known as Deceivers, Shadow Wanderers, and the Formless. Conceived in pure dark power, these were the high priests of the Dark, and they were frightful beings.

But Lord Demus held sway in the world of the Dark, and in the hierarchy was near the top; a position earned through unyielding loyalty and sacrifice. And as he strode towards the doors he was reminded of just how much he'd sacrificed in order to become a Shadow Lord.

The guards raised their heads in unison and stared back at him with dark formless faces. Fear gripped him as they peered into what remained of his soul. But one did not hesitate in this world.

"I am expected." Lord Demus declared tersely in a commanding tone.

"Yessss, Lord Demussss," they hissed in unison.

The doors opened and the guards stood aside.

Lord Demus stared at a long dark corridor before proceeding down its lengths. The corridor led into a large oval shaped chamber with huge glass mirrors covering its entirety. In the center of the room stood an iron kneeling platform with sharp spikes sticking up from it. Lord Demus walked to the platform and knelt down upon it, allowing the spikes to sink deeply into his scarred flesh.

"Master, your servant is here," he announced, "What is thy will?"

The room shook as the mirrors filled with an oozing black smoke. Then the smoke turned suddenly to flames and the fire grew thick and violent threatening to break through the glass and consume the entire room in a raging inferno.

Though only a reflection in the mirrors, the Master's arrival was a stirring experience. Even from within the depths of his prison his power was immense.

Lord Demus felt his Master's presence coiling around his mind, melding onto him, becoming one with his thoughts. Then the words came forth as if from his own mind, as if he were having a conversation with himself in his own voice.

"The Prophecies are coming to fulfillment…and the time of the Dark is nigh." Lord Demus felt his Master's anticipation rushing through his body. "Is the way prepared?"

"Everything is precisely as you ordered Master," replied Lord Demus, "All the pieces are moving into their appointed places, and the Generals are awaking."

Lord Demus smiled underneath his mask.

"Once the binding is completed, and the King reborn, the war shall begin…" and for a moment Lord Demus recalled his own rebirth in the darkness, reliving the immense pain as his old self was literally ripped apart and stripped away, and then replaced with the blinding clarity of new life and purpose.

"Master, what of …the other?" inquired Lord Demus, "What is to be done with him?"

There was a momentary pause. "He belongs to his brother."

"Yes, my lord."

"Now go forth and bring me my champion."

And then suddenly the fires vanished from the mirrors, and Lord Demus' mind was once again his own.

Lord Demus walked out of his Master's chamber filled with clarity and purpose.

An Earthy Visitor

JACK DIDN'T COME out of his room all day. This gave Thomas the opportunity to converse with Wordsworth at length about all manner of things. Wordsworth was a treasure trove of stories. He told tales about knights and dragons and wizards, about great battles and even greater heroes. Thomas loved every second, and suspected Wordsworth enjoyed telling the tales nearly as much as Thomas did listening to them

They ate dinner with Uncle Hades, who like the other night appeared drained. Until he consumed the potion, which restored him again. This time, however, it didn't restore him completely and afterwards still appeared quite weary. He left shortly after dinner to attend to some urgent affairs.

Thomas stayed up talking with Wordsworth a while longer and then eventually headed off to bed himself.

He discovered that once again he was in for another bumpy night, as the moment he attempted to shut his eyes the tree branch began rapping against his windowsill with such ferocity that any sleep was rendered impossible.

"That's it," he declared finally, at his absolute wit's end, "I can't take it anymore!" and he walked over to the window and opened it.

Suddenly the tree branch burst into the room, and Thomas backed away as it literally invaded his living space. He grabbed hold of the limbs and tried desperately to push them back. But the branch was too strong, and soon limbs had spread over half his room, with no signs of slowing.

Limbs grew out of other limbs and green leaves sprouted and formed all around him. Grass sprouted on the floor and flowers bloomed on his bed. It wasn't long before Thomas was standing in the middle of a full-blown forest.

A strong wind blew, and leaves fell from their branches like a storm in autumn. They formed into one large pile on the grass in front of him. Then abruptly the wind stopped, leaving the massive pile of leaves behind.

At first, the pile was still. But then the leaves began rustling about as if something was buried beneath them trying to get out. Until at last the rustling ceased, and then to Thomas' astonishment a woman emerged from the pile.

She had hair of green leaves, eyes like tiger lilies, and flowers of all kinds bloomed from the soil of her earthy brown skin. She walked towards Thomas, and he backed away so fast that he tripped over a twig and fell to the ground, which was thankfully covered with soft green grass.

"W-who are you?" stammered Thomas, scurrying back to his feet.

"Do not fear me child. I mean you no harm," the woman spoke in a warm nurturing tone, "I am a maiden of the earth, a servant to the Mother Herself, and it is on her behalf that I have come. I pray you take my words to heart, for time grows short."

"I-I will." Thomas promised, astounded by what was occurring.

"The Dark King will rise and claim his serpent bride. Upon their dark throne they shall plot the war to come. You are all that stands in the way of their ultimate victory. If you fall, all is lost. For the Evil Below will be freed when the hearts of the realms go dark."

"Wait—what? W-why me?" asked Thomas, scarcely able to conceive of a person more ill-suited for such a thing.

"Because you are the only one who can," replied the leaf woman.

"Well what if—what if I don't want to fight?" asked Thomas, never much of a fighter, to say the least.

"That is your right, as it is your choice to make. But know that as a result the world will descend into darkness, and the Evil Below will hold dominion over it. For though if you choose to fight the outcome is unknown. If you do not, the end is certain."

Thomas' head was spinning. *That's not really much of a choice at all,* he thought. "What do I have to do?" he asked, adding, "*If* I choose to."

"The enemy has begun preparing the way, and the realms are being corrupted as we speak. You must force them to fulfill their sacred oaths. The darkness will spread like a plague, and fear and greed and power and all that turns the mind to the Dark will be unleashed upon them. You must give them hope for the future. You must be the light in the darkness."

Thomas had no idea how to possibly accomplish such a thing. "How am I supposed to—I'm just me!" he protested.

"You have great strength inside you. The blood of the greatest heroes flows through your veins. Nor will you wage this war alone. You will have your allies, as the Dark King shall have his."

"Well, that's a good thing, I guess," said Thomas, glad to hear he'd have friends.

"But be forewarned: do not place your trust in appearances, for they will deceive you. Even in the light there are shadows," cautioned the leaf woman.

"I'll remember that," said Thomas, certain he'd never forget a single thing from this night so long as he lived.

"One final thing before I depart. No matter who your enemy may be, you cannot allow mercies, for none shall you receive. Your choice comes at the Festival of the Moon. Choose wisely…. "

Thomas awoke abruptly, and looked around the room. The forest was gone, and there were no signs that it had ever been there.

Was I…dreaming? he wondered. *Was that all just a dream*, and he quickly ran over to the window and looked out.

There was no sign of the tree branch. And when he looked down he saw that his window stood at such a height that no tree could've possibly grown to reach it. He shook his head, and returned to bed.

The Festival

THOMAS SAT UPON the edge of his bed thinking about the day ahead. It was the day of the Festival, and he had the distinct feeling that today was going to be important. Certainly everything he'd heard had made that clear, even if he wasn't sure whether the sources were all real. Nevertheless, he knew that today was going to be consequential. But to what end he knew not.

He'd prepared himself to expect the unexpected. But even he wasn't ready for how the day started. For when Thomas emerged from his room he found Jack sitting outside the door to his own. His brother appeared in a daze, staring vacantly out into space. He gave no recognition that he knew Thomas was even standing there.

"Jack," said Thomas attempting to get his brother's attention—"Jack!"

Finally his brother peered up at him.

"What are you doing?" asked Thomas, "Are you feeling okay?"

"What would you give to have everything you ever wanted?" asked Jack.

"What?"

Jack repeated the question with the same vacant expression.

"I-I don't know," said Thomas taken aback, "What are you talking about?"

"If you could have everything you've ever dreamed of, what price would you pay?"

"A lot, I guess," said Thomas, scratching his head in both the literal and figurative sense, "Why are you asking me this?"

Jack stood up and began pacing back and forth. As he did, Thomas noticed something different about him. Something Thomas had never seen before. *He almost looks...scared.*

"Would you give up a part of yourself?" asked Jack, continuing with his bizarre line of questioning.

"Like an arm or something?" asked Thomas, not taking his meaning.

"A part of who you are…as a person." Jack clarified.

"You mean like your soul?"

"Yes," said Jack. "Your soul."

"I'd have to say no. I mean nothing is more important than your soul right, so nothing could be of equal worth. It's not a fair trade," said Thomas logically.

"What if you could save millions of lives?" asked Jack, continuing to pace.

The question reminded Thomas of the story Wordsworth had told him about the woman Lilith who'd given up her soul in order to save the world from the banshees.

"I honestly don't know," said Thomas, unsure what this all had to do with.

Jack stopped suddenly and stared at Thomas with a wild intensity in his dark eyes. "What if you could get mom and dad back?"

Thomas paused, the question taking him completely off guard. "We can't," he said at last, "Their dead,"

"But what *if* there was a way?" said Jack with a strong hint of desperation.

"I…don't know." Thomas admitted, "Why are you asking me this?"

Jack appeared like he was going to say something further on the subject, but instead simply smiled and replied, "No reason. Let's get breakfast," and with that headed down the hallway.

Thomas stood there dumbfounded. *This is bizarre,* he thought shaking his head. And if this was how the day was beginning, he shuddered to think how it might end.

Wordsworth awaited them at the bottom of the stairs with the cart filled with assorted breakfast treats. Thomas ate hardily, quickly filling his belly. While Jack—and for perhaps the first time ever—was thoroughly uninterested in eating; a fact that did not go unnoticed.

"Are you not hungry Prince Jack?" Wordsworth inquired.

At first Jack didn't respond, if he heard the question at all.

"Is the food not to your liking?" prodded Wordsworth, "Do you want something else to eat my Prince? Are you still not feeling well?"

"I'm fine," replied Jack finally, though appearing like his mind was someplace else.

"You have slept late." Wordsworth informed them, "The Festival will begin shortly. So finish up and we'll head into town. Which at this hour would normally be a harrowing task. But now that you know about them we'll be taking full advantage of Janus' doors, saving an inordinate amount of time."

"Is it night?" asked Thomas, wondering how long they'd slept.

"Very nearly, the day is extremely brief, being the shortest of the year, while the night is the longest. The reason it's known as Moon's Day," explained Wordsworth.

After they'd finished eating, or at least Thomas did anyway, they followed Wordsworth through the third door on the right side corridor.

They entered into the confines of a house.

"Your Uncle keeps this place in town," Wordsworth informed them as they entered into the living room.

The house was elegant, with rich earthy tones dominating throughout. The furniture was old and of a far eastern design. There was a decent amount of dust and the place appeared little used. And like the castle, portraits hung on the walls. Thomas wondered what his Uncle used it for.

"Your Uncle will be addressing the town soon. If you go up to the top floor you'll find we have an excellent view," said Wordsworth.

The balcony on the second story overlooked the town square. It wasn't night just yet, nor could it properly be described as day. It was dusk, and the moon had yet to show its face.

The town appeared different than it had only a few days earlier. The decorations had multiplied to the point where hardly a structure lay unadorned. The white Tree of Everfall was lit with candles and encircled by torches burning with Dragon's Fire. Crowds lined the main thoroughfare and the whole town seemed crammed into it. Many were dressed in costumes, some quite elaborate.

It's like Halloween. Thomas observed. *Only the characters we dress up as are dressed up themselves*!

"The square is magically expanded to accommodate more spectators," said Wordsworth as they looked on.

I knew it appeared bigger, thought Thomas, marveling at all the wonders that magic could accomplish.

"Here," said Wordsworth handing each of them a silver mask.

"What's this?" asked Thomas taking the mask into his hands.

"Moonmasks," said Wordsworth, "They will display any creature you choose in the light of the moon. Your head will literally reflect whatever you concentrate upon."

"Cool," said Thomas, and began to slip the mask on.

"You do, of course, have to wait for the moon to actually show its face," said Wordsworth.

"Oh, right," said Thomas, hastily taking it off.

"Ah, here your Uncle comes now," said Wordsworth pointing to the platform set up in the middle of the square next to the white tree.

As Uncle Hades ascended the platform stairs everything grew suddenly silent. Even the wind seemed to cease blowing, as stillness washed over all.

"Welcome," Uncle Hades began in a voice sounding only several feet away yet not raised even a decibel over its usual whispery volume. "During the Moon Festival we honor the past and usher in the future. For Everfall it harkens back to our founding, when the first settlers traveled to this distant valley from faraway lands. They came from all over the world, and though from different backgrounds and different beliefs, in this valley they formed a common home, and started a new life together. Tonight we honor the moon which bestowed upon our founders a new life, and gives to all who come here a new beginning. For like the moon has many phases, so too does life…tonight many of you shall set out upon a new path…"

Thomas glanced over at his brother and saw him staring down intensely at their Uncle. It was an aggressive, unflinching stare. And suddenly he saw fire cross Jack's dark eyes and it caused Thomas to stumble backwards.

But when he looked again it was gone, and Jack turned and went back inside, causing Thomas to breathe a deep sigh of relief.

Uncle Hades paused and raised his arms; a gesture emulated by the surrounding masses.

"Now what?" asked Thomas, raising his arms as well.

"The invocation," said Wordsworth. "We invoke the Moon Goddess, and welcome her home as she once welcomed us. You see the moon shines in many different places all at the same time. But tonight she's here only for us."

Uncle Hades began speaking in another language and as he did the sky suddenly darkened. There was no rush of nightfall as before, instead it was like someone had simply dimmed the lights.

"What language is that?" Thomas asked as his Uncle spoke.

"The tongue of the Ancients," said Wordsworth, "The first language."

"What's he saying?"

"That's between him and the Moon Goddess," said Wordsworth.

The torches fluttered as the wind suddenly picked up. Everything rustled about and many of the decorations were blown clean off. Thomas could feel the approach of something extremely strong, and it caused the hair on his arms to stand straight up.

Finally, Uncle Hades stopped speaking and everyone looked up expectantly.

The moon at first very faint and far away drew steadily close, and closer and closer and closer still. Until it was so close that the town and the moon appeared on the verge of touching. Everything was bathed in an intense blue glow, and the crowd cheered wildly below.

"Wow," Thomas mouthed. He'd seen so many wonders since arriving in this new world, so many impossible sights, but this was perhaps the most wondrous of all. And though Thomas had felt magic before in the library, what he felt now was stronger by far.

"Let the Festival commence!" Uncle Hades pronounced to raucous cheers.

"Shall we go down and join the celebration?" asked Wordsworth, appearing anxious to do so himself.

Thomas nodded enthusiastically.

When they arrived on the street below, the festivities were in full swing. Music was playing and there was dancing in the streets. It was a frenzied atmosphere, and given the severe mismatch of heads to bodies, moonmasks were definitely out in full effect, producing a truly surreal scene to say the least.

Thomas put his mask on, closed his eyes, and concentrated on the image of a bulldog. When he opened his eyes, he gazed into a store window and saw that his head was indeed that of a white and brown bulldog, exactly as he'd pictured it. He howled with laughter.

"Hey Jack, look at—"

But Jack was nowhere to be seen.

"Jack—Jack! Oh come on, not again."

A Pirate's Life

WHILE WORDSWORTH AND Thomas were distracted, Jack slipped back into the house, and made his way to the door which transported them from the castle. He held the black gem up to the door, and as promised it opened.

Upon returning, he followed the black gem as it guided him through the corridors of the castle like a planchette on a weggie board.

As he came down the third corridor the black gem pulsated rapidly in his hand, like a heart beating. It grew stronger the further he went, pushing him towards something in the hallway, and the closer he came to it, the more powerful the beating became. By the time he reached the end of the hallway, where a single painting stood upon the wall, the gem was practically leaping out of his hand. Jack knew then he'd arrived at the right place.

The portrait was of a quintessential pirate. The tall man had a black patch over his left eye, large golden earrings, wore a long magnificent red coat and atop his head sat a black captain's hat. He had a strikingly long black beard, and a small ruby-hilted dagger adorned his thick brass buckled belt.

Jack stared up at the pirate, and suddenly the pirate stared back at him. Startled, Jack moved back a couple of steps.

"I've been waiting a very long time for you," said the raspy voice of the pirate with a smile revealing several gleaming gold teeth.

"Who are you?" Jack asked.

"Me?" laughed the pirate hardily, "But a simple adventurer and traveler of the Seven Seas," and he tipped his hat to Jack exposing his coarse black hair, "Captain Blackbeard at your service."

"And you've been waiting for me?" questioned Jack uncertainly.

"Aye," confirmed Captain Blackbeard, "And for far too long it seems."

"You're going to take me to where I need to go?" asked Jack, "To the Hill?"

Captain Blackbeard nodded. "I am. And if you do be ready, we may be on our way."

"No sense in waiting."

"No sense at all," said Captain Blackbeard, "Not when the sea calls!"

Captain Blackbeard's hand reached completely out of the painting to Jack. Who after a momentary pause grabbed ahold of it tightly, and was pulled into the painting....

Captain Blackbeard's ship, a mighty vessel known as the Queen Anne's Revenge, sailed upon the clear blue waters of a calm sea spanning as far as the eye could see. The Jolly Roger flapped in a warm ocean breeze. Like the sea below, the sky was a crystalline blue, and seagulls flew overhead basking in the golden rays of the sun.

The crew of the ship, a hardy group of pirates, swabbed the deck and manned the masts while singing bawdy songs of adventure and conquest. Captain Blackbeard stood beside Jack at the helm of the ship. He cut an intimidating figure. There was something dangerous, even unstable about him, and his face had an odd smoky quality as if on fire, causing him to appear almost demonic.

"What are you?" Jack asked as they overlooked the calm blue waters.

"Why, I told you, but a simple pirate's captain."

"That's not what I mean," replied Jack sharply.

"Ah," said Captain Blackbeard, taking his meaning, "You wish to know what I've become."

"Yes."

"Plainly said, I am a memory of the man I once was."

"Explain," ordered Jack.

Captain Blackbeard gave a slight bow. "I was once a man, a *great* man, a conqueror of the Seven Seas. But like all mortals Death came one day and took me. And for my worldly crimes, my soul was sentenced to eternal peril in the bowels of an icy prison. But my image, suiting Death's fancy, was kept and added to his collection. There my memory lived on upon his wall, while my soul resided in the dungeon. And though a man I do be on the outside, within this painted skin, I be hollow."

"But then one day a voice came to me with a proposition," said Captain Blackbeard his voice rising, "It said there was one who could save my soul, and make me whole again. I would know him by the black gem he carried. All I had to do was to wait upon my wall until he came, and then take him to the Hill." Captain Blackbeard smiled widely, "And here as promised you stand."

"So we're inside the painting?" queried Jack.

"No, we're far away from where the painting hangs. We be neither here nor there...but somewhere in between," said Captain Blackbeard, "One of the Otherworlds that dwell within."

"What about the crew?"

"Like me, soulless memories—hollow skin and lifeless bone."

"Like ghosts," said Jack.

"Ghosts be something else entirely," said Captain Blackbeard.

"So I'm to grant you your reward?"

"That do be what the voice promised," affirmed Captain Blackbeard.

"How'd you lose your eye?" asked Jack, abruptly turning the conversation's tide.

With great flourish, Captain Blackbeard pulled out the ruby hilted dagger lying in the thick of his belt. "This be the reason!"

"What's so special about it?" questioned Jack, for though a nice knife, certainly not worth losing an eye over.

"If you wish to hear its tale, then I do be pleased to tell it."

Jack nodded.

"I heard from reputable spies of a ship carrying a great treasure, including a very special item, an artifact of legend." Captain Blackbeard held up the knife, "This be no ordinary dagger. But the blade of Brutus that slayed that most famous Caesar.

"The Spanish King was transporting it along with some other booty to his castle. I and my crew commandeered the King's ship in the black of night, and slaughtered all aboard." Captain Blackbeard smiled at the reminiscence. "Knowing the King would stop at nothing to regain his treasure, I buried it deep on a secluded island. Eventually, after a grand chase, I was caught by his armada, and hauled off to the royal dungeon. I was questioned endlessly about the whereabouts of the legendary weapon—I gave up nothing, not a whisper of its location. For my silence they cut out my eye, that I may see the error of my ways." Blackbeard laughed bawdily, "Still I gave the bastards nothing! When at long last they tired of their sport, I was sentenced to death by hanging. Aye, but they knew not with whom they were dealing, and on the day of my execution I made a daring escape, breaking free and stealing one of their ships. I sailed until I reached my treasure island, and the knife that had cost me my eye. Ah, what a fine sight it was!" Captain Blackbeard gazed lovingly at his ruby-hilted child. "It stayed with me until the day I died, when I was made to walk the plank in a treacherous mutiny. Now it stays with me still, and shall forever, for we do be linked the dagger and I."

"You never regretted losing your eye?" said Jack.

"At first, perhaps. But once I held the dagger it bothered me not a wit. And I've discovered there are advantages to being one-eyed."

"Like what?" asked Jack, not seeing how it could be anything other than a handicap.

"They say that when one loses something important they gain something else. A person loses their sight and their hearing increases ten-fold; or, loses the ability to taste and suddenly can smell even the faintest scent. I lost but one eye, sacrificed only half a sense, yet gained so much more in all the rest. A bargain if I say so myself. And I'd make the same trade a thousand times over," said Captain Blackbeard.

"Why should you be rewarded with more by having less?" said Jack, having trouble with the concept.

"Because Fortune demands a sacrifice. The loss of something precious, a limb, a sense, or a great love especially wets its appetite. To obtain what you desire in life, anything of true worth, you must give up something of equal value." Captain Blackbeard belted out a hardy laugh, "Aye, Fortune be just like a woman in that respect. She'll take from you everything you possess, but grant you the one thing no one else can—herself."

Jack appreciated the Captain's wisdom, especially now that the time drew near, and soon he'd experience the fullest extent of Fortune's demand. But like the Captain knew the price to be paid was only a fraction of what he hoped to gain. *Yes*, he thought, *I understand now. To gain the world you really must give up your soul.*

Just then the skies darkened and the water below grew turbulent, as a storm approached.

Captain Blackbeard pulled a looking glass from his pocket and peered out into the burgeoning tempest. "Getting close to the Hill now."

"Good," said Jack, taking the looking glass, "I'm feeling generous."

Choices

WHEREVER JACK HAD run off to Thomas hadn't a clue, and with the streets packed to the brim it was unlikely he'd find out any time soon. Though the way his brother was acting perhaps that wasn't such a bad thing.

Wordsworth had gone off too, and was nowhere to be found. So for the moment Thomas was left completely on his own.

There were so many things to do, so many extraordinary sights to see, with attractions literally everywhere you looked. It was one big party. There were festive costumes, music, and dancing in the streets. Vendors sold interesting foods and drinks. While the most amazing fireworks lit up the night sky and performers performed astonishing feats. All made more incredible by magic.

Each of the guilds had a tent in which to sell their wares. The alchemist's tent was filled with glowing potions like those in Doctor Von Wolfenhauer's store. The witches' tent was filled with herbs and other earthly ingredients. Thomas had entered hoping to see the girl from earlier, but alas she wasn't there. The mystics, shamans, and the druids all had their tents as well.

Amidst all the revelry, however, Thomas suddenly saw something in the crowd that caused his heart to skip a beat. Only a few yards away stood Loki and Cadmus.

What are they doing here? he wondered, and sure it wasn't anything good. *Should I follow them and find out*? he asked himself.

Normally, Thomas would've never considered such a thing, but lately he'd found himself doing all sorts of uncharacteristic things. Still, after seeing what he had of those two, following them presented a whole new kind of danger. But despite the many good reasons weighing against it, decided to do just that.

But before he did, he concentrated on the image of a white mouse. Until through the magic of the moonmask his head mimicked perfectly the picture in his head.

Quiet as a mouse, he thought sneakily.

Loki and Cadmus drew away from the crowd and headed down a dark alleyway. Thomas crept quietly behind them, following as closely as possible without risking detection. They emerged from the alleyway into a far less populated section of town. In fact the Festival hardly seemed to be occurring here at all, and even the moon's light was blunted by heavy shadows. They headed into an establishment with a sign hanging crookedly that read, ***The Headless Horseman's Tavern.*** Which appeared to be closed.

Thomas saw a side window peering into the tavern. *Might as well have a look.*

The place was darkly lit, and the window rather dirty, but Thomas could see just enough to make out what was happening. And what he saw came as quite a shock: Loki and Cadmus were meeting with the Mayor. Garrick the goblin was there too, hanging closely by his bosses' side.

Why would the Mayor be meeting with those two?

He couldn't hear a thing. But from what he saw, the Mayor hardly uttered a word and simply nodded his head as Loki spoke. Then after a minute of one sided conversation, Loki handed the Mayor a velvet sack, which he greedily pocketed. In return, the Mayor presented Loki with a small golden scepter with a glowing green gem at its head.

Once the scepter was in Loki's hands, he grinned widely and then suddenly Cadmus grabbed the Mayor by his head and lifted him clean off the ground by it. The Mayor's eyes bulged with horror, and his corpulent body squirmed for dear life, futilely attempting to break Cadmus' hold. Loki nodded, and Cadmus snapped the Mayor's neck, turning his head completely around, then dropped the Mayor's lifeless body to the ground. It was all Thomas could do not to scream out.

But before Thomas could process what he'd just witnessed, something else happened, something equally disturbing. Garrick the goblin began growing rapidly in height and girth, and his entire form drastically changed. Until he'd transformed into an exact replica of the Mayor prior to his death. Thomas could scarcely believe his eyes.

It was then that Loki and Cadmus turned to leave in one direction, while the newly formed Mayor headed in the other, presenting Thomas with a choice. He made a split second decision to continue following Loki and Cadmus.

They headed outside the town walls into the surrounding hills, making their way to the cottage which stood beside the tree half filled with luscious red apples and half rotted. The place Wordsworth had said was forbidden.

The moon's light didn't even touch the cottage as black smoke poured copiously from the chimney causing a heavy black cloud to hover over it.

Loki took an apple from the tree and bit into it. Blood oozed from the apple and dripped down the side of his mouth. Cadmus grabbed several apples and consumed them all at once. Then Loki opened the door and they walked inside.

Thomas saw that the cottage door was left cracked open, as if inviting him to enter. By far the biggest risk he'd taken yet. But he had to know what they were up to. *I've gone this far already*, he rationalized to himself. So after a moment he followed them inside.

Far larger than it appeared from the outside, the cottage was like a giant museum with odd items displayed upon pedestals. Clearly dark things had occurred here, for there were symbols written in blood upon the floors and walls, along with areas that could only be described as torture chambers.

What am I doing here? he wondered, and feeling that perhaps he'd made the wrong decision.

Just then he heard voices up ahead, and quickly hid behind a pedestal with a dark black crystal ball sitting atop it. From behind the pedestal he saw Loki and Cadmus standing around an enormous ornate mirror with a huge bubbling black cauldron beside it. Another figure was present as well. Dressed in dark robes and wearing a gold mask fashioned into a skull. In his left hand he held a long black staff with flowing golden script written around it.

"Lord Demus," said Loki bowing slightly, a gesture crudely imitated by Cadmus.

"Is everything in order?" Lord Demus asked tersely.

"The town's defenses are no more, and the guards will soon be…transformed. It will be as sheep before the slaughter." Loki laughed cruelly.

"Then there is only one final thing left to be done." Lord Demus gestured towards the large ornate mirror standing beside the cauldron. "This is a very unique object, a mirror between this world and the Banishment. From this side we can affect the other. Behold."

The glass suddenly became a filmy liquid which rippled like a stone skipped across a placid river. When it finally settled Thomas found himself staring at his world, at the Banishment.

It was a city, easily recognizable as one of the world's most famous. It had been transformed into a battlefield and the wreckage and carnage were everywhere. Tears welled up in Thomas' eyes as he gazed upon it.

"They destroyed themselves. But who could blame them? Their lives were so short and utterly pointless, devoid of magic...devoid of *truth*. A wonder they lasted even this long. But now the Banished shall have their revenge...as the undead horde shall rise again," and Lord Demus pulled out a vial. Which Thomas recognized instantly as being the same one he'd seen in the forest. The one containing his blood.

"From life unto death...and from death unto life," said Lord Demus, and he poured the blood from the vial into the cauldron.

Then Lord Demus removed his gauntlet revealing a grotesquely burned hand. He took out a knife and cut into his scarred flesh allowing his black blood to drip into the cauldron. After several generous drops he touched his staff to his hand and the wound instantly closed. He then submerged his staff into the mixture and began stirring. As he did he spoke in a language Thomas recognized as being the same his Uncle had used when invoking the Moon Goddess: the language of the Ancients.

At first nothing happened. Then it started to rain in the Banishment. No ordinary rain, but a black rain. Thomas watched as the dead bodies stirred and twitched as the drops hit them. And then one by one they rose up from the ground, with eyes as dark as the rain itself.

Horror and panic washed over Thomas. *I have to do something...I have to tell Wordsworth or Uncle...I have to...*

But as he stood up, he knocked over the pedestal he was hiding behind and the black crystal ball came crashing down and shattered.

All three pairs of eyes darted instantly in his direction.

"Cadmus—fetch." Loki ordered.

Thomas got barely ten yards before feeling a familiar paw grab him roughly by the scruff of the neck.

Cadmus carried a dangling Thomas over to the others.

"Ah," grinned Loki "we caught a mouse."

Lex Talionis

THE QUEEN ANNE'S Revenge sailed through tumultuous waters towards the island ahead; a vast series of endless red hills, standing one after another like a mountain range. There was one hill at the midpoint of the island taller than the rest. That one Jack knew was reserved for him.

The sky above swirled in violent black clouds to mirror the sea below it, and lightning infused the air with deadly electricity. Blackbeard yelled out instructions to his crew, who scurried to their appointed positions, preparing for arrival. Jack stood at the helm of the ship staring out at the island marking the beginning of his destiny, and the end of his old life.

"Throw down the anchor!" Blackbeard commanded as they neared the shore, and soon they were docked a hundred yards from the island.

The stormy sea abruptly calmed as the waters soothed and flattened and grew preternaturally still. Until the surface resembled glass.

Jack turned to Blackbeard. "Am I to swim?"

"Nay, you're to walk."

"I can't walk on water!" snapped Jack.

"Aye, but you can, for the sea allows it," and Blackbeard walked over to a crewmember standing near the edge of the ship, and threw the unsuspecting man overboard. After a moment there was a sickening thud.

Jack looked over the side and saw the pirate lying in a pool of his own blood. The only liquid remaining upon the solid surface.

"You see—solid as a rock!" bellowed Blackbeard.

Jack smiled. "Wait for my return."

"Aye, for as long as it takes."

Jack was lowered onto the water's surface. As he walked towards the barren beach everything grew quiet, even the sounds of the pirates ceased, and the sky above uttered not a peep. It was the quiet before the storm, a time to reflect upon what lies ahead.

If he wished he could turn back. It was still his choice to make, and if he desired he could call the whole thing off. But he wouldn't allow himself to take the coward's way out. Even now as his body riddled with fear for what awaited him, he wouldn't succumb. He'd carry through with his plans, steadfast to the end.

As he walked the last leg of the water's length, he pulled out the black gem from his pocket and gazed into it hoping to see the girl, or his parents, or something else of inspiration or comfort. But all he saw was his own reflection staring back at him. A melancholy face appearing restless and uncharacteristically stricken with fear. Though also one that held great strength and the conviction of purpose.

He placed the gem back into his pocket. He didn't need it now, not for this. He had himself, and that was more than enough.

He paused briefly before the shoreline, marking the end of the water, and the beginning of the beach: his Rubicon. The next step would change his life forever. He strode boldly over the fateful line, and as he did, the storm began.

Jack lifted up his arms as the storm raged above. "Come and get me!" he called out defiantly.

A shrill cry suddenly pierced the air, and it brought with it others, and they brought with them others still, as the sounds multiplied and compounded all over the island.

The Furies are coming.

They emerged from all over the island, their faces hideous and beastlike, neither human nor animal but a horrifying distortion of both. Their sole reason for being was the infliction of pain, and every inch of their bodies was devoted to that purpose. Their mutilated green skin was covered in sharp protruding shards of bone. They had hooked talons for hands and feet, and writhing venomous snakes for hair. Their teeth were razor sharp and could cut through skin and bone like paper sheets.

They converged upon Jack like a pack of bloodthirsty wolves. But Jack was no helpless lamb to be slaughtered, and he picked up a rock and struck back with everything he had. His eyes burned with fire, as all that had remained dormant for so long burst forth. He fought with the frenzied blood craze of his warrior ancestors.

But they were far too many, and the Furies quickly overtook him in a furious whirlwind of teeth and claws. He fell….

They beat him unmercifully. Not allowing a single centimeter of his body to go un-bruised, or a patch of skin uncut, and every bone they broke, every ligament they fractured. Only then did they drag him up to the Hill, where the real pain would begin.

Upon the Hill stood a barren tree of mangled lifeless wood with sharp needle branches covered in thorns. The Furies hoisted Jack up upon the tree, and the mangled branches came alive and wound tightly around him holding his broken body in place, while the sharp ends of the gnarled branches pierced his skin and spread deep into his flesh like famished roots seeping into a fertile earth. He screamed out as the blood was withdrawn from his body and transferred into the parasitical tree. At the top of which bloomed a bright red rose, and as more blood was taken more roses emerged.

What seemed like hours passed, and Jack's tears were utterly spent. But still he hung upon the vile tree as it sucked the life out of him. And the tree wasn't yet filled with roses. There was still so much life to give.

Suddenly Jinn appeared upon the Hill.

"You're doing so well!" he proclaimed.

Jack had no voice in which to respond, and it was all he could do now just to listen.

"It will all be over soon. The binding is nearing its end. I know it hurts, but think of everything you will gain—think of your *future!*" said Jinn.

"I'm afraid, however, there remains one thing left to be done. The last part of the bargain, as it were," and a sharp spear appeared then in Jinn's right hand, while from out of the shadows of his left appeared the black gem. "Forgive me this my king…" and suddenly Jinn thrust the spear into Jack's left eye.

Jack let out a silent scream as Jinn twisted the spear, digging it deeper into the socket. After a few excruciating moments he pulled it out…*slowly.* The blood poured out like a waterfall from the gaping hole where Jack's eye had once been.

The black gem rose up from Jinn's hand, until parallel with Jack's face. There the gem began to transform. It stretched out, elongated, becoming no longer a gem, but a long black worm. It coiled in mid-air and then struck with blinding speed into the cavernous hole of Jack's eye. The worm burrowed deep into Jack's body and he could feel it literally growing inside him, expanding, consuming, contorting, and altering his very being. Until the black gem emerged in the shape of an eye to replace the one lost, and it filled with raging fire.

Jack saw everything, as if for the very first time—the world as it truly was. He saw the interwoven magic, the fabric of the world in all its many strands. And with his new sight came new understanding, new knowledge, and new power gained. He remembered all his past lives, and more than that, they all converged into him, becoming one. He saw the past, the present, even the future. And he knew then what a tremendous gift he'd been given.

The tree holding Jack wilted and shriveled, and the flowers that had blossomed so fully instantly died, their petals falling upon the side of the Hill like compost. The needle-like branches sticking deeply into Jack's skin turned black and rotted, and as they did Jack's mutilated skin began shedding from his body like a snake molting, and to the earth it fell, adding to the heap of refuse. Underneath was a new flawless shadowy gray skin, and a physique appearing sculpted from granite. Not even the slightest remnants of the torture he'd endured remained.

As he descended from the tree, lava burst forth from the surrounding hills and began consuming the island. The ear-wrenching squeals of the Furies filled the air of the crumbling island, and as the lava avalanched down blood red snow fell from the sky. Jinn was nowhere to be seen.

Jack closed in on the violent sea raging ahead of him. Before he reached the shore, he looked back at the island one final time and watched as it was consumed by steaming lava. Soon it would be gone, as the sea claimed its remains and buried it deep beneath its waters.

As he approached, the massive waves crashed upon the edge of the beach, breaking with thunderous force. Though this time the sea wouldn't calm to allow for his crossing. But it mattered not. He was no longer subject to its will.

Standing before the shoreline, he peered out at the tempestuous sea with a dismissive grin. *Time for a magic trick.*

He raised his hands and fire roused in his new eye. The earth quaked and grew to a furious rumble as the sea drew in upon itself. It split one side from another, parting into two separate waves, walls of water hundreds of feet high that held steady in their place, creating a pathway directly to the awaiting ship.

"There we are," said Jack, admiring his handiwork.

Now for my crown and my Queen, and suddenly his left hand twitched, *and my spear.*

He made his way between the mountainous waves, which budged not an inch. When he reached the ship a rope was lowered for him. But he didn't take it. Instead his feet elevated effortlessly, and within moments stood aboard the ship's deck.

"Your king has returned," he declared triumphantly.

The pirates all bowed to one knee, and praised Jack with hardy cheers.

"Good to have you back," said Blackbeard when the clamor died down, "Aye, and I see you've returned to us changed," he added pointing to Jack's new eye.

"A gift," said Jack simply. "Now let's go…I have so much to accomplish."

As the ship pulled up anchor and sailed off, the waves crashed back down behind them with a thunderclap, covering the sandy sea floor once more.

"Wait here my liege and I'll fetch you some clothes," said Blackbeard.

A few moments later, Jack heard a gathering of footsteps behind him. He turned to see the pirates with swords drawn and Blackbeard at their head wielding his dagger.

"There do be just a *slight* change in plans," said Blackbeard.

Jack raised his eyebrow. "You're betraying your king?"

"You do be sharp as my knife," said Blackbeard and there was a booming laugh from the pirates.

"You want more than your promised reward—more than your life restored?" asked Jack, appearing completely unfazed.

"Oh, much more than that," said Blackbeard, "We want what all pirates want— treasure!"

"Treasure?" replied Jack, "I carry no gold or silver."

"Aye, but you do have that fine new eye, and anything worth so much pain to obtain is a treasure worth having."

"So imagine what I'll do to keep it," retorted Jack coldly.

Blackbeard laughed. "Brave talk for one about to walk the plank. For can't you see, my *liege,* or are you blind, you do be between the devil and the deep sea."

"I control the sea," responded Jack.

"Aye, but not the devil," said Blackbeard, inching to within striking distance.

"Word of advice, never trust a pirate," said Blackbeard.

"And you should never underestimate a king…" and Jack's black eye roused with fire as Blackbeard lunged at him with the knife.

At the moment before the blade touched Jack's new gray skin, his hand caught Blackbeard's wrist and held it there with barely any effort. Jack twisted Blackbeard's arm, who cried out and dropped the dagger as he was brought to his knees.

The other pirates converged on Jack. But he rounded on them swiftly with fire raging in his black eye and his voice thundered: "Come not between the dragon and his wrath!" and a great fear overtook the pirates and they cowered like hares before the hound.

Jack held out his other hand—the one not breaking Blackbeard's arm—and the dagger flew up to it obediently. He gazed at the dagger of lore, and considered it's illustrious past.

"Please my liege I didn't mean too, I was confused, I was—"

"Silence!" roared Jack, and Blackbeard went quiet as a mouse.

"This knife cost you one eye…and now it shall cost you the other," and Jack jammed the knife into Blackbeard's other eye….

Jack wore Blackbeard's magnificent red coat and black hat as the ship sailed off into a blood red sunset with Blackbeard's head leading the way, stuck forth upon the ship's mast. While the crew cheered loudly, "Long live the King!"

Meetings

So far Catherine's night had been an uneventful one. It was like any other Moon Festival she'd been to before, with the exception that every mundane thing was magnified a thousand fold as she searched for higher meaning in even the smallest details. Such as when Mrs. Clause asked if she wanted to stand on the right or left side at the ceremony, or what kind of headdress to wear. To which after much debate she chose a wreath of purple roses. It was all very maddening trying to determine which decisions may prove life altering.

She was currently waiting for her Grandfather in front of Sigmund's Bookshop. It was a Festival tradition that they would meet here. Sigmund's was one of their favorite places. She'd come here with her Grandfather and listen to him converse for hours on end with fellow members of the philosopher's guild as she'd taken to calling them. There was Mr. Franklin, Lord Byron, Mr. Poe, Mr. Frederick, Mr. Milton, Mr. Church, Mr. Carroll, and Mr. Sigmund himself. She'd sit and listen as they opined on every subject imaginable, and debated every point fiercely. They allowed her to join in—indeed encouraged it. They recommended books for her to read, and would quiz her on them. It was an education separate and apart from the one she received with her Sisters, and one she found equally valuable.

Suddenly, as if sprung forth from her mind, two esteemed members of the guild, Lord Byron and Mr. Poe, rounded the corner. Plainly obvious that they'd indulged in quite a few libations as both were stumbling noticeably while engaged in a loud, animated conversation. Which she gathered had something to do with the pedigree of gnomes.

"—no, no, they're distant cousins of dwarves not leprechauns."

"Leprechauns are a form of dwarves!"

"Catherine!" Lord Byron exclaimed when he saw her. Only it wasn't Lord Byron's voice, but Mr. Poe's.

Then Mr. Poe remarked with Lord Byron's voice, "Enjoying the Festival?"

Moonmasks, she thought, shaking her head.

"So you've decided to switch heads for the evening."

"A social experiment. I wanted to see what it was like to be hideously ugly," said Lord Byron, wearing Mr. Poe's head.

"And I wanted to know what it was like to be universally disliked," said Mr. Poe.

Catherine laughed. These two always amused her.

"So what are you standing here by yourself for?" asked Lord Byron.

"I'm waiting for my Grandfather... who should be here by now actually," she said looking around as if he'd suddenly pop up. It was unusual behavior for him. He was never one to be late. Indeed to him nothing was more precious than time. "Wasting time is wasting life," he was fond of saying.

"Well the crowds are larger than I can ever remember, and it's difficult to get around," said Mr. Poe, adding, "I'm sure he'll be here shortly."

"And in the mean time we can keep you company," offered Lord Byron cheerfully, "Unless of course you'd rather we not. We wouldn't want to impose."

Catherine paused. "On one condition,"

"Name it," said Mr. Poe.

"Take off the masks."

"I thought you'd never ask!" said Lord Byron, "I could scarcely stand to look at myself any longer."

"And I was beginning to thoroughly despise myself," said Mr. Poe, removing his as well.

"That's better," said Catherine when restored to their rightful selves.

As usual, the conversation was anything but dull and jumped from topic to topic, some quite absurd. But in the midst of a conversation regarding the nature of ballehorns, Catherine caught sight of Captain Allac coming up the street, and waved him over.

"What brings you to these parts Captain?" inquired Lord Byron.

"I received word of a disturbance," said Captain Allac, looking quite serious. "Two centaurs on the verge of bludgeoning one another," his eyes darting about.

"That's centaurs for you," said Lord Byron, "They'll fight over anything."

Centaurs, Catherine knew, were notorious for their short tempers and willingness to engage in battles, usually to the death.

"Well we haven't seen anything like that," said Mr. Poe, and Lord Byron and Catherine nodded their heads.

Captain Allac appeared noticeably disturbed. "That's the third false report in the past hour."

Catherine recalled what Captain Allac had told her earlier about the town's defenses not working properly. But before she could inquire further, another First Guardsman ran up to Captain Allac. A burly fellow with a bushy brown beard and forearms the size of small children who, judging by his features, appeared to have some troll blood in him.

"Anything to report Sergeant Murat?" asked Captain Allac.

"Nothing Captain," responded Sergeant Murat.

Captain Allac emitted an audible grumble.

"But Doctor Von Wolfenhauer gave us these potions to keep us sharp and alert, free of charge," said Sergeant Murat, "I brought you one," and he pulled out a vial containing a glowing blue liquid.

"I don't need anything to keep me alert," replied Captain Allac tersely. "Keep looking."

"Yes, Captain," said Sergeant Murat, and ran off.

"I must be going," said Captain Allac turning back to them, "I have a feeling this will be a long night."

Shortly after Captain Allac left, Catherine saw two Wordspreaders walking down the street. Easily spotted by their red cloaks and the Book of Light clutched tightly in their hands. They wore moonmasks: one displaying the head of a ram, the other the head of a bull. They were speaking to one another in hushed, secretive tones.

"There up to something," said Catherine. She could feel it.

"We could follow them and find out," suggested Lord Byron, in a tone making it unclear whether or not he was joking.

"We're not doing that," said Mr. Poe.

"Why not?" asked Catherine, and they both turned towards her, "I'm serious, let's do it."

"That's the spirit!" cried Lord Bryon, "A bit of adventure—count me in."

"What about your Grandfather?" asked Mr. Poe.

"He can't expect me to wait around all night for him," said Catherine, suspecting that he'd probably ended up doing some last minute chore for his Lordship.

"Quite right," replied Lord Byron.

"I'll just leave a note in case he shows up," said Catherine.

"Well I guess I'm in too," said Mr. Poe, "But I want to go on record now saying this is a bad idea."

"Noted," said Lord Byron.

Catherine left a note attached to the door of Sigmund's shop, and then they set off after the Wordspreaders.

Wordsworth had followed Jack back into the house. But once inside, was knocked unconscious. The last thing he remembered was a dark shadow coming towards him at a blinding speed.

His attacker was undoubtedly a shadow creature of some sorts. Perhaps even one of the dreaded Formless, and the taint of dark magic still lingered upon him. The minions of the Kingdom of Darkness being in Everfall meant that the town's defenses weren't working as they should. A fact highly troubling to say the least.

He was supposed to meet Catherine. But navigating the crowds proved near impossible, and by the time he arrived at Sigmund's Bookshop he was thoroughly late.

He looked all around. But Catherine was nowhere to be found. Then he saw the note on the shop's door tied in a green bow he recognized instantly as belonging to his granddaughter. He took the note off the door and opened it up.

Grandfather,

I couldn't wait any longer. Hopefully, I'll see you later.

Love,

Catherine.

I must find her, he thought. Tonight was not the night to lose her.

The End of a Story

JACK EMERGED FROM the painting and back into the confines of the castle. He made his way to the eastern wing: the oldest section.

When he arrived he headed straight for the door he'd gone through with his brother and Uncle the day before. The one with the symbol of the tree above it. As he pulled the handle his new eye alighted with fire, and the door opened.

He followed the path through the Orchard to the small raft and rowed towards the cave beneath the World Tree. As he sailed, all the creatures carved into the Tree came alive and watched him pass. He made his way through the cave with the shadows on the walls. When he arrived, Sam was waiting for him.

"Hello my son." Sam greeted him.

"I'm not your son," retorted Jack coldly.

Appearing frailer than ever, Sam returned Jack's vitriol with a warm smile. "Ah, but you are, for I am father to all things that exist in this world...for good or ill."

"Creation doesn't make one a father," snapped Jack.

"Perhaps not. But I gave life to this world and have experienced all its joys and sorrows. I am bound to it, and it to me."

"Even worse," scoffed Jack, "To know the pain and suffering of the world and do nothing to end it. You could've fixed everything with the stroke of a pen. But you refused to lift even a finger."

Sam nodded. "I learned long ago that it is best to allow my creations to live their own lives and make their own choices...however painful. For what is the point otherwise—to be puppets on strings? Shadows on walls."

Jack laughed. "Are you claiming to have never interfered?"

"I make no such claim. If anything, I've interfered more than I should have… and it has been the cause of many of the ills plaguing this world. Every choice has a price, and mine have been quite dear," and there was a deep sadness in Sam's eyes. "But what of your choices, do they not have their consequences as well?"

"I will save this world," replied Jack defiantly, his eye rousing with fire.

"By destroying it?"

"By remaking it."

"I see…But if I am, what you say I am, a cold, uncaring tyrant, then why simply trade one master for another?"

"I am the master!" roared Jack, and the cave shook.

"Are you certain? It seems Setus now holds your allegiance."

"We have an arrangement."

"Yes, I can see that," said Sam, gesturing to Jack's eye, "Though, in my experience, Setus has never been one for sharing. Especially when it comes to power."

"It is *you* who doesn't share power," countered Jack, "Setus was a rival to your throne, and so you struck him down."

Sam nodded. "I admit I did not wish for Setus to destroy all that I had created. Though ultimately Setus is my fault. There is darkness in this world, because inside me darkness exists. In that darkness Setus was bred…" his voice trailed off.

"But," Sam began again, "in order to stop Setus I unleashed terrors upon my world. To stop a monster I created another. Samson was a weapon to end a war. But once the war ended, the weapon remained. I thought I could control it…but control is an illusion. And now, the weapon stands aimed at me."

"You deserve your fate," declared Jack bluntly. "You failed us."

Sam put his head down. "You are right. I have not been the father to this world that I should have been. But it has always been my great hope and desire that my creations will be better than I am. The reason I imbued them with wills of their own. I always intended for them to take ownership of this world. And though I wrote the world into existence, it's a story being written by those dwelling within it." Sam smiled, "All good writers know, the characters guide the author's hand, not the other way around. And I've often wondered whether I created this world at all…or whether it created me."

Jack stood utterly unmoved. "You're right about one thing, a new world is being written. A world without you in it… " and suddenly he took Blackbeard's dagger and drove it deep into Sam's chest. Then took it out and thrust it again and again and again…

The blood poured out of Sam in torrents and the cave shook as it filled the ground. Jack stood over him coldly and watched the life seep out. "Every story has an ending. This is yours."

As Jack began to walk away, he caught sight of a rolled up parchment sitting on Sam's desk. He recognized it as the one Sam had given him earlier. He picked it up and found the seal broken. He unraveled it.

I forgive you my son, it read.

Fire burned in Jack's eye and suddenly the paper alighted. He threw the burning parchment on Sam's lifeless body.

Jack left the cave with a satisfied smile as the Author's body burned to ash.

Into the Woods

When Thomas awoke he found himself propped up against a tree in the middle of the Golden Forest tied up tightly by a thick rope. He looked up and saw the one called Lord Demus staring down at him through the dark slits of his golden mask.

"Let me go!" Thomas demanded, struggling futilely to break his restraints.

"No." Lord Demus replied simply in a deep, hollow voice.

"W-who are you?" asked Thomas, "And what do you want?"

"I am but a servant," responded Lord Demus, "And only want what my Master wants."

"Who is your master?" ventured Thomas.

"He has many names," said Lord Demus, "But perhaps you know him as the Lord of Nightmares."

"You serve Setus," said Thomas.

"Yes. And soon all shall serve him, or perish," said Lord Demus.

"What are you going to do with me? Take more of my blood?"

"Perhaps. Blood is the coin of the realm, and yours is extremely valuable and can purchase a great many things. As you've witnessed for yourself," said Lord Demus.

Thomas' had seen his blood used in the mixture that caused the black rain that reanimated the corpses in the Banishment. "Why is my blood so valuable?"

Lord Demus paused momentarily, as if pondering the question. "No one has told you?" he asked finally, genuine surprise in his voice.

Not understanding, Thomas shook his head.

"Curious," said Lord Demus, "But then, this realm is filled with secrets... secrets extremely well kept."

Thomas wondered what he meant by that.

"Though, it is a peculiar twist of fate that I should tell you. Not that it will make a difference in the end."

"Tell me what?" asked Thomas anxiously.

"I assume you know the story of Prince Jaden," said Lord Demus.

"The Pretender King," said Thomas.

"I would not call him that if I were you," said Lord Demus sternly. "Particularly as your brother shares his soul."

"Jack is...Jaden's soulcestor?" said Thomas.

"And so you are his brother Abram's," said Lord Demus, "A lineage tracing back to Samson."

"The Soul of Legend," said Thomas recalling what his Uncle had told him. But the fact that he was of that line was information completely new, and difficult to fathom.

Lord Demus nodded. "Then you understand why your blood is valuable. Contained inside you is a piece of the Author's own spirit imbued with the Infinite. The weapon the Author wielded to defeat Setus in the First War."

Thomas wouldn't have believed even a single word, if not for all that had occurred over the last few days.

"But it appears that you have proven an unworthy vessel for such power. Unable even to break through a simple piece of rope. Of course your soul is far weaker than your brother's," said Lord Demus, "For with Jaden and Abram the Soul of Legend split, becoming two distinct souls. But it was an unequal split. Jaden receiving all the strengths, and Abram all the weaknesses."

"But Abram defeated Jaden!" interjected Thomas.

Lord Demus laughed derisively. "Jaden could've easily destroyed Abram. But Jaden was a plot long in the making. Setus knew Samson would be his defeat, and so within his soul planted a dark seed. For Setus understood the nature of man, and with cultivation knew the seed would blossom. Until the darkness broke free, becoming its own entity.

"Contained within the dark seed was also a binding spell, linking the soul to the Author's, for they were part of one another. The seed drained the Author's power and absorbed it, and as it grew stronger the Author grew weaker. So the Author's great champion would become his ultimate undoing," said Lord Demus, appearing to relish the opportunity to divulge his Master's genius.

"But to complete the binding required sacrifice, for all spells have their price. So instead of killing Abram, Jaden took his own life. All that remained was for his heir to be reborn in the darkness, and the Author's power would be completely drained. Tonight your brother completed the transformation."

Thomas recalled then the bizarre conversation he'd had with his brother that very morning. Then Thomas remembered the dream with the leaf woman, the dream that had felt so real. *Was Jack the Dark King she'd warned him of? Does that mean everything she said was true?* The questions mounted in his head.

But before he could ponder them further, Loki emerged suddenly from behind a bush and walked up to Lord Demus, flashing Thomas an evil grin as he did. He would never forget Loki's promise to eat his soul; a promise Thomas was certain Loki was intent upon fulfilling.

"Our guests are arriving," said Loki.

"Then let us go and greet them," replied Lord Demus.

Catherine, Lord Byron, and Mr. Poe followed the Wordspreaders into the Golden Forest. Catherine had placed a cloaking spell on all three of them so that they would remain hidden when no longer enjoying the cover of the crowds. The spell was one of her specialties, and having used it so often—mostly to sneak out at night without being caught by Mrs. Clause—had become quite proficient. Of course she'd never actually used the spell on anyone other than herself, let alone two others. But found she was able to do so without any additional effort. *My magic is really strong tonight,* she thought.

The Wordspreaders journeyed further into the forest until they came to a clearing with torches set up in a large circle. Two formidable looking individuals in black armor stood guard.

"Those are vampires," whispered Lord Byron.

"How can you tell?" asked Catherine, never actually having seen one up close.

"The eyes," replied Lord Byron.

They were blood red; a stark contrast to the extreme paleness of their faces.

"He's right," confirmed Mr. Poe, "There's no mistaking it."

"What's the Arch doing with vampires?" asked Catherine, "They're sworn enemies." Recalling the infamous Vampire Wars waged over several bloody centuries.

"And the plot thickens," said Lord Byron.

They watched as others, all wearing moonmasks disguising their identities, entered the clearing to join those already present. Many bore the distinctive robes of the guilds, of which nearly all appeared represented. There were shamans, mystics, warlocks, alchemists, and druids, along with some of the smaller guilds. Though Catherine was heartened by the fact that none of her Sisters had appeared yet.

"Let's find a place to watch," suggested Lord Byron.

They found a spot behind some bushes, close enough to see what was happening, yet far enough away that they didn't risk detection.

Dozens of figures stood in the clearing with more continuing to arrive. At the front of the gathering was a tall figure with a golden mask fashioned into the shape of a skull, holding a black and gold staff. To his immediate left were the two individuals Catherine had bumped into earlier: the one with the red hair and obscenely sharp features, and the massive ogre.

"That's a wizard." Catherine observed. For though not adorned in the attire of the Arch, who always wore white robes to denote the pureness of their spirit, the staff in his hand was unmistakable, as was the magic emanating off it. He possessed a presence that she'd never felt before. It was pure dark magic. The strongest she'd ever experienced. *A dark wizard.*

"This is becoming a truly interesting night indeed," remarked Lord Byron, "I'm bursting with anticipation to see what will happen next."

"Brothers and sisters," the wizard began when the guests had ceased arriving; "You've come from near and far to be here this night, in this place, to bear witness to the beginning of a new age. Long have we waited for this moment to arrive. For years we've hidden away in the shadows, setting the path and preparing the way...plotting and maneuvering. But our days of hiding are at an end. For our King has risen!"

The masked figures cheered uproariously. While Catherine, Lord Byron, and Mr. Poe glanced at one another warily.

The wizard quieted the crowd with a gesture. "He'll be arriving soon to greet his faithful subjects. In the meantime, I have a special treat for you all. Cadmus, bring our little friend if you would."

The ogre Cadmus went behind one of the trees and emerged shortly holding in his massive arms a golden haired boy tied up in rope, who he dropped roughly on the ground in front of the wizard. Catherine recognized the boy instantly as one of the realm's new princes.

"That's—"

"Prince Thomas," said Mr. Poe.

"Behold, I present Abram's heir! The White Lion!" proclaimed the wizard.

There was a pronounced stir amongst the gathered congregation.

"Kill him now!" one of the figures called out.

"End him!" echoed another.

"Patience my friends," said the wizard quieting the crowd, "Our King has waited long for this moment, and it would be criminal to rob him of the satisfaction of ending his own brother."

"We have to help him," whispered Catherine.

"How? There are so many of them. . .and we are so few," said Mr. Poe.

"We can't just let him be killed," said Catherine.

"We need to create a distraction," said Lord Byron, looking at Catherine.

Catherine smiled. "I believe I can manage something."

"And while their distracted, I'll grab the Prince," said Lord Byron as if that simple, "Unless Mr. Poe would rather do it. I am flexible."

"No, I wouldn't want to deprive you of the chance to get yourself killed," said Mr. Poe.

Catherine turned to Lord Byron. "Now, even though you're under the cloaking spell you can still allow someone to see you by focusing on that individual, and then in your mind's eye granting them permission. To everyone else you will remain invisible. Do you understand?"

Lord Byron nodded. "Perfectly."

"Ready?" said Catherine.

"Quite," said Lord Byron, who appeared to be enjoying himself.

Catherine took out her wand and began to speak words under her breath… Domitas…Naturan….Darandaras…. It was a nature spell, invoking the tree spirits known as dryads. As she spoke a strong wind blew, and then suddenly all the torches went out, leaving only the light of the moon.

The trees suddenly came alive and attacked the members of the congregation, assailing them with limbs and branches. While preoccupied, Lord Byron snuck around to Prince Thomas who was lying next to a bush, slightly removed from where the action was occurring. When he arrived, he focused on allowing Prince Thomas to see him, as Catherine had instructed.

"Lord Byron!" cried Thomas, thoroughly surprised, "What are you doing here? Where did you—"

"There will be plenty of time for explanations later my Prince, but now we really must be going," and Lord Byron took out a knife and severed the rope. "Now take my hand, and don't let go."

Thomas nodded.

"Let's go."

Amidst the chaos they hurried back undetected to where Catherine and Mr. Poe awaited.

"Mr. Poe," said Thomas.

"Good to see you again my Prince," said Mr. Poe, and then seeing Thomas' eyes gazing at her, added by way of introduction, "This is Lady Catherine."

Thomas paused. "A, hello."

"Hello," replied Catherine.

"Um, they don't see us?" asked Thomas confusedly.

"Cloaking spell," said Mr. Poe, "Thank Catherine for that."

"T-thanks,"

"Don't mention it."

"I don't mean to be rude, but we should probably get going," said Lord Byron.

"Right," said Catherine.

"Um, why is everything suddenly so silent?" asked Mr. Poe.

They saw then that the trees had ceased attacking, and the entire congregation was staring in their direction.

"They can't see us right?" whispered Mr. Poe.

"The wizard must have performed a counter spell," said Catherine.

"We should probably run," suggested Mr. Poe.

"Yea, um, thing about that is—I can't move," said Lord Byron.

"None of us can," said Catherine, "We're frozen in place."

"I did mention that this was a bad idea from the start," said Mr. Poe.

"Bring them here," ordered the wizard, and the figures converged upon them.

Just then a terrible, shrill ear-piercing shriek filled the air.

"What—was—that?" asked Mr. Poe, echoing friend and foe alike.

"Banshees," answered Thomas.

Wordsworth had always been able to find Catherine by way of a tracking spell he'd placed upon her without her knowledge. He'd been careful never to abuse it, and for the most part he hadn't. But tonight he had to find her.

The tracking spell led him to the edge of the Golden Forest where he currently stood. *Why would she go in there?* he wondered.

Upon entering the forest, he immediately detected the familiar charge in the air of casted magic, followed by a barrage of screams and shouts. Wordsworth hurried towards their source.

He arrived at a chaotic battle scene. Figures bearing the moonmasked induced heads of all sorts of creatures fought a pack of ravenous banshees. While Catherine, Prince Thomas, Lord Byron, and Mr. Poe were surrounded by the beasts. Prince Thomas held a sword, Lord Byron a dagger, Mr. Poe a rock, and

Catherine her wand. But they were vastly outnumbered and would be overtaken soon.

Before he could come to their aid, however, a banshee jumped out in front of him. Its sickly yellow skinned face was covered in putrid puss-filled boils and its sharp rotted green teeth were bared. Its lower half was that of a vulture, while its torso a wilder beast's. But even in his old age his instincts were sharp, and he struck the banshee in the neck with his cane.

"You've chosen the wrong old man for your meal," snarled Wordsworth, and a bright yellow light shot forth from his cane. The banshee wailed and fled.

He moved quickly to Catherine and the others, the light from his cane shining brightly.

"Grandfather!" cried Catherine as the banshees scattered.

"Wordsworth!" yelled Thomas.

"Oh thank goodness, I thought we were going to be eaten," said Mr. Poe, visibly shaken.

"Nothing like waiting till the last moment, eh?" said Lord Byron, appearing shaken himself.

"Let's get moving," ordered Wordsworth, taking charge.

With Wordsworth's cane leading the way, they moved rapidly through the forest. When suddenly Catherine tripped over a vine and fell hard to the ground.

While down, a banshee leapt out of the bushes at her. But just as it was about to sink its teeth into her neck, Thomas thrust his sword through the banshee's heart, killing it instantly.

Another banshee emerged then from the bushes, but as Wordsworth turned to face it he ran straight into a solid surface, as if an invisible wall had been erected in front of him. He moved to either side, but found himself running up against the same invisible wall. He had been trapped in a cage of woven magic.

Standing only a few yards away, Wordsworth saw a masked wizard.

"Who are you?" he demanded, his cane at the ready.

"You don't recognize your old friend? Perhaps it's because I appear so different since last you saw me…when I was being consumed by fire."

"V-v-victor?" Wordsworth's eyes widened with sudden realization.

"I am known as Lord Demus now."

"But you were—I saw—"

"I have been restored."

Wordsworth knew there were only a few ways such a thing could be accomplished, and fewer still that could accomplish it. "Restored by whom?"

"My new master."

"Setus," said Wordsworth disdainfully.

"Yes."

Wordsworth knew then what his friend had become. He was a lich; an undead wizard. "So you're just another one of the Lord of Nightmare's monsters."

"Hardly worse than serving my old master, and your current one."

"Nothing is worse than serving Setus," said Wordsworth firmly, "He is the enemy of all of creation. He seeks only destruction, and the enslavement of all creatures."

"Propaganda," retorted Lord Demus dismissively, "Lies spread by the true enemies of this world. And it wasn't Setus who threw me into the flames. It was Setus who saved me from them."

"You brought the flames upon yourself, when you opened the Dark Book," replied Wordsworth bluntly.

"Because I dared to gain knowledge that he would deny us? Because I wanted to bring back my son!" roared Lord Demus.

Wordsworth sympathized with his former friend. After all he'd once had a son of his own. But there were good reasons why such knowledge was forbidden. "You forget that he saved your life, as he saved mine."

"He saved our lives so that we could serve him. A debt that I like you repaid a thousand times over. But what did I receive in return for my countless years of service? I begged him to save my son, and he refused."

"You know the price of sparing a life."

"A price he's paid many times before," countered Lord Demus.

Wordsworth knew that there was truth in what he said. But also knew that there were no easy choices when dealing with life and death.

"I bear you no animosity Wordsworth," continued Lord Demus, "We were friends, bonded by the same shared experience, both servants of Death. But now the Dark King has risen and soon Setus will be freed, and this world rewritten.

Then my friend, Death will serve you. And all those who perished, all those you loved will return…including your son."

Wordsworth paused only momentarily before responding, "Setus will bring only pain and suffering, and whatever promises he has made to you are lies."

"You disappoint me. I thought you wise. But I see now that you are nothing more than a foolish old man. Nevertheless, I'm going to give you a gift. I'm going to free you from your servitude…" and a black thunderbolt shot forth from Lord Demus' staff and struck Wordsworth in the chest. He crumbled to the ground.

As Wordsworth felt the dark magic coursing through his body, eroding his life-force, Lord Demus stood over him, aiming his staff at Wordsworth's heart. "Farewell old friend…"

Just then the ground shook and the air trembled.

Wordsworth seized upon the momentary distraction, and fired a beam of light from his cane at Lord Demus, hurling him towards a tree several yards away.

Catherine, Thomas, Lord Byron and Mr. Poe rushed over to where Wordsworth was lying.

"About bloody time," grunted Wordsworth, in obvious pain.

"Simply repaying the favor," said Lord Byron with a smile.

"Where's the wizard?" asked Catherine, her wand prepared to strike.

Wordsworth pointed to where Lord Demus had fallen. But he'd vanished without a trace.

"He's hurt bad. We have to get him out of here," said Mr. Poe.

Lord Byron and Mr. Poe grabbed hold of Wordsworth and together ran fast as they could out of the forest.

Door of the Damned

STEPPING BACK INTO the confines of the castle, Jack turned towards the door to his right, with a symbol that looked like fire above it, opened it like the one prior, and walked through.

Jack stared down a long narrow passageway, the walls of which were covered in flames. Yet the fire emitted no heat and was cold as winter's heart. Smoke filled the space, stifling any gasp of breathable air. This, however, had no effect upon Jack, who no longer drew breath in the traditional sense. Nor could the flames even singe his skin, and he touched them freely as he strolled through the passageway at a leisurely pace.

The passage led into a sizeable antechamber, with a massive iron door at the end. The chamber's stone walls and ceiling were both engulfed in flames, while the floor was covered in pure black ice.

Upon entering the room, Jack could hear the screams and blood-curdling shrieks coming from behind the iron door. The voices begged for him to release them and save them from their endless torment, swearing to serve him forevermore.

Reaching the door in short order, he gazed at the cruel iron exterior frosted over with black ice. As Jack reached out towards the door's handle, he heard footsteps coming from behind him. He needn't turn around to know to whom they belonged.

"Hello Jack," responded the whispery voice of Lord Hades, "Or is it Jaden? Or do you go by another name now."

Jack smiled. "King."

"I suppose you can always pretend."

Jack's eye alighted with sudden flames, but then quickly subsided.

"I was wondering when you were going to arrive at my re-birthday party. I was beginning to think you were going to miss it. Did you bring me a present Uncle? Or should I call you Dorian. That was your once name wasn't it."

"Like you I've had many names…and lived many lives," said Lord Hades.

"And this will be your last," promised Jack.

"We shall see."

Jack smiled. "I already have."

"Tell me, how did you open the door without a key?" inquired Lord Hades.

"I am the key to all doors," said Jack.

"Whatever the case, I cannot permit you to open *that* door," said Lord Hades bluntly.

"And I cannot allow you to keep it closed. Those behind it—"

"—deserve to be there." Lord Hades finished for him. "I assume you know the place. It was one of Setus' infamous prisons during the war. Now it keeps his monsters from plaguing the world once more."

"Monsters?" Jack laughed. "Their crimes pale in comparison to yours. Who are *you* to judge them?"

"I do not judge," replied Lord Hades sharply.

"Oh, but you do. You keep your favorites, don't you?" said Jack, "You collect them and bring them here to play with like toys. Tell me what grants them Death's favor? Are some more worthy of life than others?"

"Yes, some are," admitted Lord Hades. "But what about your judgment?"

"I will save the world," said Jack. "By building a better one."

"And to fulfill your vision countless will be slaughtered."

"Some must fall, for others to rise," remarked Jack casually. "And unlike you, I offer them a choice. They can either join me in the new world…or perish in the old one."

"A threat is not a choice," said Lord Hades.

Jack shrugged. "All choices have consequences."

"You have always possessed the uncanny ability to justify your atrocities."

"Come, we're not so different, are we?" said Jack. "You have engineered your own world here, and filled it with those you desire. I will do the same. Only on a slightly grander scale." Jack smiled. "But I do wonder if you've chosen unwisely...brought the wrong sorts to inhabit your little kingdom in the valley? Some bad apples, perhaps?"

"I have never claimed freedom from error, or from my own personal biases," said Lord Hades, "But at least I acknowledge my weaknesses. While you're still blinded by your own ambition and arrogance. So quick to count all your victories before they are even won."

"All battles are won before they're fought," retorted Jack, adding with mockery, "King of the shades."

"You will not win," declared Lord Hades bluntly, cutting to the core, "For all your power, you shall fail."

Fire erupted in Jack's eye. "And who is going to stop me? The Author is no more," and he held up the bloody knife as proof.

Lord Hades paused only momentarily, before responding firmly, "Your brother will stop you."

Jack laughed at the absurdity. "My brother is weak. I will crush him."

"He will fight you. I will make certain of that. Even if I cannot defeat you myself, I will ensure that he is ready to face you when the time comes." Lord Hades swore.

Jack shrugged. "Even if he fights, in the end he will be just another martyr for a hopeless cause. Like all the rest who stand against my new world. Evolution cannot be stopped."

"He stopped you once." Lord Hades reminded him.

"Only because I allowed him. I took my own life, so that when I returned I would be beyond even the reach of Death."

"Nothing is beyond Death," responded Lord Hades.

Jack smiled. "You know, it's curious that we should be enemies. After all I have fed the Beast that dwells within you more than any other...and I have so much more to give. Serve me and I'll fill your belly with more lives than you could ever dream of consuming."

Lord Hades felt the Beast stir inside him. But with tremendous effort suppressed it.

"You should be far more concerned with the beast dwelling inside of you," replied Lord Hades, "Or the one you now serve."

"I can end the torment you know," said Jack, "I can free you from your burden...if you join me. I only make this offer once. And this is the moment of the offering. Choose wisely. . .Uncle."

Lord Hades hesitated only momentarily, before responding firmly, "My answer is, and shall always be, no. I will never join you no matter what you offer."

Jack sighed. "How terribly predictable. . . ." and with that he turned, grabbed the handle, and pulled. . . .

Lord Hades rushed towards him with blinding speed. But by the time he reached the door Jack was gone.

Lord Hades hastily shut the door, hoping nothing had emerged. Even a moment was long enough for something horrible to slip through.

Suddenly he felt a sharp pain pierce his abdomen. *Something is wrong.*

"Come Achilles," he called, and the massive hellhound appeared then beside him.

A door appeared out of nowhere, and they walked through it.

A Knight's Song

WITH TREMENDOUS EFFORT, Thomas, Catherine, Lord Byron and Mr. Poe were able to get Wordsworth into the fields on the outskirts of town and safely hidden behind a large hill. Catherine placed the cloaking spell back on them to ensure they wouldn't be seen.

They laid Wordsworth down gently. The blood was gushing out of him in torrents. Catherine was not a healer like some of her Sisters, of which none was better than Mrs. Clause. *If I can just get him to her.* But there was no time, and with her limited healing abilities she did what she could to stem the tide. But this was a wound created by powerful dark magic and there was no salve that could heal it.

They all hovered above her Grandfather with faces doing nothing to mask their grave concern.

"I need to speak with Catherine," said Wordsworth, his voice struggling to maintain anything over a whisper, "Alone,"

Mr. Poe nodded. "We'll keep watch," and with Lord Byron and Prince Thomas in tow headed off to the other side of the hill.

"What is it Grandfather?" asked Catherine, kneeling beside him.

"I have something to tell you…something I should have told you long ago. Please listen close for time is…slipping away."

"Grandfather it can wait, you need to rest now." Catherine insisted.

"Please," said her Grandfather grabbing her hand, "*Listen.*"

Reluctantly, she nodded her assent.

"I've not been honest with you Catherine. I've hidden things from you. But it's time you knew the truth. Time you knew my story…."

Catherine listened as her Grandfather began then to tell his tale.

"I was a knight of the Order of the White Lion. Renowned as one of the Order's best. One day I was sent upon a secret quest by the Patriarch himself to find the staff of the first wizard, Mosiah. The Arch had sought it for centuries. Rumors of its location had come and gone, cropping up here and there. Many had searched for it, all had failed. I was bound and determined to finally find it. I was so brash in my youth, so determined to make my mark on the world…to be a hero for whom tales were told—"

Her Grandfather suddenly coughed violently, spitting up blood as he did. Catherine went to comfort him, but he shooed her away. And after a moment to regain his composure, he forged on with his story.

"I left behind my beautiful young wife and infant son and set out to find the staff. The quest took me to the very ends of the world. Years upon years passed away, but no matter how far I went I would not stop...I *could* not stop. The staff was my obsession. Nothing else mattered, not my friends, not even…" her Grandfather paused, "Ultimately, I went too far, and found myself lost in a no-where place…a place no one is meant to go. And as I lay dying upon a dark desolate shore, Death himself came to me with him an offer. He told me he required someone like me, someone willing to go to the end of the world and beyond. If I served him, he would spare my life, even grant me powers requisite to the task. Having no other choice, I agreed to his terms, vague as they were.

"True to his word, I did not die, and was granted new powers and abilities. Though my youth, long gone by that point, was not restored, and I continued to age as a constant reminder of how frail and close to death I was, lest I forget my service, the thread from which my very life hung. So it is that I have served the Lord of the Dead faithfully ever since."

"Grandfather, are you—are you telling me that Lord Hades is—"

"Death," confirmed her Grandfather.

"But how could he—"

"That is a story best told by another."

"So this place is—"

"Not what it seems. The truth of it is…complicated. Far too complicated for me to fully understand, or try and explain. But this whole valley is a world unto itself, enchanted by powerful magic of the kind known only to the Dream Kings, for whom this valley was once home."

"So those who live here, are they—"

"Dead? No. They are not dead. Indeed, most have been saved from the jaws of Death."

"What do you mean…saved?" asked Catherine confusedly.

"On occasion, Lord Hades finds a life worthy of saving from the Beast, and brings them here to live out their days. You may call them the living dead. For though they live on here to the rest of the world they are very much deceased."

"Am I—was I—"

"No. You are here because I brought you here. Most do not remember how they came to be here, and what they do remember fades over time, like sand slipping through an hourglass."

"So Mr. Poe and Lord Byron?"

Her Grandfather nodded.

"Mrs. Clause?"

"Yes,"

"Prince Thomas?"

"No, he is like you."

Catherine's head was reeling from the onslaught of information. But when she thought about it, there were so many peculiar things about Everfall, so many things that didn't make sense. Like the fact that Mrs. Clause could never recall much about her past, and not just Mrs. Clause either, but a great many of her Sisters couldn't seem to remember how they came to be in Everfall, or anything before it.

"But wouldn't someone recognize them? We have many visitors," said Catherine.

"Just as you have a cloaking spell for the eyes, there are those for the mind as well," said her Grandfather.

"What if they try to leave?" asked Catherine.

"The magic of the valley restricts them from leaving," said her Grandfather, "Or at least causes them not to desire to do so."

"So they don't even know what they are?"

"How could they? To them this is their life, and they are living it. The mind is quite a curious thing. It can find ways to justify anything."

A sad fate in many ways Catherine thought. To have lived a life and have no recollection of it.

"But why does Lord Hades save them?" Catherine asked.

"His reasons are his own."

"So why can't Lord Hades save you now? If you um—" she didn't dare say the word.

"He saved me once. Now, I must save myself. Even so, this wound would be beyond even his powers to restore."

"Maybe Mrs. Clause could help. She is—"

He put his hand on hers. "Know that I love you, and that I have treasured our time together more than anything."

"I-I've treasured it as well," said Catherine tears running down her cheeks, "and we're going to have plenty more time together," she added with feigned confidence.

Her Grandfather smiled. "I must speak with Prince Thomas for a brief moment. Would you be ever so kind as to send him over?"

Catherine still had so many questions, and the last thing she wanted was to leave his side, but she nodded and granted the request. "I'll tell him."

She stood up and began to walk away, and then stopped abruptly, and turned back around. "Did you ever find the staff?"

Her Grandfather smiled. "A story for another time."

Thomas walked over to Wordsworth, while Lord Byron, Mr. Poe, and Catherine kept watch on the other side of the hill.

"Prince Thomas," Wordsworth greeted him genially, despite looking extremely grim.

"Wordsworth—you need help!" cried Thomas distressed by his friend's rapidly failing condition.

"What I *need* is for everyone to stop telling me what I need," said Wordsworth, "Now come here and sit down. We have things to discuss and not much time in which to do it."

Thomas did as asked.

When Thomas sat down Wordsworth gave him an odd look.

"What is it?" asked Thomas.

"There is something different about you." Wordsworth observed.

"What do you mean…*different*?"

"For starters, *that*," said Wordsworth, indicating the sword Thomas held tightly in his right hand.

"I found it in the forest during the battle," said Thomas admiring the sword's sharp blade and silver hilt. "I've never even swung a sword before. But somehow I know how. Actually, I'm pretty good at it," he admitted. It was the strangest thing, but when Thomas picked up the sword it felt so familiar, as if he'd held it every single day of his life. And not only that, but he'd fended off a couple of vampires with it, and even slain a banshee.

"You know how to wield a sword the same way you knew how to ride a horse even though you'd never ridden one before. It is because of your soulcestors, and the blood that courses through your veins. I have no doubt that you will discover a great many hidden talents and abilities in the days ahead. And soon you'll become the great warrior that you were always meant to be," said Wordsworth.

Thomas laughed nervously. "Me, a great warrior?"

"I have no doubt," affirmed Wordsworth. "The Festival reveals what we truly are, and the moon's light has a transformative quality. Moonmasks are worn in celebration of this transformation. But where the moonmask is merely an illusion, for those Coming of Age, the transformation is a very real one."

"Tonight is my Coming of Age?" said Thomas.

"Isn't it obvious? Since the moment you entered Everfall you've begun to change, and not simply in appearance. Some of which was due to your adjustment to the magical world, and the pastries I fed you contained potions to facilitate this adjustment. But mostly the changes were because you were nearing your Coming of Age. I imagine tonight has been quite revealing for you, to say the least."

"They say that…that I'm Prince Abram's heir," said Thomas, still not completely convinced of it himself.

"You are indeed the White Lion returned," said Wordsworth with the certainty of a priest.

"Wait, you knew all along?"

Wordsworth smiled. "I had my suspicions. But Lord Hades ordered that I not interfere, that nature be allowed to take its course. But now that we know, I wonder if you truly understand what it means?"

Thomas shook his head. "No."

"Simply put, it means you were born to save the world."

The leaf woman in his dreams had said the very same thing. But coming from Wordsworth made it all the more real. Though the shock of hearing such a thing had not changed. "I can't save the world. I'm just…just…me!" said Thomas.

"You can, and you must," said Wordsworth firmly, "The Infinite courses through your very being, and once you learn to control your powers you'll be able to do things on par with the Dream Kings, and even greater. Only your own self-doubt will prevent you from reaching your full potential. It is absolutely essential that you master yourself. Because despite all of your great power, the threat you face is greater still."

"Jack," said Thomas.

Wordsworth nodded. "He is Jaden's heir. The Dark King. And just as Jack has chosen to be the destroyer, you must choose to be the savior. Destiny only offers a door…you must walk through it."

The leaf woman in his dream had said it was his choice as well. But she had also said that if he chose not to fight, the world would surely fall. *Though if I do fight it will be against my own brother.*

"I've never defeated Jack in anything in my entire life." Thomas confessed, "Not one single thing. How can I possibly beat him in a war for the world?"

"For starters, by believing that you can," said Wordsworth.

"I'll…try," uttered Thomas weakly.

"You must do much more than simply try," replied Wordsworth firmly, "You must succeed…for the sake of all."

But before Thomas could respond, a large explosion suddenly came from the town, followed by blazing fires throughout.

"You must go—*now*." Wordsworth urged.

"But what about you?" said Thomas, "I can't leave you here."

"I am but one old man. Many more need your help now," said Wordsworth. "You must think of the greater good. It's time you began fulfilling your destiny."

"I'll come back for you," promised Thomas.

"I have no doubt," said Wordsworth with a smile, "Now go, be who you were born to be."

With great reluctance, Thomas stood up and began walking away.

"Oh, and Prince Thomas do take good care of my granddaughter would you," Wordsworth called out.

"Wait, what."

Wordsworth laid there staring up at the giant moon shining above, his remaining life-force draining away, when suddenly he heard footsteps coming his way, and felt a familiar presence drawing near.

"I knew you'd come."

"How could I not," said Lord Hades, kneeling by Wordsworth's side. "How are you my friend?"

"I've been better," admitted Wordsworth.

"It will all be over soon," said Lord Hades in a comforting tone. "You have played your part well."

"I suppose…but…" Wordsworth paused abruptly. "He doubts himself."

"Abram and Aloysius doubted themselves as well." Lord Hades reminded him.

"He needs training."

"And he shall have it."

"Victor has returned," said Wordsworth, "Calls himself Lord Demus…and is a lich."

Lord Hades stared up pensively at the moon above. "Victor always desired power. I should have seen that when I first recruited him to serve me. But his talents caused me to overlook certain things. Now it appears he has returned to haunt me…." He turned his glance back to Wordsworth. "But you need not worry about him any longer, or anything else. There is someone here for you."

Wordsworth saw the Valkyrie once called Officer Valorous standing before him. She appeared far different than the last time he'd seen her. Glowing with bright light, she wore golden armor which appeared forged from the sun itself, while a halo hovered above her head.

"Hello again Wordsworth," she greeted him, her voice nearly as angelic as her appearance.

"I see you found your way back home," said Wordsworth.

"Thanks to you. And now I'm here to repay the favor. I'm here to bring you home. To the halls of your ancestors in the World Beyond."

Wordsworth smiled. "I have waited so long to see my family again."

"Are you ready?"

Wordsworth paused for a long moment. "Not just yet," he said finally, and turned back to Lord Hades, "I have a final request."

"Name it," said Lord Hades, and Wordsworth proceeded then to do so.

When finished, Lord Hades bowed his head. "If that is what you truly wish,"

"I do."

"You understand the cost?"

"A price I pay willingly."

"Very well then…" and Lord Hades' eyes went suddenly red.

Wordsworth braced himself as the Beast of Death consumed his life-force.

The Attack

TO THEIR ABSOLUTE horror, upon entering Everfall Thomas, Catherine, Mr. Poe and Lord Byron encountered a warzone, with blood thirsty vampires attacking every living thing in sight. Thankfully, they remained hidden by the cloaking spell.

"How did vampires get inside the walls? Where was the warning—where were the bells!" cried Mr. Poe after they'd slipped behind some large wooden crates.

"It would appear the town's defenses have been disarmed." Lord Byron observed.

"You're right," concurred Catherine, "I don't sense the magic that usually surrounds the town like an invisible wall."

"None of the town's defenses are working it would seem, magical or otherwise," said Lord Byron.

"Yea, where's the First Guard?" asked Catherine.

They looked all around. But saw none.

"Wait, there's one!" cried Catherine suddenly, pointing towards a figure wearing the distinctive red cape of the First Guard standing in an alleyway directly across the street.

"I'll find out what's going on," volunteered Lord Byron, and ran over to the guardsman.

Lord Byron allowed himself to be seen as he had with Prince Thomas earlier. "Guardsman, what happened to the defenses? How did the vampires get in? Where is the rest of the First Guard?" he asked in rapid succession.

But when the guardsmen turned around, Lord Byron froze. It was the guard from earlier, the one who'd come up to Captain Allac when they were in front of

Sigmund's Bookshop. Only now he appeared…different. There was a mad look in his eyes, like a ravenous dog. And he shook furiously, as if something inside him were desperately trying to get out.

"Oh…um…you know what, I'm sure you're quite busy at the moment with the vampires and all so I'm just going to leave you alone." And Lord Byron made a hasty retreat back to the others.

The guard began to suddenly transform. Fur sprang up all over his body; his nails became claws; his teeth grew large and sharp; his face elongated and his bone structure altered; he even sprouted a tail. Before long, he'd turned into a full-fledged werewolf, and howled up at the moon above.

"He's a bloody werewolf!" blurted Lord Byron.

"It would appear so," said Mr. Poe.

"Um, the cloaking spell is still on us right?" asked Thomas.

"Yes," confirmed Catherine.

"Then, um, why is the werewolf staring directly at us—"

"—and moving towards us?" Lord Byron added.

"Because he doesn't need to see us," said Catherine, "When he can smell us."

"Oh, I see," said Mr. Poe, "Run!"

They ran down an alleyway and the werewolf gave chase. The beast's strength was nearly as impressive as its speed, and any obstacle in its path was utterly obliterated. He was on their tails and gaining ground quickly. His massive paws swiped at them, narrowly missing. It was a frantic game of cat and mouse, and no mistaking which was which.

As they rounded a corner they saw the open door of a basement cellar.

"There!" cried Catherine.

They dove inside and immediately shut the door behind them.

Catherine instantly enchanted the door to keep it closed. The werewolf banged ferociously against it.

"Everyone all right?" asked Mr. Poe.

They all nodded.

"What now?" asked Catherine, soliciting suggestions.

"We don't want to kill him do we? I mean he is a First Guardsman after all," said Mr. Poe.

"He bloody sure wants to kill us!" cried Lord Byron.

"We could wait it out. Maybe he'll get bored and go on eventually," suggested Thomas.

"Unlikely. When a werewolf gets your scent it doesn't stop until its fed," said Catherine, dispelling any notion of the werewolf simply going away on its own.

"Can't you put a spell on him Catherine, something to restrain him perhaps?" asked Mr. Poe hopefully.

"Most magical creatures possess some natural resistance to magic. Werewolves are amongst the most resistant," said Catherine, "One of the reasons they're so dangerous, aside from the obvious."

"Oh," said Mr. Poe, crestfallen.

"Well we'd better do something and soon, that door Catherine enchanted isn't going to hold much longer," observed Lord Byron, as the door started to cave from the werewolf's assault.

Mr. Poe turned to Thomas. "My Prince, I hate to impose upon you like this, but if you *really* are who they say you are, this would be a most splendid time to play the hero."

Lord Byron nodded. "I must say I quite agree."

Even Catherine gave Thomas a look plainly stating it's time to show what you're made of.

Thomas looked down at the sword in his hand, the sword he'd slain the banshee with. Maybe it was Catherine that gave him the courage, or anger for what had happened to Wordsworth that drove him. Or perhaps he was simply curious to know if everything they were saying about him was true. But whatever the case, he was ready to fight.

"I'll do it. I'll fight the werewolf," he declared bravely, not knowing how exactly he planned on doing such a thing.

"What do you need from us?" asked Catherine helpfully.

Thomas thought about it for a moment, and then responded, "A way to get through the door without being eaten first."

"I have just the thing," said Lord Byron, and he pulled the flask from his pocket, popped open the lid and took a giant swig.

"And how exactly is *that* supposed to help?" asked Catherine.

"Because in addition to its many other benefits, the liquid in this flask is also highly explosive."

"That's not surprising." quipped Mr. Poe.

"So what do you have in mind?" asked Catherine.

"Watch," said Lord Byron, and he walked over to the door and poured a healthy amount of the liquid right outside of it. "Now then we just need a little fire," and he looked around for a moment until he saw a wooden stake on the ground, and picked it up. "Catherine if you'd be so kind."

"Inferia," said Catherine with a wave of her wand and the end of the stake alighted.

"Thank you my dear," said Lord Byron, "I'd stand back if I were you," and then after a moment to allow everyone to get a safe distance away threw the flaming stake at the doorway.

There was a bright flash and an ear bursting bang, followed by flying debris.

"Go!" cried Lord Byron, literally pushing Thomas out, "While the beast is stunned."

Thomas ran into the alley, sword in hand. The smoke was thick in the air from the explosion. His eyes darted around. But the werewolf was nowhere to be seen.

Maybe the explosion scared him off, he thought hopefully.

But then the werewolf, missing half its hair, was suddenly upon him. Reacting in the nick of time, he dove to the side. But as he did the werewolf's paw knocked the sword from his hand, sending it hurling several feet away.

Thomas scrambled to retrieve the sword. But before he could the werewolf was upon him once more.

The werewolf pinned him to the ground. Its jaws mere inches from his head, the saliva dripping down upon his face. But where he should've been absolutely terrified, instead a great calm descended over him. Everything seemed to slow down, and in that moment he had a kind of out of body experience. He closed his eyes and imagined himself as a great hero, like Saint George. And in his mind's eye he watched himself battling the beast. He watched as they wrestled with one another. He watched as he out maneuvered the beast and climbed upon its back, where he wrapped his arms tightly around its neck, holding on with all his might. Until the beast fell at last.

When Thomas opened his eyes, the beast lay upon the ground unconscious, while he stood over it with his foot atop its head.

"You did it!" exclaimed Lord Byron, the first upon the scene.

"And without killing him," said Mr. Poe, highly impressed.

"Nice work," said Catherine, causing Thomas' face to go a deep shade of red.

"T-thanks." Thomas replied sheepishly, more than a little shocked himself.

Basking in the admiration, Thomas felt confidence the likes of which he'd never known before. *I did it! I defeated a werewolf*! And for the first time thought, *maybe I really am Abram's heir.*

But the joy was short lived, for far from being the only werewolf in town they soon discovered that the place was literally infested with them. And nearly all bore remnants of the distinctive red cloth of the First Guard.

"Do you recall earlier when the guardsman informed Captain Allac that Doctor Von Wolfenhauer had provided them all with a special potion?" asked Mr. Poe.

"Guess he neglected to mention that it would turn them all into werewolves," said Lord Byron, "Honest mistake I'm sure."

"I knew he was evil," said Catherine, feeling vindicated, "I knew it!"

"So what now?" asked Lord Byron.

"We could hide," suggested Mr. Poe.

"I'm not hiding," declared Catherine defiantly, "I'm not going to sit back and watch as they kill all my friends and destroy my home."

"Nor I," seconded Lord Byron. "Besides, we have the White Lion with us! They should be hiding, not us."

They all turned towards Thomas waiting for him to give the orders. Thomas had never had so much faith put in him before. No one had ever looked to him as a leader.

Thomas said nothing. Instead, knowing the power of symbols, simply put his moonmask on, and thought of a white lion.

The others followed him into battle....

Family Ties

Lord Hades surveyed the carnage with a heavy heart. He'd lost so many uniquely talented individuals, so many—*one of a kind's*. He had brought them here to Everfall to live and flourish under his protection. Now they lay upon the ground lifeless, their bodies drained of blood. And as powerful as he was, there was nothing he could do for them. He could save them from the Beast but only once. Those that did return would be vampires, and there was no reversing course. This was worse than death. This was destruction.

How did they get in? he wondered. Powerful magic surrounded the town, aimed at repelling threats just such as this one. But he had grown weak as of late, and the burden of the Beast heavier, taking more of his energy to control. And as he weakened so did the magic he'd woven. Still, not all defenses were of his making. The First Guard had many of their own, and they too had fallen. *Someone has betrayed us*. He was sure of it. There was no other explanation.

The anger seethed inside him, and the Beast stirred.

A hundred yards away from where he stood a vampire fed upon a young child. He was there in an instant and in a single fell swoop tore the vampire's head clean off. It rolled upon the ground, then, like the body it once belonged to, burst into flames, until nothing more than a pile of ash remained. Several other vampires were feeding nearby, and within a heart's beat had suffered the same fate.

Suddenly, a werewolf dropped down from a rooftop behind him. But before he had a chance to end its existence, Achilles beat him to it. The massive hellhound sinking its teeth deeply into the werewolf's neck, ripping out its throat.

While Achilles finished off the werewolf, he searched for more vampires to dispose of. The Beast was stirring inside him, and he allowed it to awaken. He dispatched with a half dozen vampires and three werewolves in short order.

But before he could continue with his rampage, he heard a voice coming from behind him. A voice from the past. One he'd hoped never to hear again.

"Hello father."

Lord Hades paused for a long moment before responding. "Dracula,"

"It has been a long time."

"Not nearly long enough," said Lord Hades turning to face his son. The progeny of his ill-fated union with a witch named Persephone. A forbidden love that spawned the horrors known as vampires, of which Dracula was the first.

His hair was long and dark. His chiseled face ghostly white. His eyes were bright red like his lips dripping with fresh blood. Appearing the same youthful age as when in his seventeenth year the full breadth of what he was took over, and his life was overtaken by death. He wore dark armor, particularly thick around the chest. He held in his hand the limp body of a woman. Lord Hades recognized her instantly as Madam Maltese, an extraordinary woman who'd overcome unbelievable hardships to achieve remarkable things. Dracula discarded her lifeless body like trash.

"No doubt you thought me long gone to the dust. So sorry to disappoint. But then, I've always disappointed you, haven't I father."

"I knew you would return one day. I felt your presence lingering, the embers of your being waiting for a spark. I see they have received one."

"The right blood can do wonders for one's health," said Dracula flashing a bloody grin. "Though I see little has changed in my absence, you still favor your adopted children over your real ones. But your collection of pets has grown since last I was here, in both number"— he licked the blood from his fingers— "and flavor."

"I gave you every chance, tried everything I could to help you. But you were, and remain, a monster," said Lord Hades bluntly.

"I am the child of Death!" roared Dracula, "If I am a monster then it is because you made me such."

"You chose to be what you are," countered Lord Hades, "I showed you ways in which blood could be obtained without taking it from the living. But you wanted no part of it."

"Yes, I recall that vile substance you tried force feeding me, that blood substitute cooked up in some alchemist's lab. It was so…unsatisfying, so unnatural…and it made me weak."

"But you were able to survive on it."

"Survive—like you?" Dracula laughed, "I'd rather meet my end. And though you claim the moral high ground now, I know the lengths you have gone to, of the wars and plagues you've started so that you may feast."

Lord Hades knew there was truth in what he said. "There was a time when I allowed the Beast to rule me, allowed my basest desires to cloud my judgment. But I learned to control the impulses…and the hunger. It can be done. I tried to teach you. But you never wanted to control it, did you?"

"And I never will. To try and control one's nature is foolishness. You cannot deny what you are."

"Then you are nothing more than a base animal," retorted Lord Hades.

"How right you are father. I am a predator and these"— he gestured around— "are my prey. But let us be honest shall we, since we are in such a mood for telling truths, you hated me from the moment of my birth…a birth that stole your beloved away from you. Even as Death you were powerless to save my mother," said Dracula, "How you wished she would've survived, and I had not."

Lord Hades paused for a long moment, before responding, "I never should have loved her in the first place. The fault lies with me."

"I was a mistake then," said Dracula.

"Yes."

"Then it's high time you started paying the price for your mistakes—in blood!" and suddenly half a dozen vampires appeared beside Dracula, each holding a citizen of Everfall.

Lord Hades recognized each and every one of the citizens.

"You fathered me, and I fathered an entire race," said Dracula, "Now we've come full circle it would seem, as my children shall devour yours…while you watch on helplessly." And he placed a glowing pale yellow amulet on the ground in front of him.

Lord Hades felt its effect immediately. It was a death ward, and as long as it was nearby he could not get near them. Its power would last only for a short while, but more than enough time for the vampires to leisurely drain the blood from their victims.

"This is a small taste of what you shall endure in the coming days," promised Dracula, "Farewell father," and with that he was gone.

The vampires slowly sunk their eager fangs into the necks of their terrified victims. Lord Hades watched on helplessly, unable to get within twenty feet of them.

But then a sudden thought came to him: if he could not go to them, then he'd bring them to him. To which, he had another weapon at his disposal.

Strands from his cape moved steadily towards the feasting vampires. Consumed by their feast, they remained unaware of the threat closing in upon them. Before they knew it the strands were wrapped tightly around their necks. They ripped the vampires from their victims, lifted them into the air, and pulled them past the protection of the amulet towards an awaiting Lord Hades.

As they hovered in the air, they kicked and flailed and pleaded for mercy. But Lord Hades was not in a merciful mood.

"Your end is here," and the strands pulled them to the awaiting Beast.

The heart of the battle raged in the town square near where the white tree stood. Thomas, Catherine, Lord Byron, and Mr. Poe fought alongside witches and alchemists, who unlike Doctor Von Wolfenhauer were anything but enemies. They used potions to fend off the attackers, while the witches cast their spells. The other guilds were there too utilizing their own particular brands of magic, while centaurs, satyrs, and other creatures took up arms as well. Together they fought back against the horde of vampires and werewolves laying siege to their town.

Thomas fought like a man possessed, and in many ways he was just that. It was a rampage fueled by rage, as all the anger pent up inside for so long burst forth and he saw in the vampires and werewolves all those that had bullied and ridiculed him throughout the years. And though never taught how to wield a sword, swung it with deadly expertise.

But as impressive of a swordsmen as Thomas was proving to be, none was more so than Captain Allac, who moved with blinding speed and fluid grace, his scimitar slicing through the limbs of vampires and werewolves alike. Beautiful in a way, like watching a deadly dance.

Slowly, but surely, their onslaught drove the vampires and the werewolves back. But just as the battle was beginning to turn, two massive giant albino vampires appeared then before them. Standing the size of three or four full grown men combined.

"What—are—those!" cried Mr. Poe, as they watched in horror as the giant vampires ripped whole bodies apart and drank blood from their torsos.

"Draugs," replied Lord Byron, "I've read about them…never thought I'd actually see one in person."

The tide turned decidedly back to the enemy as the two draugs went on a savage killing spree. But where most fled, Captain Allac ran straight up to one of the draugs and began doing battle with it. While the other draug was dealing with a spell cast by Mrs. Clause which caused roots to grow up out of the ground and wrap themselves all around it.

Though both draugs recovered quickly, and it soon became apparent that neither Captain Alllac nor Mrs. Clause would be able to defeat them alone.

Catherine, along with two of her other Sisters, raced over to help Mrs. Clause. While Thomas, Lord Byron and Mr. Poe assisted Captain Allac.

"We must work as a team!" ordered Captain Allac dodging the draug's wild blows. "Lord Byron, Mr. Poe, divert the monster's attention, while the Prince and I strike it."

"And how do you propose that we do that!" cried Mr. Poe.

"Well, if there is one way to get a vampire's attention its blood," said Lord Byron, "And mine is simply irresistible," and he cut his arm with his knife, and then began running about flailing his arms as the blood spewed out of them.

After a moment, Mr. Poe reluctantly did the same.

While the draug was distracted by Lord Byron and Mr. Poe, Captain Allac and Thomas buried their swords deep into the back of the draug's legs. The draug bellowed in pain, and was brought low to its knees. But even on its knees the draug was larger than any of them, and a formidable foe.

With a single swipe of its gargantuan right hand the draug sent Lord Byron hurling through the air, and out of the action. With its left hand it grabbed ahold of Mr. Poe and pulled him up towards its eagerly awaiting mouth.

"Help!" screamed Mr. Poe as the draug prepared to bite off his head.

Suddenly Captain Allac's sword drove up through the bottom of the draug's jaw and through its head.

The draug fell lifelessly to the ground, and then burst into flames.

Meanwhile, the witches had cast nearly every spell imaginable, but the draug kept coming. Two sisters were badly wounded, leaving only Catherine and Mrs. Clause to fight the monster. The battle wasn't going well, as both women were expending enormous amounts of physical and mental energy, and rapidly losing strength.

The draug broke free of a weakly cast spell that had temporarily encased it in a block of ice, and raced after Catherine. As she turned to run, she slipped on a pool of blood. The monster's foot descended upon her head, preparing to crush her skull....

Suddenly the monster's head exploded, drenching Catherine in blood.

When she wiped her face she saw her surrogate mother, and smiled. Mrs. Clause smiled back.

"I love you," said Mrs. Clause, and she collapsed to the ground.

Catherine ran over to her. But when she arrived it was too late. She was gone.

Catherine knew instantly what Mrs. Clause had done. She had cast one of the forbidden curses, a spell that would take another's life, but the price was the loss of one's own: a life for a life. She had sacrificed herself so that Catherine could live.

Catherine held her surrogate mother's lifeless head, and tears poured down her cheeks as she was overwhelmed by sadness and grief. But her sorrow soon changed, as a cold rage welled up inside of her, a fury brewing since the day her real parents were taken away from her.

She unleashed her rage on the remaining vampires and werewolves, obliterating her foes with a power she hadn't known herself capable of, as the very elements were at her command, and she wielded both wind and lightning to deadly effect. It wasn't witchcraft. It was pure natural magic. The rarest gift of Mother Nature.

The others were having success as well, and together once and for all drove the vampires and werewolves out of the town square.

But what a tremendous toll it had taken. Bodies laid everywhere, and the cobblestone streets were stained red with blood. Only two dozen or so of the citizens of Everfall were still standing after the battle. Many were wounded. All appeared utterly exhausted.

It was at that moment that Loki and Cadmus chose to make their appearance. Cadmus grabbed one of the remaining citizen's by his head and crushed his skull like an egg. While Loki closed in on a group of three alchemists, grinned widely, and they all spontaneously burst into flames. Seeing this awesome display of power, the will of the citizens finally broke and they turned and fled. Until all that remained in the square were Thomas, Captain Allac, Catherine, Lord Byron and Mr. Poe.

"Looks like we're outnumbered Cadmus," said Loki, grinning widely.

Cadmus grunted loudly.

"I concur," said Loki. "We'll just have to kill them all."

Just then however there was a blinding blue light. When it subsided two Stars stood before them. One of which Thomas observed was the one called Gabriel that had saved him in the Wayward Forest.

Catherine, Lord Byron, Mr. Poe, and even Captain Allac appeared astounded by the battle's newest additions.

"T-those are um—" Mr. Poe began.

"—Stars." Lord Byron finished for his friend.

"I take it this is rare," said Thomas, noting the uniformly bewildered expressions of his companions.

"If by rare, you mean once in a lifetime. Then yes you could certainly say that," said Lord Byron.

"Must you continue to interrupt, Gabriel!" roared Loki, "It is extremely rude!"

Gabriel turned to Thomas and the others. "This is our fight now. Go."

After a moment to rouse themselves from their shock, they did as ordered.

When far enough away, they all stopped and looked back. All they saw was a bright blue light emanating from where the battle was taking place.

"Stars never concern themselves with our affairs," said Captain Allac.

"Well, I for one am glad they made an exception," said Mr. Poe. "I didn't want to face those two."

"They would've been formidable." Captain Allac admitted.

It was then that Mr. Poe took the opportunity to ask Captain Allac a question they'd all been wondering about since they arrived back in town to find it under siege. "How did this happen? How did they all get in?"

"Our defenses failed completely, and the bells were silent," said Captain Allac, "They knew just where to attack us. Where we were weakest. Explosions went off all over town, and then vampires were everywhere. At first we fought them, then all the guards began turning into werewolves."

"That'll be Doctor Von Wolfenhauer's doing," interjected Catherine, speaking his name with utter vitriol.

Captain Allac nodded. "But someone must have shut down the defenses, while false reports diverted our attention away from certain areas. It was a coordinated effort."

"The Mayor," began Thomas, and they all turned towards him, "I saw him meeting with Loki and Cadmus, err, the red haired man and the ogre. He gave them a golden scepter with a glowing green gem."

"The Key of Everfall," said Captain Allac, "It controls our defenses. I never trusted the Mayor. He only ever cared for the fatness of his own pockets." It was an assessment shared by Wordsworth Thomas recalled.

Thomas then told them about what had happened to the Mayor and how Garrick had transformed into him.

"A Deceiver," said Captain Allac when Thomas finished.

"A what?" asked Thomas.

"One of the Lord of Nightmare's most dangerous weapons," said Captain Allac, "Beings capable of completely changing their form into any creature they desire. Everfall's defenses would usually detect their presence by their dark magic. But apparently our enemies have been slipping our nets for some time. If Deceivers are inside our walls, then we'll be hard pressed to tell friend from foe. "

"So how do we know if any of us are really us?" asked Mr. Poe.

"We don't," said Captain Allac flatly.

"Oh, well that's comforting," said Lord Byron.

"But even if the Mayor did give our enemies the Key of Everfall, it's only a tool," said Captain Allac, "One still must know how to use it, and that requires knowledge of all our defense's inner workings. Things only someone of high rank in the First Guard could've possibly known."

"What about Commander Arnault?" suggested Catherine, "He was of high rank, and suddenly disappeared right before all this happened."

Captain Allac nodded. "I never trusted him either."

"Hello brother," a deep voice spoke suddenly.

They all turned at once, weapons at the ready.

They stood face to face with a figure Thomas knew instantly as his brother...and yet in the same something completely unfamiliar. Appearing older, more man than boy, he'd grown larger and more powerful in stature. There was also a shadow around him, a dark aura. And his skin had turned an ashen gray. Then of course there was the black gem lodged into the socket of his left eye.

Thomas removed his moonmask. "Jack is that—is that you?" he asked uncertainly.

"I see you've made some new friends," observed Jack, standing amidst the fires burning all around him. "Why don't you tell them to leave so that we may speak privately."

"We won't leave you my Prince," declared Captain Allac, and they all nodded.

"Don't you worry Captain Allac, I'll get to you later," replied Jack flashing an evil grin.

"I'll be fine." Thomas assured them, "Go, *please*. Others need your help."

Reluctantly, they did as requested.

"What have you done to yourself?" asked Thomas when they were gone. "Your skin is gray, and y-you've lost your eye!"

"I have been reborn, and I haven't lost anything. But I have gained everything," replied Jack. "And I see better now than ever. I see the past, the present...and the future."

"And what is the future?" ventured Thomas reluctantly.

Jack smiled and replied, "In the land of the blind, the one eyed man is king."

"You mean *your* king," said Thomas.

"I see that I'm not the only one who has changed tonight. Who would've ever thought my little brother would be battling vampires and werewolves. I admit, I'm impressed."

Hearing that he'd impressed his brother was praise Thomas had longed for his entire life. But he couldn't allow his feelings to cloud his judgment. Not now.

"So we're supposed to fight each other is that it?" asked Thomas, holding the sword shakily in his hand, and feeling a fear that hadn't existed even when battling vampires and werewolves.

"We don't have to. We could be allies," said Jack.

"You mean I could join *your* side?"

"You want to be my enemy?" replied Jack, and fire flared in the black gem.

"I don't *want* to be your enemy Jack. But look around you. You're killing people!" cried Thomas.

"People die every single moment of every single day," shrugged Jack dismissively, "Just ask Uncle."

Thomas didn't know what exactly he meant by that.

"These people are innocent," protested Thomas, "They don't deserve this."

"No one is innocent!" roared Jack and the very air itself trembled.

There was a cruelness that hadn't existed in his brother before. Jack had always cared more about himself than anyone else and no one would've ever called him a saint even on his best day. But whatever warmth he once possessed had gone ice cold. And though it was still his brother, at the same time it was not.

"Why have you joined Setus?" Thomas asked bluntly.

"We have similar interests," replied Jack simply.

"He's evil!"

Jack laughed darkly. "Don't be naïve. There is no such thing as good and evil. There are only winners and losers, and the winners are always good, and the losers always evil."

"I don't believe that," said Thomas firmly, "Our choices make us what we are. Not whether we win or lose."

Jack scoffed. "You believe that life is like one of your little stories, that there are heroes and villains. But life is not light or dark. Life is shadow. Life is gray," said Jack, "Though you are right about one thing, choices have consequences. I have seen the future. I know how this will all end. If you fight you will only increase the bloodshed. But, if you join me you can prevent so much needless pain and suffering. The choice is yours…and the time has come for choosing… brother."

Thomas weighed the decision carefully in his mind. Undoubtedly a tempting offer, and certainly parts of him desired more than anything to accept it. But he knew in his heart that however high the cost of fighting, the cost not to would be the greater still.

"I cannot join you." Thomas responded finally.

"Then you've made your choice?"

"Yes," said Thomas, "I have."

A long moment of silence passed between them both.

"Now what?" asked Thomas at last.

"The war begins," declared Jack.

Thomas raised his sword shakily.

Jack laughed. "You're going to fight me—with *that*. Please. Allow me to show you true power…" and Jack's eye suddenly burned with an intense fire and Thomas felt an unbearable pain all over his body, as if engulfed in the flames. The sword dropped from his hand as he buckled to the ground.

Jack walked casually over to his brother writhing in pain on the ground and stared down at him contemptuously. "The only reason anyone will ever remember your name is because it was briefly connected to mine." and he grabbed Thomas by the throat and lifted him off the ground with the greatest of ease. Holding Thomas by the throat, he flew up into the air, ascending high into the clouds above.

At last, Jack stopped in midair and held Thomas there, thousands of feet from the ground.

"Please...Jack...please..." gasped Thomas as he dangled.

"You had your chance. You chose to be my enemy. And so you are," said Jack cruelly, his black eye raging with fire.

"Jack...please...I'm your brother."

"Not anymore," and suddenly Jack's face transformed into that of a ferocious red dragon. Then his hand released...and Thomas fell.

A Tale of Death

THOMAS' EYES OPENED wide to the sight of a massive drooling tongue.

"Achilles hasn't left your side for hours." Uncle Hades informed him as he sat up, wiped the drool off, and proceeded to pet a very happy dog.

"Is it…over?" asked Thomas, wondering how he'd ended up in the sitting room in his Uncle's castle.

"For now," said Uncle Hades.

"Wordsworth—did he—"

Uncle Hades shook his head gravely. Thomas knew then that his friend was gone.

"What about Catherine is she—"

"She is fine," said Uncle Hades. "As are Lord Byron, Mr. Poe, and Captain Allac."

Thomas breathed a deep sigh of relief.

"Wait, I'm not dead." Thomas realized suddenly, remembering everything. "I couldn't have survived that fall. No one could have."

"I saved you," said Uncle Hades.

"Saved me…how?" replied Thomas, who'd fallen a thousand feet and yet somehow stood all in one piece. "Who are you—*really*?"

At first, his Uncle said nothing, and proceeded merely to pace about the room. But then he began to speak, "I've had many names, though who I am and what I am are often held synonymous. The thief in the night…the collector of debts….the devourer of worlds…. I am Death."

Thomas was initially stunned by his Uncle's almost inconceivable revelation. But then suddenly it struck him. "Wait, are you Dorian the Great?" he asked, recalling the tale he'd read.

"I was called that once, yes," acknowledged Uncle Hades, "You know my tale then?"

Thomas nodded. "I read it in a book Wordsworth gave me. Why did you want to stop Death?"

"Because of what it took from me," said Uncle Hades. "Her name was Crystalana. An Elven princess and a beauty the likes of which this world has rarely known. I loved her more than even life itself..." he paused abruptly. "She was pregnant with my child when the Beast took her."

Thomas watched a single icy tear stream down his Uncle's face.

"Full of despair and rage, I was bent upon revenge. I devoted my entire life and all my powers to conquering Death. At last, I discovered something in the origins of Death itself. I discovered that in order for the Author to create life he had first to create Death. Death made life possible. So Death could not be destroyed, or life would be destroyed with it. But, Death could be controlled. The Beast could be tamed.

"I devised a spell using magic both of the Light and the Dark, for Death's nature is shadow. And here in this shadowy valley underneath a white oak tree I performed the binding spell. A dreadfully painful experience lasting for days as the Beast fought desperately against the binding. But at last we were bound, a part of one another, much in the way Changelings are. Only my life was shared with Death..."

Uncle Hades paused and reflected upon his own words before pronouncing at last, "Tonight is the anniversary of night I performed the binding. The night I became Death."

"So...the Moon Festival isn't about the founding of Everfall?" questioned Thomas.

"In ways it is," replied Uncle Hades. "Though that is not its origin. Every year after the comet comes I summon the Moon Goddess as I did the night of the binding, as a reminder. The date itself, however, has its own significance, as does the comet preceding it. The reason I chose it for the binding in the first place. It is a night of powerful transformative magic."

"But none of the story about the founding is actually true?"

"Every story contains truth," said Uncle Hades. "Speaking of which, now that you know what I am, I believe you've earned the right to inquire what you will of Death."

Thomas did indeed have a great many questions. In fact, he had enough to fill an entire book. In many ways he'd waited for this moment all his life—a life filled with death.

"People die all the time. How can you be—?"

"—everywhere at once," his Uncle finished for him.

Thomas nodded.

"As Death I am master of time and space, and though here before you now, I am in other places as well. Though I am not omnipotent or omnipresent. Nor am I aware of every death that occurs. Indeed, the vast majority go by without notice. Like lives, only rarely does one warrant special attention. Most being merely another morsel in the Beast's endless feast."

Cold and callous in a way. *But then how many people die every single day?* Thomas thought, and he recalled then his brother's words.

"Is that why you're always leaving?"

Uncle Hades nodded. "Death is an all-consuming occupation."

"So you control the Beast?" Thomas asked.

"The Beast and I have established certain rules, to bring balance and order to our… existence. Though it was not always so. For the longest time the Beast controlled me, causing me to do terrible, *terrible* things so that it could feed. Wars and plagues and so many other horrors have I visited upon the world."

Thomas saw a deep sense of regret in his Uncle's eyes.

"For years I struggled for control. It took every fiber of my being…even now it is difficult. Eventually, I was able to restrain the Beast—to a degree. Potions helped, like the ones you saw me drinking at dinner. Though the ones I've been consuming lately have not been helpful I'm afraid. And my focus has been waning."

"Doctor Von Wolfenhauer—"

"I know," said Uncle Hades cutting him off, "I won't be consuming anymore of his potions."

"What happens after you die?" Thomas asked next.

"The dead have many fates. But I do not know them all. For although I am Death, I have never died. And what happens in the World Beyond is very much a mystery. Some things we must simply experience for ourselves."

Even Death doesn't know what happens after you die. Thomas thought, and found that strangely comforting.

"Do you choose who lives and who dies?" Thomas continued with his questioning.

"There is no choice. In the end, we all must die. It is an inevitability of life. Nothing lasts forever, not even the Stars. The hour of death can, however, be postponed," and Thomas noted the golden pocket watch which hung from his Uncle's breast, "But only once. And for any life spared there is a price to be paid."

"But you can save someone, if you wanted to?"

"There is a moment, the last second, in which I may stop the Beast from feasting and save those I choose. But only once. The Beast cannot be denied a second time. And time given must be taken from somewhere else. Everfall is populated by those I have saved."

"So you're saying that everyone in Everfall is supposed to be dead?"

"Not everyone, but most, yes."

"Do they know?" asked Thomas.

"No. They are completely unaware. To them this is their life, and they are living it. And to the world they knew they are very much dead. I create illusions, so that life goes on and their loved ones can mourn, and bury them."

So does that mean that Mr. Poe, Lord Byron, Captain Allac and...Catherine are all supposed to be dead? Thomas wondered.

"Wait, you said you saved me. Does that mean—"

"It means I cannot save you again," said Uncle Hades flatly.

So I died...or I should have, thought Thomas. But before he could ponder the implications, another question entered his mind. "Why didn't you save my mother?" he asked bluntly.

Uncle Hades was silent for a long moment before responding, "Your mother was originally from this world. But she ran away into the Banishment. And eventually, like all who stay too long forgot who she was."

"Why did she leave?" asked Thomas.

"I do not know," said Uncle Hades. "But she was of my bloodline. And my bloodline is cursed, as the Beast has taken particular pleasure in eradicating it. The price for saving certain lives. No doubt, she watched a great many loved ones perish. The rest, however, is a mystery I've yet to unravel. I did not discover her presence until the day of your birth. But I suspect there is a great deal to her tale. After all, there is a reason the Author chose her to be the mother of his children."

"Wait, the Author is—"

"Your father," said Lord Hades.

"H-how?" Thomas stuttered.

"It was a miraculous conception. Your mother could not have children. Then, she was struck by a bolt of lightning and suddenly pregnant with not one child but two. You and your brother," said Uncle Hades, "But like Samson's mother Danya, also impregnated by a bolt of lightning, the pregnancy drained your mother's life-force. And like Danya, your mother died giving birth to your brother."

Thomas could scarcely believe what he was hearing. "She was…dead?"

"Yes. But when you emerged suddenly she awoke, and was alive once more."

"W-what brought her back?"

"You did," said Uncle Hades. "The Heirs are imbued with the Infinite and connected to the world as none other. In it they can do unbelievable things. Even restore life to the dead, it would seem."

"Even if I did bring her back," ventured Thomas, "That still doesn't explain why you couldn't save her."

"As I explained, the Beast cannot be denied twice. You saved her, and so I could not. She was only granted a certain amount of time before the Beast would come again and reclaim his due."

"So, if the Author is my father," said Thomas, "how come I've never met him before?"

"Oh, but you have. You met him in the cave."

"Sam?"

"Yes."

"Sam was the Author." Thomas repeated in a way making clear just how ridiculous such a thing sounded.

"Yes," his Uncle confirmed again.

Thomas didn't know which was the more shocking, that the Author was his father or that the old man appearing so frail, so utterly lacking in life, was the Author.

"Not quite what you were expecting," said Uncle Hades.

"No," admitted Thomas, though not quite sure what to expect. *But certainly not that.*

"Admittedly, he has seen better days."

That's an understatement, thought Thomas, and he recalled then what Lord Demus had told him about the Author's soul being linked with the one inside the Heirs, and how the soul absorbed the Author's power, growing stronger while the Author grew weaker.

"What he is now, that's because of me and Jack isn't it," said Thomas.

"Yes," acknowledged Uncle Hades.

"What will happen to him?" asked Thomas.

"Nothing anymore," said Uncle Hades, "He's dead."

"What! H-how could he be dead!" cried Thomas.

"Long ago, the Author wrote himself into the story of this world. In doing so, he became subject to the rules of the world he brought forth, including death. Your brother ended what remained of his life-force."

"The Author is gone…" said Thomas. *My father is dead.*

Thomas who was now standing sat back down on the couch. "Why didn't he say anything? Why didn't he tell us who he was in the cave?"

"He had his reasons. Though would you have believed him even if he had?"

"Probably not." Thomas admitted. "I wish I could have gotten to know him at least."

"Well, in ways you are him," said Uncle Hades, "Though I understand what you mean. I never really knew my father either. He was killed in battle when I was very young."

"What about my fath…um Mr. Darren?" asked Thomas unsure what to call the man that up until now he'd known as his father.

"Just a man. Though one cursed for reasons completely unrelated to any association with me. It is unsurprising, however, that two individuals such as your mother and Mr. Darren having known so much death and tragedy in their lives would relate to each other."

"So you were there the whole time…watching us?" said Thomas.

Uncle Hades nodded. "I kept a close eye on you and your brother. And when your mother passed I knew the time had come to bring you over. Of course, there wasn't much of a choice really, your mere presence in the Banishment was causing it to crumble. And as you came of age it broke more and more."

Thomas recalled the destruction he'd glimpsed in Lord Demus' mirror. "We destroyed the world." Thomas said as much to himself as his Uncle.

"The power you possess unbalanced the Banishment. But nothing you could have done would have prevented its destruction," said Uncle Hades.

"So is everyone..."

"There are survivors. They lie in the aftermath of the apocalypse, while this world stands at its doorstep. I have no doubt those remaining have roles yet to play in this story, as their world fades into this one."

Thomas recalled what he'd seen in the mirror, of the dead rising. "Lord Demus, he used my blood to raise them from the dead," said Thomas, "They were like...zombies."

Uncle Hades nodded. "The Undead Horde. Foretold to spread across the world like a plague of locusts consuming all in its path. Though hardly the only undead creature we face."

"Vampires," said Thomas, having seen more than his fair share this evening, their blood still staining his hands.

"Something that should've never existed, a being sustained only by the life blood of others. A parasite. And the reason they exist is because of me, and a love that should've never been. The consequences of my forbidden fruit."

"Her." Thomas realized suddenly, looking up at the portrait above the fireplace, and remembering how his Uncle had reacted when he'd first inquired about her.

Uncle Hades nodded. "Persephone. She reminded me so much of Crystalana it was as if they were soulcestors. Like Crystalana she was a witch of uncommon talents, a true maiden of nature. Unfortunately, it was because she was so remarkable that her jealous mother betrayed her, setting a terrible trap to end her life. But I could not bear to see her life ended thus, so I saved her and brought her here to live.

"Over time we fell deeply in love. She even came to dwell with me in the castle. She taught me to control the Beast, to seek harmony through balance, to understand that Death was a necessary part of life. I loved her deeply. But I was foolish to ever think I could have a child without consequence. The birth took her life, and the offspring it produced was neither dead nor alive. It was vampire…it was Dracula."

"As in Count Dracula?" said Thomas.

Uncle Hades nodded. "A monster that has given rise to a whole race of monsters, and I am responsible for them all…" his voice trailed off and he peered blankly out into space for several long moments.

Finally, Uncle Hades turned back to Thomas, "I want to show you something," and he walked over to the fireplace, whispered a word in the Ancient Tongue, and the fire suddenly parted revealing a secret passageway. "Come," he beckoned.

Through the passageway, they entered into a misty outdoor setting where lay an open gate with statues of fawns buttressing each side. Beyond the gate were magnificent gardens, by far the most incredible Thomas had ever laid eyes upon. There were flowers Thomas had never seen before. They were like bouquets crafted by a master florist. Vines traveled throughout the gardens, weaving into impossible shapes. There were shrubs shaped like unicorns, satyrs, fairies, and many other creatures, standing alongside stunning archways and elaborate fountains.

"Persephone's gardens. Just as she left them," said Uncle Hades.

"Amazing," said Thomas, a word he no longer used lightly.

"She was a marvel," said Uncle Hades with evident pride.

They continued walking through the gardens gazing at all the many wonders, with something unbelievable to see around every corner.

"Persephone said that Everfall was my garden," reminisced Lord Hades as they walked, "As she was fascinated by nature, so was I fascinated by life in all its endless variety."

"That's why you paint portraits," said Thomas.

"Yes," said Uncle Hades, "And why I save certain lives. I cannot bear to lose a masterpiece."

To him lives are like works of art. Thomas realized. *Though what makes a life a 'masterpiece?'* he wondered. But at the moment there was only one life in particular which truly concerned him.

Thomas abruptly stopped walking. "When I saw Jack he was like another person, and his skin it was gray, and his eye a black gemstone…and he could fly."

"Jack has bound himself to Setus," said Uncle Hades, "and been consumed by his darkness, and transformed by it. He has gained unbelievable powers. But the price was the loss of his humanity. Your brother, as you knew him, is no more. What remains is a monster. That you must defeat."

"How? Jack literally killed me today. I'll never be able to defeat him!" Thomas despaired.

"The Author believed in you. Wordsworth believed in you. *I* believe in you. Now believe in yourself," said Uncle Hades.

"But Jack said he knows the future, that he knows how this all will end," said Thomas.

"His knowledge of the future is based upon the past. But the future is not defined by the past, but by the present. And we define our present. So the future is constantly being written and re-written."

"What did my father say to you in the cave?" asked Thomas.

"He told me to have faith…in you."

"But he's dead."

"And you are alive."

"Thanks to you."

"And I fully expect the favor to be repaid," said Lord Hades.

Thomas smiled.

In the middle of one of the gardens, Thomas saw a large stone sarcophagus with the brightest, most beautiful yellow and purple flowers surrounding it.

"Is that—"

"Persephone's tomb," said Uncle Hades.

"Do you think you'll ever see her again?" asked Thomas.

Uncle Hades did not answer for a long time. "I have to believe that I will," he said at last. "Just as I have to believe that you will triumph. And I will do everything I can to ensure that you do. In my capacity as Death I cannot interfere in the war to come, for Death must stay neutral. But as the man I once was, as Dorian the Great, I will prepare you."

"How?" asked Thomas.

Uncle Hades turned and looked at Thomas with fierce determination in his pale gray eyes. "I will train you to master your powers. And when I am finished, you will be ready to fight this war. Come, we have work to do...and no time to waste."

Epilogue
Foreshadows

Jack stood atop the sharp peak known as Ragnarock overlooking the land of Nott. Below legions of vampires were massed alongside other dark creatures from the lands of Tartarus. They were waiting for him to claim the flaming spear standing before him, and solidify his right as their King.

The lich sorcerer Lord Demus stood upon the peak with him, along with the vampire lord Dracula, the vampire Count Lucian, and the alchemist Doctor Von Wolfenhauer. And in the distance, the dark pyramid loomed amidst churning storm clouds.

Jack was adorned in a black suit fashioned from dragon scales. Stronger than any armor, it fit his body to perfection. The symbol of a red dragon emblazoned upon the chest, and a black cape waved from his back. But the ensemble was not yet complete. Though soon it would be.

The spear had been a gift from Darmania. A weapon like no other, forged by Setus in Eternal Fire, the spear had a long curved blade at one end, which never dulled, and could slice through any armor. While the spear's black shaft was fashioned from pieces of Setus' own bones, hardened to stone. More than simply a spear, it was an absorber of life-forces, and with every life the spear claimed the stronger it became. But there was only one who could wield the spear's power. It would yield only to its true master. Any other would be obliterated.

A piece of the spear was missing from the black shaft near the blade. The broken shard that was now Jack's left eye. It had broken off inside of Jaden when he plunged the spear into his heart. The shard had absorbed Jaden's life-force, where it remained still.

The spear beckoned for him to come forth and reclaim it. It was like a lost appendage, without which he was not complete. His fingers twitched in anticipation of being whole again, while his eye burned with Eternal Fire to match the spear.

Jack strode forward, thrust his hand through the flames, and grabbed ahold of the shaft. The flames instantly ceased and an enormous surge rushed through him as he felt the power of all the lives the spear had claimed.

When he turned around, the girl from the gem stood before him in the flesh and blood.

"My Queen," he whispered.

"My King," her velvety voice purred in reply, staring at him through opal eyes.

She knelt down and held out a hard iron crown with sharp spikes around the edges. He took the crown from her hands and placed it upon his head.

He smiled. All his dreams were coming true.

He turned to the masses below and raised the spear. The earth shook from the roars, and the air shuddered.

Thomas collapsed onto his bed. Being brought back to life proved an utterly exhausting experience and he was still exceedingly weak. Sleep beckoned and he was ready to answer its call.

But just as his eyes were about to close, he saw lying beside him on the bed stand the parchment he'd received from Sam.

The seal was broken.

All thoughts of sleep vanished, and with great anticipation he unfurled it.

To his shock it was completely blank.

He quickly turned the parchment over.

Blank as well.

Why would the Author, my father, give me a blank piece of paper? It didn't make sense. And a rush of anger came over him.

Just when he'd needed words most he'd received none. How could a blank page possibly help him? He'd hoped for inspiring words or some great message about the future, or even simply a few words of advice would've sufficed. But instead he received absolutely nothing. Not a single word.

But in the midst of his mounting anger suddenly it struck him. And he remembered the Author's words: *'Our birth does not define us, nor our parents, only we decide who we ultimately become. In the end, we are all either the writers of our own tale or characters in another's... and if you don't decide who you are, someone will decide for you.'*

Perhaps he'd already received all the words he needed. Perhaps the blank page was the intended message. After all what was a blank page, but endless possibility. Anything could fill it. He understood now. He was to choose the words that would fill the page. It was time for him to write his story.

In the highest tower of Ravenstead, Lord Hades watched as the rain fell torrentially in the valley. The black smoke of extinguished fires rose high into the dark starless sky, where only but a sliver of the once full moon remained.

He had waited long for the events that had transpired, knowing they would come, as they must. Though he did not foresee how they would unfold, that his beloved Everfall would suffer so much. But in time all would come to suffer. Everfall was merely the first battle in a long, brutal war.

He hated that he was so restricted, that he could not interfere, for Death must remain neutral. It was the only way. And so he'd stand idly by as oceans of blood were shed, and lives beyond counting lost.

On the other hand, what remained of the man he once was could choose sides. And in that capacity he would train Thomas and prepare him for the war to come. But never fight his battles for him. However much he wanted to.

He'd saved Thomas' life, for the last and only time. In return, the Beast had demanded a king's ransom. He could never save another life again. But it was a choice he had to make. No matter the price.

The days ahead would be dark ones, with horrors worse than any nightmare imaginable. As things that should've never existed would awaken to terrorize the world once more. A war to end all wars. None would be spared. The Beast salivated at the feast to come, while the man trembled.

Catherine had lost her Grandfather, her surrogate mother, and friends beyond counting all within the breadth of a single night. Far from the only one of course, indeed none had been spared from loss, and as she walked the streets of Everfall the stench of the dead still lingered in the night air. Citizens continued desperately searching the rubble for loved ones, though days had passed since the battle. Soon their hope would turn to despair, and grief would morph into rage. A transition that for her had already occurred.

She'd been named Head Witch of the Primrose Coven by her Sisters, at least those still left, a little less than half. The ceremony would take place upon the next new moon. A bittersweet honor that she had accepted, if only because it was what Mrs. Clause would have wanted.

As she walked through the center of town, she saw the tree of Everfall split in half as if struck by lightning. The soul of Everfall literally, and figuratively, broken.

She passed by what remained of Sigmund's Bookshop, with books scattered everywhere, ripped in tatters. Sigmund himself had been slain during the battle.

Catherine continued walking aimlessly, making her way through the town's labyrinthine alleyways without direction or destination. Curiously, she discovered herself traveling upon the same path she'd taken with her Grandfather the last time they'd walked together. She arrived then at the crossroads, when he'd asked her to choose the way.

As she stood there, she knew not what would come next. But she was consumed with thoughts of revenge. And she swore that those responsible would soon feel her wrath. She felt the power surging through her and the ground rumbled.

But in the midst of her mounting rage, a voice suddenly spoke her name.

Startled, she turned towards the source.

Her mouth dropped.

"G-grandfather?"

THE END OF THE BEGINNING

R. F. Steinhauer is an attorney and writer. When not practicing law, he's creating intricate fantasies, intent on showing his son that anything is possible—and that magic does exist.

Steinhauer lives with his wife, son, and dog in New Jersey.

64653251R00173

Made in the USA
Charleston, SC
30 November 2016